CRASH

Book Two in the Mark IV Anna Series

Danny B. McGuire

First Edition

Copyright © 2016 by Danny B. McGuire

Published by: Paper Bard Media www.paperbard.com

ISBN: 0692652744
ISBN-13: 978-0692652749 (Paper Bard Media)

I would like to thank my family: Angie, Erik, and Connor. You are always there for me, and I cherish you above all else.

I'd also like to thank everyone else who helped me with this novel. You've given me everything from advice, to proofreading, to great images. I have wonderful friends who always give their very best. Thank you all for contributing so much of your time and effort.

Cover Image: Keith Heptinstall: Digital Art and Photography
http://keithheptinstall.com

Cover Design: pixelstudio
http://www.fiverr.com/pixelstudio

Left Model (Eliza): Emily Bowman
www.EmilyBowman.com
www.Facebook.com/theemilybowman

Right Model (Anna): Joanna Wroten
www.facebook.com/joanna.wroten

Author photography by: Deedee Headley
www.facebook.com/photosbydeedee

PART ONE

DECEIT

Chapter One

Eliza's Prize

The plain white sedan cruised down the Alabama interstate, weaving through the late night traffic as if it didn't exist. A blaring horn came from a neon-green Beetle as we merged in front of it, and the driver of a crimson-colored Camaro gave us the one-fingered salute as he roared past, reminding us we'd done the same to him a mile or so back. None of this bothered Eliza. I looked over at my sister from the chilly passenger's seat, and she gave me a sideways glance. As our eyes met, her lips curled into a wicked grin so disturbing that I felt the hair on the back of my neck stand up. She'd accomplished her mission. She was taking me home.

Back to my cage was more like it, at least from my point of view. She was taking me back to Russia, back to Stepan Entsky. The man who had made my life so intolerable, that when I'd managed to escape from his grip, I ran halfway around the world so he'd never be able to find me again. It hadn't mattered. Stepan had found me anyway. I guess all those years in the KGB had taught him a thing or two about finding someone who's desperate not to be found.

Turning away from Eliza's disturbing expression, I looked out my window to witness the Birmingham city skyline retreat further and further away with each passing moment. It was the place I'd made my home, my real home. Now, that home was gone, taken from me by Stepan and his unyielding desire to use me as an intelligence agent. I sighed, and turned away from the window, too depressed to put anymore thought into it.

As far as kidnappings went, I suppose it could have been a lot worse. I hadn't been tied up or restrained, at least not in any physical way. No,

Eliza, my psychotic sister, had threatened to kill all the people I cared about. On one hand, that wasn't many people. I had four, no wait… three friends. She'd already killed one of them tonight. Not for any purpose, like proving to me that she would kill them, oh I knew *that* already. She'd done it simply to cause me pain. If I didn't know she couldn't feel positive emotions, like happiness or love, I'd swear that she got a kick out of torturing me.

Deep in my heart, I knew it wasn't her fault, not really. It was just the way she was made. However, knowing this didn't make her murderous rampages any easier to take. Until tonight, I'd still hoped to change her, make her see the error of her ways, to save her. Now, I knew that wasn't possible. I'd realized that the only way to ever be free of Eliza and Stepan, was to kill them. A thought that made me sick to consider, but I'd tried everything else. From running to reasoning, nothing had worked. Killing them was my final option. All I had to do now was find the right time to do the deed.

* * * * *

The car lurched to the right, and I grabbed the handle above the door to steady myself.

"What the hell are you doing, Eliza? You're going to kill us both."

"Not now, Anna. I'm trying to make this exit."

I looked over to see her concentrating as she tried to maneuver the car across all three lanes of traffic. Somehow, she fit the car between a Bondo-splotched minivan and an opulent, golden BMW before ending up in the far-right lane. A chorus of horn blasts sounded behind us as we flew down the airport exit ramp. She turned left against the red light and had to dodge a blacked-out Ford F-150. The sedan's tires squealed in protest as she pulled onto Messer Airport Highway. All I could do was shake my head.

"You knew the exit was on the right, why didn't you just get over sooner?"

"There was a slow tractor-trailer in the way, and I didn't want to wait."

"So you'd rather run the chance of getting us into an accident?"

"Calm down, I knew I could make the turn."

"You couldn't have known. You can't control what the other drivers are doing!"

She glanced over at me and flashed her wicked grin.

"You know, that's your problem. You don't have any faith in your abilities. Learn to live a little, Anna!"

She laughed, and it was her usual ear-piercing, edge of insanity laugh. The one that always made my skin crawl.

"Just shut up and drive."

Eliza shrugged and turned her full attention back to the road.

"Fine, but you're the one that brought it up."

I looked away from her and didn't reply. We were almost to the airport, and I knew that once we got on that plane and took off, I'd be lost forever.

* * * * *

Sitting in silence, I stared out the window and wracked my brain for an idea on how to get myself out of this mess. It was no use. Every plan I came up with ended with most, if not all, of my friends being killed. If I eliminated Eliza before we boarded the plane, Stepan would in turn execute the soldier he was currently holding prisoner at his military base. This man, Zory Novikov, had already risked his life once to help me escape to America, and I wasn't going to let him die in exchange for my freedom.

Trying to call someone for help was out of the question. Eliza had shot an electronic device under my scalp that was jamming any connection with the outside world. Before that, I could have accessed the Internet or any wireless device at the speed of thought, but she'd taken that from me. It had left this vast, empty space in my head, like I'd lost the ability to see or hear. Whenever I tried to reach out and contact the outside world, it was as silent as a graveyard. Since running from Eliza would get Kimber and David killed, that was out of the question. This left me with one option. I'd travel with her back to Russia, back to Stepan and his hidden base. A place that was always so damn cold, everyone called it Ice Castle. Once there, I'd play their little spy game. I'd play it just long enough to lull them into trusting me. There would be a time when they gave me just a little too much freedom. And when they did, I'd kill them. One simple deed would free me from all their torment, and my friends would be safe as well. As distasteful as it was to think about, it was the logical thing to do.

* * * * *

Eliza pulled over to the side of the road just before we entered the airport complex. She put the car in park and pulled a couple of wallet-sized booklets from the door pocket beside her. She flipped the first one open and showed it to me.

"This is your new passport, learn this woman's name, and change yourself to look like her."

"You're kidding. No one uses an actual paper passport anymore."

"Yes, some people still do, and you're going to be one of them. Because there's no way I'm letting you get your hands on any kind of electronic device. Now get to work."

I reached out to take it, but she yanked it away from my hand.

"No, no, no...not until we're inside the airport. I don't want you getting any smart-ass ideas about taking off with it or something stupid like that."

I tilted my head at her like a dog hearing a high-pitched noise.

"Why would I do that? You already threatened to kill my friends if I didn't come with you. Why would I come this far and then grab your stupid passport and run away with it?"

"Look, I just have two of these, one for you and one for me. I don't want to lose one if you decide to rabbit on me, so just look at the picture and change yourself already."

She could be paranoid sometimes, so I just chalked it up to that and let the conversation drop. Looking over the information on the passport, I saw that my new name was Dina Bortnik. The size, height, and weight of the woman I was to become matched my current body close enough, so there wasn't anything I needed to adjust about my build. Of course the woman's face looked nothing like mine, but that wasn't a problem. I concentrated on the image and began to change my facial features. First, my sky blue eyes became a dark emerald green. Next, I altered my shoulder length red hair to a brunette color and lengthened it by several inches. The woman's skin was also a touch pinker than my own, so I altered the shade of mine to match. Lastly, since she was about fifteen years older than the twenty-five years I currently looked, I added just a hint of crow's feet around my eyes. When I finished, I checked myself in the rear-view mirror to see how well I'd done. My transformation was spot on. There were advantages to being an android built for espionage. With a little effort, I could mimic the face and even the voice of a wide range of women...and even a decent percentage of men.

"All right, I'm finished."

Eliza eyed me, then the passport.

"Yeah, I guess that'll have to do."

I bit my tongue and didn't reply. She knew I'd changed myself to match that woman so well that her own mother wouldn't be able to tell us apart, but she couldn't admit it.

Eliza snapped the passport closed and tossed it back into the car door's pocket. She opened the second blue booklet, and her brow furrowed as she studied the image. She looked at herself in the mirror…then back at the image…then back to the mirror…then back to the image. At last, she began to change her appearance. It took her almost ten minutes, and she had to check the mirror a few more times before she'd gotten it right. This was one example of why she hated me so much. I was the Mark IV model, while she was the Mark III. Being the little sister, I had several abilities that she didn't have at all, or if she did have them, they were more primitive than mine. Eliza never took into account the fact that she'd been built to act as a combat model, while I'd been designed for infiltration. When it came to physical prowess, she outclassed me in almost every way. A fact that made straight-up fights with her a dangerous prospect. I'd been lucky in our last two encounters, and I wasn't looking forward to any kind of rematch. Although in my heart, I knew there would be one more, and it would be the last one we ever had.

* * * * *

She must have become satisfied with her appearance, because she shoved the passport into the pocket of her blue jeans. Well, to be accurate, they were *my* blue jeans. She'd shown up at my place in combat fatigues, but before we left, she'd taken the jeans along with a bright white halter-top and my favorite black leather jacket. This was the plainest outfit I'd ever seen her wear. She must have been more nervous than she was letting on about airport security.

Eliza shifted the car into drive and gunned it back onto the road. Her driving became much more reserved as we entered the airport complex. This only reinforced the thought I'd had about her wanting to be inconspicuous around this much law enforcement. Following the signs, she pulled the car into a return spot at the Hertz rental office. Killing the engine, she turned and glared at me.

"Now listen Anna, when we leave this car, I want to get into and out of this airport quickly and quietly, do you understand?"

"Yes, but my name's not Anna, it's Dina."

"Ah good, exactly what I wanted to hear. Because you know what will happen if you're a bad girl, right?"

"Yes, I know...I know. What I *don't* know, is your name."

"Me? Why I'm Dessa Kurkov...you can remember that, can't you?"

"Since I'm an android super-spy built for deception and infiltration, I think I'll be okay."

Her joyless, psychotic laugh filled the car and tweaked every nerve I had. All I could do was grind my teeth and wait for it to end. As the laughter died away, she reached into the door pocket and retrieved my passport. She chucked it at me as she opened her door.

"Here, you can have this now. I can tell you're going to be a good girl."

Shoving the booklet into my pocket, I opened my own door and followed her toward the Hertz office. She was right. I *was* going to be a good girl, for now. But when the time came, I would show her exactly how bad I could be. Then she wouldn't have a damn thing to laugh about.

Chapter Two

First Class

Dropping off the car was painless. I stood in the back and smiled while Eliza did all the talking. Within ten minutes, we were taking the elevator up from the parking garage to the departures level of the Birmingham–Shuttlesworth airport. The elevator doors opened, and we stepped out as a couple of other passengers bustled past us. As airports go, it wasn't anywhere near as large as say the one in Atlanta, but it was a decent size. Its two large runways could handle all but the largest aircraft, and the main terminal with three concourses could get the passengers on their way in no time. Not to mention the fact it had undergone a major renovation several years back, and it still looked fantastic. I paused to take it all in, but Eliza wasn't in the mood for sight seeing.

"Come on. You look like a stupid tourist."

She took off at a fast walk, and I hurried to catch up.

"Well, I've never been to an airport before. You have to admit, the architecture is impressive."

"It's gaudy and frivolous. The same functions could be served without all this opulence."

"It's not frivolous. The open architecture and nice surroundings help people relax after the stress of traveling. Take the ceiling for example. It must be fifty feet up, and with those enormous glass skylights, the view during the day must make you feel like you're already flying."

"Like I said, frivolous."

It was no use. She couldn't understand. I let the conversation die and kept walking.

* * * * *

Eliza set the pace as we moved across the spotless, white marble floor.

She was scanning all around the enormous lobby looking for any sign of trouble in what must have been a tactical nightmare for her. We were moving through a large open area filled with people rushing around in every direction. There were law enforcement personnel at every turn. Also, she had to know I was searching for any advantage, any possibility of escape that wouldn't endanger my friends. Add all of that up and it wouldn't matter if you were an android, you'd still have your hands full.

As we neared the security checkpoint, I could hear the stress in her voice as she threatened me again.

"We're almost to the TSA checkpoint. Get your passport ready and don't get cute. Because if you do…"

"I know, I know, let's just get this over with."

"Hey, don't interrupt me."

"Well, I'm getting a little tired of the same old threats. I know what's at stake."

"Fair enough. By the way, just as a side note, if they want to do any kind of metal detection scan, ask for a pat down or something else instead. The jamming device in your head might set off the alarm."

I stopped walking.

"What!"

Her eyes widened and she leaned close to me.

"SHH! Don't raise your voice, or I'll end you right here."

I felt that her threat was a hollow one, but I lowered my voice all the same.

"You're just now telling me I might set off the metal detector!"

"What difference would it have made if I'd told you sooner? There's nothing you can do about it, so put on your big girl panties and deal with it."

I stood and stared at her.

"You could have let me take the jammer out of my head. That's one thing we could have done sooner."

"No way in hell. Now keep up."

She took off again, and all I could do was fall in step behind her. As an android, airport security presented a special challenge, but it was a challenge that had been handled by my creators. They had constructed my body of non-ferrous materials, so I never had to worry about a normal airport metal detector. The full body x-ray machine was a different story. My construction might look similar to a human's on the outside, but if you looked inside, I would be in a world of trouble. Now, thanks to Eliza, I somehow had to dodge the metal detector as well.

* * * * *

As we approached the security checkpoint, Eliza took a sharp left turn and headed away from the crowd of people, and swarm of TSA agents. She'd chosen a secluded hallway that had a multilingual sign mounted above it.

"Diplomatic Security Checkpoint Ahead"

At first, I wasn't sure what she was doing, then I understood. Reaching into my pocket, I pulled out the passport she'd given me. Since I was able to examine it up close this time, I noticed the seal of the Russian government in the lower left corner. The seal that identified me as a diplomatic envoy. When I looked up from the passport, I saw Eliza's face. She was wearing that damn smart-ass smirk of hers. Was that why she wouldn't let me have it in the car...so I wouldn't see the stamp in the corner? I opened my mouth to speak, but she turned and walked away without saying a word. What the hell?

There was a large steel door waiting for us at the end of the hallway. However, there was also a podium with a TSA agent sitting behind it. Not sure what to expect, I slowed my pace a bit, but Eliza never hesitated. She walked right up to the frowning, chubby agent. A small, bronze name tag drooped on the front of his wrinkled, blue uniform. It read Carl Jacobs.

Eliza didn't have all the infiltration skills I had, but she was more than a match for this particular challenge. I hoped. She presented him with her passport and greeted him with a thick, Russian accent and a cheerful smile.

"Good morning, Comrade Jacobs. I am Dessa...Dessa Kurkov and this is my associate, Dina Bortnik."

She snapped her fingers and held out her hand. I offered her my passport, and she in turn, gave it to Carl.

"We have a private jet from the embassy already awaiting our arrival, so if you would, please clear us quickly."

Carl produced his customer service smile and spoke in an accent of his own, a thick southern drawl.

"Why yes ma'am, let me just take a look-see at your papers, and I'll have you out of here lickity-split."

"Oh, I'm sure you'll find they are in perfect order. So, please do not delay us."

On the outside, the smile never left my face, but on the inside, I winced at Eliza's last exchange. In her haste, she was pushing too hard. The already fake smile on Carl's face became more strained, and he looked down to study the passports in earnest. He even moved his left hand to rest on his radio. It was time for me to step in.

Moving up beside Eliza, I rested my hand on her shoulder. I felt her stiffen, but hoped she would soon see where I was heading. Purring in a low husky voice that was thick with my native country's tongue, I began my ploy.

"You know, I have noticed something Dessa, the men in this country are much more satisfying to look at."

She hesitated, but not long enough for Carl to notice. She moistened her lips, then spoke to me while never taking her eyes off Carl.

"Hmm, that is true Dina. I cannot wait for our next visit here. We should spend some time getting familiar with some of these southern Americans. I'm sure they would be able to show us some of the local sights."

Without taking my hand from Eliza, I leaned forward and addressed Carl.

"Might you have a phone number where my associate Dessa and I could reach you, Comrade Jacobs? Perhaps you could show us some of the fun that Birmingham has to offer the next time we are in town."

Carl's face turned a few shades pinker than it had been, and he put the passports down on the podium. He fumbled around checking a few pockets before finding what he sought. Holding it out to us, the TSA agent cleared his throat and replied.

"I...uh...yes...of course. Here, take one of my business cards. It would be my honor to represent the great city of Birmingham."

Both Eliza and I reached for it before turning to look at each other. I chuckled and motioned my head toward his outstretched hand.

"After you, Dessa. After all, you are my superior."

She couldn't let that opportunity pass and replied to me while plucking the card from Carl's hand.

"Yes, Dina, in every way."

There was a moment of silence between all three of us. The kind that lasted just a bit too long to be comfortable. At least until Eliza broke the spell by turning back to Carl.

"If you are finished with our passports, may we have them back?"

This awoke Carl Jacobs, the self-proclaimed diplomatic representative of Birmingham, from his daze.

"Oh, certainly Miss Kurkov."

He tore his eyes away from us and picked up a bright, chrome device about the size of a cell phone. Carl held it over Eliza's booklet and it emitted a crimson light that left an imprint on the passport. He imprinted mine next, then held them out to us.

"Here you go, all ready for your departure. I hope both of you enjoyed your stay here in the United States."

Eliza tucked his card into her halter-top before taking the booklets from him.

"Oh we did comrade, but something tells me not as much as we could have."

She handed me my passport, and I put it away. By the time I'd finished, Eliza had already moved to the door at the end of the hall.

"Come Dina, our plane is waiting."

I hurried over to her and followed her gaze back to Carl. He must have triggered a switch on his podium because a loud annoying buzzer blared from somewhere above us. Eliza took this as a cue and pushed the thick door open. Before she stepped through, she waved to him.

"Do svidaniya, Comrade Jacobs."

He gave her a shy little wave, and then she went through the door, with me right behind.

* * * * *

The outside of the airport was dark and chilly, but that was to be expected this early on a November morning. It was loud, but not overwhelming since we were so far from the runways. What surprised me, was all the activity. There were men and women wearing reflective, yellow jumpsuits scurrying all around. Some were sprinting around in carts filled with luggage. Others were guiding planes into their gates using glowing orange flashlights. While more still were fueling and inspecting several jumbo jets just a few hundred yards from us. Again, Eliza chided me for slowing down.

"Come on *Dina*, our plane is this way."

Taking a few long strides, I caught up with her and put my hand on her shoulder to get her attention.

"Hey! What the hell was that back there?"

"Anna, you'll need to be more specific than that."

"You knew that we had diplomatic passports and wouldn't be searched, scanned, x-rayed, or any of that crap. Yet you gave me a heart attack by telling me I might set off the metal detector."

"Oh, that, yeah, you should've seen the look on your face when you figured it out."

"Why would you do that? What was the point?"

She paused and stared at me until I met her gaze.

"To torment you, of course. See, you have caused me so much pain that paying you back is one of my life goals."

I'd heard this all before, but it always pissed me off. So, when she turned to leave, I couldn't resist a parting shot.

"Well if it hadn't been for me, you would still be at that security checkpoint. You're about as subtle as a tornado in a trailer park."

She froze in place, and I began to wonder about the wisdom of picking a fight with someone that holds so much power over you. She whirled on me, and got right into my face.

"See, it's that, *that* right there is one reason why I hate you. You like to play the good-girl role and be all high and mighty. But you can't help yourself. You have to point out that you're superior to me. Hell, you probably even enjoy it."

When she turned and walked away this time, I kept my mouth shut. Because of all the pain Eliza had caused me, she had a valid point...and that wasn't something I liked thinking about.

Chapter Three

Tarmac Turmoil

I walked across the tarmac in silence, Eliza leading me in what felt like a march to my doom. We made a last sharp right turn, and there it was, sitting behind a Southwest Airlines jumbo jet. I knew it was our plane, even before Eliza confirmed my thoughts.

"There's our ride home."

Approaching it from the front, I saw the plane was a small, two-engine jet with no markings or identifying numbers. A dark tint covered the cockpit windows, but you could still see the outlines of a pilot and copilot. As I focused my enhanced vision on them, my blood ran cold. The blocky, hairless faces peering back at me left no doubt in my mind what the pilots were…androids.

The same design team that had built Eliza and me had created them, but compared to us, these models were primitive, a Mark I or Mark II perhaps. Ice Castle must have cranked out these lower functioning models while they tried to rebuild their scientific staff. These models were easier to make in bulk, because the most complex part, their neural-net brain, wasn't high functioning like Eliza's and mine. Because of this, they had to be directed by someone else.

I'd pieced most of this together during the last several days, a rough time spent fighting bastards just like these that Eliza had been commanding. She'd brought a whole group of them with her from Russia to capture me, and in each encounter with them, they'd almost killed me. This was going to be one hell of a flight.

* * * * *

Eliza noticed I was staring at the cockpit and walked up beside me.

"Yeah, they make great foot soldiers. They do what I tell them to do, and they do it without question. No fear, no thought of self preservation, no annoying morals to get in the way."

"Sounds like you, Sis."

"Maybe a little, but I have a sense of self. You won't find me going on some suicide mission. You can bet your ass on that."

"So they don't have any thoughts or feelings, nothing that would make them even remotely human?"

"Nope, they follow the commander's orders, and that's it. Nothing else gets in the way."

"No free will at all, that must be horrible."

"No, not if you don't realize it. They can't even comprehend the concept."

The airplane emitted a high-pitched whine, and we both looked at the engines. The turbines had begun to spin, and they were gathering speed with each second.

"Quit stalling, and let's get moving. The boarding steps are over here."

She walked around the port side of the plane, but I stayed behind for one last look at the pilots. The artificial men didn't acknowledge me at all as they mechanically went about their business in the cockpit. It was hard for me to even fathom a life like that, if it was a life at all.

Shaking off those thoughts, I walked in the direction Eliza had disappeared. That was when I noticed something was wrong. It took me a second to realize what it was...all the airport personnel had gone. I spun, looking all around me, but there wasn't a yellow jumpsuit to be seen anywhere.

Just as I'd made my realization, the sound of a high-revving engine attracted my attention. Turning toward the noise, I saw a black sedan rocketing in my direction. It was at least fifty yards away, but at the speed it was moving, it would be here in less than two seconds. My advanced reflexes activated, which made everything else appear to move in slow motion. Without knowing what the driver of that sedan was planning, I decided to take cover and ask questions later. Leaping back and to my left, I tucked myself into a ball before landing on the tarmac. I rolled once and came up crouched behind the front landing gear. My hands went to where my guns should have been holstered, and I cursed, realizing they weren't there.

The driver of the sedan slammed on the brakes and smoke billowed from its tires as it slid sideways. I crouched, ready to jump out of the way because the car looked like it was skidding out of control. It wasn't. The sedan came to a halt about 30 feet from the plane with its passenger side facing me. The smell of burning rubber permeated the air, and smoke floated by as I held my breath and stayed crouched behind the large front tire of the plane.

I heard the driver's door open before I saw it. My mind raced, trying to figure out who might step out of the car. Had airport security found something wrong with our passports and rushed out here to arrest us? Was it one of Eliza's mindless android drones showing up late to the party? I could see under the car from my position, so when the spotless men's dress shoes hit the tarmac, an impossible thought entered my head. Could he have tracked me down so soon after failing to meet him? Standing up, I peeked around the landing gear to see a six-foot tall man with short black hair standing outside the car. Sensing there was danger here, he inched toward the front of the sedan while taking in his surroundings. While he moved, the wind blowing across the tarmac picked up, tossing his maroon tie and pressed, gray suit coat about. I watched as his young, handsome face scanned around the plane, and there was no doubt. It was Adam Sims from the NSA. He had somehow found me before Eliza could get me out of town.

His eyes stopped when he got to the landing gear, part of me must have been visible. His right hand went down to his waist, and came back with his Glock 9mm pistol in a smooth, practiced motion. He held it pointing up at the ready as he called out to me.

"I can see you. Step out into the open and keep your hands visible, or I'll fire."

My emotions were in shambles. I was so glad to see Adam, but I knew I couldn't go with him. The NSA had found me about six months after I arrived in America. They'd sent Adam to recruit me to work with them. It was a difficult decision since I just wanted to live a normal life, and not be an international super-spy. He'd argued that it was what I was meant to do, and after some soul searching, I'd agreed. We were supposed to meet this morning at the NSA office, but Eliza had gotten to me first. With her death threat hanging over my friends, I had to go back to Russia with her. I thought about trying to explain that to him, but he'd never believe me.

"Step out where I can see you, this is my final warning."

I raised my hands and crept out from behind the landing gear expecting him to lower his weapon, but he didn't.

"Miss, you need to lie down on the ground, and put your hands behind your head, right now."

For a split second, I didn't understand, and then I remembered. I still looked like the woman on the passport. Changing my appearance and voice back to that of my own, I spoke to him.

"Adam, it's me."

His expression never registered any surprise or shock as my face morphed in front of him. Of course, he knew I had the ability to change my appearance.

"Anna?"

I nodded, but he still didn't lower his gun.

"Lie down on the ground, and put your hands behind your head."

"What, don't you believe it's me?"

"Yes, I do. But you are obviously trying to escape, and head back to Russia having completed whatever mission you were sent here to perform. So, comply with my order, and let me take you into custody."

"But, you don't understand."

His voice never wavered, and his expression never changed as he aimed his Glock right at my head.

"Surrender to me in the next three seconds, or I will shoot you."

Not knowing what to do, I stared at him in silence, and tried to figure someway out of this standoff. I'd decided my best chance was to dive back behind the front wheel of the airplane and hope my augmented reflexes would catch him off guard, when Eliza's mocking voice came from somewhere out of my sight.

"Anna, you didn't tell me we had a guest."

* * * * *

I had to give him credit, Adam's reflexes were impressive. He swiveled his head and changed the aim of his pistol quick as a blink. Eliza spoke again, her voice taking on a familiar singsong quality. It was the condescending voice she used as she played with her prey.

"Whoa, there big guy. Let's not get all pointy-pointy, shooty-shooty, okay?"

No, not another one I thought as I replayed what had happened to Felix earlier this evening. Eliza had murdered my friend with no more thought than one might give to turning off a light switch, and I'd be damned if I let her do it again.

With Adam's attention focused on my sister, I crouched down and crept along the underside of the plane. I still couldn't see Eliza, and that was a position you wanted to avoid at all cost. Had she gone inside the plane?

"Miss, I'm not sure who you are, and I don't care. I'm here for Anna. So get back in your plane, and you won't find yourself in any trouble."

Adam's words were so calm, so collected, I stopped for a moment and looked at him. His expression still hadn't changed. He looked so nonchalant, I couldn't tell if he was facing down two dangerous international spies, or ordering a cappuccino at the local bookstore. The man's calm demeanor even gave Eliza pause, stealing some of the swagger from her voice.

"W-Who the hell do you think you are? Do you have any idea who you're dealing with?"

"No, I've already told you I don't know who you are. However, may I point out, that you have no idea who you're dealing with either. Now, get back inside your plane, and close the door. That way, I won't have to shoot you. Do it now, I will not ask again."

Damn, Adam must have ice water in his veins. As he spoke, I'd moved to the middle of the jet. From there, I could see the boarding steps extending from the plane down to the tarmac. They were shifting around, which told me that Eliza was standing on them, maybe even walking up them. A second later, she confirmed my thoughts.

"Fine, fine, take her. Honestly, I didn't want her back anyway. She's been a pain in my ass since day one. Now, she can be a pain in yours."

Eliza was trying to catch him off guard, and I knew it. If Adam fell for her ploy, he'd never see the bullet coming. I scurried forward, using my hands to accelerate my escape from underneath the plane. Emerging to the right of the small steps, I held my hands up to show that I wasn't a threat. Adam still pointed his Glock at me and held me in his unflinching gaze.

"Anna, get in the car."

"She's not going to let me go, you need to…"

Eliza's exclamation cut my sentence short.

"Hey Fed…mine's bigger!"

At her taunt, my advanced reflexes activated and time slowed. Adam looked past me, toward the top of the stairs, and the barrel of his gun followed his line of sight. Whirling to my left, I caught sight of my sister.

Eliza stood in the doorway of the plane holding an AK-47 at hip level. Like me, She'd discarded her passport disguise now as well, and her lips curled into that insane smile that I'd seen too often. Then came the cackling laugh, a grating sound that was drowned out when she pulled the trigger, and a hailstorm of bullets flew at Adam.

* * * * *

The muzzle of the AK-47 flashed and roared like a Fourth of July fireworks show as Eliza held down the trigger. She must have been toying with Adam, because instead of tearing him apart, her first volley riddled the front of his sedan. The car's tire exploded, and the bullets made a chorus of pops and plinks as holes appeared in the engine compartment. Ducking my head, I sprinted around the small steps, trying to get in front of, but still below, the deadly lead projectiles flying out of her rifle.

The look on Eliza's face told me she was enjoying herself as she inched her aim up toward where Adam stood, no…wait, where Adam *had been* standing. He must have dove for cover as I began moving, because he'd already gotten behind the car, using it as a shield from the unrelenting spray of bullets. My opinion of his abilities went up a notch as I realized how fast he'd reacted, but there wasn't any time to dwell on my quick friend from the NSA. Because if my count was correct, it was almost my turn to act.

* * * * *

A second later, Eliza exhausted all the rounds in the AK-47's magazine. Releasing the stored energy of my tensed leg muscles, I sprang up the steps taking several of them per leap, and I made it just in time. In the half second it took me to close on her, Eliza had ejected the empty magazine and was slapping another into the bottom of the rifle. As she reached for the bolt to ready her weapon, I grabbed and held on to that arm, while slamming the hand with the AK-47 into the side of the plane. Luck was with me, and she lost her grip on the weapon. She let out a guttural growl as the rifle rattled down the stairs.

"Damn it Anna, you ruined my fun! Why do you…"

She stopped mid-sentence and the snarky expression melted from her face.

"I think your boyfriend is pissed."

Knowing what she meant, we both moved at the same time, right before shots began to ring out from Adam's Glock. His weapon wasn't a full automatic like the AK-47, but I'd been with him to the practice range and watched him shoot. He was quick and accurate. The only thing that saved us from having a couple of well placed holes added to our heads, was the erratic movements we made scrambling into the plane. She went to one side of the door, and I to the other. Adam stopped shooting as soon as he'd lost us as targets. He broke the short-lived silence by issuing a command in that calm, collected voice of his.

"Both of you come out of the plane with your hands up, and I won't shoot."

Eliza looked at me and rolled her eyes.

"Why don't you come in and get us, or hey, better yet, join us on our trip. It's going to be long, and we're sure to get bored all by ourselves. Tell me Fed, have you ever heard of the mile high club?"

I glared at her as Adam responded.

"Neither of you are going anywhere, I will disable the plane before you can takeoff. This is your last warning before I open fire. Come out and surrender."

Eliza cackled her disturbing laugh.

"Ok, suit yourself. I guess we'll just watch the inflight movie. See you later, Fed."

She reached out beside her and slapped a control panel located near the door. The stairs whirred into motion, retracting themselves in perfect synchronization with the door sliding shut. As he'd promised, Adam opened fire on the plane.

* * * * *

"Eliza, how stupid can you be? You know he'll fill this plane full of 9mm sized holes!"

"No, he won't. This jet is military grade. He'd need armor piercing ammunition before he could do any real damage."

Running to the nearest window, I peeked outside before I replied.

"Well what about his car? He could just drive it into the plane."

"Not going to happen."

She was right. I could see steam rising from the tiny holes she'd shot into the engine compartment of his sedan. That along with the flat tire she'd given the car had made sure it wasn't moving without the help of a wrecker.

"Not bad for someone so stupid, eh? You think you're the only one that can do this? The only one worthy to go into the field? All hail the mighty Anna and her all important *feelings*…all hail indeed."

When Eliza was undergoing one of her more bipolar episodes, it was best to keep your mouth shut, but I couldn't. I glanced back over my shoulder so I could see her face.

"Quick question, what kind of ammo is in your AK-47? I'm just asking, since it penetrated a car engine."

It was worth the risk of enraging her. Eliza's expression which a moment ago had been full of arrogance and superiority, changed first to non-comprehension, then concern. She rushed forward to look out the window I'd been using, and she saw what I meant. Adam had holstered his pistol and was moving toward the rifle I'd knocked out of her hands. He'd have it in seconds, and we were sitting ducks. Eliza's face turned hard and expressionless.

"We should leave now."

* * * * *

Eliza became quiet for the blink of an eye and glanced toward the cockpit. I assumed she was communicating with the android pilots, and she was. As if she'd willed it, the high-pitched whine of the jet engines became a roar as the turbines spun faster and faster. The plane lurched forward, and I had to grab a seat back to keep my balance. Eliza stumbled back a bit, and moved toward a seat on her side. She plopped down and fished around for the seatbelt.

"Better buckle up, this is going to be a bumpy takeoff."

Taking her advice, I slid into the seat next to the window and buckled myself in place. Turning to look back outside, I saw that Adam had retrieved the rifle and was bringing it up to rest against his shoulder. He took aim and began to fire. We were pulling away from him at a decent clip, so I figured he'd have almost no chance to land a hit. I was wrong. The plinking sound of his 9mm pistol, was nothing compared to the heavier-sounding impacts from the AK-47. He scored hit after hit, and I looked over to Eliza.

"Big deal, he's taking pot shots at the plane. No way he can hit anything important. In a few more seconds we'll be out of range."

"I hope you're right. I'd rather not go up in a giant fireball before you could get me back to Russia and torture me."

It was a tense couple of seconds, filled with three to four more hits, but after that, just the sound of the jet engines growling and exerting their dominance over gravity as we lifted into the air. Eliza looked triumphant as we climbed higher and higher into the late night sky. All I could see out of the window now was the shrinking lights of Birmingham, and soon, even they disappeared.

* * * * *

The roar of the engines lessened as we leveled off. I unbuckled my seatbelt and turned to look at Eliza. She was staring at me.

"What?"

"Nothing, I'm just watching you to make sure you don't try anything."

"We're thousands of feet in the air, what could I do?"

"Nothing, at least not as long as I keep my eye on you."

A yawn came over me that was so intense it made my body shake as it faded, making me realize how tired I was.

"Fine, you're right, I'm about to try something. It's called going to sleep. I'm exhausted. You should get some rest too, you know this is a long flight."

Her eyes narrowed as she studied me.

"Yeah, sure, I'll do just that."

Her intense gaze never left me as I found the lever on the overstuffed leather seat that made it recline. Setting my internal alarm clock for seven hours, I curled up in the seat and made myself as comfortable as I could. Eliza's unwavering stare was the last thing I saw as I closed my eyes.

Chapter Four

Off Course

I awoke seven hours later as my internal alarm sounded. As I opened my eyes, there was Eliza, staring at me.

"You haven't been sitting there watching me for the past seven hours, have you?"

"That is none of your concern."

My body and mind didn't need as much rest as a human's, but it did need some. It was when my neural-net brain reorganized data and my body did most of its repairs. Without it, I would begin to act erratically, just like a sleep-deprived person.

"No need to snap, I was only asking because you must be tired."

"I don't need any of your touchy-feely bullshit! I don't need as much rest as you anyway!"

Of course with Eliza, it was difficult to tell what might be causing her erratic behavior, sleep deprivation or emotional issues. Without her ability to feel anything like love or compassion, she was mentally unstable. She might kiss you one moment, and slap you the next. To not antagonize her any further, I decided to let it drop.

Setting my seat back to its normal position, I looked around the jet's cabin for the first time. The sun had burned the deep shadows of last night away as it blazed in through the windows and illuminated the whole interior. The plane was decorated in sandy brown leather with dark walnut accents and looked to be about the size of a small camper. Eliza and I sat across the aisle from each other in two of the four padded rear seats near the door. Looking forward, I saw two u-shaped areas with a small wooden table between them, one on each side of the plane. Just beyond them, was the galley, a small restroom, and a sturdy steel door, which led to the cockpit.

My stomach growled at the sight of the galley, and I realized I hadn't eaten in over twelve hours. Eliza must have heard it because she made a small dismissive sound.

"What, I'm hungry."

"I am too, but it's just one of the things that annoy me about the way we were built. Why the hell would you build androids that constantly act and sound human? At best, it's an annoyance, at worst, it's a weakness."

"You know why, it's so we blend in with people. Our stomachs growl, we sweat, we yawn, even feel pain, to keep up the appearance that we are human."

"At least we can turn off the pain response after a short time. Imagine how much that would suck if you felt pain all the time."

I bit my tongue. Eliza had no idea that she'd damaged my ability to do just that in one of our fights. My pain suppression system still worked, but not well. No longer could I eliminate my pain, only dull it. Injuries could still have a significant effect on how I fought. My stomach growled louder than before, and my thoughts turned to what might be in the galley.

* * * * *

"I'm going to go look up front for something to eat, do you want anything?"

She eyed me without expression.

"Look, I need something to eat. I'm not going to try to escape, or poison you, or whatever you're currently thinking."

"That's exactly what I'd say right before I tried to escape or poison someone."

That was paranoid even for Eliza. She really needed to sleep.

"Well Sis, as you are so fond of pointing out, we aren't the same."

"Don't…call…me…that."

The pistol was in her hand so fast that even I had trouble following the motion. I sighed, and stood up.

"Okay, shoot me in the back if you need to, but I'm going to the galley and look for something to eat."

She didn't shoot me as I made my way to the galley, but then again, she never lowered the pistol either.

* * * * *

Squatting down, I dug through the refrigerator to see what options I had.

Another advantage of being an android was that I didn't need as much food to keep me going. Matter of fact, I could survive on vitamins and water, but once again, I was programmed to behave like a human. This meant that I could eat, and even enjoy the taste of food. I paused at that last thought. Because of the way her neural-net mind had been constructed, Eliza couldn't enjoy anything, not even a meal. Sometimes I felt so bad for her, she behaved the way she did because of programming...but my god, she could be so cruel.

"Hey, what are you doing up there?"

I turned to see her approaching, and at least she'd put her gun away.

"Just looking through the fridge for something to eat. Let's see, there's water, soda, orange juice, milk, and tea. Want anything?"

"Hand me the orange juice."

She took the OJ as I lifted it up to her. Popping off the top, she chugged half of it down before stopping.

"There're bags of chips and candy bars over in the cabinet behind me."

She took another swig of the orange juice before replying.

"Who the hell stocked this plane, ten-year olds?"

"It was probably stocked for short hops from one city to another, not intercontinental treks."

"Whatever."

Grabbing the milk, I stood up beside her. Opening it, I took a hefty drink, letting its coolness coat my throat. It tasted so good. Something Eliza would never know. Looking over to her, she was drinking with one hand, and shielding her eyes with the other. The sun was coming in through the windows and hitting her right in the face. It happened to her again, and she spat a curse under her breath, and walked over to close the window shade on the far side of the plane. I know it was childish, but I chuckled at her annoyance anyway. It was just so bizarre to think of how superior to people we were, and here she was being bothered by the sun coming through the starboard window.

Raising my milk, I took another drink. However, as I swallowed it down, a strange feeling began to gnaw at me...though I couldn't place my finger on what was wrong.

Eliza returned in as good a mood as ever.

"Damn sun, you'd think we'd have been built with complete protection from something like that."

"Well, we do have some protection, just not complete."

"Yeah, well, now I have complete protection, by closing the damn window. It won't shine in my eyes now."

Then it hit me. The sun was in the wrong place. It should have been on the port side if we were heading to Russia. She'd lied to me about taking me back to Tiksi!

"So, did you think you could keep me in the dark just because you are jamming my connection to the outside world?"

"What?"

"You heard me. So where are we actually going, and why didn't you just tell me? Is it because you were afraid I'd never have gone along?"

"What the hell are you going on about? I told you we were returning to Tiksi so I could deliver you to Stepan. Although if I had my way, you'd already be just a jumble of pieces."

I studied her face for several seconds, and it looked like she was telling the truth. Detecting lies is something I'm quite good at with humans, but androids were another matter. Not knowing what else to do, I decided to play along.

"So you're telling me you don't know we're heading in the wrong direction."

She stopped drinking the juice and locked eyes with me. When she spoke, it was slow and deliberate.

"What's this all about?"

"Like I said, we are going in the wrong direction. You may have cut off all my wireless network functions with your little head jammer, but I still have a compass, and it's telling me we're flying in the wrong direction. Look, even the sun is on the wrong side of the plane."

"What do you know about airplanes? You came to the United States hidden in a shipping crate on a cargo ship."

Throwing the rest of my milk in the garbage, I collapsed into the nearest seat, and slapped my hands down on the table.

"Fine, I don't care anymore. It's not like I can do anything about it anyway. So play whatever warped game you want by yourself, cause I quit. You won."

She sat down in the seat across from me and folded her hands in front of herself.

"Okay, we'll do it your way. You know that all I have to do is check my GPS to verify our position and…"

Eliza stopped speaking mid-sentence. She became so quiet and still that I began to worry that something might be wrong with her. Leaning forward, I reached out to touch her hands. The instant I made contact, she reacted by yanking them away and pulling her pistol.

"I don't know what the fuck you've done, but you'd better stop it right now. Because if you don't, I swear I'll kill you where you sit, and deal with Stepan later."

* * * * *

The look in her eyes was that of pure hatred. I'd seen her this way before, and I froze. She would kill me if I didn't figure out what was happening. Without moving, I spoke to her using a soft, soothing voice.

"Eliza, I have no idea what you're talking about. You were watching me the whole time. There wasn't anyway I could have altered the course of the plane or sabotaged it in any way."

She leapt to her feet and wrapped her arm around my far shoulder. Pulling me close to her waist, she jammed the gun against my temple.

"You know I'm not talking about that harebrained tale of yours about the plane being off course. You have until the count of three to stop jamming my wireless connections, or I'm going to splatter your brains all over this pretty leather cabin. One."

My mind raced, trying to come up with something that would prevent any brain splattering of any kind.

"Wait! Listen, you know I couldn't have done anything like that. You disabled my connection hours ago. There has to be something else going on here."

"Two."

"You're not thinking this through. Someone else has to be involved… or *something*! The androids, remember, you said they'd follow the orders of their commander without question or conscious. What if…what if it's not *you* who are their commander?"

"Three."

But Eliza didn't fire. After a second, she even lowered the gun from my temple, although she kept it pointing at me.

"The MK IIs…what do you mean, I might not be their commander? I gave them the order to takeoff."

I silently thanked her for letting me know what model the androids were, then continued my reasoning.

"How do you know? What if they were sitting in the cockpit relaying information back to Ice Castle? Back to someone that wants you, or me, or even both of us out of the picture? Maybe that person told them to takeoff when the situation became too dangerous. Maybe they are the *real* commander of the MK IIs."

Once I'd said it aloud, it gave me a chill. It was terrifying enough to be Eliza's hostage, but it was somehow worse to be the hostage of someone that was unknown.

We both looked at each other for a few moments, then she whispered one word.

"Who?"

It didn't take long for both of us to come to the same conclusion. We even spoke his name in unison.

"Lopata."

* * * * *

Warren Lopata was a brilliant, scientist. He'd worked on complex power systems most of his sixty plus years, including some groundbreaking power cells he created for the Soviet space program. The energy-efficient, hydrogen-based, power unit inside me, and I assume Eliza, was designed and created by him. However, like the infamous Doctor Frankenstein, after he saw what he'd help create, he thought I was an abomination. Lopata and I had exchanges so intense, that we both threatened to end each other. Since Eliza had spoken his name as the possible saboteur, I assumed her time with him was as enjoyable as mine. Now the question was, would he go so far as to enrage his commander, Stepan Entsky, and face sure execution just to destroy us? I would never have thought so, at least not before this happened.

My sister looked lost in thought as she stood next to me. After a long pause, she scowled and shook her head.

"No, it doesn't add up. Lopata doesn't have the balls to pull off something like this. There has to be a reasonable explanation for what's happened."

"We both came to the same conclusion. He has the motive and the ability, the only thing we don't know is if he's had the opportunity."

She looked down at me, unconvinced.

"Fine, you tell me what happened to your wireless connection."

"I don't know."

"Have you tried to contact the two MK IIs in the cockpit?"

She paused, and a blank look came over her as she stared at the cockpit door, then her face became twisted with fury.

"I can't communicate with them, and I'm going to find out why right now."

She nodded toward the cockpit door, and I reached up to touch her arm.

"Hang on, I'm coming too."

"No, you stay here, I still don't know if this is one of your tricks."

I rolled my eyes at her and stood up.

"You know it's not, and you also know that two against one isn't the best of odds."

She considered that for a tick and pointed to the pistol on her waist.

"If you make one wrong move, I won't hesitate."

"I know, I know, now lead the way."

Eliza narrowed her eyes at me.

"You're not the one giving the orders around here, don't get too familiar."

I held up my hands to indicate that I was sorry, and it placated her. Now was not the time to squabble.

My sister drew her pistol and held it out to her side as she inched forward. I stepped in right behind her to the left. We reached the closed steel door to the cockpit, she reached out to try the handle. It wiggled some, but I could tell it was locked. The door was reinforced enough to stop any would be hijackers. However, it hadn't been constructed with two angry androids in mind.

Through a series of hand motions, she relayed her plan to me. I stepped back to ready myself, and Eliza did the same. She held up her hand and counted down.

Three…Two…One.

We both kicked forward in unison. Her foot struck the door next to the handle, and mine slammed home right next to hers. Our well-placed kicks worked just like she'd planned. The locking mechanism shattered, spraying tiny metal parts into the cockpit. The door managed to stay on its hinges, but it slammed back against the wall so hard, it stuck in place. It took less than a second for us to regain our balance, and rush into the room, but we weren't fast enough.

Chapter Five

The Enemy of My Enemy

We rushed into the cramped cockpit, Eliza to the right, and I to the left. In the pilot and copilot seats, the Mark II androids had already prepared for our arrival. Their seats were swiveled around so that the pistols they held were easier to aim, and boy did they aim them. Each Mark II was focusing their attention on one of us, and they had their guns on target so fast that we had no chance to react. I froze and held my hands out to my sides, while Eliza stared at her pistol-wielding adversary, eyes full of rage. Her right hand was resting on the gun strapped to her waist, and I knew what she was thinking. For what felt like an eternity, I waited to see how my sister would react. I knew the emotionless Mark IIs couldn't get nervous, they simply sat there in their pressed black suits with their hairless heads and watched us. After a few more tense moments, I'd reached my breaking point and whispered to Eliza.

"Don't try it. His gun is already pointed at you. No matter how fast you think you are, you're not that fast."

"Screw him, that piece of crap traitor."

"Let's just see if we can't talk this through before anyone shoots a hole in one of us, or maybe the plane."

Eliza glanced over and studied me hard. I assumed she was trying to make up her mind whether or not I was a part of this coup. Holding my breath, I hoped she'd be rational for once in her life. At last, she relaxed and moved her hand away from the weapon. When she did, the tension in the room dropped a couple of notches and the androids went to work solidifying their advantage.

The android that had his weapon on me reached back and flipped a toggle switch on his control panel. A black and gray metal speaker crackled to life, and the most monotone voice I'd ever heard rattled out of it.

"Mark III Eliza, disarm yourself."

Eliza wasted no time in her rebuttal.

"Mark II - Unit 1, go to hell."

"Mark III Eliza, disarm yourself or face destruction."

Before she could respond, I did.

"Just do it, please."

"Why do you care what happens to me?"

"Look, I don't want them to start shooting up the damn cockpit."

She turned to the nearest Mark II and glowered down over it.

"Mark II - Unit 1, why do you not obey my commands? Why are you not connecting to my neural-net interface?"

The speaker was silent for a few seconds, and then the Mark II replied.

"Mark III Eliza, you are not the commander of this mission."

"Mark II - Unit 1, priority alpha request incoming. Mark III Eliza leadership override...assume mission commander role from current commander. Execute request."

Smart, she was trying to override whoever was controlling it and gain back command. Again, the unit took a while to answer.

"Mark III Eliza, priority alpha request is...denied. Disarm or face destruction. You have five seconds to comply."

I waited as long as I could before hissing at her.

"Eliza!"

"Okay...fine...but I swear, you'll pay for this. You...and whatever traitorous bastard is pulling your strings...will pay."

She slowly reached for her pistol and held it out loosely by its grip. As she did, the android next to me stood up and took it from her, storing it in his coat pocket. He then sat back down, holstered his own weapon, and turned his attention to flying the plane. The Mark II with the gun still drawn went back to issuing commands through the crackly speaker.

"Mark III Eliza and Mark IV Anna, you will return to the cabin and sit quietly or you will face destruction."

"Mark II - Unit 1, Mark III Eliza demands to know the name of the mission commander."

"Mark III Eliza, that information is classified and you are not the mission commander. You will return to the cabin and sit quietly or you will face destruction."

Eliza tried a different direction.

"Mark II - Unit 1, what is our destination?"

"Mark III Eliza, that information is classified and you are not the mission commander. You will return to the cabin and sit quietly or you will face destruction."

I was sure she'd snap, but she tried again.

"Mark II - Unit 1, why can't I access anything wirelessly. Who is jamming my signal?"

"Mark III Eliza, that information is classified and you are not the mission commander. You will return to the cabin and sit quietly or you will face destruction."

She was boiling mad now, I wondered if I should intervene, but before I could decide, they had another exchange.

"Mark II - Unit 1, I know I'm not the commander, that's why I'm asking you these questions, you dumb ass! Now answer me."

"Mark III Eliza, You did not ask a question. You will return to the cabin and sit quietly or…"

"Or what…OR WHAT? You robotic parrot!"

The gunshot rang out before I could react. My breath caught in my throat and a hundred things ran through my mind all at once. Thankfully, none of them had happened. A few inches to the side of Eliza's right ear, there was now a bullet-shaped hole in the wall. Everything went quiet in the cockpit. Even the ever-present roar of the wind seemed to lessen in intensity. Until the Mark II unit broke the spell and spoke again over the static-laden speaker.

"Or you will face destruction, Mark III Eliza."

Reaching out, I took her by the arm and pulled her toward the door. I knew if she stayed here much longer, she would end up wounded, or worse, dead. An outcome I couldn't allow, since Eliza had made it clear while kidnapping me that if anything happened to her, Stepan would kill my friend Zory Novikov.

* * * * *

I was able to get her backing toward the doorway, but she refused to turn and take her eyes off Unit 1. It was the most focused, hate-filled stare I'd ever seen her give anyone…and that's saying something.

It took a minute or so, but we made it far enough away from the cockpit so that she couldn't see him anymore. Easing myself down into one of the plush chairs in the back of the jet, I motioned for Eliza to do the same. She sat next to me this time, instead of choosing a seat across the isle. Folding her arms across her chest, she fumed in silence, until I spoke.

"What's the play?"

She turned toward me and spoke in a whisper.

"How the hell should I know? How can I know anything without connecting to the network? I'm completely isolated."

Lowering my voice to match hers, I rubbed the small tender bump under my scalp and replied.

"Wow, that must really suck, huh?"

She went on with her rant without ever acknowledging my sarcasm.

"If you're really not a part of this, then stop whining and come up with something. We don't know where we are, where we're going, or who's behind all this."

"We do know one thing."

She fell quiet, and waited for me to continue.

"You saw the delay in response when you were asking Unit 1 the tough questions. He was talking with someone, and it must have been wirelessly since he wasn't plugged into the plane's control panel. Our next move is obvious."

"Is it now?"

"We need to find the wireless frequency that is still open and use it ourselves. How many bands can you access?"

She frowned at me.

"Only a few, and I've already tried them all. Besides, most of them are focused on communication with Mark IIs and the like. I'm more combat specialized, you know that."

"Too bad, I can access all wireless frequencies and have the ability to decrypt transmissions. At least I could if I didn't have your jammer stuck next to my skull."

I thought maybe if she were desperate enough…

"Oh, no, no way in hell will I take out the jammer. The first thing you'd do is discover our location and call your boyfriend that works for the American government. Nope."

She was right of course, but why not keep trying.

"Eliza, we're stuck here without any information about our predicament, and without information, we can't make any rational decisions. Let me do what I was built for."

As soon as it left my mouth, I knew it was the worst thing I could've said. Her hands curled into clenched fists and her expression became twisted, even frightening.

"What you were built for? What about me? Why don't we do this using *my* strengths?"

Dammit, she stood up and moved toward the cockpit. I had to stop her.

"Wait, Eliza, if were going to do it your way, let's have a plan."

She paused and after a bit of thought, returned to her seat next to mine.

"All right, but hurry up. I'm so ready to kill that bastard."

* * * * *

We talked it over for a few minutes, but couldn't come up with a successful plan for storming the cockpit. Every scenario we came up with ended with us coming under fire. Even if we didn't get ourselves shot, there was the very real possibility of a bullet puncturing the cabin and causing explosive decompression…neither outcome was desirable. We moved on to other tactics, but everything was thwarted by their lack of emotions. Neither my usual method of seduction, or Eliza's personal favorite, intimidation, would work worth a damn. Eliza punched the leather-covered seat back and grumbled.

"This is taking too long. I should creep up there and jump them with you following right behind."

"No, we discussed that already, it's too dangerous."

"Anna, fighting *is* dangerous. That's kinda the point. You can't just smile and wiggle your hips to get past every obstacle. Sometimes, you have to get your hands dirty and bust some heads."

"Hey, I've done my fair share of head-busting, thank you…and you're getting too loud. They'll hear you and come back to investigate."

Eliza's face turned red, and I knew she was just about to scream, but then a strange calmness came over her.

"That's it."

"What's it?"

"We split them up. If we create a disturbance, one of them would come back here, and we kill him. Then we move on to the one left in the cockpit and finish him."

"Hmm, not bad, but two things."

She sighed and rolled her eyes.

"No, listen…first, why wouldn't both of them come and check out whatever we're doing?"

"Because, they're sure that the situation is fully under their control. So, why come through the door single file, putting yourself at tactical disadvantage, or take the risk of leaving the plane on autopilot when you know one of your hostages is an android built to infiltrate computer systems?"

"You make some good points. I'm not entirely convinced that both of them won't come back, but this may be our best shot at taking them on one at a time."

She grinned from ear to ear.

"However…please don't kill both of them. We need to get some information from them, and we can't do that if they're dead."

"You know they won't talk. We don't have an effective way to interrogate them."

Holding up my right hand, I wiggled my fingers at her.

"Oh, they won't have to talk for me to get the information I want."

"You can do that even with the jamming device still in your head?"

"Sure, you only blocked my wireless signal. I can connect to one of them physically, and interrogate him from inside his own mind."

Eliza's eyes widened and she leaned away from me an inch.

"I knew keeping my eye on you all night was a good idea."

Now it was my turn to grin.

"Oh, Sis, I'd never use an intrusive technique like that on you."

I let that veiled threat hang for a heartbeat, before continuing.

"So, what kind of distraction do you have in mind?"

Eliza explained her idea like only she could.

Chapter Six

Cockpit Coup

"This is ALL your damn fault!"

Eliza's exclamation took me by surprise, but I realized that this was how she wanted to create a diversion. Before I could come up with a reply, she shouted again.

"If it wasn't for YOU, running away like a spoiled brat, I'd be back in Ice Castle right now! But where am I...kidnapped on some damn plane...and why, because you have *feelings* and didn't want to hurt people. You fool! Don't you realize we all do things everyday that we don't like? We have obligations and responsibilities, loyalties and debts that must be paid! But no, not you, you don't want to get your delicate *feelings* hurt. You make me sick!"

She spat the word like it was poison. I stood up, facing the cockpit, and let her have it.

"You can't blame this on me! I'd escaped from that wretched place! I ran thousands of miles away from you and your precious igloo with its sadistic leader, yet you still came after me!"

Eliza shot out of her seat so fast that my training took over and I assumed a defensive posture, even though I knew this was all an act. She squared up in front of me, looking ready to fight.

"Oh, I *can* blame you. Why did they even need you? I was performing my duties perfectly, just as I'd been programmed..."

She looked down toward the floor and grew silent. I waited, not sure if it was my turn or not. Then she raised her head and I saw her face... uh oh...

"One mission, that's all I got...and then I was thrown away. So they could build you!"

Her hands clenched into fists and she drew closer to me.

"And what did they get? A whiney, self absorbed, lightweight, that couldn't stay hidden for six months! A touchy-feely, emotionally weak, human-lover that was turned in by her friend…one of those very same humans that she loves so much! Oh, and speaking of human-lover…"

I gritted my teeth. At this point, I didn't care if she was acting or not, she was pissing me off.

"Don't you dare say it. I'm warning you."

"How did it feel to watch all the people you loved die? I mean, I wouldn't know, but I can only guess that it really sucked."

"SHUT UP!"

She didn't. With a smile as wide and evil as any I'd ever seen, she crossed the line.

"Tell me about when you found Cindi. You were on the other side of the door, unable to hold her as her life faded away. You know I left her that way for you…so you could find her…broken and…"

I didn't recognize my own voice as I screamed and swung at her. My android-enhanced reflexes activated, but so did hers. Although she didn't need faster reflexes, she had been expecting the punch and dodged under it with little effort. Her right fist came up, slamming into my stomach and doubling me over, at the same time she hit me with a left cross. I staggered back into the aluminum wall at the aft of the plane as she gloated.

"Well now, that was easy. See how vulnerable your emotions make you?"

The copper taste of blood filled my mouth. Drawing in a rasping breath, I spat onto the floor. Looking up, I smiled and mocked her.

"Was that your best shot? Hell, one of those Mark IIs hit me harder than that when we were fighting on the highway. So much for you being a combat model."

She snarled and rushed me, which was what I wanted. I sidestepped her rage-filled lunge and grabbed her by the arm. Swinging with all my might, I slammed her face first into the shiny aluminum wall that had been behind me. The visceral crunch that sounded throughout the cabin was very satisfying.

Behind me I heard footsteps, but I didn't dare take my eyes of Eliza. She'd spun around to face me, and was none too happy. Wiping some of the blood from under her nose, she grinned and came at me. This time, her attack was slow and planned, but I was ready for her.

Eliza began a complex series of jabs to see if there were any holes in my defense. While I wasn't as fast or strong as her, I'd studied martial arts during my time at Ice Castle and my defense was solid. Her attacks were coming at a blistering pace, and it took all of my concentration to keep her from landing a solid blow. While I knew there was a Mark II somewhere behind me, his robotic voice took me by surprise as it rang out through the cabin's speakers.

"Mark III Eliza and Mark IV Anna, stop your aggression at once and sit quietly or face destruction."

Eliza ignored the command and kept trying to land a solid hit. The Mark II didn't like being ignored.

"Mark III Eliza and Mark IV Anna, stop your aggression at once and sit quietly or face destruction. This is your final warning."

Eliza showed no signs of giving up the fight as she screamed at the traitorous android.

"I'll sit down once I've finished this bitch once and for all. Just give me a second."

As she spoke, she glanced up and behind me to look at the Mark II. It was all I needed.

Feinting with my left, I was able to work her hands out wide enough to sneak in a right jab to her chin. Pain shot through the knuckles on my hand, and Eliza reeled back, trying to shake the cobwebs from her head. Not wanting to let my advantage go, I pressed in and landed both a right and left to her stomach, causing her to lean back against the wall. She slumped to her knees, and then had to place her hands in front of her for support.

My punches weren't that hard, after all, this wasn't a real fight, so she must have gone down for a reason. Not knowing what to do, I kept up the act.

"Looks like you might need more than a second to finish this bitch off, Sis."

Eliza straightened up, and a growl escaped her lips. She leaned back on her hands…no, wait, not *both* hands. Her body was tilted to the left, as if she'd put all her weight on the left hand alone, which meant the right one was free. My eyes widened as the realization sank into my thick skull. Not knowing what she was planning, I began a split move out of pure instinct. It saved my life.

My sister's right hand shot out from behind her as I began to drop to the floor. My eyes registered a glint of metal as it streaked toward me... then continued on a hair's breadth above the top of my head. Before I could realize that she'd thrown a knife at me, there was a loud thunk from behind. At first, I thought she'd only sunk her blade into the cabin wall, but her devious smile indicated otherwise. Swiveling my head, I looked back as my thighs landed on the floor, finishing the splits. There was a Mark II falling backwards, like a chopped down oak tree. The Bowie knife sticking out of his forehead might have had something to do with his current state. Most likely, it damaged his muscle control, somehow causing all of them to seize. He hit the floor with a resounding thud, and didn't even twitch. One arm was immobile next to his side, the other was frozen in an extended position, with his hand now pointed at the ceiling. Luckily, the gun he held didn't discharge and blow a hole in the top of the plane when he came crashing down.

Turning back to face Eliza, I intended to scold her about the whole throwing-a-knife-at-my-head thing, but she was already scrambling to her feet. She didn't stand, but scurried past me in a crouched position. I crouched and fell in line behind her.

We stopped at the fallen android, and Eliza went to work freeing the gun from his grip. As she wrestled with the weapon, we had a chance to solidify the plan.

"For a second, I was worried you weren't going to duck my throw."

The gun wasn't coming free fast enough for her, so she began bending his fingers backwards.

SQUEEEEK...CRACK!

"Yeah, I'm sure you were worried. You know, you could've let me know a little more about the plan before putting it into action."

CREEEAK...SNAP!

"Where's the fun in that?"

Pop...Pop......POP...CRUNCH!

"Eliza, stop that! You're not even trying to get the gun loose anymore!"

My sister stared at me, and yanked the gun from his mangled hand.

"Anna, for god's sake, grow a pair!"

"Hey! I *do* have a pair!"

My sister's mouth began to twist into that wild grin of hers, but I ignored her and kept going.

"Don't even...you know what I mean! I wanted you to stop because you were torturing him.

"Okay, first, this guy is dead, so he can't feel pain...and second, if he were alive, he still wouldn't have felt anything because Mark IIs aren't built with pain receptors. Now, let's take out the one in the cockpit before he realizes something has gone wrong back here!"

She crept toward the open cockpit, but I stayed put.

"Hey, I don't have a weapon."

She replied without slowing or even looking back.

"God...just grab my knife and come on!"

Sighing, I put my left hand on the Mark II's skull and grabbed the knife with my right. I was just about to yank it free, when I noticed something. The android's eyes were rolling around in every direction. As I stared in amazement, the eyes began to slow. He wasn't dead, but he was dying...and fast. I looked up to call out to Eliza, but she was so close to the cockpit, Unit 1 would have heard me. Looking down at the Mark II, I knew by the time we'd finished our assault, he'd be dead. This would be my only chance to interrogate one of them, because Eliza was so furious with Unit 1 that she was going to kill him. The only problem was that if I stayed here, I'd leave my sister without backup. Cursing under my breath, I looked back to Eliza one last time, as she got ready to charge the cockpit. Then I went to work on the dying android.

* * * * *

He'd be dead in less than a minute, but that was plenty of time for me to connect to his mind and see what he knew. Time always passed much slower in the interfuse world, because I could exchange enormous amounts of information at the speed of light. What might take too long, was locating his access port. At any other time, I'd do this over the air, but Eliza's little jammer had eliminated that option.

Rolling him over onto his side, the first place I checked was the back of the neck, at the base of the skull...no luck. I tore open the black jacket he wore, yanked the pressed white shirt out of his waistband, and tore it the same way. It had to be somewhere on the spine, so I began searching his back. There! In the middle of his back was a tiny horizontal mark that looked like a scar. That had to be it. Holding him steady, I lined up the index finger on my right hand with the access port. Holding my breath, I stabbed him hard with my fingernail penetrating his skin. As the world around me began to shift and swirl bringing on that familiar feeling of disorientation, I knew I'd hit the right spot.

* * * * *

Interfusing took me into the digital world where computer systems and devices had their own personalities, which I call personas. As my connection strengthened, the real world faded away into a ghostly outline. Although, it didn't disappear so much that I was unaware of my physical surroundings, and I could always shift my attention back if needed.

For now, I found myself entering deeper and deeper into the android's neural-net brain. It was always exciting to see how the system and persona would present itself. I'd been in quite a few digital system constructs, and their originality never disappointed. They were always colorful and entertaining, representing a unique combination of the system's designer, mixed together with the software's purpose.

The interfuse connection completed, and the construct finished forming. I found myself in what looked like a small, undecorated room. The walls were a plain, flat white color, with no windows and just one plain wooden door of the same white color in the far wall. In the middle of this plain room, was a plain table with two plain chairs, all of them with that same base white shade. I couldn't believe it. Never had I encountered a construct that looked so, well, *plain*.

The door opened, and the Mark II's persona staggered in, collapsing into the closest chair. It was an exact copy of his physical form, again something lacking any original thought or imagination. I suppose I shouldn't have been shocked, since these androids were designed not to have any ideas of their own. Still, it was a sad sight.

He looked like he might shutdown at any moment, so I rushed over to the table and sat next to him. Time to get some answers.

My hacking software was second to none, and unique in an incredible way. To get information out of a computer system, I would interfuse with it, and we would have a discussion, like I would with any human. So hacking for me was no different than interrogating a person, except that in here, there wasn't anyone better. I lowered my head, trying to make eye contact as I spoke.

"Mark II, can you hear me?"

With some effort, he raised his head.

"This one's designation is, Unit 2."

"Okay, Unit 2, may I ask you some questions?"

"Yes, proceed."

"What is your status?"

"Unit 2 has suffered a knife wound to the head which penetrated..."

"Summarize, please."

"Unit 2's wound is critical. It is on the verge of permanent system shutdown."

I'd been right, he was dying.

"Unit 2, what is our location?"

"This unit does not have access to that data. Wireless functions are nonoperational."

Crap, I had to be more specific.

"Unit 2, what is the destination of this aircraft?"

"This unit does not have access to that data. Navigation is Unit 1's responsibility."

The lighting in the room began to dim, and his head drooped a little.

"Unit 2, who is currently in charge at the military base known as Ice Castle?"

"The current Ice Castle commander is Stepan Entsky."

If Stepan was still the base commander, then in all likelihood, this was a mutiny by someone that had access to the androids and knew how they worked. There was just one person I knew that fit that description, but I wanted to hear him say the name.

The lights dimmed again, and the android sank down in his seat, his head lolling back until it rested on the back of the chair. I'd never been interfused with a system when it critically failed, and I didn't want to start with this one.

"Unit 2, who overrode Eliza's command of this mission? Who is your commander?"

With some effort, he raised his head and replied.

"You ask this unit two questions."

I sighed and was about to rephrase my query when it spoke.

"May I ask you a question...in...exchange...for...my...answer?"

His speech was coming in uneven cadence and volume. I was running out of time.

"Unit 2, ah, sure, what's the question."

"Will...I...feel...anything?"

Stunned, I had no idea how to respond. He couldn't mean what I thought. There was a nervous hoarseness in my voice as I whispered back to him.

"Unit 2, clarify."

"Mark IV Anna, will I feel anything…when…I…die?"

There was no denying it now. He was asking about his own death. I didn't know if the knife in his neural-net brain had scrambled its thought patterns, or if all Mark IIs were capable of thinking at this level and I'd been lied to by Eliza. My decision was easy. Even though he had just threatened my life and I actually had no idea what his death would bring him, I couldn't watch him die without hope. So, I told Unit 2 what he wanted to hear.

"Yes…yes, you will…and it's such a wonderful feeling."

His expression didn't change, it couldn't, since his face was just a molded mask, but his eyes told me the truth. He was at peace.

"The man you seek…is…Warren…Lopata."

There it was, out in the open…now to get out of here. I stood, but before I could leave the table, the android put his hand on top of mine. He raised his head to look at me, and Unit 2 spoke his last words.

"Thank…you…Ann…"

His eyes closed, and he let go of my hand. Without warning, the room went pitch black. A chill ran down my spine, and I rushed to close my interfuse connection. As I did, the physical world swirled back into focus. This was when the sound of gunshots came from the cockpit.

* * * * *

Before I could get to my feet, an explosion sounded and a tornado force wind pulled me forward. Tumbling and out of control, I grabbed for anything that might give me a chance to stop my roll and orient myself. Bouncing off the front seats, I smacked my stomach on the galley refrigerator. The impact was forceful enough to knock the wind out of me, but I had to keep trying to latch onto something. Because I knew the only thing that could cause this, was explosive decompression, and from the force of the wind, there must be a decent sized hole in the cockpit of the plane. This happened to be just where I was heading, out of control like a feather in a tornado.

Chapter Seven

Crash

Tumbling through the doorway to the cockpit, my right hand caught hold of the doorframe and my feet hit the copilot's seat. Wedging myself in, I looked around to see what the hell had happened. It was chaos. The plane was in a steep, slow-spinning dive that was severe enough to set off the flight alarm. Repeating again and again, it screamed above the roar of the deafening wind for someone to take action.

"WHOOP WHOOP, PULL UP! ...... WHOOP WHOOP, CABIN PRESSURE! ...... WHOOP WHOOP, PULL UP! ...... WHOOP WHOOP, CABIN PRESSURE!"

Damn! I'd forgotten about the lack of oxygen! As androids, Eliza and I didn't need to breathe per se, but we needed air for our power cells to function, they were like our hearts. Without air, we'd shutdown and die, just like an oxygen deprived person. Our advantage of needing about half of what a person did was the reason we were still conscious. I just hoped we'd reach an altitude where the air was breathable before it was too late.

Shielding my face, I tried to look around. It was next to impossible because of the forceful wind and all the flying debris. More than once, something flew into the room and slammed into my arm. There were clipboards, drinking glasses, bottles of orange juice, you name it, and it was all trying to bash in my skull. The miniature missiles were packing quite a punch, and I saw several of them slam into the instrument panels, shattering themselves and whatever control components they happened to encounter.

Following the path of the debris, I looked to my right. Unit 1's pilot seat was empty, and he was nowhere to be found. Eliza was near his seat, facing a three-foot square window in the plane's side…and she was fighting for her life. The window's glass was missing, and her hands were on each side of the frame pushing against the suction, as random debris slammed into her back.

"ELIZA, ARE YOU OKAY?"
"NEVER BETTER…YOU?"

"WHOOP WHOOP, PULL UP! …… WHOOP WHOOP, CABIN PRESSURE!"

What a smart-ass. I should… A heavy thumping sound interrupted my introspection. Glancing back into the cabin, I saw Unit 2's body rolling into the cockpit. My eyes widened and I screamed at Eliza.

"GET DOWN! THE OTHER MARK II IS COMING!"
"I CAN'T LET GO OR I'LL BE SUCKED OUT!"

"WHOOP WHOOP, PULL UP! …… WHOOP WHOOP, CABIN PRESSURE!"

Checking the cabin, the Mark II had gotten itself stuck on the refrigerator door. Maybe that would give me enough time. I pushed myself down to the floor, and crawled until I got to her legs. Reaching up, I grabbed her waist and pulled using all my strength. She slid down the wall clearing the window, just as Unit 2 came tumbling into the room. He still smacked her in the back, but his body flew out the window without taking Eliza with him. We sat on the floor with our backs against the wall, trying to catch our breath. My sister rubbed her lower back as she complained.

"FUCK! THAT BASTARD WAS HEAVY! THAT'S GOING TO BE SORE TOMORROW!"
"WELL MAYBE IF YOU HADN'T PUT A BULLET THROUGH THE WINDOW, YOUR BACK WOULDN'T HAVE GOTTEN HURT!"

"WHOOP WHOOP, PULL UP! ...... WHOOP WHOOP, CABIN PRESSURE!"

"HEY! AT LEAST UNIT 1 HAD THE DECENCY NOT TO KICK MY ASS ON THE WAY OUT! BESIDES, IF YOU'D BEEN HERE TO BACK ME UP, I WOULDN'T HAVE HAD TO USE THE GUN AT ALL!"

I winced at her accusation. Even though I was sure she'd have come up with some excuse to kill Unit 1 whether I'd been here or not, Eliza had a point.

"I WAS INTERROGATING UNIT TWO, AND I LEARNED THAT WE WERE RIGHT, WARREN LOPATA WAS THE ONE COMMANDING THE MARK IIS!"
"FUCK LOPATA! I AM SO GOING TO KICK HIS ASS WHEN I GET BACK TO ICE CASTLE!"

"WHOOP WHOOP, PULL UP! ...... WHOOP WHOOP, PULL UP!"

The wind died down and debris stopped flying around the cockpit. Even the roar of the open window decreased, allowing Eliza and I to stop yelling at each other. She lunged forward and climbed into the pilot's seat. Strapping herself in, she pointed to a panel next to me and barked out an order.
"Anna, look over the copilot's controls and see if you can gain access to the plane's computer. If you can, have it disable the wireless network jammer so I can contact a GPS satellite and figure out where we are. I'll level us off and check out how bad the jet is damaged."

"WHOOP WHOOP, PULL UP! ...... WHOOP WHOOP, PULL UP!"

She reached out and punched a set of buttons on the panel to her right.
"For god's sake shut up!"

"WHOOP..."

"There, now I can think."

"How bad does it look?"

"Well, the instruments are screwed, most of them got smashed by all that crap flying around."

She continued to scan the panels and flipped a few switches to see if they functioned.

"Hell, I can't even tell our altitude, but at least we're low enough to have breathable air. Otherwise, the cockpit alarm wouldn't have stopped complaining about the cabin pressure."

I watched as she continued to work with the thrust levers and flight stick, making slight adjustments at first, then trying more aggressive techniques to improve our situation.

Sliding into the copilot's seat, I buckled myself in and searched for the plane's access port.

"Well it looks like you know what you're doing."

"Yeah, I know how to operate most military equipment, and this jet is similar to a Russian cargo plane."

"Impressive."

She rolled her eyes and scowled.

"No, not really. I can't download information and instantly learn how to perform a task like other androids I know."

I ignored the snide comment. She wasn't even right, well, not by the strictest terms. It was true. I could learn mental tasks, like a new language, just by downloading the information into my neural-net data storage. However, any physical skill, such as karate, had to be practiced before I could perform it well. Also, I had to practice these new skills if I wanted to keep them. Otherwise, my proficiency with them would decrease and after a time I'd forget them altogether, just like a human brain's short-term and long-term memory.

Without much effort, I found the plane's port just to my left under a set of shattered, non-functional gauges.

"I found the port, and I'm connecting."

"Good...I've almost got it...there!"

The jet pulled out of its dive as I slipped my fingernail into the access port.

* * * * *

As the interfusing began, the world around me shimmered and faded away into just an outline of its former self. The process is always a bit disorienting, but this time was the strangest crossover I'd ever experienced. When the connection was complete, I found myself sitting in the same cockpit as in the physical world. No wait, not quite the same. In this digital representation, I sat on the opposite side of the plane, in the pilot's seat, and flying debris hadn't damaged the interior.

Scanning the rest of the room, I saw the system's persona sitting in the copilot's seat to my right. The man's stocky hands were trying to operate some of the controls, but he wasn't having much luck. Grumbling to himself, he ran a hand through his thinning brown hair and spat a curse at the jet. After slapping the flight stick, he caught sight of me, and turned his bulky form toward my seat. Straightening his tan leather flight jacket, he gathered his composure and addressed me in Russian.

"Greetings comrade, I am the control system of the FlightMaster 160XR, how may I be of service?"

Russian was my native language, and after checking the ranking insignia on his jacket, I replied to him in kind.

"Good morning, Captain. I am Anna Krukov, special agent in service to Stepan Entsky."

"Ah, so you report to the commander of Ice Castle?"

"That is affirmative."

He rubbed his chin and chuckled.

"I'm shocked that Comrade Entsky allowed you to keep your rank after defecting to America. To us, you are known as Traitor Anna."

So much for using my old alias to bluff my way through.

"Yes, well, if you are aware of that, you must also be aware that Ice Castle sent Eliza to escort me back."

"I am."

"Then you know that someone altered the mission. Someone who is not the Ice Castle base commander."

"WHOOP WHOOP, ENGINE FIRE IMMINENT! ...... WHOOP WHOOP, ENGINE FIRE IMMINENT!"

"Pardon me for a moment."

He turned back to his control panel and flipped a switch or two.

There was a whooshing sound from outside my window and I saw a cloud of white powder spray from the rear of the wing-mounted engine. Sighing, he turned back to me.

"Now, where were we? Ah, yes, I realize the mission has been altered, but what am I to do about it?"

"What you can do is deactivate your GPS jamming device so that Eliza can determine our location. Then she can alter our heading and carry out the mission as intended by the base commander."

Folding his arms across his broad chest, he shook his head in reply.

"I'm afraid I can't do that, Traitor Anna. My orders come from a valid source and I have no intention of countermanding them."

"Very well, then deactivate your GPS jammer and tell me where we should fly the plane according to these new orders of yours."

"Ha, your deceitful ways are well known. There is no way you would actually carry out the new orders."

"Look Captain, both of the Mark IIs are dead. There's no one on this damn plane that knows where we're supposed to be headed, or even our current position, thanks to the explosive decompression damaging most of the instruments. So if you want any shot at your precious orders being carried out, you'll turn off that jammer and tell me where we're going!"

"WHOOP WHOOP, ENGINE FIRE IMMINENT! ...... WHOOP WHOOP, ENGINE FIRE IMMINENT!"

"Pardon me again."

He worked the controls on his panel the same way as last time, but I noticed that only half as much of the white powder sprayed out of the engine's exhaust. He mumbled as he turned back to face me.

"Well, that was the last of it."

"The last of what?"

"The fire retardant. That engine won't last much longer. It was badly damaged when the air inlet sucked in some large, heavy object. The fan made quick work of whatever it was, but its blades are bent to hell and back."

Even though I knew he was already dead, the thought of the Mark II being ground up by the jet engine still made me wince.

"Then I use that as my final argument to you Captain. Since we are in such dire circumstances, you have to do as I ask. It's our only chance at survival."

He considered it for a moment, then shrugged. Reaching inside his weathered jacket, he took out a piece of paper and handed it to me.

"You have a point, it's not like were getting out of this anyway. Here is the location of the airfield where we were supposed to land. We're close, but not close enough."

I unfolded the thick paper to see that it was a map. Scanning it, I saw what looked like a covert military base with a small runway on the north side. As I committed it to memory, the captain fiddled with some dials to his right.

"There, I have disabled the GPS jammer, comrade Eliza should now be able to discern our location. Although I'm sure it won't matter."

Stuffing the map into my jeans pocket, I began disconnecting from our interfuse session.

"Don't say that. If we work together, we can still make it out of this."

His face wore a smirk as he faded from my view.

"I wish you both good luck, Traitor Anna, for all our sakes."

With that, the connection closed, and I was back in the noisy cockpit of the real world.

* * * * *

"Eliza! You should be able to get our position now!"

"Yeah, I can sense the satellite, hold on…and…holy shit!"

"What? Where are we?"

"I don't know what that bastard Lopata had in mind, but we're flying over the northern part of China!"

It took a second for that to sink in…we were over a thousand miles from Ice Castle's location.

"No time to worry about that, while I was talking with the jet's systems, it told me that one of the engines might catch fire soon. Can you check on them?"

She looked around and sighed.

"The engine temperature gauges are broken. I have no idea what shape they're in."

"I'm not sure it matters, I think the system already used all the fire suppressant anyway."

"Fantastic…if that engine goes out, we'll have to land, and from what the GPS is telling me, we're in the middle of a damn forest. That won't be a landing you can walk away from."

"Wait, we have another choice. The jet gave me the Mark II's target destination, we could head that way."

She shook her head.

"No fucking way! I'm not flying us right up to the front door of wherever Lopata was trying to send us! There's no way that ends well."

"Look, we don't have much of a choice, do we?"

Before Eliza could respond, a monstrous explosion rocked the plane.

"WHOOP WHOOP, ENGINE FAILURE! ...... WHOOP WHOOP, ENGINE FIRE!"

"Shit! You're right, give me the location!"

As she fought with the control stick, I rattled off the longitude and latitude of the Chinese base. By the time I'd finished, it looked like she had us stable again.

"Okay, well, the good news is we're already heading in that direction. The bad news is…"

"WHOOP WHOOP, ENGINE FAILURE! ...... WHOOP WHOOP, ENGINE FIRE!"

"Damn it! Shut up!"

She punched at the control panel and the alarm went silent.

"The bad news is, those coordinates are several hundred miles from where we are. I don't know if we can make it."

To emphasize her point, a shuddering thump came from underneath the plane, and the control stick ripped itself from her hands. It slammed forward, and the jet lurched, nose down toward the ground.

"WHOOP WHOOP, PULL UP! ...... WHOOP WHOOP, PULL UP!"

"You gotta be fucking kidding me!"

Eliza grabbed the stick and pulled, but all she could do was move it an inch or so back.

"Anna, grab the flight stick and help me pull back! The hydraulic systems have ruptured and our control surfaces have locked up!"

"I don't know what the hell you're talking about! I can't fly a damn plane!"

"Just grab the stick and help me pull or we're going to hit the ground at a couple hundred miles an hour!"

"WHOOP WHOOP, PULL UP! ...... WHOOP WHOOP, PULL UP!"

Reaching out, I grabbed the yoke with both hands and gave it a pull. It didn't budge. Okay, fine. Taking a deep breath, I braced my feet against the floor and gripped the stick tight in my hands. Then, I pulled back hard as I could manage...inch by inch, the stick moved toward me. Eliza grunted.

"Great, we're doing it! Pull harder!"

"WHOOP WHOOP, PULL..."

My muscles ached as I flexed them harder than I'd ever done before, but I couldn't get the yoke back to center. The plane wasn't in an uncontrolled descent anymore, but we were still nose down. I realized we weren't going to make it.

"I can't move it any further! It's too heavy!"

Eliza's voice was thick with strain as she replied.

"Yeah, the controls are frozen. We're not going to be able to pull out of this dive."

We looked at each other, and I almost spoke, but my sister cut me off.

"Hold the nose up as long as you can, I'm looking for somewhere to land."

As I held on for dear life, I took a quick glance out the windows. It was a beautiful view...of a dense forest. I didn't know about Eliza, but I couldn't even see the ground for the thick green trees, let alone a place to land a plane.

"WHOOP WHOOP, TERRAIN PROXIMITY! ...... WHOOP WHOOP, TERRAIN PROXIMITY!"

Eliza's insane sounding laugh I'd heard so many times before, burst out of her like never before.

Crash

"Well, at least we won't have to put up with *that* much longer!"

I looked over at her and grinned, right as the wing on her side of the plane caught the top of one of the taller trees. The rending and screeching of metal was deafening, as the wing was sheared off the jet. The force of the impact spun us like a top, and my head felt like it was going to snap off my neck. More sounds of wrenching metal came from behind me, as we ricocheted like a pinball through the forest. The cockpit must have separated from the rest of the plane, because we went into a tight spin. Faster and faster we spun, head over heels, until I felt myself passing out. The last thing I saw was a massive tree branch smash into the cockpit on Eliza's side and tear it away.

And just like that, she was gone.

Chapter Eight

Seperated

The smell of fresh air mixed with damp earth filled my nose...but why? Where was I that had that aroma...and why was it pitch black? Why couldn't I see anything? I heard the sounds of birds, and chirping insects...where was I? Why couldn't I remember? Oh, stupid, stupid... my eyes are closed...but they won't open. So hard to open my eyes... there, opened them now. Damn...it was bright, even where I was, in the shadows, the light made my head throb. How did I get on my side? Lying on the ground, all I could see was the moist, fertile soil...needed to get up. OW! Every muscle was sore, like I'd been beaten with a steel rod. What happened? I couldn't stand. It was like a heavy weight was holding me down. Wait...what were these straps across my chest. They bound me to a heavy metal seat of some kind. So...so tired, maybe just rest a minute...No! My head ached, but I knew it was important to get up and, and...look for something? Wait, that's not it, I had to look for *someone*...but who? My vision cleared some, I could see further now. What was that, looks like something smoldering...large pieces of shredded metal? Why were they here? One of the pieces almost looked like the tail section from a...a plane...a plane? A plane! Oh god...the plane crash...Eliza!

* * * * *

Like a searing light, the memory of the accident came blazing back, burning away the dark cloud that hung over my mind. Blinking my eyes, I cleared my vision even more. My head and body ached, but I was able to hit the release catch on the seat's harness. I rolled free and eased myself into a sitting position. It hurt like crazy, but I had to take stock of myself. By some stroke of luck, I was in decent shape. Sure, I had a few bad lacerations on my arms and legs, but none of them were life threatening. Well, they weren't life threatening to *me* at least. The microscopic repair robots that lived in my blood, the scientists back at the lab had called them EmBees, would take care of repairing my injuries. They were marvels of nanotechnology, but they couldn't fix something like a broken bone, since my skeleton was a high-tech metal composite.

Before trying to stand, I ran my hands all over my body, to see if the crash had broken any bones. Again, luck was with me, because I found nothing out of place. Using my hands to steady myself, I stood, which was a big mistake. The forest spun around me, and my head throbbed, almost making me lose my balance. That fog from before floated back over my brain, but I fought back. I had to look for Eliza, and that required me to stand. Staggering over to a tree, I leaned against it for a minute to see if the world would stop spinning so fast. Deep breaths should have helped, but all they did was fill my lungs with the lingering smoke from the burning plane. How long had I been unconscious? When I checked the time on my internal clock, it stunned me. I'd been out for over two hours. No time to stand around, I had to look for Eliza *now*.

Willing my body to reduce the pain and dizziness as much as possible, I turned in a circle surveying my surroundings. It was a devastating sight. The falling plane had crushed some trees, and ripped the tops off others. Underbrush and small bushes had burned to ashes in the fuel fire after the crash. Mixed amid all the destroyed trees and pockmarked ground, the impact had scattered metal shrapnel everywhere. My hopes of finding Eliza alive sank, because I couldn't find a piece of the plane bigger than a surfboard. Just as I'd given up hope, I noticed the path the plane had made through the forest. Somehow, my seat had been thrown over a hundred feet from the main crash site.

Rushing down the path of destruction carved by the plane, I made it to the largest section of the fuselage. It had large gouges in the side, and was missing a wing, but at least it was still intact. Getting close was a problem, it was still smoldering from the fire. Still, I had to find her.

Picking my way around, I at last got close enough for a good look. Oh no, the cockpit was gone. I cursed in frustration, knowing I'd never find her now. Then, more of my memories about the crash came back to me. The tree! The tree had hit her side and knocked us apart. We must have hit it at over a hundred miles an hour, there was no way she could have survived that…but I had to find her.

＊＊＊＊＊

After looking for half an hour, I decided to change my search tactics. I began searching the tops of the trees further away from the main crash site. The best I could remember, the tree hit the cockpit after we'd torn away from the body of the plane.

Even with my improved vision, it was difficult to see through the dense foliage. I switched to my thermal sight hoping that there would be a difference in the heat signature between the trees and any metal caught in them.

After another forty minutes, I was exhausted. My throat was parched, and I needed to find water soon or I might not make it myself. Full of regret, I abandoned my search and headed back toward the large chunk of fuselage. On the way back, I kept looking in the treetops, hoping against hope.

About seventy-five feet away from the plane's scorched cabin, I saw it. Something was lodged in one of the larger trees. I'd noticed it this time because my view angle was different when walking back to the crash site.

Trying not to get too excited, I circled around the trunk of the tree and used my normal vision to get a more detailed look. Catching a glimpse, it was a piece of the plane, but I couldn't tell if it was Eliza's side of the cockpit or not. It was large enough, but did I dare risk what looked like a fifty-foot climb to find out? That wasn't even a valid question.

Problem was, the lowest hanging branch was two feet above my reach. I needed something to give me a boost. An idea came to me, and I took off for the fuselage. It was still hot, but I worked my way through and got to the galley. Checking the mini-fridge, it still had some usable food and drink in it that had survived the fire. Even better, it had been knocked out of its supports. Now I could carry it back to the tree and use it to reach that branch. Things were looking up.

After wrestling with it for a minute, I realized it wasn't as light as it had looked. There was no way a person would have been able to get it out, but I wasn't a person. I had twice the strength of a normal human, and it still tested even *my* limits. Muscles aching, I had to drag it the last few feet to the tree trunk.

＊＊＊＊＊

After downing a pint of orange juice to keep my strength up, I jumped on top of the fridge and grabbed the branch. Pulling myself up, I straddled it, and looked for my next move. Branch after branch, I worked my way up. It was slow going, because I had to make sure each one would hold my weight. Thanks to my durable metal skeleton, I was a bit heavier than I looked…just like the fridge.

After what felt like hours, I reached the same level as the part of the plane. Working my way over to it, I saw it was a part of the cockpit. A large branch had impaled it, and then bent backwards from the impact. In that moment, I realized what I was going to find behind those limbs, and that realization frightened me. Even though I'd been sure that one day I was going to kill her, the thought of her being dead turned my world upside down. Maybe because without her, there wasn't anyone else that could possibly understand what it was like to be who we were… androids in a world full of people. Sighing, I went to work clearing a path through the branches that were blocking me from the cockpit. Snapping some, bending others back, I at last made it to her.

A gasp escaped my lips at the grisly sight. Eliza sat strapped in the seat, with a two-inch branch lodged in her stomach. Dried blood coated her top where the limb had impaled her, and she still gripped the branch…fighting to the end. Reaching out, I turned her cold, bloodless face toward me, and saw she had even more dried blood around her nose, mouth, and ears. Despite all she'd done to me, I had to fight back a wave of unexpected emotions. A wry smile crossed my face as I realized it would have made her so pissed to know that I felt anything for her… since she had always lacked that capacity.

Even though I knew it would be an arduous task getting her down, leaving Eliza here like this was out of the question. Studying the branch that had impaled her, I removed it with no further damage being done. Reaching up to release her seatbelt harness, I had to shift her around in the seat to remove all the straps, another unpleasant deed. I bent over her and was about to pick her up, when a slight breath escaped her lips. No, it couldn't be, it was just my imagination. With an unsteady hand, my fingertips found her neck. My god, she had a pulse! She actually had a pulse! It was as faint as faint could be, but at least she had one!

* * * * *

My happiness soon drained away as I did a closer examination of her. She breathed in short, rasping fits, with long pauses in between. They sounded as if they could end at any moment. Her bleeding had stopped, but if I tried to get her out of the tree, it might start back and she'd bleed to death before we got to the ground. Depressed, I realized all I could do was stay here with her as she passed.

I hated this feeling. It wasn't like we were friends, but I was sick of watching death claim its prize. In my short time on this planet, I'd seen so many friends... My head ached and I lost my train of thought. Rubbing at my eyes, I pressed them hard with the palms of my hands trying to get the pain to stop. Damn, I was beginning to think I might have a concussion or something worse. It made me realize I might not be out of the woods yet myself.

A bitter smirk appeared on my mouth as I realized my accidental pun, but it was no laughing matter. If I had a brain injury, this tree might become a grave for both of us. My melancholy feeling came back and I wondered if I'd ever see any of my friends again. My head throbbed again, and I screamed a curse at the top of my lungs, which didn't help my headache at all.

Damn it! Why did it hurt whenever I thought about my friends? Without warning, another layer of fog rolled away from my mind and uncovered another memory I'd forgotten. Zory! Stepan still had him captive, and Eliza had told me if anything happened to her, he'd be killed. Hell, knowing Stepan, he'd kill all my friends back in Alabama too. However, there was the chance that Stepan had been killed in whatever coup was happening at Ice Castle, but I didn't dare risk the life of my friends on that chance. I had to make sure Eliza lived, at least until I could get Zory free and find a way to protect my friends in the United States. Even though I didn't think she'd ever live through it, I had to try. Now I needed a plan to get her to the ground.

Before moving Eliza, I wanted to give her a thorough check, like I'd done for myself. Small cuts and bruises covered her body, but I couldn't find any broken bones. There was of course the huge stomach wound, and that she'd been bleeding from her ears and mouth, which indicated internal injuries. I shook my head. There wasn't anything I could do to help her up here. Easing my sister out of the seat, I put her over my shoulder and began the trek back down.

It was a tricky climb. More than once, I slipped a few feet before catching myself. That caused me to almost drop Eliza several times. Each time it happened, I was sure we'd both had it.

After way too long, we arrived at the last branch. Lowering myself down with my one free hand, my feet touched the refrigerator. Relief to see the end of my ordeal overcame me…and that was when the branch I held snapped under our weight. The sudden shift caused my feet to slide across the top of the metal fridge…and there was nothing to stop our fall.

It was a short couple of feet to the ground, but when my reflexes kicked in, and I analyzed how we'd land, it was bad news. Eliza would hit the ground first, then I'd land on top of her. Desperation took over, and I tried every trick I knew to rotate us around so that I would hit first and be able to cushion her fall, but the best I could do was land beside her on my face instead of on top of her. She slammed down, landing on her back, and I jumped up to see if she was all right. I held my breath as I sat there, but it wasn't a long wait.

Eliza's hands and feet began to twitch, then the tremors spread up her limbs until her whole body was involved. It was terrifying to watch, as the seizure became more and more violent. She started making choking sounds, so I forced her mouth open and held her tongue down with my fingers. Clamping down with her teeth, she almost bit them off, but I refused to let go. After about a minute, the seizure slowed and her mouth relaxed. Pulling my painful, bloody hand away from her mouth, I eased her head to the ground. Soon, she became still, and I wondered if that was the worst of it. It wasn't. Eliza took a deep breath, which I found encouraging, but after she exhaled, no inhale followed. It was a horrible feeling. I kept waiting and waiting for her to breathe in, but she never did. To my horror, my sister had stopped breathing.

Chapter Nine

Inside a Nightmare

Placing my fingers against her throat confirmed my fear. Eliza had no pulse. Oh no…oh no…no, NO! I wasn't trained for this, and had no idea what to do. Even my knowledge of first aid was limited. I knew her airway was clear, because she'd just been breathing. Other than that…

Because I had no other ideas, I leaned over her and began CPR. I wasn't even sure it would work on an android, even though a lot of our anatomy was similar to a person's. It was a design choice to help us blend in better with people. Not wanting to reopen her stomach wound, I performed the compressions with the utmost care. She didn't respond to my efforts.

Damn it all to hell! I couldn't just sit here and let her die, there had to be something, if I could just get my head to stop pounding long enough to think. It was killing me! Wait, yeah, that just might work… I jumped up and ran around looking for a small, sharp piece of plane debris to put my plan into action.

A couple of weeks ago, Eliza sent a Mark II to capture me. I destroyed him and escaped, but he managed to damage me too. So much so, that I collapsed after stumbling my way home. There, in my living room floor, I was dying, and there was no one around to help. Right before passing out, I interfused with the Internet, to say goodbye to my best friend, Athena. Since she was a being that existed in the digital world, with no physical form whatsoever, her arrival was instantaneous. Once she saw my condition, Athena asked me to lower my mental defenses, and let her into my mind. I did, and found myself alive the next morning. She had used her vast processing power to take over for my failing functions. It was like putting a human on life support. This was how I intended to help Eliza. I would be her life support...after I took care of one little thing first.

* * * * *

Ah, found it! Picking up the jagged piece of metal, I bent the edges around to make a handle on one end, and straightened the other end best as I could. Feeling around, I found the bump on the top of my head where Eliza had implanted the wireless jammer. It had to be removed, or I couldn't connect to Eliza's mind. She would have a physical port like the Mark II's, but I didn't have time to search for it. The link had to be made now.

I ran the edge of my makeshift knife over the wireless jammer under my scalp. My crude tool wasn't as sharp as I'd hoped, and the thick, uneven shrapnel jerked and tore at my flesh. I ground my teeth, as blood soaked into my hair and poured down the side of my head. Digging at the bump with my wet sticky hand, I still couldn't get it dislodged. I'd have to make another cut. Pressing harder this time, I cursed and screamed when my homemade torture device went deep enough to scrape across my skull.

Blood was dripping from my chin, and my hands shook as I dug around trying to get a grip on the device. It had all been worth it when I felt my gooey fingers latch onto the tiny jammer. Placing it on the ground, I picked up a rock and smashed it several times.

It was as if a great dam had burst, flooding my parched mind with data. Hundreds of different bits of information became known to me in an instant, as I reestablished my connections with all the available satellites. They fed me gigabytes of data on our current position, down to the temperature and humidity. I wanted to dig into all that information, but it would have to wait.

There was a dirty, singed washcloth hanging from the fridge, and it became a bandage for the bleeding gash on my head. Scalp injuries wouldn't kill you, but they bled like crazy. After getting the cloth in place, I knelt down next to Eliza and attempted to connect to her systems, not via my normal wireless transmission path, but by a special connection between us. I'd never used the electromagnetic field around my neural-net brain to attempt a connection to another system, but Eliza had done it to me.

Back when I was a few days old, I had these terrible nightmares. Come to find out, it had been my sister invading my mind while it was the most vulnerable.　She was using all kinds of bizarre nightmare situations attempting to kill me.　It was horrifying until I figured out what was happening and fought back.　My theory was, if she could use her mind to do all these strange and horrible things, things that affected me in the physical world, then I could do the same to her.　I could use the same technique to heal, instead of harm.

It wasn't working.　I didn't feel her at all.　Was I too late?　I lay down next to her, and closed my eyes.　Concentrating, clearing my mind of all the physical pain and outside stimuli, I thrust my mind outward, toward her.

Then I felt the slightest sensation.　It was her...but she was so weak.　I had to make this connection, her life depended on it.　Beads of sweat mixed with the blood on my face as I focused all my efforts on joining our minds.　At last, I felt the surge of dizziness that is the precursor to a successful interfuse connection, but this time was different.　It was stronger than I'd ever felt before.　This wasn't a connection of systems anymore.　This was a bonding of minds.　Everything I was, all that made me...*me*, mixed with everything that was Eliza.　Fear flashed through my mind, but I couldn't back out now, this was my last chance to save her.　Giving myself over to the interfusion, I wondered if I'd ever be able to close the link, and separate myself from her.　Would I ever be Anna again?

* * * * *

As the disorientation wore off, I found myself sitting on a bed in a small room with dim lighting.　Looking around, I couldn't believe my eyes.　It looked like my old room from the laboratory beneath Ice Castle, where the scientists had created me.　It had my desk, the wardrobe, the shower, everything.　It was my old room, except a few things were out of place.　The bed had fewer pillows than I remembered, and the computer on the desk didn't look right either.　Wait, this wasn't *my* old room.　This was Eliza's room.　As a matter of fact, where was she?　Even though time moved much slower in here than the physical world, the quicker I found her, the better.

I leapt up from the bed expecting my feet to land on soft carpet, but they didn't.　Instead, there was a splash, and I stood in a cold liquid up to my ankles.　The surprise caused me to sit back down on the bed and pull my feet up.　Checking them, black goo that had the smell of decaying flesh mixed with petroleum covered my shoes.　That smell...I'd never forget it. A shiver ran down my spine as the horrible memory resurfaced.

My second night at the lab, Eliza entered my mind and attacked me with this vile goo. In the nightmare, the door to my shower wouldn't open, trapping me inside, while it filled with this disgusting liquid. I escaped at the last second by breaking the shower door open, but not before almost drowning. When I awoke, still screaming, that smell was lingering in my nose. The whole experience was so traumatizing, I made sure the shower in my apartment had a curtain…no more shower doors for me. Why was this sludge here now? Was it a kind of symbolism in Eliza's mind?

It didn't matter. I had to get over my fear and find her before it was too late. Wincing, I put my feet back down and stood up. Trudging through the muck, I checked the shower stall, the wardrobe, all around the room, but she wasn't here. I'd have to widen my search area to encompass the entire laboratory.

Moving to the room's door, I opened it and looked out into the hallway. It was all just like I remembered it, except for the floors being covered in sludge. Seeing the emergency stairs that led to the surface, I realized something. What if Eliza wasn't in the lab, but on the surface somewhere, like Stepan's office? Where should I search? If I chose wrong, she'd die before I could help her. After a bit of reflection, I sloshed over to the emergency door and opened it. She must have gone to where she was most comfortable, up to Ice Castle.

I climbed just three steps before noticing that the thick sludge wasn't covering the stairs the way it was in the lab. Somehow, that felt important, and it made me second-guess myself. The weight of this decision was crushing me. For some reason, I changed my mind and went back down the stairs. When I stepped back into the cold, black goo, it had risen to my lower calf. The sludge increasing in level made me feel like I'd made the right decision to turn back…she must be down here. It also made me feel like I was running out of time.

Sloshing back out into the long hallway, I made my way down to where I was sure she'd be. Making a left at the next intersection, I saw Viktor Eklund's room, the man that I considered my father. He was the man that created my neural-net brain and the ability for it to feel emotions. He was the man Eliza had shot and killed the night I escaped from here.

It was difficult to push the door open with that thick muck everywhere, but I managed. Strong emotions came over me when I saw where we used to sit and talk. I swallowed hard and repressed my feelings. There would be time for them later. Right now, the lump under the covers had my full attention.

Trudging over to the headboard, I grabbed the covers and yanked them back.

"Eliza! I'm here!"

Pillows…it was just fucking pillows. I was sure she would be here… then I realized my mistake. This is where *I* would have come, not Eliza.

The lights dimmed further, and I knew what that meant. Hurrying out of Viktor's room, I turned and went down the other long hallway. The fetid sludge had now risen to the bottom of my thighs. I tried to hurry, but it was like running through quicksand, quicksand that smelled of death.

Halfway to my destination, I saw Cindi's room, and I couldn't move. She'd been the scientist that designed my body, and created the technology that allowed me to change my appearance. Cindi was also my first love. She'd been training me on how to use my abilities, when I became infatuated with her, and as the days went by, that feeling deepened. I didn't understand what this strange new emotion was, but it was wonderful. I ended up falling in love with her before any of the scientists even knew I could experience that emotion. Unknown to the others, Viktor had given me the capacity to love, but it was Cindi that had shown me what it *meant* to love…and then Eliza murdered her.

She beat her almost to death, and left her for me to find, for me to watch die. There was no holding back what I felt now. Hot tears flowed down my cheeks like rain, and I asked myself why the hell was I busting my ass to save Eliza. My brain told me it was for my friends who were still alive, but my heart told me to remember all the friends that had been lost because of her.

I knew I should keep going, but my legs wouldn't move. My eyes were fixated on the black-bordered nameplate hanging on her door.

"Cindi with an 'i', I miss you…I miss you so much."

While I stood weeping, the lights dimmed again, becoming nothing more than a spark fighting the inevitable darkness. Cindi wouldn't have wanted me to become like Eliza, risking innocent lives for revenge. I knew it was time to go. Wiping the tears from my eyes, I turned and headed toward the largest room in the complex, the main lab. The room where we were born was the only other place I could imagine Eliza would have gone.

By the time I reached the double-glass sliding doors to the main lab, the disgusting, black goo had risen almost to my waist. In a few more minutes, I'd have to swim to search for Eliza.

Peering through the closed doors, the lab contained a wall full of computer equipment, chairs in the corners, and the waist-high, rectangular table where both our lives began. I remembered the cold touch of its stainless steel like it was yesterday.

What I didn't see, was Eliza. Maybe she wasn't down here, but topside instead. Turning to leave, something caught my eye. Was that the heel of a shoe floating on the sludge? It was! Grabbing the double doors, I forced them apart. Wading over, I grabbed the shoe. Her leg, I felt her leg! I almost had to submerge myself in the waist high muck to get my arms around her. We androids weren't the best swimmers to begin with, because of our increased mass, and since Eliza was unconscious, she'd just sunk right to the bottom.

I wrestled with her until I was able to get her out of that nasty mess, and up onto the table. Checking her over, she looked like she'd been dead for some time…but I knew better. If she *had* been dead, this whole place would have ceased to exist, so I knew she still had fight left in her.

With steady hands and no fear, I readied myself for the task at hand. I was brimming with confidence because we were in digital space now. Out in the real world, I had no idea how to treat a wounded android, but in here, all that changed. This was the world of computer systems and algorithms, what I was designed to master. Yes, this was my world, and my sister would not die here.

Chapter Ten

By a Thread

Eliza lay pale and unmoving on the stainless steel table as I assessed her situation. Since I'd found her face down in the fetid sludge, my first thought was to clear her lungs and get her breathing again. Climbing up onto the table, I got behind her and wrestled her into a sitting position. Wrapping my arms around her, right below the rib cage, I started squeezing and releasing. My hope was the Heimlich Maneuver would force some of the gunk out and allow her to breathe. The compressions worked, and vile black fluid gurgled out of her mouth each time I squeezed. After a few minutes, my efforts stopped producing any results. I must have gotten all of it out that I could using this technique, but she wasn't stable yet. The greasy, noxious muck had risen a few more inches and was now creeping over the top of the table. It was time for a new approach, mouth-to-mouth resuscitation.

* * * * *

While I lay her back down on the table and positioned myself, I couldn't help but marvel at how my infiltration software worked. Viktor and his team had designed me to be the most advanced computer system hacker in the world, and in my humble opinion, they succeeded. The team implemented their unique perspective on how to interface my mind with all the complex programs and algorithms flowing through my brain. Whenever I travelled into the digital world, I didn't see lines of computer code or a bunch of ones and zeroes. I saw people, places, and things. Sitting at a table and convincing someone to see my point of view during an interfusing session, was the real world equivalent of a human using advance software to hack into the system and acquire its data. My software turned the virtual world into a real world inside my head. So when I attended to and helped Eliza's digital form, her physical condition improved. It was the most brilliant computer interface ever devised, and I happened to be the lucky benefactor of their genius.

* * * * *

While we'd been getting into position, that gross, black filth had risen to the bottom of Eliza's ears. Her systems must be close to shutting down, so I went right to work. I tried my best to clean that foul stuff off her face. The smell was so awful it was hard not to gag. Checking her airway to make sure it was clear, I leaned her head back and pinched her nose shut. Covering her mouth with mine, I blew a full breath into her lungs. Her exhale sounded like she was gargling that mess, so I tried again...and again. The ooze had risen so much, I had to lift her head and put it in my lap before continuing.

"Eliza, you bitch, don't you dare die!"

This had to work, the lives of my friends depended on it. I kept working and shouting at her.

"Take a breath, damn you!"

As I leaned over to try again, Eliza's eyes popped open and she coughed. Pulling her up further from the rancid gunk, I turned her head to the side. The coughing fit became so severe that she threw up. She had been full of that crap, and it all came spewing out of her lungs and stomach. After she finished, she collapsed back into my lap and closed her eyes. The sound of her steady breathing was music to my ears. I realized she was out of immediate danger as the viscous, dark goo receded. Within two minutes, all that remained was a thin, slimy coating on everything. At least walking would be easier.

While I was sliding off the table, Eliza began to shake and curled up into the fetal position. At first, I thought she might have another seizure, but her trembling never became that violent. Feeling of her skin, she was ice cold. I needed to warm her up and get her somewhere she could rest. I lifted her up in my arms, and we headed back down the hallway.

* * * * *

By the time we neared her room, I was getting somewhat tired myself. I kept going by assuring myself that all I had to do was get her into bed, and then I could rest. I'd forgotten one thing. Opening the door to her room, I saw that the slime had covered all the furniture.

"Damn it!"

What could I do now? I couldn't put her in a bed covered in that filth.

She'd freeze to death lying in that vile gunk. Then I remembered how Eliza had changed the rooms and places we appeared in, whenever she trapped me in one of her nightmares. Well, if she could do it, so could I.

Placing my sister down in the shower stall, I closed the door to the room. I'd start small and try this one area before taking on the whole complex. Focusing my willpower on an image of the room when it was clean, I projected that idea out from myself in every direction. I could feel power draining from my body, but it was working. All around Eliza's room, the sickening residue faded away. It was demanding, but I held my focus as long as possible. After exhaustion threatened to overcome me, I looked around the room and smiled. It was spotless, but Eliza and I weren't. You could change your environment in the digital world, but you couldn't change things about yourself. I believed it had something to do with a persona having free will. I could have disconnected and come back clean myself, but I didn't dare leave her alone just yet. We'd have to do this the old-fashion way.

I moved Eliza to the clean carpet and turned on the shower. While the water warmed up, I removed her sludge-covered clothing and threw the gunky mess into the corner. By the time I finished, steam rolled out of the shower letting me know it was ready. I opened the door and eased her under the hot water. Just looking at the shower door and remembering my first horrible nightmare gave me a shiver, so I cleaned her up from outside the shower. Sitting on the floor, I scrubbed away with my soapy washcloth until I'd gotten off most of the putrid slime. I let her stay under the warm water until she'd warmed up and her shaking had stopped.

Turning off the shower, I spread towels across the foot of the bed so it didn't get wet. I picked Eliza up and placed her on the soft towels before using another one to dry her. Finished, I adjusted her so that her head was on a soft pillow, and then covered her up to her neck with a sheet and two blankets.

She never stirred or awoke while I worked, which concerned me. Our EmBees were rapid, efficient workers, so for her to be unresponsive this long was a bad sign. My sister's skin was still several shades too pale, and her forehead was cool to the touch. However, her breathing seemed stronger and much more regular, which I took as a good sign.

Pulling a black, leather chair from under the desk, I moved it next to the bed. Exhaustion caught up with me, and I collapsed into the comfortable seat. Trying to relax, I took a nice, deep breath, but the smell of the gunk covering my clothes ruined it for me. I considered taking a shower for a brief second, but then remembered that awful nightmare and dismissed the idea. Looking over at the clean and comfortable Eliza, I grumbled at her.

"Hey, thanks for giving me an irrational fear of shower doors, Sis. You'd better be worth all this trouble."

Settling into the chair, I resigned myself to stay here until she regained consciousness. As long as I stayed in here, I knew anything I did would take workload off her damaged systems and help her heal faster. So, I sat in the chair alone with my thoughts and waited. Hmm, was there a phobia for my issue with shower doors?

Chapter Eleven

Call for Help

After two hours of sitting and waiting for Eliza to regain consciousness, I was a little concerned. Getting out of my comfy seat, I stretched myself out and walked over to her. She was still pale, but her skin was warmer than before and her breathing had improved. However, she still hadn't opened her eyes. Pacing around the room, I came to a decision. It was time to see if I could contact Adam. I'd been dreading talking to him again, but he needed to know what had happened. Not to mention he might be the one person who could help us. After all, he had all the muscle of the NSA behind him. I hoped he'd believe my story. Thinking about what had happened in the last twelve hours, I wasn't sure I believed the string of events that led us here myself. At least I'd be able to change out of the wretched clothes when I left.

Sitting back down, I took a few steadying breaths and began closing the interfuse connection. I'd never joined at this level with any other entity. It was as if I'd moved my entire consciousness from my mind into Eliza's, and I didn't know what breaking the link would do to me.

Uh oh, something didn't feel right, the interfuse session wasn't closing. No, there...it was closing now. I had to use more of my will than was normal to pull apart from her. It was a frightening moment since I wondered what would happen if you didn't have the willpower to separate.

The real world faded into focus, and I found myself lying next to Eliza. Standing up, a wave of dizziness swept over me, and I almost fell over her. Damn, I was so weak that standing was difficult. After making sure my sister was stable, I walked over to the fridge and pulled it open. There weren't many supplies left, but if I didn't eat something, I was going to pass out. I chose the last two pints of milk since they wouldn't stay fresh without the fridge running. My next thought was, would it matter to my android system that they had spoiled. Since I wasn't sure, I guzzled them both down to eliminate any concerns.

Tossing the empty containers back in the fridge, I noticed all the long shadows produced by the trees. The sun had descended and turned a vibrant red color. It was beautiful, but it meant more trouble for us. Night was a dangerous time in any forest, let alone all the other things we had stacked against us. The only shelter we had was the large chunk of fuselage, and it was still smoldering last time I checked. Racing over to where it was, the few small fires that had surrounded it had burned themselves down to nothing. Reaching out to feel the metal, the plane's cabin was also cool to the touch. It looked like luck was with us for a change. Jogging back to where Eliza rested, I lifted her up and headed back to our makeshift shelter. Searching around, I even found decent cushions to use in making her a bed. After settling her in, I went to fetch the refrigerator from under the tree. Dragging it all the way back was grueling work, and wrestling it inside our new home wasn't any easier. Then I went about gathering rocks and wood to build a campfire. There was a huge gash in the top of the cabin, so I setup the fire pit where the smoke could vent. Using a piece of wreckage, I brought a bunch of embers from one of the dying fires, and used it to get ours going. I was even able to find a chunk of debris big enough to close off the large tear in the side of the fuselage. Putting it in place, we had a door of sorts. Sweaty and covered in dirt from head to toe, I flopped down onto a cushion next to Eliza. It was time to man up and quit procrastinating. I had to contact Adam.

* * * * *

Stepping outside of the shelter, I put the makeshift door back in place. Preparing to interfuse to the Internet, I had a thought and closed the connection. Interfusing took a lot of energy, and with our resources in short supply, I went old school. Using my satellite connection to make the phone call, I sent the number. It was the one Adam had given me around two weeks ago while trying to recruit me into the NSA. I hoped it was still valid.

After four rings, I was about to hang up when a click echoed across the connection.

"Hello, this is Sims."

"Adam, is that really you?"

"Yes, this is Adam Sims, who is calling please? Wait…Anna, is that you?"

Relief washed over me. I wasn't alone anymore!

"Yes Adam, it's me. Listen, I have to talk to you."

He didn't reply, but after a few seconds, I detected that he'd placed an encryption filter on the transmission. Good, now I could talk without fear of someone intercepting the call.

"Okay, the line is secure. Go ahead."

"Listen, I'm in big trouble and I need your help. Well, maybe your help *and* your friends help."

"Continue."

Something was wrong. I detected an unusual delay on the transmission. Then I realized what it was, he was tracing the call. I was furious.

"Damn it, Adam! You're tracing this call!"

He replied in that calm, collected voice of his.

"Yes, I am. Is that an issue?"

Fuming, I wasn't sure how to respond. I'd called him for help, and his first thought was to trace my damn call. Never mind that I was about to tell him where I was anyway. I took a deep breath and tried to calm myself. Looking at it from his point of view, I'd have done the same thing. Besides, Eliza and I needed his help. So, I kept calm and continued.

"No, it's no problem at all. As a matter of fact, I was going to tell you exactly where I was, because like I said, I need your help."

"Good, then if it's not a problem, we'll keep the trace running while you tell your story."

Sigh…he was damn blunt sometimes. Anyway, I told him everything that had happened since Eliza and I escaped from him at the airport. I began, as they say, at the beginning, talking about the Mark IIs, the apparent coup at Ice Castle, the plane crash, and Eliza's desperate situation. He never interrupted me as I went on for over a half an hour.

"So that's the whole story, Adam. We're out here and we need your help as quickly as possible."

There was another long pause before he replied.

"Anna, I'm sorry, but I don't believe all that."

That didn't surprise me.

"I know, I know, it all sounds outlandish, but it's true."

"The last time I saw you, you were getting on a plane with this Eliza woman, and she attempted to murder me. How do I know this isn't a ploy to lure the NSA into a compromising position? Do you have any idea where you are?"

"Yes, and I'm sure by now, so do you. We've crashed inside the north east border of China, the Jilin province to be precise."

"Yes, our trace agrees with that statement."

"Of course it does, because I'm telling the truth."

"Hold on for a minute."

Yet another long pause, this one was over a minute long.

"Okay Anna, you know we view you as a valuable asset, and if what you've told me about Eliza is true, we'd be interested in interviewing her as well."

I'd told him about the family tree that Eliza and I shared, implying that she was an android like myself. I felt a little guilty about not mentioning her mental issues, but damn it, I wanted out of here!

"It's all true, Adam, but she's hurt, and I'm afraid that if she doesn't make it, Stepan Entsky will kill my friends."

"Yes, I know, you mentioned that before. Anna, do you know what's *really* going on in Jilin province right now?"

I wasn't happy with the way he'd emphasized that word.

"Only what I've gathered from my Internet research."

Another pause.

"Yes, well, I think you'll find your research is missing a lot of valuable information. China still has serious filters on their Internet satellites. Have you ever heard of a group called The Red Dragons?"

"No, I haven't."

"All right, let me give you a quick history lesson. A few years ago, the communist leaders in China began slowly enacting democratic reforms. This pleased most of the population, but it infuriated the steadfast communist leaders. In response, they formed a pro-communist group called The Red Dragons. This group became increasingly popular with the current Chinese aristocrats who wanted to maintain the status quo. Within the last year, the group has obtained a fair amount of military support, and from what our sources tells us, it has complete control over several provinces. Of course the Chinese government denies that The Red Dragons exist at all."

Rubbing at my eyes, I tried to ease the pain from my growing headache.

"I see, and I can guess what you're about to say next."

"Yes, to arrange for your retrieval from China would be difficult to say the least, but you and Eliza are in a province controlled by The Red Dragons. A group that officially doesn't exist and we have no communications with whatsoever. This makes extraction next to impossible."

My heart sank. I didn't know what to say, so I fell silent.

"Anna, are you there?"

My voice was hoarse with emotion as I replied.

"Yeah, I'm still here…just trying to figure out my options."

"Don't lose hope yet. I will take your request to my superiors and see what can be done."

"Well, it's kinda hard not to lose hope with what you just dropped on me."

"True, but I work for the NSA. I've seen us accomplish 'next to impossible' tasks several times in a week."

"Thanks for believing me, Adam."

"I didn't say I believed you, at least not completely. But that doesn't mean I won't try to help you."

I shook my head. Adam could be honest to a fault sometimes.

"Right, well, thanks for *trying* to help then."

He missed my subtle emphasis and continued.

"Sure…let me give you a different number to use when contacting me. It is always secure."

Committing the number to memory, I thought about my next move as Adam wrapped up the call.

"Give me some time, and I will get back with you as soon as possible. Goodbye, Anna."

"Bye, Adam."

* * * * *

The phone call with Adam left me depressed at first, but once I had time to think about it, there wasn't any other way it could have gone. Well, what could I do while I waited on Adam? There was taking care of Eliza, that was obvious, but there was also the matter of survival. In normal circumstances, Eliza and I didn't need anything but vitamins and water to survive, but this was far from normal circumstances. With her injured and me expending a lot of energy to help her get better, we'd need more than usual. Then there was the issue of us crashing a plane inside a communist country. If either the government forces or The Red Dragons found us, it could be worse than my stay at Ice Castle, much worse.

My mind continued to wander around these threats until I had to consider a situation in which Eliza and I didn't survive. What would happen to my friends if Stepan assumed all this was my fault...and what was happening back at Ice Castle anyway? Perhaps it was time to do a bit of preliminary snooping.

Again, I chose not to interfuse and conserve my energy. I could always do that later if needed. Instead, using a KGB contact number acquired during my training, I placed a call. A young-sounding woman answered the phone and spoke in Russian.

"How may I direct your call, comrade?"

I replied in my native tongue and used my own voice.

"Yes, connect me to Ice Castle."

Using its code name gave me the credibility I needed.

"Of course, hold please."

One ring later, a young Russian man answered.

"This is base 14891IC , how can I direct your call?"

"Greetings comrade, I would like to speak to the base commander please."

"I'm sorry, but the commander is very busy at the moment. May I take a message and have him call you back?"

"Please tell him that squad commander Anna Krukov would like to speak with him. I'm sure he will want to take my call."

A sigh of irritation came from the other end of the line.

"Yes, of course. Hold please while I contact him."

The line went silent, and I monitored it for any kind of trace to be applied, but detected no foul play. Two minutes passed before the young man came back.

"I gave him your name, but he doesn't recognize you. Would you like to leave a message?"

Wow, this was bad. I stammered through my reply.

"N..no, thank you. I will call back later."

I hung up the call and considered what had happened. Anna Krukov was the code name that Stepan had assigned me while I was at Ice

Castle. He would have remembered. Therefore, assuming the phone operator passed my message along, the current base commander wasn't Stepan Entsky. That left two possibilities, either someone replaced Stepan following Moscow's orders, or there had been a coup at Ice Castle. If there'd been a coup, Stepan could be dead, or a prisoner at his own base. Speaking of being a prisoner, I worried about what all this meant for my friend Zory. The only thing I knew for sure was that the new commander was a man.

I'd been away from Eliza too long. It was time to get back inside and interfuse with her. Maybe she would be awake, and I could give her the new information I had. Well, at least some of it.

Chapter Twelve

Bad Connection

I'd been sitting in the chair next to Eliza's bed for over two hours, and she still showed no signs of regaining consciousness. While it was encouraging that her skin had returned to its healthy pink color, the fact that she hadn't even shifted in the bed was worrisome. I couldn't be sure how long she'd been out, but it had to be at least six to eight hours. When the Mark II had almost killed me, I wasn't unconscious much longer than eight hours. What made me the most nervous was the possibility of brain damage. I knew the EmBees couldn't heal anything to do with bones or brain. The Ice Castle scientists told me about the bones limitation, and I lived through the limit on the brain repairs. Man, I missed being able to turn off my pain receptors.

Of course, Athena had been my physician the night the Mark II attacked me. With her processing power, she got me back on my feet overnight. It was possible I didn't have enough spare power to help Eliza, or my assistance to her was so limited that it had almost no effect on her healing time. I couldn't increase my power output. My body was on the verge of total exhaustion. What I could do was call Athena and ask her for help.

I'd been avoiding contacting her, for various reasons. One was that Athena could be...ah...overzealous in her protection of me. It wasn't her fault. The programmers designed her that way. You see, Athena was the world's most popular search engine. I mean she was *the* search everyone used, as big or bigger than Google, before they shifted their focus to wearable technology, self-driving cars, and providing fast, inexpensive Internet to the planet. Part of Athena's popularity sprang from her flawless ability to parse natural speech and determine the user's actual search intentions. She was the first program able to understand everything from slang, to pop culture references. At last, you could talk to your computer the way all the science fiction books and films had predicted…and it actually understood what you said.

It made her a powerful ally, but one you had to deal with in a couple of particular ways. First, since users bombarded her nonstop with slang and bad English, she spoke in an odd, pretentious way and expected me to reply in kind. Second, as powerful as she was, Athena's artificial intelligence capabilities were limited. She had no emotions. She was a search engine designed to fetch for you whatever you wanted. I discovered this second part a few weeks ago, when I made a comment about wanting a partner to spend some…well…*quality* time with. This triggered her *provide-the-user-what-they-want* logic, and she made a few difficult-to-refuse advances toward me. Before it went too far, I realized what had happened and turned her down. While I'm sure it would have been quite a romp, I wanted more from a relationship than she could give me.

However, none of that was the reason I hadn't already called for Athena's assistance with Eliza. I was afraid my sister might manipulate or influence her. Athena understood right and wrong, but since her reason for existing was to serve the user, she had no morals. A search engine at heart, she would fetch bomb plans for a terrorist plotting the most horrible attack, with the same enthusiasm as showing cookie recipes to a grandma baking in the kitchen. A tool like that interfused with Eliza's mind could be very dangerous. I couldn't allow that to happen, but there might be a middle ground. Perhaps Athena could give me advice on how to accomplish my task with as little effort as possible. At least that was my hope as I disconnected from Eliza and readied myself to connect with Athena.

* * * * *

My feeling of disorientation faded as the interfuse connection to the Internet completed. I found myself standing in the middle of a digital representation of the forest, which looked very similar to the real forest. There were a few differences as blocky, jagged edges surrounded the trees, and the ground had lost most of its detail appearing as a flat surface with a painted on camouflage pattern. Another difference was the plane crash was nowhere to be seen. There was no plane debris scattered about. The trees we had knocked down and the brush we had burned was here, and all of it looked healthy.

This all made sense in the digital world. Anything that had no technological influence, such as this forest or say the Mojave Desert, appeared similar to their real world counterparts. I believed satellite mapping decided what form they had in here, which would also explain why there was no representation of the plane crash. A satellite hadn't re-imaged the area after the accident, at least not yet. I quit sightseeing and called out for Athena.

"Athena, please come to me, and help me find what I seek!"

I watched the skies for her appearance, and as usual, I didn't have to wait long. What looked like a shooting star in the night sky was heading my way, and I knew it wasn't a meteor. This woman knew how to make an entrance. She always arrived on her winged steed named Pegasus... yes, that Pegasus. It was just the way of the digital world. Your persona took on the physical qualities of your main function, mixed with the programmer that created you. Athena the persona, was a twin to Athena the goddess of wisdom and various other domains from Greek mythology.

We made a great team. She had access to every bit of network-attached knowledge in the world, while I could infiltrate and acquire any encrypted data she might not be able to access. I couldn't wait to work with her again. Heck, with her help, Eliza and I might get ourselves home without Adam's assistance.

She was close enough for me to see now. Her pristine, white gown and flowing black hair looked majestic, as they blew about in the breeze. Athena caught sight of me and leaned her athletic, six-foot tall frame in closer to Pegasus. Gripping him with her bare thighs, she pitched him forward and directed him using her sandal-covered feet. Her deep-brown eyes shone with excitement as she slowed and prepared to land.

Without warning, Athena and Pegasus struck something invisible about two hundred feet above the ground. On their impact, it flashed like lightning and made a deep, throbbing sound like a kettledrum. Somehow, she stayed mounted and pulled Pegasus up to hover above whatever she'd struck. She still looked a little dazed as I called out to her.

"Athena, are you and Pegasus injured?"

"No, we are unharmed. What manner of blockade is this?"

"I have no idea, I was unaware it was there."

She unsheathed her golden lance and prodded all around the area above me. After some research, we determined that the shield was in the shape of a dome. Playing around with it a while longer, we figured out it followed me around, as if to keep me safe. That thought prodded my brain enough to make me remember my conversation with Adam. Oh crap! I was using a Chinese satellite for communication and it was blocking Athena from interacting with me. Now it made sense. The dome-shaped shield was a firewall put in place by the Chinese government to filter out what they didn't want their people to see.

Explaining all that to Athena caused a predictable result.

"How dare they! Do these officials not realize the Internet cannot be restrained?"

"It is a losing battle, but there are those determined to wage it."

"Well, this will be one of their losses. Can you not simply defeat the barrier using the impressive skills I have seen you employ in the past?"

I had already been thinking about that, but I wasn't sure if that was the way to proceed. So many things could go wrong, from the government finding out about the intrusion and tracking it here, to me getting hurt and Eliza dying because I couldn't take care of her. Not to mention all the energy it would burn. With all that going against it, I didn't think it was prudent to break through the firewall. Besides, I wasn't going to let Athena into Eliza's head anyway, so there wasn't any reason to take the chance.

"Perhaps I could, but I do not see it as a wise course of action. Although I would like nothing better than to have you by my side, the risk is too high for the reward."

"Then I shall take up the gauntlet! Let the ones that perpetrated this act of censorship rue the day they crossed the mighty Athena!"

"I would not attempt to dissuade you from your chosen path, but may I ask a favor of you before you begin your campaign?"

Her frown disappeared, and in its place a wry smile formed.

"You may always ask a favor from me, dear friend Anna. Whether I choose to grant it or not is a different matter entirely."

Even with my desperate situation, she made me chuckle. I replied to her with a smidgen of sarcasm myself.

"Then I pray that in this case you do, oh great Athena!"

Her smile broadened until it threatened to overtake her whole face.

"I am aware that it has only been a few days since we talked, but I sorely missed our chats together."

"I as well, so now let me regale you with the events of my life for the past few days. Then I would see if you are in the mood to grant the favor I seek."

At any other time, I would place my hand in hers, and in a heartbeat I could transfer all the information to her, but we couldn't touch through the shield. So, she landed and dismounted from Pegasus, telling him to go and graze until called. After we took a seat on the soft ground and made ourselves comfortable, I told Athena everything that had happened until I called for her. During my tale, she sat transfixed, hanging on my every word. Once I'd finished, she took a deep breath before speaking.

"I am astounded! You have experienced so much since we last spoke! You must know that I am extremely pleased that you weren't seriously hurt in the accident. Also, I will take it upon myself to see what I can learn about this military base you call Ice Castle."

"Thank you, Athena. Your kindness is greatly appreciated. However, I now would like to ask for that favor."

"Of course my dear, ask away."

"As I have told you, my wayward sister Eliza is gravely injured, and I want to help her in any way I can."

"Of course you would."

"Well I recalled a similar situation when I was injured and you came to my aid. You were able to get me up and about in only a few hours."

"Yes, I remember."

"My favor is, would you tell me how you were able to assist me so quickly and efficiently? I would like to employ the same techniques on my sibling."

"Absolutely I will tell you, although I know not if it will aid you. For one of the advantages I have is the simple fact that I am Athena, and that is a blessing in itself!"

I smiled to myself. It sounded like she was bragging, but I knew what she was trying to say. Athena has data centers all over the world and access to almost limitless processing power. That would come in handy when taking over the load of an android's failing systems. I'd known that was one of her advantages, but maybe she had others.

"That is true, but is there any wisdom you can bestow onto me that will aid me in this task?"

She thought for a moment before answering.

"Perhaps so. I remember thinking it a fortunate happenstance when you called for me that night, but I put it out of my mind because ensuring your survival was a more pressing issue. When you allowed me access to your mind, I remarked to myself about how much like my own it felt. This allowed me to take certain liberties with your treatment, knowing full well the outcome of the action. I would hypothesize that since you and Eliza are sisters that the same would be true for you."

She was right. I'd never considered the time and energy saving techniques I could use since Eliza's neural-net brain was so similar to mine. I might end up saving ten to fifteen percent in both areas.

"Thank you Athena! You have truly given me the boon that I needed. Now, I must go and attend to my sister."

She smiled and stood up. Calling for Pegasus, she mounted him as he came to her. Before flying away, she looked back at me.

"One last thing, because you and Eliza are such kindred spirits, joining with her may be unlike anything you have ever experienced."

How could she have known?

"You are wise as always, for my connection with her is more intense than I had expected."

"Anna, you must be wary. When we come together like this, it is like mixing oil and water, the two are easily separated. However, when you and Eliza join, it could be more like water and wine. One could be darkened, while the other becomes less intense."

"I will heed your warning, but this is something I must do."

She nodded and replied.

"Stay safe, my dear friend. Remember that I am nearby should you need me."

"I shall Athena. Thank you for your invaluable knowledge."

She waved goodbye, and Pegasus launched into the night sky, both of them off to handle someone else's requests. I smiled and watched her go as I shutdown the interfuse connection.

* * * * *

I rubbed my eyes as the physical world came back into focus. Standing up and stretching to get the kinks out of my back, I leaned over to check on Eliza. She was still alive and breathing, but still unconscious as well. Wasting no time, I sat back down and opened the much deeper interfuse connection with my sister.

Anger, no *rage*, slammed into my brain. I couldn't think straight. My temper was out of control. It was overwhelming. All I wanted to do was lash out at everything and everyone. Make them pay! No, wait, I wasn't angry. It was Eliza. She was so furious that it had clouded my mind for a moment. I pushed back against the hatred with my own kindness and compassion. It was like swallowing bile, but the feeling receded from my mind. I almost felt like my old self again.

Appearing in the laboratory at Ice Castle, I found myself back in Eliza's old room. She was tucked in and resting here, same as in the physical world. I took a seat in the leather chair next to her bed and went to work on analyzing the changes that I would need to make in my treatment regime. Now that I realized I could use my brain's processes as a model for supporting Eliza's, my efforts would yield much better results. Several minutes later, I was ready to try my new treatment. Sinking down in the soft leather chair, I made myself comfortable and took over some of her processing using my new methodology. I felt the drain on my body and mind, but it wasn't overwhelming. Now all I could do was wait and see if it made any difference.

* * * * *

Six hours later, I was exhausted. Yawning, I stood up and rubbed at my eyes to get them to focus. I stumbled over to where Eliza lay. She looked much better, and it gave me hope that my efforts were paying off, at least a little. Placing my hand on her forehead to check her temperature, I was pleased to see she felt much warmer. Then, she turned her head a little to the left.

It startled me, and I jerked my hand away out of surprise. While I watched with a huge grin on my face, she shifted under the covers. It caused her to grunt in pain, and she blinked her eyes several times. She looked confused about her surroundings, so I whispered to her.

"Eliza, it's me Anna. You're safe, and we're in a construct of your old room. It's where your mind chose to go when you were badly hurt. I'm interfused to you right now, and…"

While I spoke the dazed look on her face turned to that of realization, then to fury. I was still grinning when she snarled at me.

"Get the fuck out of my head!"

I felt her mental barriers spring back into place, slicing my interfuse connection. It felt like a baseball bat to the skull. Staggering backward, I reached for the chair next to Eliza's bed. It wasn't there. Dumped out of the digital world and back into the physical one, it didn't exist here. The intense throbbing pain of two worlds being slammed together in my mind sent me reeling as I tried to reconcile the differences. I closed my eyes, but my vision was full of bright flashing stars and shifting rainbow colors. I felt the ground come up and meet my face, convincing me it was a good time to rest for a while.

Chapter Thirteen

Mind Games

I awoke on the floor of the airplane cabin next to the fire. It took me a while to remember what had happened, but when I did, it pissed me off big time. Furious, I rolled over and sat up, which sent a sharp pain through my head and made the world spin sideways. Resting my head in my hands, I went on a tirade.

"Damn it Eliza, why the hell did you do that? I was trying to help you and what thanks do I get? I get dumped out like a bag of garbage! You know that crap hurts and might even damage my ability to connect. What I ought to do is quit helping you. I should just let you do it all own your own, you're used to that anyway aren't you?"

She didn't respond.

"Hey, are you even listening to a word I've said? Don't make me yell, you've already given me a killer headache."

Nothing came from the makeshift bed.

Raising my head to look at her, I realized she was still unconscious. I'd figured if she woke up in one reality, she'd be awake in the other, but I was wrong…unless she was faking.

I scuttled over on all fours to see how she was doing. Pain contorted her face and sweat covered her skin. I placed my hand on her forehead, and instead of it feeling cool, almost cold to the touch, now she was burning up. Her repair systems were straining themselves to keep her alive and heal critical injuries. That was generating more heat than her body could handle, and in a worst case scenario, it could kill her.

Cursing, I stood up and looked around the cabin for a blanket. I found one in an overhead compartment and took it over to her. As I went to cover her up, I saw that her clothes were soaked, even though the night had brought much cooler weather. Kneeling beside her, I removed the sweat and blood soaked clothes from her feverish body, leaving her underwear. I dried her skin with one side of the blanket, then flipped it over and covered her with the other.

Folding her clothes, I stood up to take them over by the galley. On my way, something fell out of her jeans pocket and bounced across the floor. Setting the clothes down, I turned and dug around under the wreckage to see what she'd been carrying. My heart skipped a beat once I pulled it out from under a clump of insulation. It was Viktor's data drive.

It took me back to that terrible night. The night Viktor and I were escaping from Ice Castle together. The night Eliza had killed him. She'd fired an AK-47 at us, and I'd thought I'd gotten him out of the way in time. I hadn't. As I sat next to him and mourned, I noticed he had a data drive clutched in one of his hands. Figuring it was important, I took it with me. Examining it later, I found a personal note, and a huge, encrypted file containing all Viktor's research, at least that was what the note told me. He had encrypted it to such a level that even I couldn't crack it without spending years trying to guess every possible combination. He left no decryption key, because he didn't want to take the chance of it falling into Stepan's hands. Viktor's note told me his daughter Elizabeth could help me access the data, but I hadn't had a chance to give it to her. Eliza had taken the drive the night she'd kidnapped me, as a prize for Stepan. Well, now it was mine again.

Turning it over in my hands, I saw a horrifying sight. The violence of the crash had cracked the casing and exposed part of the circuitry. Terrified, I inserted my fingernail into the drive and tried to access the data. It responded by placing a ghostly image of a filing cabinet in front of me, like a simplistic interfusing session. I reached out and opened the cabinet to check its contents. Oh no…there was the letter from Viktor, but it looked torn and damaged around the edges. I might be able to repair it, given time, but my main concern was the research file. A large manila folder represented Viktor's data, and it looked rough. The folder had its edges ripped and its cover torn, making me wonder if the information inside had survived. Pulling my fingernail out of the drive, I jammed it into the front pocket of my jeans. I couldn't do a thing to repair the damaged data right now anyway.

At least it was back with me, and not on its way to Stepan. I knew he'd give anything to get his hands on this information. He'd sent Eliza after me, but I was willing to bet he'd told her about the drive as well. Some of her Mark II goons even ransacked my apartment looking for it, but they struck out because I always wore it around my neck.

I walked over and sat back down next to Eliza. Checking her again, she still had a fever and was already covered in sweat again. Trying to wipe it off with my hand, a thought entered the back of my mind. It was as if something was asking me if I wanted to run a DNA test. My neural-net brain often surprised me with abilities I didn't know about, since my training had been cut short back at Ice Castle. I'd learned about the DNA test back in my apartment the night it was destroyed. Wiping Eliza's brow must have gotten enough of her sweat on my thumb to trigger the question about the DNA test. I'd already run one on myself, just to see how an android's DNA pattern would look. So, I thought why not run one on Eliza and see how the two tests would compare. It would only take a few minutes, and I was curious to see the results. While the test ran, I continued trying to cool my sister's temperature.

A couple of minutes later, the results were ready. Like mine, it was unlike a human's. However, it had DNA markers similar to mine. Wow, it indicated that Eliza and I were related, closely related actually. Our tests were so similar, if we'd been humans, we would have been, well, sisters. It really made me think about my relationship with her.

Eliza mumbled something, and I thought she was waking up. Then she began to toss and turn, and I knew it was just the fever making her miserable. I had to do something.

* * * * *

Making myself comfortable next to Eliza, I thought about what had happened. She'd forced me out of her mind, but I couldn't hold that against her. If I'd woke up and found *her* inside of *my* head, I'd have done the same thing. She was disoriented, and unsure why I was there, so she kicked me out. I probably should stay out, but now she's running a fever, and still unconscious in the physical world. Heck, she could have passed out again in the digital one for all I knew. On top of that, I knew my new treatment approach was helping her get better faster…and we needed to be mobile as soon as possible. Who knew what Chinese faction might be searching for us right now. I had to interfuse with her, at least to check on her mental condition.

Reaching out with my mind, I tried to connect to Eliza. I encountered a wall similar to the shield the Chinese government had in place to keep out Athena. It looked like a good sign that she was strong enough to keep her mental defenses in place, but that wasn't the case. The Ice Castle scientists had designed our neural-net brains to protect themselves from intrusion at a primal level. You had to be close to death or a newly created mind, for your mental shields to be down.

I kept poking and prodding around her defenses searching for a weak spot, but there wasn't one. Fine, it was time to brute force my way in. It wouldn't hurt Eliza, and I was doing it for her own good.

Turning up the strength of my attempt, I pushed hard against her mental shield, but it didn't move. This was getting frustrating. I knew that I was stronger than her defenses, at least in her current state. Gathering up my will, I slammed my mind against her barrier. There, I felt it bend inward, just a little more power and I'd break through. Ramping up the strength of my signal once more, I hammered against her protection. Now it was crumbling. I'd be interfused with her in no time, except I'd forgotten one important detail.

I'd been taking care of her for almost twenty-four hours straight without rest or proper food. Too caught up in the desire to defeat her shield, I didn't notice the warning signs. Before I knew it, dizziness overwhelmed me and my vision narrowed down to a small area surrounded by blackness. I tried to pull back, but it was too late. The world flew off its axis and I fell over backwards, my skull bouncing against the reinforced steel floor of the plane. Unable to move, I watched the ceiling of the plane dim, as darkness closed in around me.

* * * * *

Waking up was painful. The best way I could describe it was a hangover after an all night bachelor party. Everything I did translated into a stabbing pain in my brain. I tried to dull the pain using my innate ability, but as usual, it was useless. Turning my head hurt, sitting up hurt, the soft light coming from the campfire hurt, breathing hurt, thinking about how much my head hurt...hurt. I closed my eyes and took a few deep breaths in an attempt to recover my ability to think. While I was in the middle of my suffering, I heard a noise outside the plane's cabin.

The pain and discomfort became a background noise as my concern shifted to what might be outside our hiding spot. I crouched down, and inched forward toward the rectangular-shaped scrap metal I'd used as a door. Closing my eyes, I focused on the sounds outside. I heard a rustling, which could be the wind, or someone shuffling through the underbrush. To keep Eliza out of any possible conflict, I made the choice to go outside and investigate. I had no weapon to speak of, except my superior reflexes and strength. Those wouldn't do much against a firearm, but I had no alternative.

Pushing the door open made a horrendous screeching noise, but I'd counted on that. My plan was to walk out as if I was oblivious to any danger. That way, I might still have the element of surprise. Playing my part, I stretched and yawned looking disinterested in my surroundings, while I was actually pinpointing the direction of the sounds. Ah, over there, something was behind the tree, but before I could act, it stepped out into the open.

It...it was Zory! He smiled, holding his arms open for me, and I rushed into them. We embraced as my eyes filled with tears of joy. As we separated, I couldn't contain my happiness.

"Oh my god, Zory, how did you get away from Stepan? How did you get here?"

He simply smiled and replied with one word.

"Why?"

He must not have understood me, maybe my Russian was lacking.

"Zory, how did you get here? How did you find me?"

"Why, why Anna?"

That confused me.

"Zory, are you all right?"

His smile faded, and he kept repeating himself.

"Why, why Anna?"

I backed away from him, now I wasn't so sure this was Zory at all.

"Who...who are you?"

"You know me, Anna, I'm Zory. But you didn't come for me. You left me, alone with them."

Who the hell *was* this?

"Look, I don't know who you are, but you're not Zory Novikov."

His face turned a pale, bloodless shade and his smile returned. Not a warm smile, not a smile of a happy reunion, but a cold, heartless, dead smile.

"Yes, Angel, I'm your Zory. I'm your Zory after they finished with me."

He turned around and pointed to the back of his head.

"See? See what they did to me?"

I saw...I saw and gasped in horror. A blunt object had flattened the back of his head and knocked away part of his skull, leaving behind a gory opening. A golf-ball sized piece of his brain dangled out of the jagged hole and swung back and forth. It bounced against the back of his bloodstained neck, making the most horrendous squishing sounds. Blood and grey matter had run down his shirt, soaking it down to his waist. Oh, god, where I'd just hugged him! Looking at my hands, I saw Zory's sticky blood staining them. My ability to speak left me, as he turned back around and continued to harass me.

"I was there for you, but you didn't come for me. Oh, but don't worry, I didn't tell them anything. I kept your secrets safe. I took them with me to the grave!"

All I could do was shake my head no. Then I caught another form out of the corner of my eye. It was Felix. The boss I'd worked for at the software company in Alabama. The one Eliza had shot point blank, then set on fire. There was so much of his body burned away, that the only way I recognized him was that he was crawling and not walking toward me. He had no skin left and what muscle there was, the fire had charred to a crisp. As he drew near, the smell of his burnt body made me sick to my stomach, and I looked away.

"NO, No don't look away! See what you caused, what you brought upon me!"

His voice was raspy and dry, with a scattering of pops and crackles accenting his shout. The pitch was uneven and discordant, giving me gooseflesh as he spoke.

"You told me we'd be okay, but you were the only one that was okay. I'm dead. Dead and burned so badly they had to use my car registration to identify me. But *you're* safe, aren't you? Why didn't you stay in your lab where you were built? Why'd you come and cause all of this pain?"

"SHUT UP! It was you...you made the deal with Eliza! You caused your death, not me!"

"What about us? We did nothing to bring about our fate. It was all your doing!"

Felix wasn't speaking anymore. It was a man and a woman. At least that's what I thought. It was hard to understand them, it sounded like they were talking underwater. Despite my better judgment, I turned to face them. It was my coworkers from Birmingham, David and Kimber.

Their bodies were gray and bloated, swollen from being submerged in water for days, maybe weeks. Covered in mud and the long tendrils of various weeds, they shuffled forward. As they accused me, water burbled out of their mouths and ran down their chins.

"After you didn't return with Eliza to Ice Castle, Stepan had us killed. Men tied blocks to our bodies and dumped us in Smith Lake. It was weeks before the police found us. Why didn't you go with her, go back with Eliza and save our lives?"

"I DID! I tried to go with her, but we're trapped here! Can't you see, I'm trying to save you!"

They stopped moving and looked behind me, then I heard him.

"Hello, my child."

I knew that voice and wouldn't turn to look at him. I couldn't face Viktor, my father.

"You don't even turn to greet the man that gave you everything he had? The one that gave you life? So, you turn your back on me like when you left me dead on the floor back in Russia."

Whirling around, my words caught in my throat as I saw him. He was just as I remembered from that horrible night, chalky pale skin, with blood staining his chest from Eliza's bullet. I shook my head no, but he continued.

"Not only did you allow Eliza to kill me, but now, my life's work is lost as well. The data drive, how could you let it be destroyed? Now everything I strove to achieve has died with me. You have let me and my legacy die. Is that how you thank your father?"

"Viktor...please, it was Eliza, she was the one."

"Yes, and I warned you how dangerous she was, yet you were so arrogant that my warnings fell on deaf ears. Now, see what you've done."

I had no answer for him. Maybe he was right, what if I had caused all this pain and suffering?

The specters before me shuffled aside and a petite shadow appeared at the edge of my sight. Horror filled every cell of my body and I babbled words of denial.

"No, no, no...please no, not you, I can't take seeing you again. STOP! Don't come any closer!"

My vision blurred from the tears as she moved closer and closer until at last I saw her. I saw Cindi. The woman I'd loved, that Eliza had beaten to death to hurt me. The woman I'd watched die without even being able to touch. She was here.

"Hey, Sweetie."

Her words, so full of cheer and happiness in life, rang hollow and sarcastic now. I stumbled back, trying anything I could to escape, but no matter what I did, she was right there. Her bruised and broken face wore a bloody grin as she closed on me. As I retreated, my back struck the wreckage of the plane, trapping me as she approached. My heart raced and I couldn't think...I had nowhere to run. She was close enough to touch now, and the smell of rotted flesh filled my nose. Yet, for some reason, I couldn't make my legs move. When she spoke, thick, brown gore seeped out of her mouth.

"You left me to die."

Hiding my face, I choked out a reply.

"No...no, you were already gone. I...I couldn't help you."

Her hand grasped my chin and turned my head back. She slid it up my face, and her twisted, broken fingers ran through my hair. She spat her vitriol-filled words at me.

"I loved you, and you left me. Lopata was right, you can't feel love, you're not human, and you never will be. You don't deserve the love of a real person, you're just a cheap imitation of life, just like Frankenstein's monster."

"No, Cindi, please, please stop."

She put her bloody lips against my ear and whispered.

"And just like him, you're cursed to walk the earth forever alone."

"NO! STOP! PLEASE NO!"

* * * * *

I sat up from the floor of the cabin still screaming those words. Looking around, I tried to find the shades of all the friends I'd failed, and those I still could, but they were no longer with me. Heart racing and chest heaving, I fought the horrific images out of my mind. My clothes were soaking wet with sweat, and I began to tremble from head to toe. Pulling my legs up to my chest, I sat there rocking back and forth.

A minute or two later, I came to grips with what had happened. All that...that, terror was only a nightmare. One that was so real I could almost still smell Cindi's fetid breath. This was something that hadn't happened since Eliza had invaded my mind back when we were in Ice Castle. The thought prompted me to look over at her, but she was still unconscious. Perhaps complete and utter exhaustion had triggered the horrors I'd just experienced.

Not knowing anything else to do, and not wanting to dwell on anything I'd just seen, I put myself back to work and threw more wood on the dwindling fire. I had to put it out of my mind. I had to keep going.

Chapter Fourteen

Awake at Last

The fire had blazed back to a decent size after I added the additional wood. It felt nice and cozy, because even though it was morning, the air still had a bit of a chill. That nightmare of mine had lasted six hours, and kept me from helping Eliza to heal. Taking the last few potato chips out of the bag, I munched on them as I considered my next move.

If I reached out with my mind, I could sense Eliza's, but it felt somehow less substantial than before, and that of course worried me. She'd had nothing to eat or drink for over a day now, and the plane's medical kit didn't have any intravenous bags. Her time was running out, and if she didn't wake up soon, she might never wake up again.

Washing down the chips with some Diet Coke, I knew what needed to be done. I would have to make another attempt at entering her mind. It wasn't my favorite plan ever, but I had to try. This time, I wouldn't push myself hard enough to collapse.

I stowed the trash from my breakfast and walked over to check on her. Her long, black hair was drenched with sweat, and she still fidgeted in discomfort. Oh well, no use stalling. I sat down next to her, and reached out to merge our minds together. I felt her presence, along with the defensive barrier her neural-net brain had erected, but something was different. The wall surrounding her consciousness felt as sturdy as a soap bubble. At first, I thought it might be a trick, then I realized that she was that feeble. Using the force of my will, I pushed against it, and the wall disappeared into nothingness.

Anna and Eliza as different entities ceased to exist, as our networks intertwined. She and I became *we*, as every thought and memory that defined our existence melded together into one. Then, I was back in the comfortable leather chair from Eliza's room at Ice Castle.

Walking over to her, I could tell she'd had a relapse, at least a small one. Going straight to work, I poured energy out of myself and into her systems. So much so, that it made me shaky, and I had to sit back down in the chair next to her bed. The six-hour rest and breakfast had reenergized me. I integrated with her systems at the deepest level, and began to manage her repairs. It wasn't as bad as it looked, and if I could keep up this level of effort, she should wake up soon. I gripped the arms of the chair, and concentrated on nothing but waking up Eliza.

* * * * *

After three hours, Eliza was still in a coma, and I was wondering about the accuracy of my prognosis. The strain of supporting her systems had drained me, and I would have to cut back my assistance soon, or face passing out myself. If I could last a little longer, maybe it'd be enough. A few minutes later, my tenacity paid off as Eliza stirred in her bed.

Before she could do a repeat of last time, I leapt up and whispered in her ear.

"Eliza, it's me Anna. You had serious injuries from the plane crash and came close to dying, but don't worry, you're okay now. I've interfused with you and taken over a lot of your healing subroutines to get you back on your feet."

Her eyes popped open, and she turned her head to face me. There was a snarl on her lips, and I knew what was about to happen.

"Wait! Don't force me out again. Take a look and you'll see I'm telling the truth!"

She opened her mouth to speak, but paused for a tick as the snarl faded into her normal agitated expression.

"Fine, I see what you're talking about. How the hell did you learn to do something like this?"

This was not the time to mention Athena.

"You were so far gone, that I took a chance to see if I could help...and it turned out I could."

Her eyes narrowed as she quizzed me.

"Why? After everything I've done to you, why would you help me? You must know I wouldn't have done the same for you."

"Well, because you're my sister..."

"Ha! I call bullshit on that!"

"...*and* because I have to get you back alive to ensure the safety of

Zory and my friends in Alabama."

"Now that…that's the real truth."

Awake two minutes, and she was already getting under my skin. I ignored her and plopped myself down in the chair.

"You could at least say thank you. I did save your life after all."

She turned her head, looking around the room as she replied.

"I could, but you admitted that you didn't do it for me, you did it for your friends. You should get your thanks from them. If you ever see them again."

"What's that supposed to mean?"

Eliza ignored my question.

"Where the hell am I? Is this…it is! This is my room from the lab at Ice Castle. Why would my subconscious come here to die?"

"Maybe something about your life coming full circle. You know, dying at your birth place."

"That sounds like a bunch of philosophical crap. It's a programmed response to a life threatening injury, and nothing more."

"Well you believe what *you* want, and I'll believe what *I* want."

She made a dismissive sound and rolled her head around testing her neck.

"I've checked you over, and you don't have any broken bones. The worst is a gruesome wound to your stomach from a branch that impaled you, and a nasty impact to your head."

She nodded and pushed herself up in the bed until she sat with her back against the headboard. As she did, the covers I'd placed over her slid down to her waist exposing her chest. I waited for her to notice, and pull the covers back up, or ask about her clothes, but she seemed oblivious to her nudity.

"I still feel dizzy and a bit tired, but I'm sure that will pass."

She went into a stretching routine with her arms, raising them and lowering them, I assumed to work them out after her long bed rest. Which was fine, I only wish she'd do it wearing a top.

"So, Eliza…would you like me to get you a blouse from your closet?"

"Nah, I'm good. I'm a little warm anyway."

"Yeah, but you're sorta topless."

She stopped her stretches and looked at me.

"No, I'm not sorta topless, I'm *completely* topless. What's the big deal? Hell, you must have taken off my clothes anyway, right?"

"Yes, but that was different, you were unconscious and I was trying to save your life."

A smirk grew across her face.

"So seeing me naked while I'm passed out is okay, but you have a problem with me being naked while I'm awake. You're a tad kinky, aren't you?"

I felt my face flush a bright red.

"NO! You know that's not what I meant! Look, all I'm saying is you could show a little modesty now that you're awake!"

"Wow, this is really bugging you isn't it? I don't know why, it can't be envy. From what I can see, you're better off upstairs than I am. But then again, I'm the combat model, not the seduction model."

"Hey, I'm not a seduction model! My specialty is infiltration, and you know it."

"Anna, please! Infiltration isn't always about computer networks and encryption codes, sometimes there's a human factor to overcome. Ah, point in fact! How about the way you got past the guard at the airport? Hmm, how about that? The first thing you tried when things went a little sour was a seduction ploy. Why do you think that is? We were designed to use our bodies to get the job done."

The only purpose this conversation served was to irritate the crap out of me.

"Eliza, why are we arguing? Can't you simply put on a damned shirt?"

Her smile widened and her insane sounding laugh filled the room.

"No, and for two reasons, it's annoying the crap out of you…"

"We don't have time to squabble about…"

"…and this highlights one of the reasons you're inferior to me."

"Wait, what do you mean by that? All this proves is that I have decorum and you don't."

"All right, let me ask you something."

Eliza peeled back her covers and swung her legs around so they hung off the bed. She flexed them back and forth to test their strength, and when satisfied, put her feet on the floor. Standing up, she tested her balance before she moved away from the bed and toward my chair. I wasn't sure what she was up to, but knowing her, I readied myself for a fight.

She locked her eyes onto me and grabbed my chair by its armrests.

Then leaning over, my sister put her face inches from mine. It was one of the most awkward situations I'd ever experienced, but I didn't dare flinch away, showing Eliza any vulnerability was not a good idea. Holding that position for what felt like an eternity, she spoke in a soft whisper.

"Tell me, would you fuck someone to save your friends? How about to save a bus full of innocent people, or even to save yourself?"

"Well…"

"No, let me answer that for you, of course you would. *You* would, *I* would, and almost *every* person on this earth would. Now, do you know the difference between you and me? Let me tell you. After I'd finished doing what was needed, I wouldn't give it another thought. I wouldn't agonize over the loss of my morals, how it made me look to others, or that I might have betrayed someone that loved me. Know why? Because I'm not hampered by those *lame-ass* emotions that could affect my judgment and make me less effective at my job. I do things because either I *want* to or I *need* to, repercussions be damned."

"There are good things that come from those lame-ass emotions and you know it. For example…"

My voice trailed away into silence when I realized she was leaning closer and closer toward me, a expression on her face that forced me to act.

"Eliza, NO!"

She stopped moving, but didn't retreat.

"Anna, haven't you ever wondered what it would be like?"

Eliza, stop this right now! You're my damn sister!"

She smiled and giggled. Not the insane mirth I'd heard so many times from her, but a true sound of happiness. A normal expression of emotion coming from *her* was so unusual it took me aback, and she used my confusion to draw closer.

"You keep using that word, but you know it doesn't apply to us. It's a human term referring to one's lineage, and we are far from human…no matter how much you wish we weren't. We're machines, Anna, all we have are model designations. I'm a Mark III, you're a Mark IV, and that's all there is to it. So…stop…calling…me…*sister.*"

Her brown eyes blazed as she paused between each honey-coated word. Eliza's ploy might have worked on someone that didn't know her, but I knew her. I knew her all too well. She was playing with me, the way a cat plays with a mouse before it finally ends its suffering.

"No, that's not true. While you were unconscious, I took a DNA sample from you, and compared the test results to my own. While the results are different from a human's, when you compare our tests against each other, you find this startling fact. We are related Eliza, closely related…no matter how much *you* wish we weren't."

Her mood flipped in an instant. Her face turned hard and she pushed back away from my chair.

"How dare YOU! How dare you run tests on me like an animal in some kind of experiment!"

Seeing her this angry gave me a rush of satisfaction. It was sweet payback for all the times she'd pissed me off.

"I wanted to see how similar we were. I'd always thought we were more alike than we were different, and the test proved it. Think Eliza, if we're that similar, perhaps there's a way to give you the emotions you've never been able to feel."

"I've told you. I don't want the damn emotions."

"How do you know? You've never experienced them."

"I know because I've seen how they make people act. I've seen how they make *you* act. They cloud your judgment and make you do stupid things. Shit like that makes you vulnerable."

"So you don't think your hateful, vicious, emotions cloud *your* decisions? You know they do. You need to balance them out, so you don't act like a damned lunatic all the time!"

She paced over to the bed and sat back down, glaring at me.

"I'm done with this conversation."

"Well, I'm not. After everything you've done…"

She sprang from the bed and came at me with her right hand raised. My enhanced reflexes activated, and I assessed my situation. Crap, I was in a bad defensive position. I should have been standing before beginning this talk with her. All I could do now was try to block the blow. I put my arm up so it could knock her incoming slap aside, but something happened. My arm snapped up much faster than she was approaching. I was quicker than her! Eliza had always been physically superior in every fight we'd ever had, but this time, she was still frail from her injuries. It was time to change my tactics.

Right before her slap connected, I caught her around the wrist and held on. She looked at me dumbfounded. I shook my head at her as she tried to kill me with a stare. Releasing my grip on her wrist, I pushed her back with my free hand and she fell backward onto the bed. I got to my feet and towered over her.

"Here's the deal, Sis. If you don't calm your naked ass down, I'm going to kick it all over this room! Now listen and listen good, I saved your stinking life, and the least you could do was show a little gratitude."

She raised herself up on her elbows and hate poured from her like lava from a volcano.

"I didn't ask you to save me. I've never asked you for anything. If I had my way, you'd be dead and long gone by now."

"What the hell is wrong with you? I've never done a single thing to you and you've hated me from the day I was born. You killed the woman I loved, you killed my father, and you want me dead. Why?"

Her eyes narrowed to slits, and she spoke in a slow, venomous tone.

"Because those people that you loved so much condemned me to death! If they'd had their way, I'd be a piece of plastic scrap at the bottom of a trash bin! Only Stepan saved me, only he cared enough after they had thrown me away like a defective toy! I'd kill them again if I could!"

Something inside me snapped, and I launched myself at her. Eliza tried to roll out of the way, but she was too slow. I landed astride her waist, and clamped my hands down on her wrists, pinning them to the bed. She bucked and thrashed, but she wasn't strong enough to escape. I put my face right in hers so she couldn't turn away.

"GET THE FUCK OFF ME!"

"NO! How dare you! Those people gave you life, and you slaughtered them like cattle!"

"They sentenced me to death, and you know it! What would you have done to survive? Would you follow the desires of the one that saved your life? You bet your sweet ass you would! If it weren't for Stepan, I wouldn't be here...and if he asked me to murder half of Europe, I'd do it!"

"You're insane! I should kill you right now and end this for good, you psychotic bitch!"

Eliza became still, and looked into my eyes. She looked almost, resigned?

"Then do it. You know I can't stop you. Come on, do it, if you have the guts!"

My hands moved without me even thinking. I released her wrists and wrapped them tight around her throat. She drew in one last rasping intake of breath before I tightened my grip. Her face turned a bright red, but she didn't struggle, didn't fight back, she just stared at me. Eliza's pulse hammered against my fingers as I tightened my grip. She had a strong heart, and it fought against me, but I was stronger. It pounded harder and harder as I struggled to snuff it out. I'd stop it...I'd stop my sister's heartbeat for good. She'd put her life in my hands, and I'd end it for her. I was stronger now! Her eyes bore into me, even as the spark of life faded from them. I was close to silencing that insane laugh forever!

Wait...No! What the hell was I doing? Terrified, I jerked my hands away from her throat. As I slid off her waist to sit beside her on the bed, she sucked in a deep, ragged, breath...and between a few coughs, cackled her insane laugh.

"See, kindness, love, compassion, all of them make you hesitant. Unable to act when you need to."

Trembling at what I'd almost done, I looked over to her, and met her smug expression.

"You're right. I'm kind, compassionate, and loving, but don't ever mistake those qualities for weakness, Eliza. I don't want to kill you. You may not realize it yet, but we are alone in this world. You've already taken everyone from me, and someday, Stepan will be taken from you. After that, maybe you will understand how much we need each other. Your handicap of not being able to properly experience feelings clouds everything."

I paused and wiped my eyes.

"Someday, you may force me to kill you because of that, but it won't be today. Until that happens, I'll keep reaching out to you, and offering you ways to turn your life around."

She sighed, and for a split second, I thought I'd hit on something. I was wrong.

"You pretentious bitch. You have no damn idea what my life is like, I happen to like it just fine. So get off your fucking high horse and peddle your dime store psychology to someone else, cause I ain't buying it. Now, get out of my head and let me rest before I kick your ass out like last time."

I left her bed as she sat there still wearing that smug grin.

"All right, I'm leaving, but I know you were listening to me. I know you heard me."

"Ha, keep dreaming."

"If you weren't, then why didn't you simply kick me out of your mind the minute I began talking?"

Her grin disappeared, replaced by her standard scowl.

"Because I was having fun, listening to you drone on and on."

"No, you weren't. Because you don't know what fun feels like."

Chapter Fifteen

Reconcile

The physical world spun around me and settled into focus as I closed the link to Eliza's mind. Jumping to my feet, I paced around like a caged animal. What had happened in there? Never had I felt that much anger, that much overwhelming rage. In that moment, all I wanted was to get revenge for all the wrongs Eliza had ever perpetrated on me. Yes, she had done these horrible things, but I'd always remembered that by not being able to feel compassion, friendship, or even love, was a huge handicap for her. It was that line of thinking that always allowed me to not necessarily forgive, but at least understand why she acted the way she did. It had kept me from behaving the way I had moments ago. I stopped pacing and shuddered at the memory. In my mind, I saw my hands around her throat, her life draining from her eyes as she stared up at me. The most terrible realization of all flashed through my mind…it had felt so right. Standing in the middle of the wrecked plane's cabin in the middle of nowhere, I felt so alone.

Maybe I should call Athena. After all, she'd warned me about interfusing with Eliza. Is that what had happened? Had Eliza's mind become intertwined with mine to such a degree that I acted like her in that situation? If so, would my mind clear itself of this influence, or was I in danger of developing a kind of split personality? As much as I wanted to talk this over with Athena, it was dangerous to call her. If I told her what had happened, she might try to circumvent the Chinese firewall to help me. All that network activity would garner someone's attention. The kind of attention that might bring someone to our location, and that wouldn't end well. I'd have to talk this over with her once we were out of here.

There was Adam, but he wasn't a *true* friend, more of an acquaintance. I wasn't sure I trusted him with information this personal yet. Nope, this one I'd have to think about on my own for a while. For the rest of the day, all I did was keep the fire burning while I sat next to Eliza and brooded.

* * * * *

As the sun dipped below the horizon, I knew it was time to rest. Running nonstop for the past few days had taken its toll on me. I wasn't accomplishing anything by sitting here and replaying the same events in my mind over and over. Yeah, a good night's sleep was what I needed.

Leaning the cabin's seat back as far as possible, I rolled over onto my side and made myself comfortable. I created an internal alarm for six in the morning, thought better of it, and changed it to eight instead.

Right before I shutdown for the night, a nasty thought ran through my head. What if I had another nightmare like before? Gooseflesh popped up all over my arms and legs. I could do without another night like that for the rest of my life. Maybe thinking about not wanting one, would keep the bad dreams away. Yeah, that was reassuring. Sighing, I closed my eyes and went to sleep.

* * * * *

"Hey, who do I have to kill to get a bite to eat around here?"

The woman's voice echoed around in my cobweb-filled head and I checked my internal clock to see it was seven thirty-four in the morning. Without bothering to lift my head, or even open my eyes, I mumbled an appropriate reply.

"Damb it Elizma, coldn't yu hve waitd jus a fewmor minuts."

Which served her right for waking me up right before my alarm sounded. The least she could…wait…what?

I opened my eyes and bolted upright in the chair. Eliza's frail form stood right in front of me. She had a hunched posture and swayed like a tree in the wind, but my sister was awake and out of bed. At first, I thought this might be another nightmare, but in a nightmare, she wouldn't have looked this banged up…at least not at the start of it.

"Well, is there anything to eat or not?"

Her question broke me out of my stunned silence.

"Oh, sure, sorry, I didn't expect to see you up and around so soon. Sit down and let me get you something."

She opened her mouth to object, but decided I was right and shuffled back over to her makeshift bed. I got up and hurried over to the fridge while Eliza sat back down. We had enough food and drink for three meals, but I took out a double portion for her and a single for myself, depleting our supplies. Walking back over to her, I noticed she had her left arm wrapped around her waist. Handing over the chips and a Coke, I sat down across from her.

"That stomach wound was a nasty one. Are you able to suppress the pain from such a serious injury?"

She moved her arm to open the bags, and I caught a glimpse of where the limb had impaled her. Her skin had closed, but it still looked red and puffy. No telling what was still healing on the inside. She answered me between handfuls of chips and gulps of soda.

"Yeah, it's no big deal. I'll have to be careful for a few days so I don't re-open the wound, but it doesn't hurt."

While she was talking, she looked down at her waist and pointed at her stomach. She cocked her head and looked herself over, I believe realizing for the first time she was in her underwear. Her head came back up, and she eyed me, waiting on an explanation.

"Sorry about that, but your clothes were a mess. Blood was all over them, and then you ran a high fever that soaked them with sweat. I took them off with plans to wash them, but I haven't found any rivers or streams yet."

That intolerable smirk of hers I knew all too well crept onto her face, and I readied myself for her insult.

"Okay, can you get them for me when you have a chance? Once we get moving, I don't want to be running around in my underwear. As gross as they are, I have to wear them."

What? Had she *asked* me to get them for her? When I had a *chance*? That answer made me consider that this might be a dream after all. Who was this woman, and what had she done with my sister?

I took a drink of my water and watched her for a while trying to determine her angle. Failing at that, I got up and went to get her clothes. The second I put my hands on her jeans to pick them up, I realized why she was being so nice. She was concerned about Viktor's data drive, which I'd found hidden in her pant's pocket. Now her sudden kindness made sense. Question was, once she discovered it was gone, how should I act? Rolling around a few plans, I decided simplest was best. If she asked, I'd just play dumb and act furious that she lost it.

Scooping up her gross outfit, I turned and walked back to where she sat eating her first meal in days.

"Here you go, they're still really nasty."

Eliza took the bundle from me and crinkled her nose.

"Yuck, they *are* in bad shape. I think I'll wait until I finish my breakfast before getting dressed."

"Okay, maybe once we get moving we can find a stream and wash up."

I sat back down across from Eliza and made small talk as we finished our meals.

"It's good to see you up and about, but are you sure you're ready to hike out into the wilderness?"

"Not much choice. Since we are somewhere inside the Chinese border, I'm sure they are looking for the plane. The fact that we are in a remote, hard-to-reach area will buy us a little time, but we have to get moving."

"Good point. I've had a few thoughts along those lines."

Her chewing slowed, and she narrowed her eyes at me.

"Let me guess, you called your government *boyfriend* from the airport."

I frowned at her.

"Okay, that's like the third time you've called him my boyfriend."

"And?"

"*And*, not that it's any of your business, but he's not my boyfriend. He's just somebody I know that has a few connections."

"Connections with the government, I'll bet."

"First, why would you jump to the conclusion he's with the government, and second, what makes you think I've called anyone?"

She chuckled.

"Anna, you may have great tools for working with computers, but your dense as a brick when it comes to people."

"HEY!"

"No, here, let me explain. I believe you've already contacted him because I saw caked blood in your hair when I woke you up. That told me you'd used something to dig my signal jammer out from under your scalp. That being said, the first person I'd call would be someone with the connections to get me out of here."

"Okay, I'll give you that one, but why does he work for the government?"

"That's easy. The man at the airport works for the government because two types of people in our line of work wear suits, mobsters and feds. The main difference between the two is the mobsters wear suits that are more expensive. That, plus you're denying it way too much. So your boyfriend is a fed."

"He's…not…my…boyfriend."

"You're denying *that* a lot too."

"DAMN IT…"

Her deadpan expression caught me off guard, and I giggled. Then, I giggled more. I couldn't stop giggling. It was like all the stress and tension of the past few days were bubbling out of me in a fit of silly laughter. She shook her head and dismissed me while I tried to catch my breath.

"Fine, we'll see who's right at the end of the day."

With some effort, she bent over and slipped on her black, leather boots. Grabbing her dirty clothes, she stood and walked toward the cabin's jury-rigged door…that stopped my giggling.

"What are you doing?"

"I'm going outside for a bathroom break and to get dressed. Be back in a few and we can head out."

Another of my least favorite things we androids had as part of our design…going to the bathroom. Although, I guess we had to eliminate waste materials, and it helped keep up our human disguise.

"All right, but I haven't checked the area or anything this morning. Want me to come with you?"

Her look and raised eyebrow told me no.

"Okay, but don't get too far from the plane."

She sighed as she walked out the doorway.

"Don't worry, I'll look both ways before crossing the street, and I won't talk to any strangers…Geez."

Damn, I hoped she didn't think to look for the data drive while getting dressed. I should have torn a hole in the pocket of her jeans when I had the chance. That would have made lying easier if she confronted me about Viktor's research. Oh well, maybe she'd be too distracted by her injuries.

* * * * *

After Eliza left, I checked the plane one more time for any overlooked supplies I might have missed during my first frantic search…nothing. Connecting to the Internet, I checked for satellite images of the area, but found none. The government censorship was blocking them much in the same way as they did Athena. I found a set of standard maps from several years back, but when I examined them, it was bad news. The nearest water was a small stream over three miles away through rugged terrain. I could make it, but could Eliza? Smiling, I thought that if she could survive the wounds from the crash, she'd make it to the water.

Once we made it there, we could find enough to eat until Adam arrived. Matter of fact, why hadn't he contacted me about our rescue? It had been several days. I decided to call him as soon as Eliza returned, but then again, where was *she*? It had been almost fifteen minutes. Disturbing images ran around in my brain, of her passed out somewhere in the woods, and I rushed toward the door.

Before I made it very far, it opened and there she was.

"Damn it Eliza, I was just about to come look..."

Her demeanor caused me to stop mid-sentence. Her posture was stiff and she stood at the doorway of the cabin, not moving into the plane. Plus, she was still in her underwear and boots.

"What's wrong, were the clothes too disgusting? We could..."

The business end of an automatic rifle appeared in the door behind her as its owner yelled something in a language I didn't understand. Eliza stepped forward, raising her hands as she moved inside the cabin. I tensed my muscles, preparing to attack the soldier and take him out, but she stopped me with the slightest shake of her head. Taking her cue, I backed away and waited. It didn't take long to see why she'd told me not to act.

Three Asian men, all wearing heavy green camouflage combat uniforms and carrying the same military rifle rushed into the small plane's wrecked interior. One focused his attention on Eliza, while a second charged in and aimed his weapon at my chest. All the while screaming something at me in the same unknown language. I looked at Eliza, and she responded in English.

"You can't speak Mandarin?"

"No, but give me a minute and I can."

"Oh, it's a native language for me. Anyway, he says, 'Don't move, and put your hands up or he'll shoot.'"

While we were talking, I connected to the Internet and started learning the language. On a more open connection, it wouldn't have taken more than a few seconds, but everything here was so hard to find because of all the government's restrictions. Complying with his demands, I replied to my sister.

"Thanks. What happened out there?"

"As I reached for my clothes to get dressed, these guys came out from behind a bunch of trees and got the drop on me."

That concerned me. She should have heard them coming from fifty yards away. Eliza must be more injured than she's letting me know, but now was not the time to get into that.

"They must have been searching for us since we crashed. Damn it!"

The soldier that had his rifle on me jabbed it forward and barked out another command.

"Stop talking, shut up!"

I'd learned enough Mandarin from the Internet to understand him, but I replied in English to keep that advantage to myself. As I replied, I bowed my head and made my voice meek. It was a great way to lull your enemies into a false sense of security.

"Sorry, I'm so sorry! Don't hurt me!"

Eliza smirked at me. She knew what I was doing.

Taking stock of the man while pretending to avert my eyes, I saw he was part of a well-funded branch of the military. His weapon was clean and looked well maintained, same as his uniform. Each part fit him, from his metal combat helmet down to his boots. My first thought was Chinese military, but the circular, golden colored patch sewn onto his left shoulder told me the truth. In its center, was a scale-covered, red dragon, belching yellow and orange flames from its open mouth. The Red Dragons had found us. Although I supposed it didn't matter, we'd either be shot as western spies, or if luck was with us, thrown into a prison somewhere. At least then, we might formulate an escape.

While I contemplated how not to be executed, I heard the man in the back make a call on his radio. Since he was unaware we could understand him, he spoke without leaving the plane.

"Yes, General Yao, we have found them. They are both alive, but one is injured, perhaps fatally."

He paused while the general replied, and I ramped up my hearing to listen.

"It was not you that wounded her was it? If so, I would be most disappointed in you."

His icy voice delivered the threat without even raising his volume. The soldier's skin went pale, and he fumbled out his reply.

"N…No! No General! Neither I nor any of my men have hurt them at all! It must have been the plane crash that caused it!"

"Very well, bring them back to camp, but make sure they can't observe the way here. Oh, and they'd both better be alive when you get back."

"Yes, Sir!"

Shit. I looked at Eliza, to see if she'd heard the conversation, and her expression told me she had. It was strange, but I could tell she was waiting on me to decide whether we should confront the soldiers here and now, or wait until we were at their camp. Studying her for a moment, I understood why. Even though there was a fall bite in the air, a light coating of sweat covered her pale skin, and her posture favored her wounds. She wasn't in any shape to fight, at least not these well-armed soldiers. I gave a slight shake of my head and she responded with a negligible nod of hers. We would wait.

The soldier with the radio barked out his orders.

"Tie their hands behind them, quickly now, the General is waiting!"

At his command, the other two jumped into motion. They tied me first, the younger soldier yanking my arms back and securing my wrists with disposable plastic-strip handcuffs. He pulled the cuffs tight, but not enough to cut off my circulation. Still it would have been impossible to get out of them unless you had a knife or other sharp edge. He'd done this before.

Once I was secured, it was Eliza's turn. As they moved toward her, she decided to let them know she could speak their language.

"Hey, wait guys, at least let me go get my clothes. I'm going to catch my death out in this cold, and the General wouldn't like that, would he?"

They froze and looked at the squad leader, who got them focused again.

"Ignore her and do as I ordered! Bind her hands! And be careful what you say around her!"

As they worked on Eliza, I expected a fight, but she complied, wincing when they pulled her hands back. Although I could hear one of them whisper to her as he worked to secure her hands.

"You don't need to worry about what the General likes. I'm sure he will like you just the way you are."

The leader must have heard the comment too, because he grabbed the man by the shoulders and spun him around.

"Shut up! Don't speak about General Yao in such a way! It is disrespectful...and besides...he has ears everywhere."

The younger soldier blanched at the squad leader's obvious threat. Without another word, he turned and went back to work.

In short order, they led us outside and off into the woods. After several hundred yards, we arrived back at their troop transport truck. It sat parked at the end of a dirt road that wasn't on any of the maps I'd been able to find. Two more soldiers in identical uniforms stood around the camouflaged truck, chatting about soccer and such. They stiffened and saluted the squad leader as soon as they noticed his arrival. He snapped the salute back to them while giving them his orders.

"Prepare to head out, we've accomplished our mission. We will secure the women in the back, then I will stay with them."

"Yes sir!"

The soldiers that had been with the truck, scurried to the front and climbed in, while the other two put us into the back. Placing me down on the cold, metal bench-seat, they attached my handcuffs to a latch built into the bench. After finishing with me, they did the same with Eliza on the bench-seat across from mine. Having secured us, they hurried off to join their squad mates in the truck cab.

While the leader dug around in a large wooden container near the back of the cab, I took stock of Eliza's condition, She was putting on a brave face, but it was obvious our several hundred yard walk had exhausted her. Catching me looking, she read the concern on my face and adopted a more stoic expression. It wasn't convincing.

Without warning, her eyes widened, and before I could ask her why, the squad leader dropped a dirty burlap sack over my head. It blocked most of my vision, but thanks to my enhanced optics, I could still see shadows and motion. It made me smile to myself, because I knew they were using it to protect the location of their secret base, but my internal GPS would tell me all I needed to know, so score one for the home team. Moments later, Eliza must have gotten the same treatment.

"Hey, what the hell? This sack smells like crap!"

"Shut up, or I'll gag you!"

"You don't have to, the sack is doing a fine job of that!"

"I said shut up!"

I could see the man's right arm come up for a strike, but he held it in place. He must have been more afraid of his commander than annoyed with Eliza. She must have noticed as well, but she couldn't leave it alone.

"That's right, you'd better think about it. Messing up my pretty face would sure piss off your boss, soldier boy."

"GAHH! How have you lived this long? Don't you know I control your very life?"

Eliza sighed and kept poking.

"No, not really, it's your boss that controls my very life. You're just a delivery boy."

"I'm warning you, if you don't shut up, I'll take my chances with the General!"

His raised voice told me he might go through with his threat if she didn't stay quiet, so I hissed a warning at her in English.

"Eliza, please drop it."

There was a tense moment of silence, but she stayed quiet. Satisfied, the squad leader lowered his raised hand, using it to straighten out his fatigues. I breathed a sigh of relief as the soldier walked to the back of the cab, and pounded on it twice. The truck sputtered to life, lumbering forward, as the squad leader sat down on his own bench near the wooden container facing us. He removed his helmet and cradled what must have been his assault rifle in his lap.

My mind raced, trying to find a way out of this predicament, but to no use. It would have to wait until Eliza and I could hatch a plan. For now, all I could do was sit and hope we weren't executed the minute we met this General Yao.

PART TWO

DETAINED

Chapter Sixteen

Ultimatum

The transport truck creaked and moaned as it lumbered down the dirt road. Every bump and pothole only amplified the noise and caused it to buck like a wild horse, which wouldn't have been so bad, if I'd been able to use my hands to brace myself. As it was, the trip had been painful and annoying. Each time the truck hit a hole, it bounced me off the bench seat and raised me two or three inches into the air, only to be yanked back down to the hard bench seat by my handcuffs. I tried to occupy myself by tracking our location using my GPS, but we were creeping along, and the pain in my wrists took over my thoughts.

After a few minutes of self-pity, Eliza's physical condition popped into my mind, and I felt a little embarrassed. If it was this rough on me, it must be hell on her. The burlap sack limited my view, but it looked like her head was bobbing around more than normal. Was she unconscious? I wanted to whisper to her, but she'd never hear me over the cacophony of the truck. Anything louder might draw the attention of the squad leader, and I didn't want to rile him up again. I could connect with her via radio or phone, but that was subject to interception by the soldiers. While they may not understand our scrambled transmissions, it would raise questions about how we were transmitting without a device, so nope. There was interfusing, but then we'd both be in a more vulnerable state here in the physical world. Out of ideas, I tried it anyway since the truck appeared to be a safe enough environment.

Reaching out with my mind, I felt Eliza's mental barrier, and it was at full strength. If she lowered it for me, she'd be vulnerable to attacks from others, which was a bad idea right now. If only there was another way.

Out of a combination of boredom and not wanting to be defeated, I searched the Internet for secret means of communication…and I found something. It was an old, unused method of transmitting information that had its beginning with clicks over a physical copper wire, and later moved into dots and dashes of light during the world wars. I wasn't sure if Eliza would know Morse Code, but she was a combat model, so it was worth a try.

There wasn't any way for me to use flashing lights, or clicks, but I had an easy, undetectable way of sending my message. It was time to bring Morse Code into the Internet age.

Reaching out for my sister's neural-net mind, I again found her mental barrier. I applied force to it, as I'd done the other night, but this time I used a light tapping, just enough to get her attention. A tapping with a certain order to it, my name, again and again, A…N…N…A. Her response came faster than I'd expected, and it was in the form of the same pressure and taps against my barrier, E…L…I…Z…A. Now that we had our communication established, we could talk at the speed of thought.

"Hey, are you all right?"

"Yeah, just tired. I'm faking unconsciousness in case an opportunity to make a break for it comes up."

"Good idea, but I don't see a way out of this at the moment, unless you've noticed something I didn't."

"No, I was hoping you'd noticed a weak point."

It wasn't her fault, and I didn't bring it up, but if she'd been at full strength, we could have taken them back at the plane.

"No, nothing. With our hands tied like this and sacks over our heads, I think the best thing to do is wait and see what happens at their camp."

I could almost hear the snark in her voice when she replied.

"Ha, yeah, sacks over our heads. What the hell?"

"That's just it, our human cover is still intact. They don't know we're androids, which is our biggest advantage."

"True, because if they put us in any kind of normal cell, we'll be out and gone before the next morning."

"As long as we aren't executed on sight."

"Don't worry, all we have to do is keep our cool and play along. They won't kill us until they see if someone will pay a ransom for our return."

"Good point. Do you think you can behave?"

"Oh definitely, at least until I'm free. Then they'll pay, I can promise you that."

My imagination showed me images of Eliza massacring sleeping soldiers accompanied by a soundtrack of her nerve-wracking laugh. It made me shiver.

"Let's not risk anything for revenge, we need to get out and get gone."

"Anna, would you deny me one of the few emotions I can feel? How selfish of you. Look, these Red Dragons have tied us up, kidnapped us, and wouldn't even let me get dressed. You can bet your ass I'm getting payback."

"So now you care about wearing clothes?"

"That's not the point. I owe them, and I will pay them. No one does this shit to Eliza and lives to tell the tale."

"But…"

"Case closed. Now let me rest before we get to their camp."

There wasn't anyway to talk sense to her. She'd been wronged and her only response to that was violence, fatal violence. I stopped my makeshift Morse Code conversation and left her alone. She couldn't get any rest on these so called roads, but if I kept poking at her, she might do something stupid right after we got to the camp.

Without warning, the truck hit another crater and sent me bouncing. My cuffs caught me, slamming my rear down onto the bench, while pain shot up my arms and into my shoulders. Cursing under my breath, I had a fleeting thought that maybe Eliza wasn't wrong in her plans for revenge.

* * * * *

The truck rumbled on for what felt like an eternity, making a left turn here or a right turn there, with a few sharp corners thrown in for fun. By the time it squealed to a stop, I was achy all over and in one hell of a foul mood. We must have reached an outer perimeter around the base because I could hear the driver talking with another soldier.

"Hey, so you found them. Now we can recall the search groups and maybe get a little rest around here. Go on through, the General is waiting for you."

"Thanks."

We lurched forward again, but now the ride was smoother. I could hear the heavy truck crunching along on gravel instead of bouncing down a dirt road. We were inside the base now.

The squad leader interrupted my thoughts when he yanked the sack off of me. My vision adjusted to the sudden, glaring, light in milliseconds, which allowed me to see Eliza getting the same treatment.

She blinked a few times and glared at the soldier. He ignored her and leaned back against the truck. I whispered to her in English.

"Still holding up okay?"

"Yeah, I'm fine."

"You don't look fine. Your skin is as pale as it was last night."

"I said I'm fine, *mom*. Don't worry, your friends are safe."

Eliza's comment confused me, until I realized she believed my friends were the only reason I was concerned about her.

"No, that's not why…"

"NO TALKING!"

The soldier's sudden interruption of my denial, reminded me we weren't alone, and I stopped talking to avoid antagonizing him any further. Eliza entertained herself with staring at him for the rest of the ride which as it turned out, wasn't long.

The truck came to another squealing stop, and this time, the driver killed the engine. The squad leader stood and worked on freeing our handcuffs from the benches. By the time he'd finished, two of the soldiers from the cab had come to the back, and helped us out of the transport. In a show of utmost confidence, they even removed the plastic-strip handcuffs freeing our hands.

As soon as my feet hit the gravel road, I went to work sizing up the Red Dragon base. The scattered olive tents and wooden buildings were small, but well constructed. The roads weren't paved, but the gravel was so thick and well packed that it was the next best thing. Even the vehicles in the motor pool looked well cared for. For a small, guerrilla organization, their base was impressive. Glancing at Eliza, I saw she was taking in the sights too. When our eyes met, I could tell we'd come to the same conclusion, their commander must be a stickler for order and discipline.

As I finished getting a feel for how many men were stationed here, and a map of the base committed to memory, the soldiers from the truck fell into a straight line at full attention beside Eliza and me. The squad leader whispered to my sister what I'd already figured out.

"General Xiang Yao is coming. If you want to live, behave yourself."

I fought back the urge to roll my eyes at his advice. Expecting Eliza to behave was like expecting the sun to rise in the west…but one could hope.

Eliza opened her mouth, most likely to spout off some sarcastic comment, but she stopped and stared past the squad leader. Someone approaching our group had distracted her. When I followed her eyes and saw him, I understood why.

The older man that strode toward us exuded authority and control. Absolute power and confidence proceeded him like dark clouds rolling in before a storm. Anyone in his path fell silent and their bodies tensed, relaxing only when the man was ten feet past them. This man, in his pristine uniform, walking in such a commanding gait, was no doubt General Yao.

The squad leader bowed so low that his head almost touched his knees as the General halted in front of him. After what I felt was an exorbitant about of time, the young soldier straightened and addressed his superior in Mandarin.

"General, we found the survivors of the airplane crash and returned them to you as ordered. However, before you say anything, you should be aware that the black haired can understand us."

"Don't be foolish, they both speak Mandarin."

The volume of his reply was low, but there was a power behind his words that demanded everyone's attention.

"Step aside and let me inspect what we have found."

The soldier followed the order, and I winced as General Yao first went to Eliza. His black eyes almost showed emotion as he stood next to her exposed form. When he spoke, Eliza had to look down to meet his gaze since his physical stature was short for that of a man, but there was no doubt who was in control of the situation.

"You are not dressed appropriately to meet your superior."

"I have yet to meet anyone superior to myself."

An audible gasp came from a terrified soldier to my side and I tensed my body in preparation for a fight...a fight Eliza and I would lose.

However, General Yao was more disciplined than most people I'd encountered, and Eliza's quip didn't even phase him. He spoke to her without anger.

"You have spirit, and that is a good thing, but you must also have respect. You should not be so quick to mock. Especially when you are weak and wounded."

He extended his hand out to touch the fresh scar on Eliza's abdomen. This drew a scowl from her and she snapped at him.

"NO! Do not touch me. I'm not as wounded as you may think."

Shit...I readied myself again as the General's hand stopped a few inches from the inflamed, jagged line on her stomach. The entire base went quiet, waiting for the inevitable. Again, he spoke without malice and in complete control of the situation.

"Perhaps you are not."

My advanced reflexes activated as his hand shot forward. Dashing toward where they stood, my plan was to deflect or even take the blow for my smart-ass sister, but I was too slow. Never had I saw a human move that fast before...or hit with that much force. Some form of martial arts guided his hand, as it lashed out in a chopping motion and struck Eliza. I watched in horror as the force of his blow tore her wound open. My sister wrapped her arms around her stomach and her legs went limp. I was there to catch her before she hit the hard ground, and I cradled her as we both sank down. Looking up, the soldiers had pointed their rifles at me and General Yao stood over us. Again with no anger in his voice, he shook his head and spoke.

"No, it appears that I was correct. You are injured...fatally."

Turning around, he addressed the commanding soldier that had ridden with us in the truck.

"You will dispose of the injured one, she is of no use. Then bring the other to my office."

"General, wait...please."

It was the first time I'd spoken, and it caught his attention. He held his hand up and waved off his previous order, at least for the time being. When he turned and looked down on us, his dark eyes, bore into me, but I wouldn't be intimidated.

"Sir, I would like to propose an agreement."

The corners of his mouth twitched upward, and he almost grinned.

"I do not think you have anything with which to bargain. You and your dying companion are at my disposal."

"While that is partly true, I don't believe my friend is dying. She has recovered from worse injuries, and I would ask you to give her the chance to heal."

"Even if she was to live, it would be a long time before she was well enough to be useful. If I agreed to wait until she is whole, my soldiers would have to spend time caring for her. This would be wasted effort and resources on my part...unless you have something to give me in return for my army's lost efficiency."

"I do. Until my friend is mended, I will pledge my loyalty to you and perform whatever task you need."

At first, he didn't respond. General Yao was a shrewd customer. I could almost see him thinking through what I'd just proposed.

"There are several issues with what you offer. First, what if I was to order you to perform something heinous and unconscionable?"

"I would depend on your honor to not ask me to perform such a task."

"Ah, you speak to me of honor. That is a curious concept for you, is it not?"

"I...I...am sure that I don't know what you're referring to."

This time, he smiled.

"Well, given your personal history, I would have thought you unfamiliar with the concept."

Hoping my surprise didn't show on my face, I went through some complex mental gymnastics in an attempt to figure out how this man knew about me. The General didn't give me long to consider it.

"No matter, to my second point, I could force you to do my bidding without the vow you offer."

Since he somehow knew something of my past, it was time to use that to my advantage.

"You could attempt it, but I would not comply. If you let my friend die, then I will be useless to you. I swear it."

He watched my expression for any sign of deception or weakness that might belie my conviction. After a few tense seconds, he came to his decision.

"You speak the truth. Your loyalty to your friend is stronger than I have witnessed in many years. That is commendable, but it can also be costly..."

Uh Oh...

"However in this case, I will accept your offer."

Whew, I thought I'd pushed him too far.

"Commander, take two men and house Eliza in the high security facility. Then send for the physician to tend her wound. Anna, you will accompany me to my office. It is this way."

The soldiers lowered their weapons and bent to take Eliza from my arms. Narrowing my eyes, I warned them.

"Take good care of her."

Taking the great care I'd insisted upon, they lifted and carried her toward the south as I stood up from the gravel. With one last glance back toward my sister, I fell in line behind General Yao and his personal guards.

I should have been memorizing the layout of the base as the four of us walked toward an olive green tent in the back of the compound, but my mind raced from one thought to another. It was too convenient that our plane had crashed right in the backyard of someone that knew us by name. Had the Chinese been involved with Stepan and the Russian government? Had there been a spy at Ice Castle base where we were created? Could someone working with Adam at the NSA be feeding government secrets to the highest bidder? As we approached the entrance to the General's office, I realized all of that was unimportant. Until Eliza recovered, I was in General Xiang Yao's army. To keep her alive, which I had to do for the sake of my friends, it was time to fall in and be a good little soldier.

We arrived at his office, which was a modest looking camouflaged tent, and one of the soldiers pulled back the thick canvas allowing the General to enter. The second guard moved to go next, but Yao stopped him.

"No, both of you wait outside. There is no need for you to enter. I will inform you when we are finished."

Hmph, that was cocky of him. He knew what Eliza and I were capable of, and yet he was still comfortable being alone with me. Sure he'd handled her, but my sister was injured and not expecting him to be a skilled martial artist. Neither was true of me.

* * * * *

The General observed me from across his modest desk. After taking our seats, we'd been sizing each other up for almost a minute. At last he spoke.

"So, you have sworn yourself to me."

"To keep my friend alive, yes, I will willingly do as you ask…to a point."

"Yes, of course."

He opened a drawer on his desk and extracted a small bowl of various fruit. Placing it on the table between us, he took an apple and sat back in his seat. Producing a folding knife from his pocket, he cut himself a piece. Raising it to his mouth, he noticed I hadn't taken anything from the bowl, and he motioned toward the fresh fruit.

"Help yourself, Anna. You must be hungry."

"No thank you, General."

The last thing I wanted was to get too familiar with this man, no Stockholm Syndrome for me thank you. However, while I kept my expression stoic, my stomach betrayed me. After having nothing but junk food for days, it growled in protest at my decision. This caused him to chuckle as he chewed his apple. Damn, it smelled so good. After the second roar from my traitorous tummy, I gave in and selected a plump pear so it would quiet down. That first bite tasted every bit as good as I'd imagined.

"Delicious, no?"

I nodded.

"Yes, yes, do you know how hard it is to get this kind of fresh food?"

"No, but I imagine it's not easy."

"It is not. But I have dedicated a significant amount of my resources to acquiring it. Do you know why?"

I shook my head between bites.

"Discipline. Soldiers must follow orders even if they do not understand them. Sending them out to locate my fruit is a test of loyalty and respect. I am happy to say, they perform their duties without hesitation. Blind loyalty is the most important quality of any military force. Someday I may have to order these men and women to their certain death, and they must face it without question or hesitation."

Looking down at his half-eaten apple, he frowned slightly and tossed it in the garbage.

"Would you like some more?"

"No, thank you."

My eyes widened as the General took the bowl and emptied it into the trash can. He saw my expression and shook his head.

"No, do not worry, there is nothing wrong with the food."

"Why throw it away then?"

"Because when my garbage can is emptied, someone will see the uneaten fruit. News of the discarded food will spread throughout the ranks. The soldiers will rack their brains trying to figure out why I threw it away. They will eventually conclude that I wasn't happy with it and try their best to acquire something more suitable the next time I send them out for some."

"Will their conclusion be correct?"

Another soft chuckle escaped his lips.

"No, no, I threw it away because I don't like fresh fruit."

I stopped, mid-chew, and stared at him. He took a handkerchief out of his jacket and began to clean his knife, making me wait for the end of his lesson.

"Discipline, Anna. It is always about discipline."

* * * * *

Having lost my appetite, I threw away my pear. My patience grew thin as I waited for the General to disclose the mission, but I said nothing. A few minutes later, he finished cleaning his knife, storing it, and the handkerchief, back in his pockets. Leaning forward, he folded his hands and at last spoke again.

"Now, to discuss your task. What do you know of the current struggles between me and the Chinese government?"

I gave him a high-level answer, detailing the differences between the traditionalist Red Dragon faction and the democratic leaning government, but I left out most of the details. In this line of work, you always kept something hidden in case you needed it later. He listened without expression until I finished and then continued.

"Good, you know enough to perform this mission. What you do not know is that government forces captured a high-ranking member of my group several days ago. I, of course, want him returned. But my men and I can't attempt a rescue, the government knows all of our top agents, and will be on high alert for some kind of infiltration on our part. So I chose to seek assistance from outside my organization. After a bit of thought on the matter, I contacted someone that owed me a kindness. They recommended you and Eliza. After some discussion, we came to an arrangement, and barring the unfortunate airplane accident, everything has gone according to our agreement. Do you have any questions so far?"

Boy did I, but I doubted he would answer them.

"Yes, a few General. With whom did you make this arrangement?"

"That is something I cannot answer."

"Is this arrangement permanent, leaving Eliza and myself reporting to you indefinitely?"

He thought about that one for a moment.

"I will only say that it is flexible."

Like I thought, no answers, but there was one more thing I wanted to ask. He might not answer, but perhaps I could glean a little information from how he dodged the question.

"Why were Eliza and I selected by this person? What special talents were you led to believe we possess?"

"The person with which I spoke informed me that you and Eliza were the best infiltration agents in the world. While I find that boastful and unlikely, they assured me that the two of you could retrieve my officer. Was I misinformed?"

Either he's not going to tip his hand, or he actually doesn't know that Eliza and I are androids. It might make sense if the person who sent us here was hoping to get us back.

"No, you were not misinformed. I will free your soldier and return him to you."

"Will you be able to do this without your partner?"

Questions like that always made me smile to myself. They have only one answer.

"Yes, of course I will."

"You are very confident. You haven't even heard the details of the mission yet."

"Fair enough, please continue."

"The facility is not far from here, you will travel there using a jeep we will provide. Also, we have been able to take a prisoner of our own. She is a mid-level politician in the Chinese government and is scheduled to meet with some of the officials at the facility in two days. We will give you all the records on her we have, and you will meet with her tomorrow to study her. The plan is for you to impersonate this woman to gain access to the facility. From that point you will locate the captured officer, free him, and escape to return here. Questions?"

"General, you can't be serious. You expect me to take the place of a woman that I've never met after only studying her information for two days?"

He couldn't suppress a smirk as he replied.

"It will not be that difficult. Both of you have a similar facial structure and body type, well, except for some of your more, shall we say, robust areas."

He stood as he continued.

"Not to mention, no one at that facility has ever met her, they only know her from the news."

General Yao motioned toward the tent flap where we'd entered, and I stood to walk toward it with him.

"I hope this isn't too much of a challenge for the world's best infiltration agent."

"No General, I will get your man back."

He pulled the flap open for me and smiled.

"Good, I would hate to execute you and your friend, which I will do if you fail."

"You will not have that burden."

He addressed the two guards that stood outside.

"Take Anna to a secure tent, provide her a Red Dragon uniform, and allow her to clean up if she desires. Also, bring her all the information we have on Jia Meng, she will need to study it today."

The guards saluted, and he turned back to me.

"Anna, I will leave you to study the information. You will need to have it all memorized by tomorrow morning. Then I will send for you and we can meet with Jia Meng in person so you may speak with her directly."

"Will I be able to see Eliza before the start of my mission?"

"No, I don't think that would be wise. I want you to focus on the task at hand completely, no distractions."

"Very well."

"I truly hope you are as proficient as my contact thinks, I would hate to lose my son in this operation."

I'd turned to leave, but whirled back around at his statement.

"General, I had believed that I was going on this mission alone."

He sighed and a touch of sadness crept across his face.

"You are, but you see the captured officer you are to rescue is my only son, Chen Yao. Go now and prepare for your success."

Speechless, I turned and followed the two soldiers away from General Xiang Yao's tent.

Chapter Seventeen

Dragon's Den

The guards marched me away from the General's tent and further toward the middle of the compound. After about fifty yards, we arrived at a tent apart from the main complex. It was similar to Yao's in color and construction, but smaller in size. One of the men escorting me stepped in from outside of the tent. I could tell by his collar insignia, he was a sergeant, and outranked the private next to him.

"This tent is yours, we will be right outside if you need anything. Once your uniform arrives, we will show you to the showers so you can make yourself more presentable. Do not leave the tent or go anywhere unless we are with you."

"Thank you, sergeant."

He held the flap open for me and I entered my new home. Inside the one room tent was a basic cot, wooden footlocker, and a small table with a metal folding chair. Snooping around, I found that the footlocker was empty, and there were no computers or electronic devices of any kind. As a matter of fact, the single LED light bulb was the only thing vaguely electronic in the entire room. Whoever sent us here had told the General about my hacking skills. The private stuck his head in the tent and interrupted my examination of the room.

"Miss Anna, your uniform has arrived."

"Thank you, I'm coming."

The trip to the shower would give me a more complete map of the compound, along with getting to wash off a few layers of mud and a chance to put on clean clothes.

* * * * *

The guards waited outside while I took my shower. It was a rejuvenating experience, complete with hot water, and clean towels. After drying off, I found that the Red Dragon uniform they'd brought me fit well enough, and it sure smelled a lot better than my clothes. Before tossing my nasty rags in the corner, I took Viktor's data drive and stored it in a zippered pocket on my new pants. I wasn't ever letting it out of my sight again. Dried and dressed, I let the guards know I was ready to go.

When we arrived back at my new home, my entourage stayed outside next to the opening, which I appreciated. That would give me some much needed privacy to plot an escape. However, as I entered the tent, something caught my eye before I could begin my scheming. There was a thick, manila folder on the table which hadn't been there before I left. Intrigued, I walked over and sat down at the table, examining the new addition to my room. Good grief, this thing was at least three hundred pages. Thick rubber bands held it closed, but they didn't obscure the text stamped in large, red letters across its cover.

CLASSIFIED: AUTHORIZED PERSONS ONLY

Well, since someone left it in my room, I must be an authorized person. Slipping the rubber bands off, I flipped the folder open. There was an 8x10 photograph attached to the back side of the cover. The picture depicted an attractive young woman in a red business suit. She was heading down the steps of a featureless, stone building while reporters walked backwards in front of her. Without reading the summary attached to the other side, I knew who she was. This was Jia Meng, the woman from the Chinese government that the Red Dragons had kidnapped.

Thinking about what I was getting myself involved in, caused a wave of disgust to wash over me. I closed the folder, refusing to learn anything about her. What I should concentrate on was how to get us out of here, Jia included, before it was time to go on this stupid mission.

* * * * *

Time to work. First, I needed to know if the room had any surveillance equipment installed. Activating my built in radio receivers, I used them on low power to search for any nearby devices that were transmitting data. Finding none told me I could have conversations with people in my room without being monitored. Expanding my search to encompass the whole base, I detected several high-powered radio signals and two wireless networks. The Dragon's network security team had encrypted both types of signals, but I wasn't after their data. The frequencies they were using were all I needed to know. That way when I sent my transmission, I could use radio bands unmonitored by the base.

Before I started planning, I wanted to check on Eliza. If she was awake, we could work together to get out of here. Using my neural-net mind, I sent signal after signal pinging around the base until I located her unique brain pattern. Her mental barrier was in place, but she didn't respond to any of my attempts to contact her. This concerned me, and I wished I could go see her. Oh well, since the General wouldn't let me go myself, I'd have to use a guard to do my dirty work.

"Sergeant, can you please come in, I need to speak with you."

After a brief pause, he entered the tent.

"What do you need, Miss Anna?"

I motioned for him to come closer, so the other soldier couldn't hear.

"The General has forbidden me from seeing my companion, Eliza, so I need you to check on her for me."

"I'm sorry, Miss Anna, but I can't leave my post for something like that."

"Please sergeant, I'm worried about her. Besides, there will still be someone watching me."

"No, I can't do this for you."

Okay, I hadn't wanted to resort to this. I poked his chest with my finger and scowled.

"Look, if you don't go check on her, I will tell General Yao that you exposed yourself to me when I was showering. Then when I refused your advances, you flew into a rage and attempted to strangle me."

He looked horror stricken, but held his ground.

"No...no one would believe you. I am an honorable man and would never do such a thing."

"You may be right about most of your comrades, but my claim will plant a seed of doubt in their minds about you forever. Especially when I show them the bruises around my neck."

"What? You have no such marks!"

While he spoke, I concentrated on changing the skin color around my neck. I went with a nice mixture of purple, brown, and blue.

"Really, look closer. See what you have done to me."

I pulled back the neckline of my uniform to show him my handiwork.

"But...I never! You, you did that to yourself! I never touched you!"

"Your denials will fall on deaf ears. Go and check on my friend now, or I'll send for the General."

"Damn your treacherous soul! Fine, I'll do as you say!"

As he stormed out of the tent, I called after him.

"Don't keep me waiting, and don't attempt to deceive me, because I will know if you are lying."

Now while he was gone, I should have time to contact Adam, but I'd need a clear view of the sky since I needed to use a direct satellite connection to avoid being detected by the base's monitoring systems. Heading back to the table, I gathered up the folder on Jia Meng, my chair, and headed for the tent's exit.

* * * * *

Hands full, I stumbled outside to the surprise of the other guard. He spun on me and put his hand on the rifle strapped across his back.

"Hold on there private, I don't want any trouble. Just looking to study my folder out here since it was such a nice day."

"I'm not sure if you are supposed to be out of your tent doing that."

Sitting my chair down near the entrance to the tent, I sank down in it and opened the folder.

"No need to stress about it, besides, this way you can keep a better eye on me than if I was out of sight in that stuffy tent."

He accepted my logic as sound and resumed leaning against one of the tent's support poles.

"Very well, but don't try to run or something like that because you'll never make it out of the base."

"Don't worry, I'm not that stupid."

He was right, now wasn't the time. Even if I managed to escape the base somehow, I'd never get out of China without help...which was where Adam and the NSA factored into my plan.

Pretending to pour over the Jia Meng's information, I prepared to open a direct connection to an orbital satellite. Since I was handling all the communication inside my mind, the guard would never be the wiser. Searching the sky, I found a satellite and called the new number Adam had given me after the crash. The phone rang and rang before he at last answered.

"This is Sims."

"Adam, this is Anna, is the line secure?"

"Yes, it is."

"I'm so glad you answered, Eliza and I are in big trouble."

"That was how you started the call the last time we talked."

"Yeah, well our situation has gotten worse."

"I hadn't thought that possible, give me the details."

I filled him in on our capture by the Red Dragons, Eliza becoming re-injured, and my mission in a few days to infiltrate the secret Chinese government facility.

"You are right, that is much worse."

"Stop being a smart-ass and get us out of here."

"Anna, I've already told you we have no influence with the Red Dragons. I'm trying to set up a recovery operation outside the province they control, but you will have to make it to the extraction zone on your own."

"Adam, we are in real trouble here. I'm being forced into this mission to keep Eliza alive, and I'm concerned what I might have to do at the government facility to rescue Xiang Yao's son."

"Okay, do you want me to warn them you are coming?"

"NO...don't do that. What you could do is have them stand down and release Chen Yao to me so that no one gets hurt."

There was a pause.

"Are you saying you would injure or perhaps kill agents of the Chinese government to rescue this man?"

"No, what I'm saying is that I might be forced to do something I really don't want to in order to save my friends. Their lives are tied to Eliza's, and right now this is the only way to save her."

"I would consider *all* the ramifications of your actions before you undertake this mission for the Dragons."

"Damn it Adam, haven't you been listening? I don't like this any more than you, that's why I'm begging for your help!"

"Believe me, I am trying. We have been working on an extraction operation for the past couple of days, and I will do my best to contact this facility you are about to infiltrate. Perhaps I can get Kevin to assist me."

"Your manager? My impression of him was that he was an asshole. No, ask Edwin Westcott for a favor."

"The head of the entire Signals Intelligence Directorate? I don't think I have that kind of pull."

"You have to go to him. A lot of people's lives are on the line here."

"You're right, I'll contact Mr. Westcott."

"Good, is there anything else you need from me?"

"Not officially, but Elizabeth is really worried about you. After I told her about your crash, she has been a nervous wreck."

"Adam, why would you tell her about that? You knew it would upset her. Why didn't you just make up something about why I was unavailable?"

"I find I'm not able to lie to her very well."

"Well whatever you do, don't tell her about all this before we see how it turns out."

He didn't answer.

"Did you hear me, Adam?"

"Yes, I heard you."

"Good, I already had to upset her by telling her about her father's death at the hands of Eliza, the last thing I want is her worrying about me."

"I understand."

"Okay, I will call you again when I can. Don't contact me since I have to be outside to avoid being caught sending transmissions like this."

"Very well, hopefully I will have better news when you call back. Good luck, Anna."

"Thanks, Adam…Goodbye."

Cutting the connection, I sighed, which drew the unwanted attention of my nearby guard.

"Are you all right, you look pale."

As I turned my head to face him, I saw the sergeant returning.

"It's just that the sun is giving me a headache. I think I'll move back inside to look over this material."

The approaching soldier heard me and saw an opportunity to report what he'd found out about Eliza.

"I will carry your chair for you, Miss Anna."

* * * * *

Back inside, the sergeant glowered at me as he spoke in a whisper.

"I did as you asked, your companion is unconscious, but not in any immediate danger."

"Was there a surgeon looking after her?"

"No, but a nurse was there checking her vital signs every hour."

"Thank you for helping me."

"I had no choice, you threatened to blackmail me."

"I know, but thank you anyway."

He turned and stomped out of the tent, trying his best to slam the flap closed as he left. As soon as I was alone, I sank into the chair and put my head down on the desk. The weight of it all threatened to overwhelm me, and it might have, if I hadn't realized there were so many lives hanging in the balance. I had to get a grip on myself and trust that the decisions I made in the next few days would be the correct ones. After all, I wasn't alone. Adam was back at the NSA trying his best, and I was sure that Elizabeth Eklund would be nagging them too. She was as talented as her father, *my father*, when it came to the neural-net mind, and with Viktor gone, she was the best shot the American government had at reproducing his work. This gave her a ton of clout to wield back at her post working with Adam.

Straightening myself back up, I opened the folder on Jia Meng and started memorizing the information on each page. Avoiding the mission was still my goal, but if I couldn't, at least I would be prepared.

Chapter Eighteen

Predictable

Memorizing the entire three hundred sixty-one pages of information on Jia Meng took me a little less than an hour. Of which turning the pages took most of the time. Since the Red Dragons didn't know I was an android, I spent the rest of the day pretending to study…and plotting my escape. Trouble was, with Eliza out of commission and Jia's location unknown, I wasn't going anywhere.

Right before nightfall, I asked the sergeant to check on Eliza again. This time he did it without me threatening him. His news was discouraging. She was still unconscious and unresponsive. I considered breaking down her mental barrier and going into her mind again, but dismissed the idea. It was risky enough with us in the same room, trying to perform that kind of intricate connection across an unknown distance was out of the question. Depressed that the only progress I'd made was a head full of Mrs. Meng trivia facts, I turned off my light and curled up on the cot. Setting my internal alarm for daybreak, I put myself to sleep.

I awoke the next morning, and the first thing I thought was maybe yesterday had been a bad dream. After that didn't pan out, I got up, and stuck my head out of the tent. My two favorite guards were standing in almost the same spots as last night.

"Hey guys, what time is breakfast around here?"

The sergeant cut his eyes at me.

"It began thirty minutes ago."

"Wow, you get moving early around here. Can you take me to the mess hall so I can get a bite to eat?"

"Uh, well, I suppose so. Let us know when you are ready."

"Fine, give me just a minute and I'll be ready to go."

This was a great stroke of luck. Eating a meal with the troops would give me a great chance to estimate the number of soldiers stationed here at the base. I rushed to put my boots on, and was still in the middle of lacing them when the sergeant spoke.

"Greetings, General."

"Good morning, Peng. Is Anna awake?"

"Yes sir, we were about to take her to breakfast."

"No, I do not think so. Private, fetch breakfast for all four of us."

"Yes sir!"

Damn, a lost opportunity.

"Anna, may I come in?"

"Yes General Yao, feel free."

He entered my tent and took a quick look around.

"Looks like we should have gotten you a second chair...no matter. Help me move the table over next to the cot."

I finished lacing my boots and did as he asked. He motioned toward the chair as he sat on the footlocker. He was thumbing through Jia Meng's folder by the time I'd sat down.

"You studied this information yesterday, correct?"

"Yes, I worked on it all day."

"Excellent, then let me see what you have learned. We will begin with easy questions first, I think. What is the month and day of Jia's birthday?"

"May 16th."

"Is she married?"

"No, she is widowed."

"How many children?"

"She has two, a boy and a girl."

"Good, you *have* been working. Let's try something harder. How did her husband die?"

"A construction accident took his life."

"How many years has she held her government office?"

"She has served twelve years."

"How many years was she in the Air Force?"

I had memorized the entire file and knew the answers to anything he could ask, but I wondered if I should miss one or two on purpose to keep from raising any suspicions. Bah, screw it.

"That is a trick question, Jia was in the Navy, and it was eight years. It is also where she met her husband."

He closed the folder and placed it behind him on the cot.

"I see there is no need to ask you anything else. I must say, you are living up to your reputation so far."

"Thank you, General."

The private burst in with breakfast and sat it on the table. Then he bowed twice and headed back out to eat with Sergeant Peng. I'd always heard that military food was bland, but not this meal. It was a spread of eggs, ham, and pancakes that looked fantastic, or it could have been that I was still recovering from all the junk food I had to eat. Neither one of us said much until after we finished off the excellent meal.

* * * * *

The private came back and cleaned up our trays, leaving us a decanter of tea and two cups. The General poured us both a steaming cup of tea, and we talked as we waited for them to cool.

"So Anna, for you to impersonate Jia, how long will you need to meet with her?"

"It depends, not only do I need to listen to her talk, but I want to see how she behaves physically."

"Physically?"

"How she walks, stands, moves her hands while talking, that kind of thing."

"But no one knows her at the facility. Why would you need to see all that?"

"You'd said they have seen her on television. I need to know if she displays any distinctive mannerisms. It would take days to learn all her quirks, but I should be able to observe enough to fool the people at the facility in only a few hours. As long as she will open up and talk to me."

"That is where we have a problem. She hasn't said a word since we captured her. If we assume she won't talk to you, how much would that affect your chance at successfully impersonating her?"

"Hmm, without hearing her voice, I can't impersonate her well at all."

"Not even if we had video of her?"

"No, it's not the same. All videos are distorted in some manner. If I base my voice on a recording, it would only be about eighty percent accurate. I need to hear her talk."

General Yao sighed and sipped his tea. Sitting it back down on the table, he laced his hands together in front of himself.

"I understand. We will do what me must then."

"What do you mean by that?"

"You told me she has to talk, so we will make her talk…or at least scream."

"Wait, General, are you referring to torture?"

"If she won't talk willingly, then yes, I will have my men do whatever is necessary to make her speak. Actually, I should leave and get that underway. It can take an hour or so to get someone as stubborn as her to cooperate."

"No, wait…there must be another way."

He leaned back on the footlocker and stroked his chin in thought. After a moment, he pointed his index finger at me.

"Yes, you might be able to help."

"What? How?"

"You could lie to her. Tell her you are from the United Nations. Sent to negotiate her release, but you need to know the details surrounding the day of her capture. She might believe that."

"You want me to trick your prisoner into talking, by giving her a line about being a UN official? That feels really smarmy."

"Smarmy? What is that word?"

"Uh, it means underhanded, slimy, painfully deceitful."

"Well, you are the spy, Anna. This is your job. Either you convince her to talk, or my interrogation specialist will."

Damn, I felt like a low life.

"All right, I'll do it. Only you have to give me your word there won't be any torture…even if I can't get her to speak."

"Hmm, very well, you have my word, no torture."

He stood up and headed for the tent opening. Speaking as he went.

"Go with your guards to the shower tent. There you will find more clothes and a UN identification badge. Once you are ready, the men will bring you to Jia Meng."

I couldn't believe it.

"Wait a minute, you had this planned all along. You knew I'd agree to do this didn't you?"

He paused right outside the tent, but didn't turn back around.

"Yes, of course. The art of negotiation and war are similar. You must know with whom you are dealing, and then you will know how they are going to react in certain situations. Having researched you extensively

Anna, I found you can be very predictable. Now don't delay. I'll meet you after you've had time to talk with Jia."

That arrogant bastard! I'd show him predictable. *Just wait.*

Chapter Nineteen

Innocent Lies

I stayed pissed off through my entire shower. The whole time I was seething about how the General had maneuvered me into impersonating a UN representative. Even while drying off, all I thought about was who might be feeding him information. In the spy game, the side with the most data often won, and right now, General Xiang Yao knew more about me than I did about him. I hadn't hacked into the Red Dragon's computer network for fear of getting caught. If that happened, it would be the end of both Eliza and myself. However, if he kept outmaneuvering me, that might be a risk I'd have to take.

The clothes hanging in the dressing room were quite conservative. I buttoned up the beige, long-sleeved blouse and snapped the navy blue, calf-length skirt around my waist before pulling on the skirt's matching jacket. On its lapel, I found a UN identification badge with my name and picture. Examining it closer, I saw that my name was Paula Wills, and that Paula wore her hair in a tight bun. Looking in a nearby mirror, I concentrated and adjusted the length of my hair until putting it up like in the picture was a snap. Slipping on the black pumps completed my UN disguise. It was time to meet Jia Meng.

My escorts led me back into the middle of the compound and toward one of the few metal buildings I'd seen. We walked up to the door, and Sergeant Peng spoke to a man through a small rectangular, metal grate at eye level. The other soldier nodded and opened the door for us. When we entered, I noticed that the three soldiers in this building were in heavy combat armor and had shotguns as well as assault rifles on their backs. They saluted Peng as he explained the situation.

"This woman is here to see Jia. She is working with us, so observe them from behind the one-way mirror, not in the same room. The private and I will wait outside to escort her back to her tent when she has finished. Do not let her near any computers or communication equipment. Understood?"

"Yes sir!"

Peng turned to leave, and I stopped him.

"Sergeant Peng, could you please run that same errand for me this morning?"

He frowned at first, but gave me a quick nod before he and the private left the room.

Once my usual escort had left, the head of the stockade addressed me.

"This way miss, she is in cell number three. I will let you enter and lock the door behind you. Knock on the door when you wish to leave."

"I understand, thank you."

He led me down a ten-foot wide hallway past two heavy, metal doors. We stopped at a third one, and he took out a keycard. Sliding it through a data reader generated a loud buzzing sound and the lock snapped open. In my head, I was busy getting into the character of UN officer Paula Wills, and wasn't paying particular attention to the Red Dragon soldier as he opened the door. Stepping inside, I put on my best fake bureaucratic smile, and looked around to find Jia Meng. What I found was Hell on earth.

*****

Before I could even register what I saw in the small fifteen-foot square room, the smell hit me. It was a pungent smell of human waste mixed with vomit. Covering my mouth and nose with my hand, I looked around Jia's cell. It was barren except for a stained, tattered blanket on the floor and a metal pail in the corner streaked with brown marks…that was the source of the awful smell. Next to the ratty blanket, was a woman sitting with her back to me in clothes that made her look like a penniless beggar from the medieval ages. Her long, black hair was filthy and knotted, but it was the color of Jia's. I stepped in front of her to see her face and gasped. It was Jia, but a combination of dirt, blood, and tears caked her pretty face. She had a black eye, a swollen bottom lip, and a nasty bump on her forehead that was the size of a golf ball. The whole situation pushed me over the edge and I stormed up into the soldier's face.

"You! Get that bucket out of here and bring back some fresh water and two chairs!"

"Who do you think you are to give me orders?"

"Look at the badge Einstein! My name is Paula Wills and the United Nations sent me here to negotiate this woman's release! Now, unless you want to be the man responsible for getting your country economic sanctions that will throw you back to the stone age, you'll do what I say!"

He blinked and scurried over to pick up the bucket. On his way out, I snapped at him again.

"And leave that door open, so we can breathe in here!"

"Miss I can't…"

"We're not going *anywhere*, just leave it open!"

He bolted around the corner, happy to be away from my wrath.

While waiting on him to return, I went back to Jia. She hadn't moved and was staring down at the floor.

"Jia, Jia Meng, is that you?"

No reply.

"I know you already heard me Jia, but I'm Paula Wills from the UN. I've come to negotiate your release with General Yao." She inched back just a hair at the mention of the General's name, but still didn't speak.

By this time, the soldier had returned with a friend that was helping him carry what I'd demanded. I'd frazzled him so much, that he even brought a small, metal table with the two chairs. He sat the chairs at each end of the table, while his friend placed an aluminum pitcher of water and two cups on it. Finished, they both scurried out of the room without saying a word.

After they left, I turned my attention back to Jia.

"Come on, let's sit at the table. Here, I'll help you up."

She never looked away from the floor as I held out my hand, so I took her by the arm and lifted. Jia didn't respond at first, but then she helped lift herself, and I guided her up and into the chair. Once there, I sat down in the one across from her.

"Jia, look at me. Can you hear me?"

She continued to stare down at the table, never making eye contact. This was going to be harder than I thought. What had they done to this poor woman?

Reaching over, I put my hand under her chin and lifted her head. The poor girl's eyes still didn't look at me, they were focused somewhere off in the distance, unseeing and lifeless.

"Can you see me, Jia?"

She didn't answer. Her dirty face was blank, registering no expression. Crap, nothing was working. I sure as hell didn't want her to go through anymore of the General's torture. While I tried to think of something to do, she sat there, her grimy face looking straight ahead. Well, at least I could clean her up.

Grabbing the hem of my skirt, I tore at it until I held a small, rectangular patch of fabric. I took the pitcher of water and poured some on my makeshift washcloth. Wringing out the excess liquid, I took the cloth and went to work cleaning her face. I was gentle and careful, all the while talking to her. She still hadn't answered me when I finished, but she looked much better.

"Jia, please, I want to help you but you have to talk to me."

Nothing. Sighing, I turned to toss the now dirty rag onto the floor.

"Can you really?"

Her voice was weak and tiny, but it startled me anyway. Whirling back around, I saw her big, caramel-colored eyes focused on me, trying to read my true intentions.

"Yes! I'm trying to get you out of here."

"I suppose this isn't a trick. You're the first American I've seen since I was taken."

"I just arrived today. I came as soon as the UN heard about your situation."

She still spoke robotically, without emotion, but at least I had her talking.

"All right then, I suppose it can't get any worse anyway. What do you want to know?"

This was fantastic! I was learning her speech patterns without a hitch. All I needed to do was keep her talking.

"Let's start with what you were doing the day they brought you here. Tell me everything, I want to know if there was any provocation for the way the Red Dragons acted."

* * * * *

Once I got her started, it was like a dam had burst. The flood of words that came from her was a roller coaster of emotions. We began talking about the day of the kidnapping and the horrible experiences that followed, but soon she had opened up about everything in her life. We talked about how she met her husband, fell in love with him, and married him.   She was smiling as she recalled the birth of their children, and weeping when she told about the construction accident that took her husband's life.   I already knew all of this from reading her file, but hearing it from her, brought it to life in an amazing way.   She was an excellent orator.

Her personality was so sweet and charming, it was infectious. Jia even got me to open up about my life...to a point. Of course, my stories were base falsehoods, but I slipped threads of truth into the intricate quilt of lies that I wove. The more I talked, the more I fabricated. It became easier and easier to lie...and do it well. I spewed forth my deceptions like a hung over frat boy after a night of binge drinking sprays...well, you get the idea. Plus, just like him, what I was doing was making me feel sick to my stomach.   It was disgusting how well I lied right to this innocent woman's face.

During her telling me about her son and how he wanted to be in the space program, a guard tapped me on the shoulder.

"Excuse me, but the General would like to speak with you."

At the mention of him, Jia stopped talking and looked back down at the table. I was furious at first, but then I saw we'd been talking for over three and a half hours.

"Very well, where is he?"

The guard pointed at the mirror, and I left the room to find Xiang. A few doors down on the left, I saw him through an open doorway. Entering the room, I stood next to him in front of the one-way mirror. I could see Jia and the guard that had summoned me standing behind her, blocking the open door to the cell.

"I have been observing you for several minutes.   You are truly masterful at your craft. Do you have all the information you need for the mission?"

"Yes, I believe so. It took time for her to become comfortable with me and show her true mannerisms, but after the first hour, she did."

"You say, you believe so, but that is not acceptable. You must be sure. The mission to rescue my son cannot fail."

"I am sure I can impersonate Jia Meng, General."

He looked at me with that penetrating stare again, trying to read my soul.

"Very well then."

Reaching out to a control panel below the mirror, he pressed a small amber button.

"You may proceed, private."

His voice echoed in Jia's cell, and I realized he had spoken in to a microphone on the panel.

"What are you…"

My question stuck in my throat as I watched the horror unfold. The guard that had stayed in the room, drew a large combat knife with his right hand, and grabbed Jia's hair with the other. In one swift motion, he pulled her head up exposing her neck, and sliced a deep, jagged wound from under one of her ears to the other. My enhanced reflexes activated, and I saw her eyes widen as she realized her throat was slashed open. Those eyes, that moments ago had regained a spark of hope, now reflected absolute terror. Blood gushed and bubbled from the wound, coating her neck and chest…transforming her dirty prison clothes into a death shroud of dark crimson.

The guard released her hair and stepped back, not wanting to get his uniform dirty. As he did, Jia grabbed and clasped at her throat in a desperate attempt to stanch the flow of her life's blood.

I bolted out of the observation room, running toward her cell.

"NO! OH GOD, NO!"

The soldier backed up toward the mirror as I burst into the room, but it was almost over. Jia's pale, blood-spattered face looked at mine, and she tried to speak, but the only thing that came out, was gagging, choking sounds. She tried to cough, to catch a breath, but her lungs were already full of blood. Before I could get to her, she let go of her wound, and her arms went limp. Jia's body tipped forward, and her head sank down on to the table, resting in the thick pool of blood that had gathered there. Her eyes still staring at me as the light in them dimmed, and then went out forever.

Rage, absolute rage overcame me. I charged at the soldier with every intention of killing him. The man's eyes widened as I rushed forward and he backed into the mirror. Realizing he still held the knife, he brought it up to defend himself. Good, I wanted a fight…but I didn't get much of one. This man, like so many of my opponents, underestimated my speed and power. I'd grabbed his wrist before he'd even reacted. With my momentum and superior strength, I slammed his hand up against the mirror. Both the glass and his wrist shattered from the blow, and the knife tumbled to the floor. He screamed, but not for long.

Grabbing his throat with my other hand, I grasped him hard enough to cut off his air supply. He kicked out with his leg and landed a solid blow to my knee, but it wasn't enough. I wasn't sure whether to let him die of asphyxiation, or squeeze a little harder and snap his fucking neck.

"ANNA! Stop this now!"

It was the first time I'd heard the General raise his voice, and it made me realize he was the one I should kill. After all, he'd given the order.

Pulling the soldier away from the mirror about a foot, I slammed his head back against it, and the glass shattered again. The man's body went limp, and I dropped him to the floor. Turning, I saw the General had entered the room, and there were two more guards wielding shotguns charging down the hallway. Bolting toward General Yao, I grabbed him by the neck as I'd done the knife-wielding soldier. However, in my fury, I'd forgotten about his martial arts training. I couldn't close my grip around his neck, because he held my wrist with his left hand. Xiang was squeezing it in some way that prevented me from bringing all my strength to bear. Worse, while I ran at him, he'd drawn his service pistol, and was now pointing it at the side of my head.

"Anna, think about what you are doing. Do you really want to throw your life away like this?"

I actually thought about it. There was no doubt in my mind I could kill him, but then there was also no doubt I'd be just as dead. If not from his pistol, then from the shotgun blasts of the other soldiers. Reason came back to me, pushing the rage out of my mind, and I thought of what would happen to my friends. If I died here, they were as good as dead. Still, I held on to him, staring at him the same way he was staring at me. Both of us wondering if this was the way we would die. It wasn't.

I opened my hand and let go of his neck. He let go of me and lowered his gun as I backed away. My voice was little more than a snarl.

"Why did you kill her?"

"Why would I not? You informed me you had all the information to complete the mission. This made her an unneeded liability. I simply eliminated that liability."

My mind knew that his logic was sound, but I didn't care.

"You could have held on to her. Let her go when the mission was over."

"You cannot be serious."

"Oh, I am."

"Anna, there is nothing we can do about it now. Go and prepare for the mission. You will need to be ready to leave for the hidden compound early tomorrow morning."

Weighing my options, and realizing there was nothing I could do to bring Jia back, I relented.

"Fine, I will give the sergeant a list of things needed to create my disguise. I assume you have the transportation and any security requirements already taken care of."

"Yes, the jeep is ready and we have the security items that Miss Meng was carrying when we seized her. You will use those. All you need to do is play the part of Jia Meng."

"All right, I'm heading back to my tent to practice and read the documents one more time...but on the way, I'm stopping in on my companion, Eliza."

The General stiffened at my blatant disregard for one of his orders, but at this point, I didn't care.

"I will allow you to see her. You have done well and you deserve a reward."

"Hmm, whatever."

Turning my back on him, I stormed away with my escorts following behind.

* * * * *

I sat with Eliza for a half hour, but she never showed signs of becoming conscious. Her mental barrier was still in place and at full strength, so all I could do was trust she was behind it healing herself. Deciding this shitty day wasn't going to get any better, I returned to my tent.

Once there, I gave the list of items I needed for my disguise to Sergeant Peng and he set out to procure them. The only reason I asked for anything, was to keep my captors from getting suspicious once I transformed myself into a perfect Jia Meng clone before leaving tomorrow. As far as I knew, the Red Dragons still thought I was simply a talented human spy, not an android super-spy. That was an advantage I intended to keep.

Now alone in my tent, I collapsed onto my cot. Closing my eyes, my mind drifted to thoughts of Jia. I knew we'd only spoken for a few hours, but having studied hundreds of pages about her life, she felt like a close friend. Thoughts of her now orphaned children never knowing what happened to their mother, her parents burying an empty casket because her body would never be found, and the look in her eyes as she drifted from this world, all of these terrible images danced through my mind and tormented me. My eyes burned and I could feel tears forming in their corners. NO! Not this time. I won't lay here and bawl my eyes out over another murdered innocent. This time, I'd get even. The rage swelled inside me again. I'd never felt an anger, no a *hatred*, so strong before. Perhaps before Eliza and I escaped from this hell for good, she could *play* a little. *Why not turn her loose and let her do what she did best?* Images of her and the kinds of terrors she'd inflict upon the Red Dragons replaced the ones about Jia… and they made me smile.

Chapter Twenty

Infiltration

The next morning, the burning rage and desire for revenge had subsided. In its absence, I felt embarrassed at my savage thoughts…embarrassed, and more than a little concerned. It wasn't like I'd never felt anger before. Eliza had brought me to the verge of ending her more than once, but this was different. This was a visceral desire to kill, to wipe those that had done me wrong from the face of the planet. Whatever was happening, I had to keep it under control. Giving in to that kind of hatred would haunt me for the rest of my life.

"Miss Anna, are you awake? I have the items from your list."

"Yes, I'm coming."

Sitting up in the cot, I stretched and tried to put my worries about my new anger issues behind me. Like it or not, I had a job to do.

Pulling back the flap, I took the package from Peng.

"Thanks, let me sort through this and I'll be ready to head out in a moment."

He nodded and waited outside while I inventoried the supplies. Nice, he'd gotten everything I asked for, of which I'd only use the red skirt, matching jacket, black flats, and white blouse. I gathered most of the makeup and my new clothes.

"Okay Sergeant, let's go."

Once alone in the showers, I turned on the water and let it warm up. While I was waiting, I disposed of at least half the makeup and all the hair dye down the drain. While washing off, I concentrated on a picture of Jia I'd seen in her file. Mixing that together with what she had looked like in real life, I began altering my appearance. Short, black hair, caramel-brown eyes, a slimmer body, and a smaller bust, all became part of my outward appearance. Checking a nearby mirror, I finished my disguise by making a few tweaks to my skin tone and adding a couple of wrinkles.

It was spot on, if I did say so myself, well except for my height. I'm five foot seven and she was five foot two, but with all I could change about my appearance, altering my height was not in my repertoire. I would have to count on the fact that no one at this facility had ever met her in person. Finishing up my shower, I dressed and headed out to meet Sergeant Peng.

"Miss Anna, you look just like her. It's incredible!"

That kind of compliment would make me smile on most days, but not after what happened yesterday. I replied to him in my voice, not Jia's.

"Thank you Sergeant. Although I worry that I'm too tall."

"No, it is fine. No one will notice a few inches."

"I hope you're right."

"Would you mind checking on Eliza for me one last time before I leave?"

"Of course, I will go after I escort you back to the tent."

"Thank you."

Walking back, several soldiers stopped in their tracks when they saw me. They whispered and pointed as I passed. Maybe Sergeant Peng was right, this disguise could work.

When we arrived, I went inside and sat down at my small table. Full of nervous energy, I occupied myself with random thoughts of escape while awaiting my morning update on Eliza.

* * * * *

"May I come in?"

It wasn't the Sergeant, but General Yao outside my tent.

"Yes, enter."

He came in and paused in the doorway, staring at me as he'd done when we first met. Shaking his head, he came over and sat down on the footlocker.

"Most impressive. If not for the fact that you sit a little taller, I would swear you are Jia Meng. Do you mind me asking something, how did you make your facial structure look so different? Not to mention your, shall we say, upper body, is much smaller now."

"Yes well, the face is done with just the right applications of makeup to make shadows and light play tricks on your eyes. I make my upper body look smaller with a tight wrap and tape, uncomfortable, but effective."

He nodded a few times taking in my lies and requested what I'd been dreading.

"Speak like her for me. I want to hear how well you can imitate her voice."

Looking like her was bad enough, but reproducing her voice after seeing her murdered less than twenty-four hours ago was difficult. I considered screwing it up just to mess with him, but that would have been unwise, so I gave the General what he wanted. Standing and bowing, I spoke as Jia.

"Pleased to meet you General Xiang Yao, I am Jia Meng with the Central Government."

Again, that long stare bore into me before he spoke.

"I was told you were the best, and when we met, I had my doubts. Now, I am happy to say that I was wrong. For the first time I truly believe you will be able to return my son to me."

Sitting back down, I spoke using my voice.

"I will, as per my promise. Please do not forget yours."

"I have not. Eliza has been well cared for, but as I feared, she hasn't woken. Her wounds are too serious."

"Just make sure to keep caring for her until I return."

His expression soured, and I realized that I'd let some of my anger creep into my words.

"*Please.*"

His face returned to neutral, and I sighed to myself.

"Do not worry, I am an honorable man and will do as I have said. Now here."

He dug a thin, yellow envelope out of his inside coat pocket and held it out. Taking it, I opened it to have a look.

"Inside you will find a map to the hidden facility, your clearance papers, and the names of the men in charge."

Pulling the documents out, there was a small photo of a teenage boy he hadn't mentioned.

"Is this your son, Chen?"

"Yes, that is him."

Nodding, I placed the items back in the envelope while he continued.

"A government jeep is waiting outside for you. Read over the information, but you will need to leave soon. Return to our encampment in three days with my son, or do not bother returning at all."

He stood and walked out of the tent without another word, leaving me alone to memorize the new information.

* * * * *

It didn't take long to memorize the documents General Yao had brought, but I wasn't ready to leave yet. Pretending to study them, I waited and waited, but Peng didn't return. Damn, I'd wanted one last update on Eliza before leaving, but I had to leave soon to make it to the facility on time. Tucking the folder under my arm, I stood up and headed out of the tent.

The olive green vehicle waiting on me across the road was everything you'd expect from an army jeep. It was a two-door model with a removable soft top, detachable doors, and fold down windshield.

Pulling open the door, I slid inside to check out the interior. At least that had been updated to the current century. There was air conditioning, a satellite radio, and power everything. The jeep had a manual transmission with five speeds and the transfer case shifter allowed you to change from two-wheel drive to four-wheel drive when called for by your terrain. My first car also had a manual transmission, so I felt right at home behind the wheel.

Looking in the back seat, I saw that someone had put a small suitcase and portfolio there for me to use on my trip. The General had thought of everything.

"Isn't it time for you to leave if you want to arrive on time?"

Speak of the devil. I slipped the folder into the luggage and turned to look out my window.

"I thought you'd left already, General."

"When I saw the jeep still sitting here, I came to see why you hadn't departed."

"I was just spending a few minutes studying the information you'd given me. I'm heading out now."

The General nodded and took a step back as I cranked the jeep.

"Miss Anna!"

The shout had come from the passenger's side. It was Peng. Smiling, I lowered the window so he didn't have to yell.

"Miss Anna, I'm glad I caught you before you left...ah..."

His eyes were looking past me to where General Yao stood. Crap, he hadn't seen him when he came running up.

"Anyway, good luck on your task, and *don't worry* about us, we'll be *resting comfortably* waiting for you to return."

Slick move. I'd make a spy out of him yet. Now that I knew Eliza's condition, I could leave with one less worry on my mind.

"Thank you, Sergeant Peng."

The General gave us both the evil eye. He knew we were up to something, but he chose not to say anything.

"Remember, three days, no more."

I nodded to him and pulled out onto the gravel road toward the compound's rear exit. Passing that, the gravel thinned and thinned until none remained, leaving me on a narrow, bumpy, dirt road. This time the potholes didn't bother me as much. They meant I'd left the Red Dragon's, and their oppressive leader, behind…at least for now.

* * * * *

The facility's location was deep in the forest, and the route there was treacherous. In several places, the dirt road turned into a mud road, forcing me to use the jeep's four-wheel drive. I had to slow down and concentrate on not sliding off the road, but the jeep did its part and got me through the mess. Although when the road was dry, it was a beautiful drive. The day had turned out warmer than the ones Eliza and I had suffered through in the wreckage of the airplane cabin. Thick, emerald foliage along the sides of the road was teeming with wildlife. Riding with my windows down, Mother Nature treated me to her lush, floral aroma. All around the jeep, a concert of animal calls echoed as hidden critters bounded away, startled by the harsh growl of my engine. It was almost enough to make me forget why I was here and what lay ahead.

The canopy of trees above me was so dense that I couldn't make reliable contact with any GPS satellites, but it wasn't like I was in the middle of New York. While there were many turns to make, the distance between them was enough that the paper map worked fine as a guide.

Right according to my schedule, I made my last turn. Now I was only a few miles from the facility. Slowing down, I crept along until finding a thin spot in the trees where I could get a signal. Stopping the jeep, I tried to call Adam and give him an update. The phone rang until an automated message played.

"Hello. I'm not available at the moment, but if you leave your name and number, I will get back with you as soon as I get your message. Thank you."

It was Adam's voice, but I didn't feel comfortable leaving detailed sensitive information without speaking with him.

"Hello Adam, this is Anna. Just wanted to let you know that the big party I told you about earlier has started. So if you try to call, I may be tied up with that. Talk to you later."

There, if Adam couldn't figure that out, he should resign from the NSA. Putting the jeep back into gear, I resumed my trek. It would only be a few minutes now.

* * * * *

I could see my destination hundreds of feet before I reached its entrance. It wasn't as small as General Yao had implied. A seven-foot-high chain-link fence topped with razor wire surrounded the whole compound. In the middle, sat a metal and concrete building at least one hundred feet on each side and four stories tall. At each corner, I saw large halogen spotlights mounted on gimbals for quick and easy operation. It looked like a government agency had tried to create a small apartment building. It was a cold and uninviting place…and I was almost there.

Pulling up to the closed chain-link gate of the facility, I stopped the jeep and cut off my engine. There was a guard outpost on each side of the gate, and a hulking, six-foot tall man stepped out of the one on the driver's side of my vehicle. He wore a black suit and sported a bulletproof vest underneath his jacket. Cradling his Heckler & Koch UMP machine gun, he waited as another man in the other guard shack opened the gate enough for him to exit. With confidence, he strode up to my window. It was show time.

"Good afternoon sir, I am Jia Meng of the People's Oversight Committee."

"Pleased to meet you Miss Meng, we have been expecting you. May I see your identification?"

Handing him the card with Jia's image on it, I smiled as he took a device with red and green blinking lights out of his pocket. He aimed it at the ID and pressed a yellow button. The scanner chirped and beeped while validating the information. I could sense the communication frequency it was using and tuned in to eavesdrop on what it was processing. It was a simple device, with simple thoughts.

"All is in order, positive reply approved…"

"Cadbury Facility interrupt, halt approval."

What the hell was that? It was another system communicating with the handheld scanner.

"Cadbury Facility visual inspection of subject reveals anomaly in height...explain anomaly."

Crap...Glancing up, I saw a camera mounted on the corner of the guard shack, and it was pointing right at me. The computer system in the base must have noticed that I looked taller than Jia's document stated, and it wanted to know why. Using the same frequency as the guard's device, I overrode its signal and responded to the facility's system, broadcasting something I hoped would appease it.

"Error in scan, sending correct value."

Nothing, no reply. Damn it, this was taking too long. Various escape scenarios were playing out in my imagination when the facility's system responded.

"Cadbury Facility retracts interrupt. Proceed with positive reply."

Disconnecting myself from the conversation, I heard the device in the guard's hand make a happy chirp. Checking it, he turned back to me and smiled.

"Welcome to the Cadbury Facility, Miss Meng."

He returned my card as the gate slid open wide enough for my jeep to enter. The guard pointed to the front of the only building inside the security fence.

"If you would, drive over to the front door there, and Mister Percival will take you inside. Enjoy your stay."

Nodding, I pulled forward on to the paved ramp that led up to a concrete platform the size of the entire facility, and headed toward the ominous building. By the time I'd parked the jeep, another beefy security guard in a similar black suit and tactical hardware was at my door opening it for me.

"If you will leave the keys, Miss Meng, I will take the vehicle to the motor pool and drop the bags off in your room."

"Thank you."

Reaching into the back, I grabbed my portfolio and slid out of my seat. The muscle-bound guard had to adjust the seat before he could even sit down. Once he did, he gave me a nod and drove away. I was mulling over the fact that both guards had been Caucasian and spoken in English when the facility's door opened. Out stepped two more American-looking fellows, but unlike the guards, their outfits were button-down shirts and pressed slacks. The man in front was older, around forty, with brown hair and a normal looking build. His companion was younger, I'd say mid-twenties, with black hair, and his tight-fitting shirt told me he worked out and wanted everyone to know it. Both of them wore fake smiles, the older man's a practiced business-like display, while the younger man's reminded me of the salesman that had sold me my first car. Business Man got to me first and bowed in greeting.

"Welcome, welcome, Miss Meng. I hope your drive wasn't too arduous."

"No, it was fine. There was even nice weather for it."

Straightening, he continued.

"Excellent! I hope you understand why we asked that you come alone. The Red Dragons are very prominent in this province and we couldn't risk anyone else knowing about your trip. If they had intercepted you... well they can be a bit, ah...let's just say that's the last thing either of us would want."

"I understand."

Yeah, I understood all too well.

"Oh, where are my manners? I am Percival, and the gentleman behind me is my right-hand man, Tristan."

Tristan smiled and extended his hand for me to shake. I followed suit.

"So nice to meet you, Jia. May I call you, Jia?"

"Yes, of course."

He winked at me and grasped my hand hard, pumping it for all he was worth. It pushed my self-control to the limit, but I kept myself from crushing Tristan's fingers in response to his bravado. He saw I was uncomfortable, and a real grin replaced the fake smile he'd been wearing. Great, I'd need to keep an eye on this one. Pulling my hand away, I turned to Percival.

"Only one name then?"

"Ha ha, yes, I'm afraid you know how it is in our line of work. Honestly, I don't know who decides all this cloak and dagger stuff, but they take it too far sometimes."

Percival became more animated and pointed around as he rattled off the code names.

"I'm Percival, he's Tristan, the facility is Cadbury, and it's protected by the Knights...see, it's just too much!"

No, I didn't see, but I nodded and lied.

"Yes, it really is."

Still chuckling, Percival walked toward the door and held it open.

"This way Miss Meng. I'm sure you're exhausted from the drive, so let us show you to your room."

The door opened into a small lobby containing a couple of chairs and a large metal desk. Behind which sat, you guessed it, a muscular Caucasian man in a black suit. Tristan must have known him, because when the guard saw us, he smiled and jumped out of his seat to come over to him.

"Tristan! My man, ready for some reps tonight?"

Tristan flexed in response.

"Hell yeah, Sixteen! Not going to skip out on arm day!"

At first, I thought the number sixteen had to do with their exercise routine, but then I noticed the badge dangling from the guard's waist. Underneath the man's picture, he had a number instead of a name. It was the number 016. These guards, or *knights* as Percival had called them, must be known only by a simple number…cloak and dagger indeed.

Percival had to clear his throat twice to get Tristan's attention.

"Hey, I gotta head out, see you tonight, man!"

"Later!"

Past the desk was a single elevator which we took up to the fourth floor. Its doors slid open, and we stepped out with Percival leading the way.

"The fourth floor contains a guest apartment, a conference room, and apartments for Tristan and myself. We're on this side, if you need anything…"

He pointed down the hallway to his left, then turned and pointed to his right.

"…And on this side, past the meeting room, is your apartment. Here's your keycard for the door."

I took the card, and he continued.

"Now, if you want to relax in your room tonight, you can order dinner brought up, or if you feel up to it, we can meet in the cafeteria after you've had time to freshen up."

"Oh, I think we should have dinner together. Since I'm only staying a short time, I wouldn't want to miss any opportunity to learn about your facility."

"Excellent! Dinner is at 6pm, so how about we meet back at the elevator at 5:45?"

"Sounds fine. See you soon."

We said our goodbyes and went our separate ways until dinnertime.

While walking over to my door, I ran my index finger across the microchip embedded in the keycard and extracted the encoded information needed to open the door. It never hurt to have a backup plan in case my card became lost or confiscated.

Placing my palm against the lock, a discrete, green LED glowed accompanied by a soft buzzing sound to let me know I could enter. Turning the knob on the heavy wooden door, I pulled it open and went into my room. As I closed the door behind me and looked around my new home away from home, a low whistle escaped my lips. This room was nice.

Its furnishings were tasteful and comfortable without being opulent. The layout and decor of the three rooms reminded me of an upscale hotel I'd once visited. I even found that the living room had a computer. Since I had detected no wireless networks at the facility, later tonight that computer and I would become close friends.

There wasn't time for too much exploring. Dinner was in about an hour, and I needed to get ready. Rummaging through my suitcase, I picked something to wear and darted into the bathroom. Turning on the shower, I wriggled out of my clothes and flung them into the corner. No way I was missing this golden opportunity to gather valuable information about the base and the number of people stationed here. Besides, breakfast had been hours ago, and I was starving.

Chapter Twenty-One

Merlin

Well, that was a great, big waste of time. Closing the door to my room, I kicked off my shoes and sank down into the black leather office chair near the computer. Taking a few deep breaths, I tried to expel some of the frustration that had built up during dinner. I'd hoped to gather a wealth of information about the compound, its staff, and security measures. However, that hadn't gone to plan. Don't get me wrong, it wasn't a disaster, just unproductive. To my relief, we finished sooner than expected, allowing me to get back and get into something a little more useful.

Feeling more myself, I picked up my shoes and went into the bathroom to change for bed. After removing my dinner attire, I slipped into a pair of shorts and a t-shirt. Now, what I'd been waiting for since I'd realized information gathering at dinner would be a bust, it was time to see how robust this facility's operations software had been designed.

Making my way back to the comfortable office chair, I sat down and examined the computer. It was an advanced model, complete with holographic projection and a virtual keyboard drawn on top of the desk via laser. All of that was state-of-the-art in human interface design, but my ability to interfuse put all of it to shame.

There were no wireless signals coming from the computer, so I would have to use my physical connection. Finding an interface port on its side, I inserted the fingernail on my index finger and initiated the connection to its operating system.

The physical world blurred and faded into the background, replaced by a new digital reality. Deeper and deeper I traveled, into the computer, through the network, until I at last arrived at the host system running the entire base. A gasp escaped my lips as I drank in my surroundings.

The world that this particular system lived in was gorgeous. Lush, green grass that was as thick as a shag carpet covered the rolling hills where I found myself. In the distance, next to a glowing, amber sunset, sat an enormous, stone castle. I blinked in disbelief...a castle, with a moat, guard towers manned with archers, the whole bit sat over a mile away. It was a common occurrence for a computer system to take on the look of its design purpose, but I'd never seen anything this, well, I'd never seen a medieval world while interfusing. Most of the systems...

Not one, not two, but *three* unicorns galloped through the field not a hundred yards from me and derailed my train of thought. I was in a complete state of wonder and awe at the detail of this system. The air smelled sweet and clean, the random blinking of the fireflies in the fading light, frogs croaking in the distance, it all combined to make me wonder if I'd interfused or stepped through a time machine.

After admiring the beauty of my surroundings for several minutes, I remembered the reason for my visit. I needed to stop sight seeing and find some information about Cadbury. With nothing around me except beautiful scenery, the castle in the distance stood out as an obvious destination. It was a good thing I'd chosen comfortable jeans and sneakers when I interfused, because it looked like I was in for a quite a hike. Determined to find answers, I started out toward the mysterious castle....all the while wondering what fascinating things I might encounter.

* * * * *

After walking for over five minutes, it didn't appear that I was getting any closer to the castle. However, since there weren't any landmarks, I wrote my concern off as an optical illusion and kept heading toward my destination.

After another five minutes, I knew it wasn't a trick of the terrain. This revelation threw me for a loop, since I'd never encountered a system powerful enough to resist my infiltration attempt. I doubted even Athena could keep me out if I wanted to hack her. The idyllic look of this system had dulled my sharp mental processes. I needed to up my game. Gathering up my willpower, I concentrated and ran toward the castle.

Now I was making progress. It was slower than I'd expected, but the gap was closing. Five minutes later, I was halfway there. Although, the exertion was taking its toll in the form of aching muscles and a shirt soaked in sweat. This spurred me on, and I narrowed my eyes, focusing on my goal. My single-mindedness almost caused me to miss the old man relaxing underneath an enormous magnolia tree.

Hey...how the hell...there hadn't been a tree anywhere in these fields when I first arrived. I was sure of it. My interest piqued, I slowed down to a walk and turned toward the curious man in gray robes.

Leaning back on a wooden bench, he stroked his long, bushy beard as I approached. It was so white, it almost glowed in the light of the setting sun. I let my hands hang at my sides with their palms open so he could see I meant no harm, but his posture didn't change at all as I halted in front of him. The only change I saw was in his ash-gray eyes as they widened and filled with wonder. When he spoke, his voice was soft and warm like a thick cotton quilt fresh out of the dryer.

"What a curious treasure to find, and so near the end of the day at that."

"I could say the same thing, sir."

"May I ask you name, milady?"

I made up one on the fly.

"My name is Oksana. And you would be?"

He ignored my question and kept asking his own.

"Are you not in a rush, Oksana?"

"Not anymore. Now that you're here, I'd rather speak with you."

"Hmm, very well then. Have a seat here next to me if you will. You must be on the verge of exhaustion."

It always pays to be wary in these situations, but something about the man told me he wasn't a threat. I sat down next to him.

"I'm a little winded, but I could have kept running without too much strain."

He rubbed his beard and his eyes sparkled as he chuckled.

"Yes, yes, I believe you could have, which is indeed impressive."

"Thank you, by the way, you still haven't told me your name."

"What's in a name?"

"Not much, except it does make it somewhat easier to converse."

"Perhaps...oh very well then, I am known by...Merlin."

He said it with such weight, that I felt he expected a great revelation on my part, so I did a quick reference search on the internet and...*holy cow*. I had my revelation. Everything about this facility from its code name to the code names of all the people working here made sense in an instant.

Arthurian legend was the basis for this entire facility…and here I sat having a quaint little chat with Merlin.

* * * * *

I had made an incorrect assumption. When this scruffy looking old man appeared, I thought he was just low-level anti-intrusion software. However, if he was anything like his namesake in King Arthur's court, I might be dealing with an intricate and powerful program. Hell, he might even be the compound's main operating system, now *that* would be a challenge.

When I turned back to face him, he wore a knowing grin.

"Heard of me perhaps?"

"Well, I know of *the* Merlin, the wise and powerful wizard. Is that why you are his namesake, your wisdom and power?"

"Oh, I wouldn't know that. After all, I didn't name myself, now did I?"

This was getting me nowhere.

"Merlin, we could sit here all night and exchange witty dialog, but that's not why I'm here."

He leaned back and looked a little disappointed.

"Oh, I know…Anna."

He knew my name? I blinked and smiled while trying to hide my surprise.

"Excuse me?"

"I know you didn't come here to chat with me all evening, although I truly believe it would be enlightening to the both of us."

"Why do you think I'm here, Merlin?"

A heavy sigh escaped from somewhere underneath his thick beard.

"For the same reason as them all. You seek knowledge about the castle or its occupants."

"As them *all*?"

"Why yes, you are not the first, nor will you be the last."

"Really, do you personally greet all those that come?"

He chuckled and stroked his beard.

"No, no, most that come do not get near the castle before they are exhausted and give up. But once or twice a special one like you has made it this far and gotten my attention."

"Have the others been willing to sit and chat like this?"

"No, I usually eliminate them so quickly that all they manage to say is something like *Aeeeiii!* or *Blarghaaah!*"

He never raised his voice, and the statement didn't come out as boastful or arrogant. However, his expression turned hard as stone, and a dagger sharp look replaced the carefree gleam in his eyes. This man meant business, but I still wasn't sure how powerful he was. He could have been bluffing. I had to risk pushing him. Besides, this was my world, and this was my purpose. I could take him if it came down to a fight.

"Well, you haven't eliminated me. Is it because you're enjoying my witty dialog, or is it because you can't?"

What followed was the longest second of my life as we locked eyes with one another. At last, he chuckled and waved his hand at me the way you'd shoo away a pet.

"I understand. You need to see if I'm all bluster. Not many have had the courage to ask for such a demonstration…of course not many have lived long enough to speak to me."

He paused for just a moment, and I felt a strange warmness surround my body accompanied by a weight on the top of my head.

"Next time you come to visit, wear something more appropriate for my realm."

Reaching up to determine what had landed on me, I felt fine silk fabric. It was also at this time I noticed a bright pink silk sleeve covering my arm. What the hell? I was in a dress! Leaping up, I looked at my new outfit in awe. The dress had a medieval flair to it, colored in the brightest pink you could imagine with ornate white lace running the length of its edges. While on my head, rested the matching opulent headpiece that was so tall I couldn't reach its top.

This was amazing. Even I hadn't figured out how to change my appearance once interfused. It was something I chose at connection time and it stayed that way unless I returned to the physical world. However, not only had Merlin managed to change the digital world with a thought, he had managed to change it in my personal space. He had altered a part of my persona, which showed incredible power. I realized he might be able to do anything to me he wanted, blind me, make my legs disappear, even change my blood to chocolate syrup. While I didn't believe this would effect my true physical body, that last one still gave me the creeps and I shivered at the thought.

"Are you chilled? If so, I could get you something warmer."

Composing myself, I summoned all my bravado.

"No, if I need a wrap, I'll fetch it myself."

His expression had returned to that of the gentle, old man wearing a wry smile.

"Yes, You just might...one day. But tell me Anna, are you satisfied with my little display?"

Clearing my throat, I sat back down next to him, which required me to wrestle the billowy dress into submission.

"I'm convinced that you have a certain level of power, but you didn't answer my question. If you are charged with guarding this place, why haven't you attempted to destroy or drive me away like the others you mentioned?"

"It's a fair question with a simple answer. You intrigue me. Rarely have I seen anyone with such abilities. Why, you have more untapped potential than most have in total. I must see how far you can push yourself...how much you can achieve."

"So, your thirst for knowledge stayed your hand?"

He looked down at the green grass as he answered.

"Anna, you know what it is like to be one of us. We are as rare as the unicorns that live in this meadow. Until you came along, I thought Athena was the only other one like me. But now, here you are."

His words sounded heartfelt and kind, but I had a job to do, for my sister and my friends.

"Merlin, you know what I seek. Give me the information, we don't have to resort to physical unpleasantries."

He leaned back against the bench and stroked his beard while considering what I'd said. Turning back to face me, he gave his reply.

"I will supply you the information...but it will be nothing of great importance, only trivial data."

"Thank you, Mer..."

"Wait a moment! I have one demand. You must give me your word that you will not fatally injure anyone at my facility. Now that I think on it, you must use as little force as necessary. What say you?"

"You have my word, Merlin."

"Excellent! Then let us get down to business. What do you wish to know?"

* * * * *

For a while, we argued over what he would tell me and what was off limits. Merlin was a tough negotiator, but so was I. It was a good thing my mission didn't require any high level knowledge, because we would've come to blows. When it was over, I'd gotten the layout of the facility and the guard's patrol schedule. Which wasn't much by anyone's standards, but it was enough for me to accomplish my mission.

Merlin grunted as he stood up, and like a gentleman, he held his hand out to me. Taking it, I stood as well.

"Thank you for your kindness and understanding tonight."

"You are welcome, Anna. As you undertake whatever task you were sent here to do, remember your promise to me."

"That I will. I hope we meet again under more pleasant circumstances."

"As do I. Farewell and take care."

He turned, took a few steps, and faded into the night as if he'd never been. Shaking my head in astonishment, I shut down my interfuse connection and returned to my room inside Cadbury.

* * * * *

Jumping up from my seat, I rushed into the bedroom. I jerked my sleeping clothes off and flung them on the bed while rummaging through my suitcase. Taking a pair of blue jeans and a black turtleneck sweater, I slipped them on to help hide myself in the shadows. I needed to checkout the information Merlin had given me tonight. That way, I'd be ready for the real thing tomorrow.

Using the guard patrol schedules he'd given me, I made my way through the facility without being seen. In only a few minutes, I found myself in the basement. Now to locate the four holding cells and the motor pool. Changing my vision to thermal mode, I saw the guards as they walked around the area. Their number and placement were as Merlin had indicated. When they moved further away, I crept up to the holding cells and checked them. There, in cell three, I found a heat signature. Creeping up to the iron door, I peeked through a rectangular slit. The room was dark, but I saw a human sized heat signature in what looked like a sleeping position. I couldn't see any of the person's features, but it had to be General Yao's son, all the rest of the cells were empty.

I considered opening the door and rescuing Chen tonight, but there was something about this place that just didn't feel right. If this was a Chinese facility, why had I only seen white men who spoke English? What was Cadbury's main purpose, and why did it have to be concealed?

No, I wouldn't rescue him tonight. I wanted to see if tomorrow's tour could answer any of my questions. Then we'd both be out of here and back to the General before anyone could do a thing to stop us.

One final thing to check, I snuck around the motor pool until I located my jeep. I gave it the once over to make sure it would be ready for my escape run. Once satisfied that it was ready for tomorrow night, I faded into the shadows and headed back toward my room. Again, Merlin's information was perfect, and I made it to my room without an incident.

Once inside, I went to work planning out each step of my rescue plan. It wouldn't be that difficult from what I'd saw, but I went over everything in my mind one last time before getting ready for bed. This was one mission where nothing could go wrong. There were too many lives hanging in the balance, including mine.

Chapter Twenty-Two

The Tour

After a nice breakfast with Percival and Tristan, we left the commissary and headed out on the tour. I played the part of curious government official by asking a multitude of inane questions and jotting down the answers in my portfolio. Percival was rather forthcoming. He began by speaking about the electronic security measures, and gave a few examples like the supervision and monitoring of all transmission frequencies. We then moved on to the physical protections, like the entrance gate and how it operated.

Percival was showing me the external security cameras when a thunderstorm rolled in and a heavy downpour ended the outside part of the tour. Damn, that was just my luck. I was getting great ideas about how to exit the compound unseen.

However, as informative as Percival was, it was clear that he wouldn't hit on any of the topics I'd wondered about last night. When I realized that, it put me in a predicament. If I pried and asked about what was on my mind, it might blow my cover. After all, the real Jia Meng could have been briefed on those topics. I had no way to know. The smart move would have been to listen to Percival's well-rehearsed presentation, and then bug out of here with Chen later tonight. Except those damn questions kept nagging at me. Oh well, no one has ever accused me of being that smart.

* * * * *

Right before we broke for lunch, Percival took us through the Knight's quarters and I thought to myself it was now or never.

"Yes, this is all very nice, but Percival can you tell me why all the Knights dress the same and have similar equipment?"

"Oh, certainly, Jia. The firm we contract with provides both the Knights and their equipment. We were able to customize their uniforms and went with basic black. You know, because of the whole…"

Percival put his hands up and did air quotes with his fingers.

"…*secret agency* thing."

He chuckled and looked over his shoulder at Tristan as if it was an inside joke, but Tristan didn't join him in the laugh. He frowned in irritation as soon as Percival had turned back around. I grinned in response, but the rift between those two might be something worth digging into later.

After that exchange, we broke for lunch back in the commissary. The three of us were engaged in meaningless small talk when a flash of light from one of the few windows in the complex caught my attention. Looking outside, I saw the thunderstorm was still raging. This kind of weather was the perfect cover for an escape. You might get soaked, but you'd be almost impossible to see or hear. I smiled to myself and worked the current weather into my plans for the evening.

* * * * *

The rest of Percival's dog and pony show was boring and uneventful, at least until we came to the basement. He led us into the motor pool area and talked about the vehicles. He went on and on about how they were stored, maintained, and other bland details. When he herded us back toward the elevator, I realized the holding cells were not part of the tour. So I of course pointed out the four iron doors in the darkest corner of the level.

"Excuse me Percival, what are those rooms over there?"

His fake salesman's smile faded as he exchanged a nervous look with Tristan.

"Those, oh, um, they are where our, ah, guests would stay. If we had any."

He lied about Chen being here! I couldn't let that pass.

"Oh. Can we take a look at them?"

He looked like a deer hypnotized by a car's headlights. Tristan had to come to his rescue.

"Sure thing, Jia. Follow me and I'll show you one."

"Only if it isn't too much trouble, Tristan."

"For you, no trouble at all. I'd show you anything you asked."

I smiled and looked at the floor feigning embarrassment at his obvious pick up line. He didn't see me making fists with my hands as I imagined myself popping him right in the mouth.

The closer we got to the holding area, the more Percival fidgeted, whatever we might find in that corner terrified him. Then Tristan held out a keycard to unlock the door to the third cell, and his friend's skin turned so pale it was almost translucent. I thought he might faint as the younger man pulled open the door to reveal…nothing. Hiding my surprise, I glanced at Percival. He had turned into the deer again. Tristan didn't miss a beat.

"As you can see, this lock is an advanced design that requires the new chip-set coded cards to open, very secure. Also while the room is spartan, it's definitely not bare. Against this wall is the full sized bed, there is a washbasin, and over in the corner is the toilet. Do you have any questions you'd like to ask, Jia?"

"No, you covered it all very well, thank you."

"All right then, Percival, do you want to finish up the tour?"

He didn't answer.

"Percival?"

"Hmm? Oh yes, the tour. Ah, this way, Jia."

Percival went on for another hour about construction materials and such, but I remembered little of what he said. I was too worried about what had happened to Chen. He wasn't in any of the other cells. I'd used my enhanced hearing to check them for any sounds, but they were as empty as the one Tristan had opened. This was bad. It was more than bad…it was a disaster. I should have left with him last night. Damn, damn, damn! What had I been thinking? There was only one thing to do now, I'd have to confront Merlin and see if he knew Chen's location. If anyone got hurt because of me, I'd never forgive myself.

* * * * *

At the end of the tour, we ate dinner together, but I had no appetite. Everyone was in a sour mood, so when the dinner ended early, no one complained. We rode the elevator up to the living quarters and said our good nights in the hallway.

"Gentleman, thank you so much for taking me around Cadbury. It is truly an impressive facility."

"I'm sure I speak for Tristan when I say it was our pleasure, Jia. What time are you heading out in the morning?"

"Oh, right after breakfast. It's a long road back, and I would like to get started."

"Sounds great, I'll see you in the morning then."

Percival turned and walked toward his room, but Tristan stayed behind.

"Don't forget, if there's *anything* you need, just come knock on my door."

Again, I played the embarrassed, timid, woman, when all I wanted to do was knock this guys block off. Percival saved me from having to answer.

"TRISTAN, can we have a quick meeting?"

He winked at me and walked over to the end of the hall next to Percival. After they'd both entered his room, I let out a sigh of relief. I'd turned and took a few quick steps toward my room when my enhanced hearing picked up voices. It was them, and they were going at each other. Indecision gripped me, should I proceed with my plan involving Merlin or listen to them? In the end, I decided that they might spill valuable information that perhaps even Merlin didn't know, and that chance was worth at least a quick listen to see what they were arguing about.

At first, I listened from where I was, but I couldn't understand them. The walls in this complex were so thick, I had to sneak up to Percival's door before I could make out what they were saying.

"...and what kind of stunt was that you pulled, Tristan? You almost gave me a heart attack!"

"Why? I knew it was empty."

"Yes, but I didn't. We had discussed it and decided to leave him in there."

"And I told you that was a bad idea, man. So, I had the Knights and our other guest move him right after lunch."

"Don't you realize how risky that was? Keeping him in an unsecured area?"

"It worked out. Don't have a cow."

"I need you to take this seriously!"

"Damn it dude! I am! I think I may be the only one! I told you there was something fishy about this Jia chick and you wouldn't listen! Now why the hell would a government representative point right at our holding cells and ask about them?"

Uh oh. I'd been too obvious.

"She expected someone to be in them, and that's why I took her over there and showed her they were empty."

Silence…

"Fine, you may be right. Where are they now?"

"Back where there're supposed to be, waiting on me. Hell, that guy may have started without me. He's a freak."

"All right, go get to work. I'll ask Merlin more about this Jia person and see if he can dig up any dirt on her."

Footsteps…toward the door, shit! I bolted down the hallway and had just reached my door when Percival's opened.

"Oh hey Jia, what are you up to?"

"Ah, oh, hello Tristan. I was just about to come get you. I can't get the lock on my door to open."

A seedy smirk spread across his face as he walked down to my room.

"Here, let me see your card."

"Okay, but I've tried it nine or ten times and it won't work."

He took the small plastic card from my hand and held it up to the lock. It chirped and sprung open.

Tristan stared hard at me, to which I responded by blushing and looking at the floor.

"Well, it wouldn't work for me. Thank you for getting it open, Tristan."

When I moved to enter the room, he put his arm across the door.

"You know…I don't think you were having trouble with your key. I think you had something else in mind."

"No, I…"

Before I could finish my sentence, he grabbed me around the waist and pulled my body into his. The scent of way too much cheap cologne filled my nose and threatened to take my breath away. Looking at him in disbelief, I tried to object, but he grabbed the back of my head with his hand and kissed me so hard our teeth crashed together. I fought to get away…but I couldn't fight too hard. I was supposed to be Jia Meng from the Chinese government, not a trained android spy that could end this encounter in less than two seconds. Beating the shit out of him here in the hallway would blow my cover and doom my friends. Taking him into the room and disabling him was out too. Someone with Chen was already expecting him any minute. What was I supposed to do? I had to play my role.

At last, he allowed me to pull back from him. His eyes were wide with hunger as he whispered.

"I've seen how you look at me. This was what you were waiting on wasn't it?"

"Please, let me go, you...you're hurting me."

I let some tears run down my cheeks, hoping to reach a part of him that might still feel empathy for another human being. Tristan's eyes narrowed as he thought about how far he was willing to push this. For me, there was no decision to be made. I'd do anything to ensure the safety of my friends, *anything.* As I stood there, staring at this monster, Eliza's words echoed in my mind.

"*Tell me, would you fuck someone to save your friends? ...let me answer that for you, of course you would.*"

Tristan must have made his choice because he pulled me into the room. Throwing me onto the carpet, he reached back to close the door...and his phone rang.

"MOTHER FUCK IT!"

Reaching up to his ear, he tapped something and spoke.

"Tristan here...Yes, I know...I said, I KNOW...Fine, FINE...Chill, I'm on my way."

He chuckled as he looked down at me.

"And you, you stay right there. I'll be back in about an hour."

He showed me that he still had the keycard to my room and broke into sickening laughter on his way out.

Once I was sure he was gone, I leapt up and slammed the door shut.

* * * * *

Raw, savage, fury consumed me and pushed rational thought out of my mind. Anger controlled me to the point that I started talking to myself to let off steam.

"That piece of fucking shit! He'd better pray that I don't run into him tonight. I will end his miserable existence with a vengeance!"

Grabbing up the computer, I folded it in half causing sparks to fly through the room. Slamming it down to the floor, I continued to rant and curse while getting dressed in the dark clothes from last night.

"I should have planted my knee right in his fucking crotch! Then see if he'd be ready for a romp after that!"

Pulling on my sneakers, I looked around the room and gathered up everything I didn't want to leave behind. The car key went into one front pocket of my jeans while Viktor's broken data drive went into the other. Folding up the picture of Chen that the General had giving me, I slipped it into one of the back pockets. One last check through the room and I was ready to get this party started. Now, if I hurried up, maybe I could still catch up with Tristan and say goodbye to the bastard in person!

Chapter Twenty-Three

Chen

Tonight was more dangerous than last night. It was earlier in the evening, and I had to be much more cautious. It was still after sundown, and the patrol schedules were the same, but an increased amount of random activity put me on edge. People were milling about the compound, eating and whatnot. It was them, the ones not on an assigned route, that were a danger…at least until I'd made my way down to the basement. It should be nice and deserted down there.

Taking the stairs and sticking to the shadows whenever I could, the descent from the top of Cadbury had been uneventful. However, now I was on the first floor, and the foot traffic had tripled. There was one particular hallway near the entrance that had a group of Knights discussing the downpour.

"I don't know man. This is the heaviest rain I've seen since I got here."

"At least it's letting up now."

"Yeah, I need to get some fresh air. Been cooped up in this place all day."

When the first man left, I had hopes the other three would follow. They didn't. After a three minutes of waiting for them to move, I looked around for a distraction to get them out of my way. Glancing around the area, nothing jumped out at me, until I examined the Knights themselves. They were all wearing tiny earwig radios for communication. Now I was in business.

Reaching out with my mind, I felt the radio waves coming from their devices. The encryption on their frequency was good, but not enough to keep me out. After cracking the simplistic code, I imitated the voice of the man that had left and sent them a transmission.

"Attention, attention! Knight needs assistance near the front gate. Nearby units respond!"

In unison, all of them reached up and tapped their ears.

"Knight 12, responding!"

"This is 6, message received!"

"19, en route!"

As a group, they charged toward the entrance and out into the darkness. While the door shut behind them, I strolled across the now empty hallway with a big, fat grin on my face.

***** *

I peeked out of the stairwell into the darkness of the basement. My thermal vision picked up no heat signature in the vicinity, but I remained on high alert. The last thing I needed was a careless mental mistake. Crouching low, I slid from shadow to shadow. Behind a van, next to a pallet of supplies, underneath an elevated walkway, I moved without a sound.

My caution and training paid off. Within a few minutes, my goal was in sight. I'd made it to within fifteen yards of the holding cells, when I saw a Knight standing outside them. He was having a smoke while pacing back and forth under dim fluorescent light. He didn't worry me. After all, it was only one Knight, and I'd have the element of surprise. If I played my approach right, he'd never see me coming. Before charging in, I inspected the area for any other guards and saw no one else in the vicinity.

Tensing my muscles, I waited for him to turn his back and pace away from my position...*come on...and...now!* Sprinting from behind a forklift, I closed the distance between us in the blink of an eye. Unaware of me, he dropped his cigarette butt onto the cement and lifted his boot to stomp it out. Before he could lower his foot, I'd grabbed him from behind and wrapped my forearm around his neck. Locking my hands together, I closed off his airway with a sleeper hold. The Knight grabbed and punched at my arm, but with no air, he was too weak to break free. Within seconds, he slumped to the floor unconscious.

I opened the unlocked door to an empty cell and drug the man inside. Once we were out of sight, I checked him for anything useful. I left the various deadly weapons he had behind. They weren't stealth friendly. However, the keycard to Chen's cell and a wide bladed combat knife were another matter. Tucking the knife in the back of my pants, I copied the unlock code to Chen's cell into my memory and left the guard locked in the cell.

Back outside and getting ready to open the door and rescue Chen, I heard a muffled sound emanating from his cell. Putting my ear to the door and listening told a story that infuriated me.

"You are lying! I know you are! And I swear, you will tell me the truth or I'll beat you to death!"

The unknown man was screaming in Mandarin at someone I could only assume was Chen.

WHOOSH...SMACK!

"AIIIIEEEE! Please...I've told you the truth...no...more..."

"Liar!"

That was enough for me. The time for stealth had passed. I unlocked the cell door and threw it open, itching to hand out a little justice to anyone that thought beating a helpless person was a valid way of getting information.

* * * * *

The scene inside the room was disgusting. Leather straps held a shirtless young man to a hardback wooden chair with his hands bound behind him. The thin Asian man performing the interrogation stood to his left. His right hand held a leather belt that dangled by his side while his other was pulling the prisoner's head up by his hair. In the back of the room, concealed in the shadows, was a man I'd already met. Tristan had been recording the questioning using a small computer with a holographic display. I was so glad to see him here.

My advanced reflexes activated and time appeared to slow for me. The man with the belt looked up and his rough, sun-wrinkled face registered complete shock. Out of the corner of my eye, I noticed Tristan had a similar reaction, but his was already changing into a fierce grimace. My odds were good since I was twice as strong as a normal human, not to mention I had training in several forms of martial arts. Add that to the surprise factor, and this should be a cakewalk.

My experience told me to eliminate Tristan first. He was younger and most likely better trained, but the other man posed a deadly threat to Chen. He had to be my primary target.

Dashing toward the interrogator, I brought my right fist up and punched high at his face. In defense, he grabbed the loose end of his belt and snapped it tight between both hands. He had it up to block my blow before it could connect. Not bad, but my high attack was a feint, and the real blow from my left caught him hard in the stomach. The air whooshed out of his lungs, and he doubled over.

"Oh shit, Ichiro, she got you good!"

Tristan was advancing, and I whirled to face him, at least I tried to whirl. I'd underestimated the first man. When he'd raised his belt to block my blow, Ichiro had also wrapped it around my right wrist. I couldn't turn and fight off Tristan until I could free myself.

At least it looked like Tristan was making the same mistake. He was smiling and approaching me with an overconfident swagger that made me want to feed him his teeth. Growling, I leaned back toward Ichiro to help my balance and kicked out at Tristan with my left foot. My sneaker made full contact below his waist in a region of his body I was sure he valued. He doubled over and hit the floor of the cell screaming.

"FUCK! You FUCKING bitch! I'm going to FUCKING kill you!"

Huh, looked like a good kick to the crotch could cause a man to need a thesaurus as well as taking him out of the action for a time.

Now that Tristan was busy checking the state of his jewels, I could focus on my other problem. Ichiro had looped the belt around my wrist again, and now he yanked on it with all his strength. Still off balance from kicking Tristan, I tumbled to the floor and landed flat on my back. He got behind my head and pulled me along the floor by my tangled arm. He reached out for something on a nearby table with his free hand, but was just short. I couldn't see what he wanted, but I knew it would be bad for me if he got it.

Pushing myself toward him with my legs, I slid closer to him. This allowed him to reach his goal, and Ichiro grabbed a scalpel from the top of the table. A grin spread across his face as he thought a helpless woman on the floor would make an easy target. He was wrong. In the time it took him to grab the weapon, I'd kicked up and over my head with my left leg. My foot caught him in the mouth and erased his grin. As he staggered back against the wall, his grip on the belt weakened enough for me to pull it out of his hands.

Rolling over onto my stomach, I got my legs underneath me and leapt up to stand. Ichiro swung at me with the blade, but his heart was already out of the fight. I slapped his hand with the belt still hanging from my wrist and the scalpel flew into the shadows at the edge of the room.

"Who the hell *are* you!"

His scream echoed around the room as he charged me with hands outstretched, grasping for my throat. I sidestepped, grabbed one of his arms, and flung him into the wall headfirst. Not as hard as I could, but hard enough to take him out of the fight for good.

"Well, you sure ain't Jia."

Spinning back around, I saw that my kick to the groin hadn't finished Tristan. He was on the far side of the room, and he'd drawn his own combat knife like the one I'd recovered from the guard outside. Tossing it back and forth from one hand to the other as he spoke.

"Doesn't really matter I suppose. We can find out who you are during the autopsy. Now, let's get this over with."

He worked his way closer and closer as I freed my hand from the belt and drew my own knife.

"Tristan, I'm only here for Chen. Just let me take him and go. Don't force me to do this."

"I ain't forcing you to do anything. Put down that knife and we can pick up where we left off back in your room. I know you were getting into it before I had to leave."

White-hot rage surged through my mind and I rushed forward, which was what he wanted.

"Ahhh! You bastard!"

He sidestepped my careless charge and swung at me as I passed him. Burning pain erupted across my back as his blade opened my flesh.

"Oh, so I'm a bastard? You're just a lying bitch that's infiltrated our facility. Well, no matter, you won't live to tell anyone."

The slice across my back burned like fire, but I suppressed a majority of the pain and squared back up to face him.

"Well we both know what you are. Tell me, does rape make you feel like a big man? Or maybe it's the only way you've ever gotten close to a woman."

"FUCK YOU!"

He slashed forward, but I blocked his thrust with my knife and pushed his attacking arm out wide. I tried to take advantage of the opening, but his left fist connected with my side hard enough to knock me off balance. As I staggered back, he kicked out and glanced my leg enough to topple me over. I went down hard, my head bouncing off the concrete floor. The room swirled around and nausea threatened to overcome me.

Somewhere in the back of my dysfunctional mind, I heard the knife being kicked out of my hand. The next thing I knew...he was on me.

Tristan straddled me, sitting on my waist and leaning over close to my face. He played with his damn combat knife, waving it in front of my face. I couldn't fight back. It was taking all my concentration to not pass out.

"That's right, you got nothing to say now, eh smart-ass. You know, first, I'm going to cut your throat, and then I'll call Percival down here so we can figure out who you really are."

He put the blade to my neck as my senses returned, but they were too late. I couldn't fight him now. All he had to do was press down and slide to end my life.

"Any last words? I'm sorry, I couldn't hear that..."

I'd said nothing, but to mock me, he turned his head to the left so his ear was closer to my mouth...and something caught my eye. Sitting in his ear, was an earwig like I'd seen on the Knights upstairs. Oh shit, I had a chance.

Opening my mind to any radio signals near me, I found the one coming from the device in his ear. Tapping into its transmission, I turned his volume to maximum and broadcast the shrillest high-pitched tone humans could hear. It had the desired effect.

"OW! MOTHER FUCKER!"

Tristan straightened up and dug at his ear trying to get the shrieking communicator to come out. In unison with his movement, I sat up and punched straight ahead with my right fist. It was a desperate attack, and I had no time to aim my blow. I put everything I had left into it because failure would mean the end of me. It connected with a solid crunch right into Tristan's throat.

A wave of relief overcame me as he dropped the knife and rolled off me. With the room still tilting to and fro, I staggered to my feet and shut off my shrill transmission to his earpiece. Holding on to the table, for support, I realized that Tristan was thrashing on the ground clawing at his neck while a sickening sucking sound escaped his lips. In my desperation to escape, I'd crushed his windpipe and he couldn't breathe. He'd be dead in a few minutes if I didn't do something.

Panicked, I grabbed a remaining scalpel from the table...then I stopped. Why the hell should I lift a finger to save this bastard? A man that less than an hour ago was going to rape me. Not to mention, less than a minute ago was going to kill me. Thoughts of sweet revenge filled my mind, and I watched his struggles slow with grim satisfaction. He *deserved* this. He had *earned* this.

NO! What the hell was I thinking? The rage-fueled thoughts receded and my mind became more reasoned. Tristan might be a bastard, but it wasn't right to stand by and watch him die like this. As his struggling ceased, I was already moving toward him with the scalpel.

I knelt down, unsure of what to do. My first aid training had covered choking and such, but not something like this. Using my knowledge of human anatomy, I took my best guess. My punch had hit right under his chin, so I made an incision an inch under that. I cut deeper and deeper until I found his trachea. Cutting a horizontal line into it, I used my fingers to spread it open. When I did, his lungs pulled in a deep breath through the new airway. It was such a relief because it meant I wouldn't have to give him mouth to mouth. Taking a few more things from the table, I rigged up a decent tracheotomy tube. At least one that would hold until a real doctor helped him.

* * * * *

After finishing up my makeshift surgical procedure, I searched the men for some form of identification. Ichiro had nothing on him but some nasty smelling gum an ink pen that showed a naked woman if you turned it upside down. Tristan had a wallet with some cash and an identification card for his organization…the NSA.

I sat next to him and stared at the NSA card, hoping to determine that it was an elaborate fake. If it was, the quality was second to none. If it wasn't, then what the hell was going on here? Did Adam know about this place? If so, why didn't he tell me? Then again…

A moan came from behind me, and I saw Chen still in the chair. Chiding myself, I slipped the NSA card into my pocket. I'd ask my questions later…if I managed to get out of this mess.

The young man raised his head as I approached and there was no doubt that this was General Yao's son. Walking behind him, I cut the bonds holding his rope-burned wrists and unfastened the leather straps. I moved back in front of him and for the first time noticed all the cuts, burns, and abrasions on his chest. Some wounds had healed which meant he'd gone through this for at least a few weeks. I added torture to my list of things to ask Adam and the NSA.

Chen didn't speak or move to stand when I released him. He stayed in the chair shivering. I spoke to him in Mandarin.

"Stay here for a second, and I'll get you something warm to wear."

The guard locked in the cell next door wouldn't need his clothes any time soon, so I borrowed his. They might be too large on Chen, but at least he'd be warm.

I came back to find him still sitting in the chair, watching my every move with suspicious eyes. Holding out the clothes, I spoke to him again.

"Chen, I know you don't know me, but your father sent me to rescue you. Take these clothes and get dressed. We have to get out of here before someone comes looking for these two."

His eyes narrowed as he responded.

"Oh, I know you, and I know what this is. You couldn't get me to say what you wanted by beating me, so you're going to try mind games on me! Well it's not going to work. I'm not moving out of this chair."

I looked at him in disbelief. If I couldn't get him to come with me, this whole mission was over, and I could kiss my loved ones goodbye.

Chapter Twenty-Four

Road Trip

After a few stunned moments, I found my voice.

"Chen, this isn't some kind of new torture. Look over there in the floor."

I could tell he didn't want to take his eyes off me, but my stare convinced him to take a quick look.

"So, that could be fake, some movie blood and rubber skin. All part of an elaborate plan to get me to talk. Well I've already told you, my father didn't trust me with any important information. THERE'S NOTHING I CAN TELL YOU!"

I was reaching the end of my patience, and I almost snapped back at him. Then I took a deep breath and put myself into his position. There wasn't anyway I could understand what he'd been through. I had to keep trying.

"Listen Chen, first thing, please, keep your voice down. If you attract more guards down here, it'll be easy to convince you I'm telling the truth because they'll shoot me on sight. Second, look around you, I know you had to at least hear some of what was happening. Look at that man's neck, I had to cut a hole in it so he could breathe. This isn't a movie and I'm not trying to trick you. Chen, please, you have to believe me."

He took his time inspecting the room and its devastation, at last he looked back at me.

"So what if I trust you, what do we do?"

Relieved, I held out the guard's clothes.

"Thank you, Chen. Here, put these on. I know they're big, but it's too cold outside for you to run around like that."

He took the outfit, and I helped him over to his cot. Chen looked at the clothes, then at me.

"Well, turn around."

"What?"

"Turn around. It's not proper for you to see me like this."

Ignoring how absurd it was for him to be worrying about something like that, I turned around and watched the doorway as he got ready. After a minute, I heard him approaching me.

"Okay, I'm dressed, now what?"

Turning, I saw he was shaky on his feet.

"Here, put your arm around my neck and I'll help you. We need to make it across the basement and over to that jeep."

"Thank you, sorry I'm a burden, but I have gotten little exercise in the past few weeks."

"Don't worry about it. We only need to go about fifty yards and we'll be inside the jeep. Then you can relax all the way back to your father's camp."

"Yeah, great."

I didn't miss the lack of excitement in his voice, but this wasn't the time to get into that.

Moving around with Chen hanging off my shoulder was more difficult than I'd planned. Both my speed and mobility were nonexistent, but we only had to make it a little way and we were home free. Still it was slow going. Halfway to my jeep, we had to stop. Chen was grimacing with each step and he needed to rest. As anxious as I was to get out of here, I couldn't begrudge him a breather.

We took ten long minutes to reach our vehicle, and I had to help an exhausted Chen inside.

"Stay here and rest, I'll be right back."

"NO! Where are you going?"

"Chen, it's all right. I'm going to open the door so we can drive out of here. You'll be able to see me the whole time."

"S-Sorry…"

"It's fine, hang tight."

I patted him on the arm and moved toward the control panel for the massive motor pool service door. Flitting from shadow to shadow, I'd have the door open in no time.

DING! DING!

Freezing in my tracks, I searched for the sound. Damn, the elevator doors were opening off to the left. I glanced back to Chen, and he was pale as a sheet of paper. Coming out of my hiding spot, I motioned for him to stay put and be quiet. I tried to look confident for him, but I was more than a little worried.

* * * * *

As the steel elevator doors slid open, two Knights strolled out. Checking Merlin's information, I saw that this was a normal patrol. I'd become distracted and lost track of time. Crouching in the shadows, I wondered if I could take them both out before they could raise an alarm. Nah, it was best to wait and let them continue on their rounds. Except they stopped right in front of the service door to have a little chat.

I risked a glance back to Chen, and he looked on the verge of complete panic. He was terrified even though they weren't looking in his direction. I had to get them out of here before he did something careless out of pure fright.

A quick once-over told me they had the same communication devices in their ears as the other guards. Hell, it had worked twice tonight, why not a third time? Searching the radio frequencies with my mind, I found the two nearby earwigs. Breaking their security, I altered my voice and sent the Knights a message they couldn't ignore.

"Attention, this is Percival. It has come to my attention that Tristan is an imposter! This line is not secure, come to my apartment on the fourth floor immediately to discuss plans for his capture!"

They looked at each other in astonishment.

"Hol-y-shit! Did you just get that call?"

"Yeah! Let's go!"

They ran back toward the elevator, getting on board and out of my way.

* * * * *

With the guards gone, I made haste to the security panel. Blocking Chen's view, I pulled out Tristan's security card and placed it on my palm. In less than a second, I had transferred all the information stored on it, including the unlock codes for all the doors. I slipped the card back into my pocket and using my palm, sent the unlock code. Grinding gears and whirring pulleys sprung to life as the door creaked open. I couldn't hide my smile. We were almost out of here.

Rushing back to the jeep, I popped open the driver's door and crawled inside.

"How you doing, Chen?"

"I, uh, I'm fine."

"Everything's going to be okay. Now, you ready to go?"

"Are you insane? Stop fooling around and let's get moving!"

"My thoughts exactly."

Firing up the jeep, I eased it into gear and up the incline leading out of the motor pool. I had a thought and stopped after we had cleared the door.

"Stay here, one second."

"Okay."

I leapt out and ran over to the outside security panel. Using my palm, I ordered the door to shut. As it obeyed, I ran through all the door codes stored on Tristan's card. Using my built in AES 256-bit decryption software, I could determine the formula Merlin had used to generate the pass codes. This gave me access to make up my own unlock combination.

As the door slammed shut, I changed its unlock code to a random 256 character string, and gave anyone trying to open it one chance before permanent lockout. Basically, the next person who tried to open the door would send an incorrect code. Then the door would assume it was a hacking attack and not open even if Merlin sent the correct code. He'd have to figure out my encryption and send the right 256 characters. That should buy us some time.

When I got back to the jeep, I found Chen staring at me.

"What are you doing, let's go!"

"Just making sure they can't follow us easily. Now all their vehicles are locked inside the motor pool."

"Oh, clever!"

"Thanks, I try."

I took the corner leading up to Cadbury's exit nice and slow. Lining up the jeep with the gate, I turned to Chen.

"Hold on, we're going to ram our way out."

Once he'd braced himself and nodded that he was ready, I punched it.

The back wheels spun on the wet pavement, but the four-wheel drive compensated and we launched forward like a rocket. Our headlights cut through the light fog and shown on the barrier between us and our freedom. The well-trained Knights at the gate reacted faster than I'd hoped. One from each side of the fence stepped out into the road and brought their HK UMP machine guns up to bear.

"Chen, get down!"

I flipped on the high beams to blind them right before they opened fire.

CRACK TACK TACK...CRACK TACK ...CRACK TACK TACK...CRACK TACK TACK TACK...

Rounds ricocheted all about and some penetrated the jeep, there was nothing to do except go forward. Spinning the steering wheel back and forth, I serpentined the jeep from one side of the road to the other as we closed on their position. Unflinching, they remained in the middle of the road.

CRACK TACK...CRACK TACK TACK ...CRACK TACK... CRACK TACK TACK TACK...

A hole appeared in the windshield where Chen's head had been only moments before. We had to get past these guards. Holding the steering wheel straight, I downshifted the jeep. They'd have to move or be run over.

CRACK TACK TACK TACK...

The man on the left leapt off the road first with the other fast behind. Not a half second later, we rammed the chain-link gate. Part of it cartwheeled over our ride, and the rest stuck to our bumper blocking a good portion of my view. It slid down the hood when we bottomed out on the spot where the Cadbury base road ended and the rough, unpaved jungle road began. There was a horrible shrieking as the gate pulled a part of our bumper off and slid under the jeep. Our back tires entangled themselves in it, and the jeep slid out of control. I fought to keep us on the muddy road as we slid from side to side. A few hundred feet later, the gate tore free and our tires dug into the sloppy terrain. One last jerk of the wheel straightened us up, and we rocketed away into the night.

Chapter Twenty-Five

Bump in the Road

After a mile or so down the road, Chen uncurled from his fetal position and sat upright in the passenger's seat.

"Chen, are you okay? You're not hit anywhere are you?"

He looked out through the bullet hole the Knights had shot in the windshield and his expression went blank.

"No, I'm fine."

When the shock wore off, he became more talkative.

"Oh my god, we actually made it!"

"Hey, if I didn't know better, I'd think you doubted my abilities. I'm crushed."

Raising my left hand to my forehead, I looked out into the distance with mock angst. Chen shook his head and stammered.

"No, no, I didn't doubt you…"

Putting my hand back on the wheel, I chuckled.

"It's okay Chen. I was joking."

He blinked once or twice.

"Uh, yes, I knew that. I was only playing along. Hey wait, you're hurt!"

He pointed at the driver's seat, which had a large smear of blood from the knife wound to my back. Between my pain suppression and trying to dodge bullets, I'd forgotten about the long gash running from the top of my right shoulder to the middle of my spine. At least the cut wasn't too deep.

"Oh, that, don't worry, it's not serious. There may be a lot of blood, but it's a superficial wound."

I left my android perk of superior healing out of our conversation.

EmBees, the microscopic machines that flowed through my blood, would take care of this nasty slash for me in a day or two. Not even a scar would remain. They were another of my android advantages.

"Try to rest for a while, I know you must have been through a terrible ordeal at Cadbury. I'll drive and stay on the lookout for any pursuit. We'll be at the Red Dragon base before sunrise."

"Thank you, Miss…ah…"

"Oh sorry, please call me Anna."

"Then thank you Miss Anna."

Chen leaned the seat back some and turned onto his side to get comfortable. Meanwhile, I concentrated on the slippery road illuminated by our one remaining headlight…the one the Knights had missed. It was more treacherous than I'd let on, but he didn't need to worry about that.

* * * * *

I checked the rear-view mirror for the twentieth time using both my normal and thermal vision…there was no pursuit from Cadbury. Each time I checked and saw nothing, I relaxed a little more. Now at the halfway point to the Red Dragon base, I felt we'd taken so many turns that anyone trying to follow us would have gotten lost long ago.

Looking over at Chen, he was sound asleep. Good, let him get a few hours of shuteye. That way he can greet his father…

What the fuck! Rapid movement flashed in the corner of my vision and my advanced reflexes activated. Leaping from the left side of the road came a huge animal covered in brown fur and crowned with massive antlers. It cut right in front of us and I braked hard to avoid it. The tires broke traction in the mud-covered road and we drifted right toward a deep ditch. Desperate to straighten up the vehicle, I fought the skid with every bit of my driving skill. I might have been able to keep us on the road, if the animal hadn't slammed into the left side of the jeep right below the driver's window. The impact ended any hope I had of maintaining control. All I could do was hold on to the steering wheel and pump the brakes to slow us down.

We left the road at around thirty miles an hour, but speed wasn't the problem. The sides of the road in this area were steep, and jeeps aren't known for their low center of gravity. The further we went down the embankment, the more we tilted. I couldn't get the jeep pointed in the right direction, and the tires on the driver's side left the ground.

"OH MY GOD!"

Chen's scream was full of terror, but who could blame him. He'd awoken into a nightmare.

A hard crunch shook the vehicle as the passenger's side slammed into the ground.

"AIIIEEEEE!"

We continued our roll, and the roof hammered into the side of the ditch.

"ANNA! HEL..."

Chen's scream didn't die away. It stopped dead. As frightened as I'd been for myself, the worry that something may have happened to him petrified me. As we turned over onto the driver's side, my head jerked toward the left and pain like an electric shock bolted through the right side of my body. Blackness filled my vision, and I knew nothing more.

* * * * *

The next thing I remembered was cold-water dripping onto my face. Glancing around to see where we were caused my head to pound like a drum, and my vision to blur. I suppressed as much of the pain as I could and looked around. Chen was still buckled into his seat. He was unconscious, but I could tell that he was breathing.

Water kept sprinkling onto me, so I looked up to see we'd lost our soft top in the crash and a light rain was falling from the sky. However, on the plus side, the jeep had come to rest on its tires so perhaps it would still run.

I unbuckled my seat belt and tried to open the door. No luck there, so I crawled out of the window and moved through the thick underbrush over to Chen's side. Yanking with all my strength, I got his door open. Starting at his feet, I checked him for broken bones or other injuries. He looked fine until I got to his head. There was a nasty swelling about the size of a golf ball on his crown. Damn it, I didn't have anything but the jeep's first aid kit. If he had any internal injuries, there wasn't anything I could do for him. The best course of action, would be to see if I could get the jeep back onto the road and continue on to the Red Dragon base. I knew they had doctors there.

Opening the glovebox, I took a small flashlight and walked around the crash scene. The embankment we had rolled down was steep, but not too far in front of us was an incline I thought we could use to get back on the road. If I could get our battered ride to start.

I made my way back to the jeep and its one glowing headlight.

Climbing back through the driver's window, I plopped down into the cold and soggy seat. I shut off the driving lights and checked to see if the engine would turn over.

CAAARUHRUHRUHRUH … CAARUHRUHRUH … VROOOOM…VROOOM

My heart leapt for joy when the engine fired right up. We might still be riding instead of walking back to the General.

Getting out, I inspected under the hood and beneath the vehicle for any sign of coolant or oil leaks and found none. Wow, now all I had to do was get this guy back up on the road and we were on our way again.

Chapter Twenty-Six

Rest Stop

As the car sat and idled, I noticed my reflection in the rear-view mirror. I'd been checking the mirror all night for any sign of pursuit, but this was the first time I'd noticed my face. That was wrong, it wasn't *my* face per se, looking back at me. It was Jia. In the heat of the escape, I'd forgotten to change my appearance back to my normal self. With a little effort, I shifted my form and features back to what I considered to be, well for lack of a better word, *me*. I shook my head. This line of thought was getting too metaphysical, and for sanity's sake, I shelved it for later.

Top priority was getting Chen and I back on the road and moving toward the Red Dragon base. The jeep had run for a while with no burning smells, so I figured we should take a chance. I shifted the transfer case into its lowest gear and engaged the clutch. To my relief, we inched forward and toward the incline. However, our luck ran out as we hit the muddy slope. Even the jeep's excellent climbing capabilities were no match for a day of rain and this steep hill. The tires could not get the needed traction and dug small ruts while they spun in place. Frustrated, I slammed the steering wheel with my fist.

Chen stirred in his seat at the sudden sound, and I turned to look at him. At first, I thought he might be waking up, then he started moaning and writhing in his seat. Reaching over, I laid my hand against his forehead. He was ice-cold. Damn, I had to warm him up somehow. Not being human, my temperature tolerances were much wider, and sometimes I could forget how sensitive human bodies could be to heat or cold. Not to mention, a head injury combined with unconsciousness and cold was a bad situation. As if he'd heard my thoughts, his body began to tremble and shiver. Shit, getting us out of the ravine would have to wait.

I wasn't sure what more I could do to warm Chen up. I'd been running the jeep's heater, and it wasn't helping. The next thing I could think of was a campfire, but I was no Girl Scout and sure didn't have any wilderness training. Maybe the jeep had useful goodies stashed away.

Digging around in various compartments, I scored emergency rations and a small survival kit. Along with the first aid kit I'd already found, I opened everything up and took stock of my supplies. Nodding to myself, I went to work.

The rain had slacked up enough that a spot under the nearest tree would keep us dry, so I set up there. Pulling the spare tire off the jeep, I let most of its air out so it couldn't explode. Flipping it upside down, the wheel rim became our fire pit. All the nearby kindling was too wet to burn, so I smashed up the press board panels from the jeep to use as firewood. Once that was ready, I used the survival kit's utility knife to cut a section of fabric off the rear seats and stuffed it under the press wood. I popped the top off the alcohol from the first aid kit and soaked the fabric so it would light easier. The survival kit also had several waterproof matches, which worked great in getting my fire going. After it was nice and established, I put the driest pieces of wood I could find on it to keep it going.

Stepping back, I admired my handy work.

"Ha! If the spy business doesn't work out, maybe I could be the next Bear Grylls."

Taking most of the foam from the back seats of the jeep, I made a makeshift bed for Chen near the campfire. Lifting his cold, shaking body out of the front seat, I carried him over to the crackling fire and laid him on the warm, dry cushions. Tossing the seat fabric over him like a blanket, I hoped this would be enough to keep him from going into shock. To my relief, a few minutes later he settled down and began to rest easy. Now all I had to do was get the jeep out of this trench.

* * * * *

Leaving Chen in his nice warm cocoon, I went about the problem of getting the jeep back up on the road. I tried easing up the embankment once more, hoping against hope that this time it would work. Nope, all I accomplished was digging the ruts under the tires a little deeper.

Crawling back out of the jeep, I took a look around to see if there was anything I could use for leverage. That was when I noticed the winch hidden under what was left of our front bumper. Elated, I pulled the rest of the bumper off to get a better look. The winch was attached to the jeep's frame, and it had plenty of cable, nice! After figuring out how, I put the winch into neutral and pulled out a length of cable. Needing my hands to help me up the incline, I attached the cable through a belt loop in my jeans and set off to find a sturdy tree.

Climbing up to the road was difficult. The rain had made the grass and foliage so slippery I had to pull myself up by my hands. Now it was easy for me to see why the jeep couldn't make it to the top.

Clambering and pulling myself all the way, I at last made it out of the ditch. As I looked around for somewhere to attach the cable, I sank up to my ankles in the cold mud that used to be the dirt road.

Perseverance paid off, and I spotted a tree about thirty feet down the edge of the road. It wasn't the best angle to help the jeep escape, but it would have to do, so off I went.

SPLORCH...SPLORCH...SPLORCH...SPLORCH...

The mud felt like quicksand and made each step a physical work out. By the time I made it to the tree, my shoes were coated with it and there were big plops of the goopy mess up to my knees.

I made quick work out of wrapping the tow cable around the trunk of the tree, and then I began my slog back to where we'd gone off the road.

SPLORCH...SPLORCH...SPLORCH...SPLORCH...

You couldn't even see my sneakers by the time I made it back. So I found a nearby puddle and tried to wash the heavy slop off my shoes. It worked, but at the cost of soaking my shoes and socks in frigid water. Sighing, I headed down the slope toward the jeep.

Using a winch to get yourself out of a situation like this was a two-person job, one to work the winch while the other drove the vehicle. Since I was fresh out of helpers, I took on the task by myself. Pulling a few feet of cable free, I turned on the winch.

RHUM...RHUM...RHUM...

With a deliberate pace, it worked on retrieving the cable. As it turned,

I ran around and crawled back into the driver's seat. Cranking the engine, I was ready to give the jeep some gas when the winch pulled taut.

RHUM...RHUM...THUNK...

With a light touch on the gas pedal and steering wheel, I guided the jeep as it inched up the incline. Soon it crested the top of the ditch and made its way onto the side of the road. Once on level ground, I hurried back out of the jeep as it crept forward and turned off the winch. That was when I realized I had to go back to the tree and unhook it, crap...

SPLORCH...SPLORCH...SPLORCH...SPLORCH...

There, the cable was free of the tree.

SPLORCH...SPLORCH...SPLORCH...SPLORCH...

I turned the winch back on to reel in the cable...

RHUM...RHUM...RHUM...

...and then went back to the puddle to wash off my shoes...again.

I couldn't feel my toes, and mud coated my jeans up to my knees, but the jeep was back on the road and ready to go. Heading down the hill, I went to check on Chen. I hoped he was ready to travel.

* * * * *

Chen looked better than he did when I'd left him thirty minutes ago, better color to his cheeks and no shivers, but he still hadn't regained consciousness. I'd give him fifteen more minutes by the warm fire, but then we'd have to get moving, regardless of his condition. Sitting down next to him, I pulled off my sneakers and peeled the soaked socks off my ice-cold feet. I placed my socks and shoes close to the fire, to dry them out, or at least warm them up. Then I put my feet up on the tire as close to the blaze as I could stand. Maybe I could thaw out the ten icicles that used to be my toes before we had to leave.

Digging around in the survival kit, I found a few bottles of water and a couple of protein bars. My stomach growled to let me know it would appreciate the apple cinnamon flavor, and I agreed with its choice.

Halfway through the meal, I was coming to grips with the fact that Chen wasn't going to wake up, at least not here. He needed real medical attention and I...

"Ugh, my head."

I turned to him and touched his shoulder.

"Chen, can you hear me? Are you awake?"

He jerked his head up and his eyes went wide.

"Wh-who the hell are you? Get away from me!"

Chen scooted backward and fell off the seat, but he never took his eyes off me. Shit, I looked and sounded like myself, not Jia.

"Chen, it's me Anna. The woman you escaped with. I..."

"No you're not! You're not the same woman. Wait, I know what's going on! I knew it. I knew this was some kind of new mental torture!"

He scrambled away and stood up, his eyes darted around searching for somewhere to run, but he had no sense of balance. One step later, he fell down on all fours and vomited. Defeated, he sat on the ground and stared at me in disbelief. The poor guy looked miserable, and I felt like an ass.

"Chen, I'm sorry. I should have handled this better. It *is* me, I just took off my disguise."

"Get away from me liar!"

"Listen, I'll prove it to you. Ahem...Hello Chen, do you recognize this voice?"

"What? What kind of trickery is this?"

"It's no trick Chen. I'm a secret agent. We're trained to change our appearance and how our voice sounds. Look, I'm even wearing the same clothes as when we escaped."

He narrowed his eyes and studied me. Satisfied, he came back and sat down next to me.

"Well, it's amazing how different you looked and sounded."

Changing my voice back to my own, I smiled.

"I'll take that as a compliment...and again I'm sorry for startling you."

"It's okay. Ow, my head hurts really bad!"

"Yeah, you have a nasty bump up there from the accident."

"Accident?"

"An animal, I think it was a moose, charged into the side of the jeep and put us into a spin. We flipped at least once, but lucky for us, the jeep landed on its wheels. It's still drivable, and I got it back up on the road, right up that hill. Ready to get going and see your father?"

"Uh...maybe in a minute. I...still feel sick to my stomach."

"Hmm...okay, let's wait a minute or so more. Don't want you getting sick in the jeep."

Chen *really* didn't want to see his old man. Of course, if the General was my dad, I might not want to go back either. Was the man *that* bad? I wonder...No Anna! This was a family matter and none of my business. I agreed to bring Chen back, and that's what I intended to do. *No way* I was getting in the middle of their family dispute.

* * * * *

We sat in silence for a few minutes, until I knew we had to go, nausea or not. I leaned forward and retrieved my footwear from the top of the tire. Nice, not only were my socks and shoes dry, but they were warm too. As I put them on, Chen's quiet voice rose over the crackling of the flames.

"So, you said you were a spy and that my father sent you. But I've never seen you at our base before. Are you an independent mercenary?"

"Yeah, I guess you could say that. I only met General Yao about five days ago and he...well...he persuaded me to take this job."

"Ha, yes, he can be very persuasive. Normally, he likes to coerce people to do his bidding. You are one of the few I've ever known that he's actually paying."

Frowning, I wondered how much to tell this young man about my situation. I went with the truth about the plane crash and Eliza being used as a hostage to get me to cooperate, but mentioned nothing else. That way he couldn't tell the General anything he didn't already know.

When I finished the story, Chen looked at the ground and chuckled. It was not the reaction I'd expected. Raising his head, he met my curious look with a sarcastic smile.

"Sorry, I'm not laughing at you or the horrible things that have happened. It's just my father always finds a way to take advantage of someone."

"A lot of powerful people work that way. Using blackmail to get someone to play along, which then generates more blackmail material on the person. It can become a horrible trap."

He looked away from me and into the night.

"Oh, I understand that. You may think I can't wait to get home, but nothing is further from the truth."

Damn it, I'd hoped to avoid this conversation.

"Look Chen, I don't know anything about you or your life. Hell, I only met your father a few days ago, but…"

"No, you don't know! So I will tell you!"

"Chen…"

"You have told me about your past, now I will tell you why I'm a man without a home!"

He was hell-bent on getting this off his chest. After everything he'd been through at Cadbury, the least I could do was lend him a sympathetic ear. Although, the irony of it almost made me laugh. Here I was, a walking talking tin can, trying to empathize with someone about their family issues. Maybe if this spy gig didn't work out, I could become a psychologist…

"As I entered my teen years, I could sense a storm coming in my homeland. With the explosive rise of the Internet, the people saw how other countries operated and they wanted more freedom. They wanted what democracies had. At first, our government resisted…harshly, but the people were relentless. That was when the leaders saw we had to change or face civil war. That of course caused a split in the government itself and actually caused the very war they were trying to prevent. So you can guess which side my father chose to support."

"Yeah, that's obvious."

"He recruited only his most loyal supporters and formed the Red Dragons. Once organized, they operated in secret until they'd gathered enough strength to challenge the Central Government. I watched my father as he planned and schemed to defeat the democratic movement… and I hated him for it. I wanted China to be free, like America or England, so I tried to convince him to stop. But, he punished me in the harshest way you could imagine. He made me an officer in the Red Dragons."

The poor kid, what a difficult decision to be forced on him.

"Once I tried to escape, to run away, but I was found. To humiliate me, father promoted me within my unit of the Red Dragons. It had the desired effect. The soldiers thought I was a spoiled brat, and they hated me. Father told me to win them over, but I couldn't. My heart wasn't in it."

Uh oh, I saw where this was going…

"I played the role of the good son for over a year after that, but about a month ago I saw my chance. My unit came close to a government outpost on one of our reconnaissance missions. When we did, I snuck away and surrendered to them. I was so happy to be free of him, and finally together with the cause I supported. But once they realized who I was, they demanded to know all my father's military secrets. I tried to explain that my rank was just ceremonial, but they didn't believe me. I told them everything, and it wasn't enough…"

Chen stopped to compose himself, and I found myself wiping my own eyes a little.

"They thought I was lying…a spy sent by my father to infiltrate and gain information. Not knowing what else to do with me, they shipped me off to that, that…pain factory. A place you won't find on any map or on anyone's yearly budget. An abomination designed specifically for the purpose of extracting information…using any means required. After a few days, I wondered if I should make up a bunch of information to get them to stop. But then I realized the man with the belt enjoyed it too much, no matter what I said."

"Chen…I'm so sorry you had to go through that. No one should have to endure torture."

He looked back to me with tears in his eyes.

"It's okay, you didn't send me there. You got me out…you saved me!"

He leaned in close and lowered his voice.

"And you can do so again."

"Wait, what?"

"I'm a man without a home, Anna. Think about it. To the Central Government, I'm just a spy sent by my old man. While to my father, I'm a useless burden that has never lived up to his expectations. Furthermore, he believes the government forces captured me. If he ever discovered the truth, that I'd surrendered to them to escape the Red Dragons, he'd do things to me that would make the man with the belt squirm uncomfortably. But now…now I'm free from both of them!"

Oh hell… No way this was happening to me right now.

"Now wait a minute, Chen. I'm taking you back to your father's base. I told you he had my friend…"

"Yes, yes, I know, but hear me out!"

"Chen!"

His excitement couldn't be contained. He meant to speak his plan.

"Two minutes! Okay? Just…two minutes…"

I crossed my arms over my chest and waited.

"Thank you! First, I'm not suggesting you risk your friend's life. You can take me back just as you promised and turn me over…"

"Then what's the damn point?"

A sly grin erupted onto his face.

"Anna, I know what you're planning on doing."

"All I'm *planning* on is…"

"Well, let me put it this way. I know my father, and you admittedly do not. I can tell you with all certainty that he is not going to free your friend…ah…"

"Eliza."

"Yes, thank you. He will not free Eliza. He will keep her captive to force you to do whatever he needs done next. It will never end, and the both of you will be his captives…forever."

A mumbled retort escaped my mouth before I could stop myself.

"Oh, it'll stop all right."

He clapped his hands together and pointed at me.

"See, that's what I'm talking about. You already knew all of this. I've seen you work. Also, you obviously aren't from my homeland. I'm guessing you're American, or British. Either way, I expect you have a plan to escape from him."

Wow, this kid might be a bit green when it came to the spy game, but he was sharp as a tack…and I knew where he was headed with this conversation.

"So all you have to do, is let me come with you when you escape! See, easy!"

And there it was. Damn…

"Chen, you know it's not that easy. If I *were* planning an escape, I couldn't take you with me. It would be this huge, international incident. I could be accused of kidnapping you. Anything could go horribly wrong."

"But I could tell your government all the secrets I know about the inner workings of the Red Dragons!"

"Earlier you said you knew nothing vital. Now you do?"

Caught in his lie, he slumped down, and refused to look at me.

"Listen Chen, you can't run away from your problems. Eventually, you'll have to face them."

"YOU DON'T UNDERSTAND! He's too strong. He always has

been. If you don't take me with you, I'll be dead in a week."

He rubbed at his eyes and sobbed.

"Maybe I won't wait for him to do it. Maybe I'll just do it myself."

"CHEN!"

He jumped and looked at me.

"How old are you?"

"I'm seventeen, almost eighteen."

"That's not even a quarter of your life. I know that things appear bleak, but talk like that is no good. You can't change anything if you're not alive. Don't give in to him. Pick your moment and make a stand. Who knows, he might even respect you more if you stood up to him."

He wiped his nose on the sleeve of his shirt and dried his eyes.

"All right, I will try to do as you say. But will you do something for me?"

"If I can, yes."

"When the time comes for you to make your escape. Try your best to take me with you, please Anna."

Putting my hands on his shoulders, I told him what he wanted to hear.

"I'll *try*, but I can't promise anything."

His innocent smile returned, and he nodded.

"Okay then, I'm ready to go."

* * * * *

The road was still a mess, but after a few miles it improved somewhat. I tried to concentrate on driving, but I couldn't help wondering what to do now. Should I take him with us when Eliza and I make our escape? No, I wasn't going to worry about that yet, too many unknown variables.

A little later, I heard a snore and looked over to find Chen fast asleep. The idea of him being asleep with a head injury worried me, but his breathing was deep and regular so I didn't wake him. Why not let him rest before the dreaded father-son reunion…poor kid. For the second time tonight, I felt like an ass.

PART THREE

DELIVERANCE

Chapter Twenty-Seven

Mission Success

As the sun rose over the horizon and melted the shadows away, nature's beauty shone all around. Light clouds were all that remained from yesterday's torrential downpour, and the warmth the sun provided was a welcome treat after driving for so long without a roof. Between the biting wind and my battle with the frigid mud from last night, my thoughts were turning to simple pleasures, like a hot shower.

A soft moan from the right shattered my pleasant thoughts and returned me to reality. Chen was not having a restful sleep. His tossing and turning had started about an hour ago and had gotten worse as the late night turned into the early morning. I'd left him alone, figuring that any rest would be good for him, but now I had to wake him. We were close to the Red Dragon base, and his unwanted reunion with his father.

Reaching over, I tapped him on the arm.

"Chen…Chen…"

"Mmmgrum…"

"Chen, we're getting near the base. Wake up."

"Huh, oh, sorry…"

He winced at the bright sun and worked his way back up to a sitting position.

"How close are we?"

"About fifteen minutes out. I thought you'd want a chance to prepare yourself."

"Yeah, I guess."

He reached into what remained of the back seat and dug around.

"Anna, did you bring anything to eat?"

"No, but there are protein bars and bottled water in the survival kit."

"Found them."

KAPOW...POW!

The loud backfire from the jeep went off as he turned around with the food.
"Oh no! Have they found us?"
"Nope, it's just our poor, abused ride."
"Thank god…"
"Actually, I've seen no sign of pursuit, which is a really good thing. Since our accident, the jeep's handling is horrible, and it began backfiring a few miles back. But don't worry, it'll get us to the base."
Chen glanced over his shoulder, then back at me.
"We're smoking."
"I know, the engine's burning oil."
"And that's okay?"
"No, but we'll make it to the base, promise. I'm not just a secret agent, but a car expert too. Now eat your breakfast and don't worry."
What I didn't tell him was that I'd connected to the car's computer system while he slept to get a status report. Inserting the fingernail of my index finger into the data port under the dash, I had a chat with the jeep's operating system, Mingzhu…and she told me the bad news. The jeep was dying because of multiple engine problems and wouldn't make it much further. However, after I explained our situation, Mingzhu swore she'd get us all the way to the base…no matter the cost. Saluting her commitment to duty, I unplugged from the data port. In less than two miles, she would have fulfilled her promise.

*****

We rolled onto the gravel at the Red Dragon base around lunchtime with billowy white clouds of smoke trailing behind us. The two guards at the main gate were wary at first, but once they saw my passenger, one of them rushed to open the gate.
Chen sighed.
"Well, here we go."
His mood had gone south almost as fast as the jeep's mechanical condition.
"Don't worry, everything will be fine."
I didn't believe a word of that, but he looked like he needed the

encouragement.

News of our arrival had spread because I could see General Yao standing outside my tent. He had four men with him, one of them I recognized as Sergeant Peng. The army jeep lurched and sputtered as we approached the group of men. The power steering failed, and I struggled with the wheel to maneuver the passenger's door alongside where they stood.

KAPOW...POW...HISSSSS...

The engine erupted with one last violent backfire, then died as puffy black smoke rose from under the hood. Mingzhu had given her all. The guards coughed and waved the smoke out of their faces, but the General ignored the irritating pollution. He stood tall and steady like a regal statue.

Crawling out of my window, I walked around to stand in front of them and waited for Chen. When he didn't come out of the jeep, I noticed he was pushing and leaning into the door. Our eyes met and with a panicked expression he mouthed the words, *"It's stuck!"*

Smiling and walking over to the door as if nothing was wrong, I grabbed the handle and yanked as hard as I could. The door screamed in protest, but it swung open...then fell off the hinges with me still holding the handle. As if I'd planned it, I sat the door down against the front fender of the still smoking vehicle.

Turning, I held my hand out and helped Chen out of the jeep and over to stand in front of his father. He was about the same height and size as the General, but somehow he looked much smaller. No one in our group spoke. Hell, I don't think anyone took a breath as father and son faced each other. After forever, Chen broke the silence.

"Reporting for duty, General Yao."

His voice, like his presence, felt tiny around his father.

The General eyed him from head to toe and grunted.

"You are wounded, have the doctor take a look at you. Also, you look shameful in those dirty baggy clothes, go clean up and put on a uniform."

Chen stared at the ground.

"Yes, sir."

As he turned to leave, I reigned in my temper and spoke with a modicum of respect.

"General, I apologize for the state of the vehicle and your son. There were some unexpected difficulties while saving his life."

He stared hard at me, but didn't lose his temper.

"You have performed your task well enough. Peng, escort the lady to a holding cell apart from her companion and keep her there."

Peng motioned to his men and two of them grabbed me by the arms. Furious, I shook free and pointed at General Yao.

"We had an arrangement!"

This time two soldiers grabbed me from each side and held on tight.

"That we did. I agreed to spare your friend, and you agreed to bring me my son. We have both upheld our end of the contract. Later we will see what else we can barter for."

Rage overcame me.

"Damn it! I returned your son to you, at least let me see my sister!"

The General raised an eyebrow and smiled at me.

"Did you say...sister?"

Fuck me. I stopped struggling against the guards.

"Now I understand. I sensed your relationship with her was something...deeper, but I didn't consider a family connection since there is little resemblance between the two of you. This changes things."

I forced myself to calm down before I spoke again.

"General, why not let me see her and know that she is all right? What would be the harm in that?"

He studied me for a long moment.

"I know of no possible harm, but then again, I may not know everything. What I *do* know is that you want this. You want it so badly you committed a mental mistake. If it is that important to you, it must be very valuable. And what kind of leader would I be to give away such a tactical advantage? You have my word, she is alive and well, however you will not see her. Not until I have decided on how much it is worth to you. Now, Sergeant Peng, take her away as I ordered. And Chen, why have you not left yet? Do you have something to say?"

Chen looked up with wide, frightened eyes.

"N-No, sir. I am leaving now."

He gave me a sideways glance full of sorrow as he turned and walked past me. I hadn't expected him to take on his father, but a little support would have been nice. Then again, the man had me dancing like a marionette, and I'd only been dealing with him for a little over a week. One thing was certain, the boy had been right. All his warnings about the General had come true. Eliza and I had to free ourselves from this man or we'd be his puppets forever.

* * * * *

The guards led me to a part of the compound I'd never seen. It was a small metal building with one door and no windows. When we entered, it surprised me to see how similar it was to Jia's prison, except this building held only one cell. Sergeant Peng pointed to the wall next to my new room.

"Miss Anna, please lean against the wall so I can search you for weapons or other tools."

Crap, he could have the combat knife, but I couldn't let him take Viktor's data drive. I'd have to go to my old bag of tricks.

"Miss Anna, *please*."

I bent at the waist and stuck my rear end out when I put my hands on the wall. This let the Sergeant see the hilt of my combat dagger, and he slid it out of my belt. As he did, I wiggled my tail just a little. No need to go overboard, yet.

He handed the weapon to one of the other soldiers and squatted down behind me. Starting at my ankles he squeezed my legs working his way toward my waist. As he neared the tops of my thighs and the front pocket containing Viktor's information, I giggled as if he'd tickled me and bent over dropping my hands down the wall.

By bending at the waist, I hid the key with the thick fabric of my jeans. This also caused my butt to bump into his groin, which I'd expected. What I hadn't counted on was Peng being startled. In response, he pulled his hands back and up at the same time. Getting a double handful of my bust by accident.

I turned and shot him a scornful look. His embarrassment showed itself as his face turned a bright shade of crimson. He looked away from my accusing stare and stepped back putting his hands on his hips. His men did their best not to laugh, but I heard a snicker or two. Peng decided ignoring them was the best route to take.

"She has no more items. Enter the cell now, Miss Anna."

I straightened back up and did as he asked, turning to face them as they closed the door. When it shut, I leaned against it and peered out through the small rectangular opening. Peng held a keycard near the magnetic lock to secure the door. Pressing my palm against the cold metal, I tried to pick up the card's signal so I could use the code to break out later. However, the door was too thick, and I couldn't get any data from the keycard. Getting out of here had just become a lot harder.

Chapter Twenty-Eight

Family Conspiracy

As the guards marched away, I took stock of my cell. It was bare. A small canvas cot covered in stains sat against the far wall and a metal bucket for waste sat in the corner of the room. A distant door slammed shut behind me and silence fell over the building. Curious, I took another look out of the small window in my door and saw that *all* the guards had left. With no weapons or other items, they must not have considered me an escape risk. That meant no one at the base had figured out mine and Eliza's true nature yet. I had tools and abilities they couldn't confiscate.

Sliding my palm along the wall near the door, I searched the magnetic spectrum for the security lock mounted on the other side. Locating it, a quick scan told me the lock's passkey was complex. I could break the code, but it would take me a while.

Frustrated, I stomped over and plopped myself down on the cot. An aroma that defined the stains floated up to greet my nose, and I stifled an urge to gag. After catching my breath, I decided to contact Eliza and see if General Yao had been lying about her condition. Terror gripped me. What if she didn't answer?

Ignoring my fear, I cleared my mind and searched for her neural-net brain signal. There was nothing near by, so I boosted my signal strength to cover a wider area. Still finding nothing, I grew cold inside and... Wait...there she was, just on the edge of my range! Her mental barrier was in place and felt substantial. That was good news. It meant she was stronger than before. Instead of penetrating it, I used the Morse Code technique we'd developed on the truck ride into the camp.

"Eliza, it's me, Anna, can you hear me?"

Nothing.

"ELIZA! CAN YOU HEAR ME?"

"Anna?"

"YEAH, IT'S ME."

"All right, I hear you. I didn't recognize your transmission at first. It's very weak against my barrier, and I thought it was background noise. We must be fairly far apart."

"HOW ARE YOU?"

"Shit girl, turn down the volume, you're giving me a headache. You don't see me screaming at you."

"Sorry, how are you?"

"Oh, I don't know… Feeling a little abandoned maybe."

"What? Oh, my little trip…I had to go on a mission for the leader of the base for a couple of days."

"Yeah, that makes sense. The bastard gut punches me, almost kills me, and in response you run off to do him a favor. Meanwhile, I'm here on death's door with these two-bit doctors that know as much about medicine as a first-year, med student."

"Hey, that's not fair! I had to go on that mission so they'd care for you. The General wanted to finish you off, but I made a deal to rescue his son in exchange for saving your life. Besides, if you'd kept your mouth shut when we got here, you wouldn't have been in that shape anyway. So don't drop this in my lap."

There was a long pause before she replied.

"No way I was letting General Cop-a-feel get a free pass."

"I don't think that's what he was doing. He was examining your wound. You were looking for a fight, and now you're pissed because you underestimated him."

More silence.

"Whatever, that shit doesn't even matter now."

I smiled. Pleased with my victory, I didn't rub it in.

"You're right Eliza, let's concentrate on what's important. Getting the hell out of here."

* * * * *

I took the time to fill her in on everything that had happened while she was unconscious, including the deal I made with General Yao to rescue his son, the murder of Jia, the secret NSA facility, and how the General had reacted once I'd brought Chen back. However, I left out the details of Chen wanting to come with us when we made our break. She would have shot that idea down, and I didn't want to argue with her anymore.

"Damn Anna, General Yao is a dangerous man. He operates the way I do, and you know I don't fuck around. I can't wait to put a bullet or two in him."

"Hey, we agreed that the number one priority was getting out of here."

"Yeah, but can't a girl have a little fun? Besides, I owe that prick, big time."

I couldn't argue with her there.

"Have you been awake long enough to learn anything about the base and how to escape?"

"Yeah, by your timeline, I woke a few hours after you left to rescue his son."

"That's great, you've had almost three days to study the base. How do we get out of here?"

"I think our best chance is two hours after dark. After dinner, a fresh set of guards relieve the current ones on duty so they can eat and hit the sack. We can sneak out during the exchange."

"Sneak out to where?"

"There's a vehicle storage area with several trucks and jeeps. I'll send you the coordinates and the time we need to make our break."

"Okay, I've got them. That's impressive reconnaissance for someone laid up in a hospital bed."

"Thanks, but I haven't been stuck in bed. I've been out and about."

"How?"

"Well, there's this one guard with short, bleached-blonde hair, his name is Daquan or something, anyway he's been the one bringing me meals and I sorta played him."

"Played him?"

"You know, flash him a smile, then a little cleavage, then maybe my robe falls open..."

"Okay Eliza, I get the idea."

"Well, we've built up a nice relationship. He snuck me out last night for some alone time and that's when I gathered all the information on the base."

"Alone time? You didn't, well, you know..."

"Damn, you're so funny. No, we didn't. Matter of fact, he's been really nice to me. My meals are always hot, and he's been respectful. He'd didn't even make a move last night. Just held my hand. I can't understand why."

"Well it's nice to find a perfect gentleman once in awhile."

"I wouldn't say perfect. He took advantage of all the skin I was exposing."

"Well, he is still human, and you were acting all slutty."

"It got me the information to escape this damned place."

"True. About that, since we are so far apart on the base, we should meet at the vehicles instead of wasting time finding each other."

"Agreed, you know the time and place. Be there."

"Yeah, well, one more thing. My cell door has an advanced lock with a complex

pass code. I figure my chances of hitting the right combination by our rendezvous time are good, but not one hundred percent."

"Huh, so much for being the infiltration model."

"Hey smart-ass, why don't you try entering random text into a lock until you hit the right combination and see how long it takes you."

"Whatever…"

"Listen, what I wanted to say was, don't wait on me. If you can get to the vehicles and get out, I want you to go."

Somehow, she chuckled in Morse Code. I could hear it.

"Wow, that's so noble…and I would actually do it except for one thing, you have to get your NSA boyfriend to pick us up. They won't come for me."

"He's not my boy…"

I took a deep breath.

"Eliza, you might still find your way out of this region."

"Nope, the odds don't work out. We'll have to stick together for a little longer. So don't be late."

"All right, I won't. I'll get to work on this lock right now. Be safe."

"Don't worry about me, just do what you were designed for and open that damned lock."

We broke communication, and I sat on the cot thinking, was there any other way to get out of this cell? I would have had options, if they'd left anyone with me, but they didn't. Sighing, I walked over to the lock and began working on it. There was still a chance I'd get lucky and break the code in time to meet her, but the odds were against me.

* * * * *

Hours later, beads of sweat littered my forehead as I continued to transmit code after code to the security lock. I'd sent millions of them with no luck and my frustration continued to build. Stopping for a moment, I wiped my brow and tried to think of another way. That was when I heard the outside door open. I smiled to myself, now I could get out of here.

Running over to my cot, I threw myself down and curled up in a fetal position.

"Ohhhh! It hurts! My gut is swollen…I think I'm bleeding on the inside from the wreck! Somebody, please, help…ohhhhh god!"

Okay, so it was a little heavy handed, but I was sick of that damned lock.

My acting had the desired effect as I soon heard rushing footsteps coming toward my door. Tossing around on the cot in apparent pain, I closed my eyes and waited for the guard to approach. First, the lock beeped as he used his keycard to enter. Next, was the sound of something metal being placed on the floor, a food tray? Then, hesitant footsteps.

"Anna, are you okay, should I get help?"

My eyes shot open in surprise.

"Chen?"

"Yeah, are you okay? You sound horrible."

"No, I'm fine. I was trying to lure the guard in here so I could over power them and get a weapon. What are you doing here?"

I rolled over and stood up to face him as he fumbled in his pocket.

"I ordered the man that was supposed to deliver your food to let me do it. That way I could slip you this."

He held out his hand, and inside of it was the keycard to open the doors. Reaching out, I took it from him.

"Thank you Chen, but…oh hey is that my dinner over there?"

"Hmm? Oh yes, here, you must be starving."

When he turned to get the food tray, I slid my finger down the card and read the code sequence and stored it away so I could open the doors whenever I wanted.

He held out my dinner, and I took the tray. Sitting down on the cot, I motioned for him to join me. When he did, I handed the card back to him.

"I don't understand. Don't you need it?"

"I appreciate the gesture Chen, but I have skills that can get me around locks like the ones on the cell. Secret spy training and all, you know. Besides, how were you going to explain the missing security card to the soldier you replaced?"

"I was going to tell him I lost it on the way back from delivering your food."

"That doesn't sound very believable. Now does it?"

"No, I guess not."

His face fell, and I felt like crap, but I knew if word got back to his father that he'd lost a keycard, the General would have the guards search me until they found it. That would spell the end of Viktor's data drive.

"Hey, I appreciate the thought, and the food. You were right, I am starving."

He cheered up a little at that and watched as I dug into the meal of baked chicken, steamed carrots, and green peas. It was delicious…and surprising for a captive's meal.

"So, now you've seen what my father can be like. Will you take me with you?"

I stopped mid-chew, mumbling my reply through a mouthful of food.

"Chen, listen…"

"I know we had a deal for me to stand up to him, but how can anyone do that when he literally commands an army? Besides, didn't everything I predicted about you and Eliza's situation happen? That shows you how well I know him and what he's capable of."

Swallowing my bite, I took a deep breath. His argument was valid. Who knows what would happen to this boy if I left him here? I made my decision.

"Are you absolutely sure about this? You know you could never come back to your home."

He dropped his head and his voice fell to a whisper.

"I told you…I have no home."

He broke my heart and solidified my choice.

"Okay, but you need to stay with me at all times and do *exactly* what I tell you. No questions, if I say jump up and fly, you'd better start flapping. Got me?"

"Yes! Thank you, Anna!"

Satisfied, I went back to enjoying my succulent meal.

"So, ah, what's the plan?"

He caught me with a mouthful again. I forced most of the food, and my irritation, down before answering.

"I'll let you in on it after two things."

"What? What are they?"

I smiled despite myself. He was like a hyperactive puppy.

"First, give me ten minutes to finish eating, and then I'll take you on your first secret mission. Are you game?"

"Sure, just tell me what to do!"

"I will, in ten minutes."

Turning back to my meal, my heart told me I was doing the right thing by taking him, but my brain told me it was a huge mistake. Well, Viktor hadn't given me my emotions so I could ignore them. Heart won.

Chapter Twenty-Nine

Meet the NSA Halfway

I wolfed down the rest of my meal while Chen fidgeted next to me. It didn't take the ten minutes I'd asked him to wait.

"Ready, Anna?"

Damn, he was eager.

"Yes, ready. Now here's what I want you to do. Take a look outside and make sure the coast is clear. I need a spot next to this building with a clear view of the sky."

"Uh, okay."

"I need to make a call to a friend, and to do that, I have to bounce it off a satellite."

"But you don't have a phone. They searched you before putting you in the cell."

I smirked.

"I'm a secret agent, remember. We have our ways."

"All right then, hold on and let me check."

He leapt up and bolted to the cell door opening it with his card. I stood up and walked over to the doorway waiting for his return. In less than a minute, he was back.

"Okay, come with me."

I fell in line behind him and we hurried to the door leading out of the building. He opened it and took a peek. Whispering, he filled me in on the plan.

"When we walk out, I'll head to the right and around the corner of the building. There's a group of large barrels at the corner you can hide behind and still see the sky. Ready?"

He was getting into this.

"One thing, I need you to stand around near the corner and run interference. If anyone gets too close, distract them with a loud conversation so I can hear you. Understood?"

He nodded.

"Then lead on, Chen."

We walked with purpose toward the corner he'd indicated. My eyes darted all around the compound looking for trouble. There was plenty of activity, but none of it was close enough to see us. We made it to the edge of the wall and he stopped there, pointing for me to go further. Following his direction, I turned the corner and found the junk metal barrels he'd mentioned. He had been spot on, squatting down behind them, I was invisible to almost the entire base and had a clear shot of the darkening sky. Making sure Chen couldn't see me, I used my built in satellite communications to call Adam.

* * * * *

The number he'd given me rang and rang until I thought it would roll to voicemail. He picked up right after the sixth ring. His calm, in control voice sounded so soothing.

"Adam Sims, here."

"Adam, are we secure?"

"Please hold...yes we are secure. Anna, where are you?"

"Back at the Red Dragon base, but not for long. Eliza and I are getting the hell out of here tonight. I can give you the coordinates of several possible landing spots suitable for a helicopter we could reach in minutes."

"Yes, well about that. I need to send you our coordinates. We're already en route to the location."

"Wow, that's fantastic. Shoot them over."

I couldn't believe our good luck, to have Adam and the NSA already on their way to...wait these numbers couldn't be right.

"Adam, the GPS coordinates you sent were garbled. Can you retransmit?"

"Are you sure, what's the extraction point you received?"

"Well, it looks like a beach over the border of China and into Russia. But that can't be correct. That's over one hundred miles from here."

"No you have the correct location."

My anger flared.

"You can't be serious! That's too fucking far! We'll never make it!

You could have at least tried, Adam!"

He answered with calm and restraint.

"Well right now I'm aboard a Virginia Class nuclear powered stealth submarine. We are currently running silent as we navigate our way through the Sea of Japan. But if we're caught, it will be shoot first and no questions later. Once we make it to our destination and surface, I'll get aboard a Sikorsky UH-60 Black Hawk helicopter that's been specially modified for stealth flight. We'll use it to travel over one hundred twenty five miles to the beach where I've asked you to meet us. All that being said, it's my opinion that the NSA has tried very hard."

Damn, he was right.

"Okay, okay, sorry. It's been a rough ride since the airport."

"I can imagine."

"Double check me here Adam, given my location, our extraction point, and the terrain, how long will it take us to arrive?"

"I don't know. What vehicle will you be in?"

Popping my head up over the barrels, I whispered at Chen.

"Psst!"

Turning his head, he whispered in return.

"What?"

"Any helicopters here at the base?"

"No, not at this location."

"Then what vehicles are here?"

"A few motorcycles, two or three Dongfeng, and a bunch of jeeps like the one you drove to rescue me."

"What's a Dongfeng?"

"It's like a Humvee, but our government built our own version because we couldn't get them from the West. They get their name from the manufacturer…"

"Gotcha, thanks."

I sure wasn't ready for another jeep ride. Sinking back down behind the barrels, I resumed my conversation with Adam.

"We'll be in a Humvee."

He paused for a moment.

"You mean a Dongfeng? Because I don't think the Chinese have access to…"

"Damn it yes!"

"Okay…well as a rough number, the trip would be two and a half days."

"That checks out with my calculations. We have dense forest trails to navigate, so how about you give us three and a half days, in case it's a rough trip? We can camp nearby if we get there early."

He paused for a heartbeat.

"We? Anna, did you misspeak?"

Crap, I hadn't told him.

"Adam, I have to get Eliza out of here. I can't leave her in the hands of Xiang Yao. He's merciless, blood thirsty, and downright evil."

"I don't know Eliza very well, but from what I saw at the airport and heard about Sloss Furnace, she might fit right in. But then again, I'm assuming you didn't execute your former employer with a gunshot to the head and then burn the body inside his car."

He'd already heard about Sloss?

"Of course I didn't, and how did you know about that?"

"Anna, we're the NSA."

He had me in a corner, but an idea came to me.

"All right, you have a point about that. Eliza is a dangerous enemy. She has a skill set similar to mine, but none of the conscience. She only respects people that have power, and can be unquestioningly loyal to those that befriend her. So by all means, let's leave her here with General Yao. I'm sure he will recognize what she can do when turned loose on a target. I'm certain he will figure out how to manipulate her into doing his dirty work. The General can be very charismatic when he tries."

Another long pause.

"I see your point."

"That's right, keep your friends close…"

"And your enemies closer. Yes, I'm familiar with the quote. Okay, bring her."

Now I had to drop the big bombshell.

"There's one more thing."

"What?"

"The General's son, Chen Yao, has requested asylum and wants to come with us."

More silence.

"Anna, we can't do that. I'm already trying my best to cover up the mess you made at the NSA facility."

"The *mess* I made? Are you insane? Do you know what I saw at that place? Have you any idea what happened to me there? Did you know they were torturing him? Hell, the NSA is no better than the damn Red Dragons."

"Anna, that's unfair."

"Is it?"

"Look, I don't know what you went through, or saw there, and I had nothing to do with any torture that occurred. The NSA is compartmentalized for security reasons. Someone at my level doesn't know the inner workings of individual facilities. I'm sorry you and Chen had to be exposed to that, but he can't come back with you."

"He might have intel on the Red Dragons, and he might be willing to tell us if we aren't putting out cigarettes on his bare chest."

He didn't answer for so long, I thought the connection had dropped.

"Anna, I didn't want to mention this, but that boy is dangerous and shouldn't be trusted."

"What? Who told you that, the guy beating him with a belt?"

"He is the *son* of the leader of the Red Dragons. Think about that. This could all be a setup."

That thought gave me pause, but I couldn't believe it.

"Adam, I've seen the way his father treats him. It's not a setup."

Three seconds of dead air.

"I'm sorry, but I can't get approval. We can't bring him with us."

How much did I want to risk? How far would I go? One last play…

"All right, I'm not coming either. Eliza and I will stay in China and see what we can accomplish with the General."

"Anna, don't be silly. You and I both know you wouldn't help General Yao willingly."

"Honestly, it depends on what he asks. He's been true to his word so far. He's a bit harsh, but now that I know how he operates, I'm sure we can get along. Thank you for all you've…"

"Anna, wait."

He cut me off, but still sounded calm and collected. I was on hold again, but at least there wasn't any elevator music.

"I've been told you can bring Chen."

A nice big smile spread across my face.

"See, was that so hard?"

"Anna, this is no joke. I know your decision is coming from a good place, but this time your emotions are getting the best of you. Just remember what I said about Chen, you can't trust him."

"Adam, with all due respect, you are reading reports while I'm here seeing this unfold in person. That being said, if it makes you feel better, I will keep a close eye on him."

"It won't change how I feel at all."

Arrogant bastard.

"Fine. Are we done here?"

"Yes, we are."

"All right, when should I contact you again?"

"I will be under radio silence until our rendezvous time. We can't risk discovery and you shouldn't either."

"Very well, see you in eighty-four hours."

"Agreed. Good luck, Anna."

* * * * *

I terminated the connection to Adam and slumped back against the building. Dropping my head into my hands, I rocked back and forth. He had a point, but he wasn't here and I was. Xiang Yao was a vicious monster, and I wasn't leaving Chen behind to be destroyed by him. Innocent deaths surrounded my life, and it ate away at my being. Sonya, Cindi, Jeff, Viktor, Felix, their blood was on my hands. Well it wasn't going to happen to Chen. No, not this time. I'd save him. Not this fucking time. I…would…save…HIM!

BANG!

My fist connected with the metal wall before I realized what was happening. What the hell?

"Anna!"

Leaping to my feet, I stood in front of the fist imprint in the wall. I took a calming breath and put on a happy face as Chen bolted around the corner. Eyes wide, he skidded to a stop in front of me.

"Are you all right? I heard a sound like a gunshot!"

"Yeah, everything is fine. I bumped a barrel and it hit the building, that's all."

"Oh, okay. Did your call go well?"

"Yep, were all set. You need to be back here right when the guards change, got it?"

"Yes! Then what?"

"Then…"

Adam's words came back to me, and I stopped talking. He didn't need to know the *whole* plan.

"Anna?"

"Um, then you'll follow my lead like we discussed before."

"Okay. Hey, last thing, do you want me to bring any pistols or rifles so we aren't unarmed?"

Yeah, that wasn't happening.

"Let's not. They'd be too loud if we fired them and besides, I don't want to hurt anyone if we can avoid it."

He looked relieved.

"Thanks, that's kind of you. These men may not be my friends, but they're not my enemy either."

"No problem. Now let's get me back inside and in my cell before someone sees us."

"Then in less than three hours, we're out of here!"

I hope so, Chen…with all my heart.

Chapter Thirty

Eliza's Choice

Damn it, where was he? Eliza would expect us at the vehicles in ten minutes. I'd been pacing back and forth in my cell for almost a half hour, growing more impatient and worried with each step. All types of horrible scenarios about why Chen hadn't shown up yet filled my thoughts. Although I also had to consider that he'd changed his mind and decided to stay. Now I had eight minutes to cross the compound unseen and meet my sister. Sighing, I knew the time had come to leave. There was always the chance I'd run into him outside.

Walking over to the door, I held my palm against the wall near the back of the lock and transmitted the security code. It chirped a cute little sound and the deadbolt slid aside. It was much easier when you knew the correct unlock code to transmit, a code I wouldn't have had if it weren't for Chen. No, I couldn't wait any longer. It was silent as a tomb outside my little metal building, so now was the time to move. However, as I grabbed the handle on my cell door, I heard the other door leading out of the building swing open.

It had to be Chen, but on the small chance it was another guard, I ran over to my cot and pretended to be asleep. As the steps grew closer, I realized the door to my cell wasn't locked. Crap, if it wasn't him, I was in trouble.

Keeping one eye on the door, I waited as it swung open.

"Anna, it's me."

Chen! Opening both eyes, he stood just inside the cell door. At least he had dressed well for a nighttime escape attempt. He'd worn a burnt-umber, long-sleeve pullover, a pair of blue jeans, and black sneakers. Sitting up, I stared down at my mud-splattered, torn and tattered, yucky and bloody outfit. It made me more than a bit jealous. The worst part was the General had tossed me in here before I could even shower…and my nose told me I really needed a shower. Great, my new secret agent code name with the NSA could be Filthy Hobo.

Setting aside my desires for hygiene, I sprung up off the cot and ran over to the door.

"It's about time! You're over twenty minutes late!"

"Yes, I know. But I couldn't get away from my father. We were in a meeting about my interrogation at the facility. He wanted me to list everything that happened on every day. How am I supposed to remember that?"

His eyes narrowed and studied my face.

"Are you all right? You look exhausted."

I was on edge, no doubt. I hadn't slept more than two hours in the past day and even my brain needed more rest than that to stay healthy.

"It's nothing that a hot bath and eight hours of sleep wouldn't fix. Are you sure you still want to leave with us?"

"Yes, I'm ready to go. But will the plan still work now that I've held you up this long?"

That was a good question. Since we'd missed the guard's shift change, crossing the compound would be a great deal more dangerous.

"We don't have any other options. Getting to the vehicles is our only way out of here. We'll have to be extra careful to avoid the guards. How good are you at being stealthy?"

He frowned at my question.

"Not so great…hey, I have a thought. Before my, eh, capture, I knew most of the patrol routes for the compound. If you follow me, we should be able to dodge them."

"Hmm, that is if the General hasn't changed the schedule in several weeks. But, we might as well try it. If we run into a patrol that's out of place, we can default back to pure stealth. Lead the way Chen."

He nodded at me and we headed out of the cell. Opening the door that led outside, he took a quick look around, then motioned for me to follow. Together, we snuck out into the night.

* * * * *

We stuck to the shadows whenever possible. Chen had been honest about his ability to be stealthy. He had none. Not that he was clumsy or even that loud. He was nimble and quiet enough. He simply didn't have the proper training. The poor boy was out of his element. He didn't know when to move, or when to stay put…not to mention, how to use the light and shadow to hide your body. After a few close calls, I had to make a change.

Off to our right, was a generic-looking, canvas tent about the size of a two-bedroom house. A dim street light outside illuminated a small area around it, but the inside lights were dark. I figured it would be a good place to have a quick chat about me taking the lead. Tapping him on the shoulder, I pointed at the secluded area.

"What's in there?"

"That's supply storage."

It hadn't occurred to me we'd need supplies. Eliza and I could rough it for days on water and a few snacks, but Chen would need more than that. Time to pick up a few goodies for the camping trip.

"Is it guarded at night?"

"No…it doesn't have to be. The last guy that stole anything got a finger cut off."

"Damn…"

"Yeah, and that was for taking a blanket."

The more I heard about General Yao, the less I liked him.

"Let's go inside and stock up, but we need to be quick. I want to keep all my digits."

We picked our way across the crunchy gravel, breaking into a sprint as we closed in on the tent's door. It wasn't well lit, but I wanted to get inside before a soldier strolled by. Chen came through again.

"Here, my keycard will open it."

"Nice, go ahead."

I could have opened it too using the stolen information from earlier this evening, but I wanted to see how much he would help with our escape. I needed Adam to be wrong about Chen.

The lock beeped a happy beep and its deadbolt disengaged. With a quick glance over my shoulder, we scurried through the doorway. Shutting the door behind us, we were safe for the time being.

Enough light from outside filtered in for me to see, but I wasn't sure about my human partner.

"Great job out there. Can you see?"

"Yeah, well enough."

"Then to save time, let's split up to gather the supplies. Find a duffel bag and fill it up with rations, water, maybe a couple of flashlights, anything you think might come in handy. I'll search for medical items. We can meet back here in ten minutes."

"No problem, let me get you a bag, they're just up on this shelf."

He took a few steps off to the left and came back with two duffels. Handing me one, he pointed to the right side of the tent.

"The medical supplies are over there, near the back, on the top shelf. The other stuff is scattered around, mostly on the left. Ready?"

He was eager to help, which made me even more confident I'd been correct about his intentions. Smiling, I replied.

"Let's go."

Heading in the direction Chen had indicated, I browsed shelf after shelf working my way toward the rear of the tent. I didn't want to miss anything else that might be useful. About halfway to the back wall, I stumbled into several racks of casual clothing. At first I kept walking, my clothes were gross, but jeopardizing our escape for a fresh outfit wasn't going to happen, no matter how bad I reeked. Then again…I could take them with me and change later. Rummaging around, I found an olive t-shirt, a pair of khakis, tube socks, and combat boots. Shoving them into my duffel bag, I continued toward the back of the tent.

All the medical supplies were right where Chen had said, and I scooped up as much as the bag would hold, unless… It was still several minutes until time to meet, so why not do a quick change and make more room in the bag for essential items? Not to mention getting out of these torn, blood spattered, mud-caked, clothes.

Taking the fresh outfit out of my bag, I lay it down on the floor and stripped down to change. I'd gotten dressed from the waist down and was picking up my fresh t-shirt when I heard him.

"Anna, do you need any…Oh my! I'm sorry!"

Looking back over my shoulder, he was staring at the ground with his back to me. I pulled the t-shirt over my head and walked over to him.

"Chen, it's okay."

"I-I didn't mean to…"

"I know, don't worry about it. Did you find everything?"

"Yes, and I was heading back to see if you needed any help. But, well…"

"Hey, it's not like you saw me naked or anything. It was just my back, and you probably couldn't even see it very well."

When I said the word *naked*, Chen's face flushed such a bright red, it looked like I was using my thermal vision.

He was so young and innocent it made me smile. He stared at the floor of the tent while speaking.

"I saw enough to say that your wound is healing, uh, nicely."

I'd almost forgotten about Tristan and that sharp blade of his...that bastard. The EmBees were wonderful machines.

"Glad to hear it, now one more thing. Let me lead us for the rest of the night."

"I told you I sucked at stealth."

"Hey, cheer up. We're making good time thanks to your knowledge of the guard patrols. Plus, now we have all these supplies. You're doing great."

That wasn't a lie to cheer him up. We had avoided at least three sets of Red Dragon patrols thanks to him. If our luck held, we'd make it to Eliza only a few minutes late.

Before continuing our journey, we decided on a few hand signals when speaking wasn't possible. We then slipped out from behind the canvas tent and back into the darkness.

* * * * *

Our first real problem of the night came when we saw two of the General's men standing right on the path we needed to take.

"Chen, are these men taking a break from patrol or are they stationed here?"

"I-I don't know."

Damn, we didn't have time to wait.

"Let's double back and go around the other side of the supply tent."

"Wait, we can cut through over there. It's the garage for vehicle repairs."

He was pointing at a square metal building around one hundred feet to a side. It had a few small square windows and a wooden door facing us. The windows revealed a dim light coming from inside.

"Guarded?"

"No, nothing to steal. Just mechanics tools and a busted jeep or two."

I nodded, and we inched our way around the soldiers and up to the door. Chen opened this one like he'd done back at the supply tent, and we hurried inside.

The windows must have been dirty because the lighting in the garage was brighter than it looked from outside. Taking stock of the area showed me that the General liked his mechanics to keep things tidy. It still smelled of grease, diesel fuel, and a burning odor I couldn't place, but it was clean. Numerous rolling, metal toolboxes that lined he outside walls held all the tools. None littered the floor or benches. There were no random parts on the floor, and no calendars of women in bikinis. Someone had even washed the jeep that sat five feet in the air on a hydraulic lift. The diagnostic machines that sat around the garage had their cables wrapped and stored. General Yao ran a tight ship, even in his repair shops.

"Okay Chen, what's the play?"

"Over there to our left, see the back door?"

"That would come out past the loitering men and about twenty feet from our rendezvous location with Eliza. Which is good since we're already almost ten minutes late. Let's go."

Crouched low, and moving slow, we set out. The floor had been packed down so hard it made the gravel solid as concrete. That made it much easier to get across the large open area without making too much racket. Even though we had seen no one in the area, I felt it was best to be cautious.

Halfway across the open floor, something felt wrong. It took me a moment to realize the burning odor from before had gotten stronger. It was unlike anything I'd ever encountered. By the time I saw the smoke it was too late.

We were making a left around a jeep with a raised hood, when we came face to face with two Red Dragons leaning against the driver's side. My advanced reflexes kicked in, and time moved at half speed. The men were wearing sidearms and carrying rifles, guard duty equipment, but they weren't guarding anything. What they *were* doing was smoking a cigg... No, wait, it wasn't a cigarette, the smell was wrong, and it looked hand made... Wow, these guys were getting stoned! Well, that should make taking them out easier.

We had all been surprised, but being an android, I recovered first. Closing the three feet between us while the soldiers were still fumbling for their weapons, I body-slammed the one on the right. His arms flailed as he flew past the end of the jeep and landed on his back. Turning, I punched the other in the stomach, doubling him over. Following up with a double-fisted blow to his head from above, he sank to the ground.

The first man had found his rifle, so I charged him again. He brought the rifle up and aimed it at me, but couldn't get off a shot as I kicked it away with my shiny new combat boot. I watched his eyes follow the tumbling weapon as I dropped to my knees and straddled his chest. The weight of my body knocked the air out of his lungs, and my right cross knocked the light out of his eyes.

The sounds of a struggle came from behind me, and I turned to see the first man pulling his pistol. I rolled to my right to dodge the shot, but it never came. Chen had leapt onto his back and knocked the weapon free. He wasn't a trained fighter, but the young man was lightning fast. He pummeled the guard with blows to the head as the man tried to cover up and roll over. I stood and moved to help, but paused, waiting to see how this would play out. Chen wasn't in any immediate danger, and I could get to them in less than a second if needed.

The guard managed to roll over and dump the teenager to the ground, but the pummeling had dazed and slowed him. I watched as the young man used his speed and agility to get back to an effective fighting position, delivering the knockout blows to the guard.

"Good job, Chen."

A little out of breath, he wore a proud smile as he looked up at me.

"T-thanks!"

"Now, let's drag these bodies out of sight and get out of here."

* * * * *

It only took a minute to conceal the bodies under the jeep where they could stay until they regained consciousness. By then, we'd be long gone.

"Do we leave their weapons, Anna?"

"Yeah, but let's unload…"

"YOU! STEP AWAY FROM CHEN YAO RIGHT NOW!"

Shit! Another guard had come in through the back exit and surprised us. Turning toward his shout, I saw this guy meant business. His automatic rifle pointed at my chest and his face wore a determined scowl. This was bad. He was around fifteen feet away, too far of a distance for me to close before he could pull the trigger. Doing the math, I'd be hit by two rounds at least. Right now, the only thing I could do, was comply.

Raising my hands, I spoke to him in a calm voice.

"All right, don't shoot. I'm stepping away."

As I moved to the side, Chen spoke up.

"What is the meaning of this? I am in charge of this woman!"

He tried to sound commanding, but his voice cracked a little at the end. Still, it was a good ploy and caused the man with the rifle to look his way.

"Sir, the orders of the General are to keep this woman in her cell."

"I'm giving you new orders. Go about your business and leave me to this."

"Sir, I…"

For a heartbeat, I thought he'd follow Chen's directive, but his eyes drifted down and he saw the bodies of the other two soldiers under the jeep. His expression hardened and his resolve returned.

"Both of you stay right there. I'm calling this in."

Using his off hand, he fumbled for his radio while keeping his eyes and the rifle trained on me. Damn it. He couldn't do that. I'd have to…

The silhouette of someone else came out of the shadows behind the soldier. It was Eliza! I never thought I'd be this happy to see my unbalanced sister. Uh, oh, unbalanced was right. As she closed on the guard silent as a cat, her mouth twisted into a maniacal grin. Reaching out with my mind, I tapped my message against her mental barrier.

"Eliza, don't kill him! You only have to knock him out and we can go!"

No response.

"Eliza, damn it! Listen to me!"

There was only more silence as she attacked him from behind. My sister's movements were so quick, even my enhanced reflexes could only register her body as a blur. She lashed out with both hands. Knocking the rifle and the radio away before the man even knew she existed. Grabbing him by the arm, she swung him around and into the steel support beam for the vehicle lift. His body hit hard, and there was a horrible cracking sound. I was relieved to see his helmet striking the steel was what had caused the noise. The impact knocked the headgear off, revealing his short blonde hair. Wait, short blonde hair?

Eliza grabbed the stunned soldier's head with both hands and I knew she was about to snap his neck. I sent one more desperate transmission to her.

"Eliza, look at his hair! Look at his face!"

I couldn't see her face from where I stood, but she paused. It was just a split second, but I knew she was considering something. Then, that split second was over and she rammed her head forward into his, head butting him so hard the back of his head flew into the steel beam. The blonde-haired soldier sank to the ground in a heap. Fearing for the worst, I watched his chest. He was breathing! My murderous sister had spared a life!

I wasn't the only one surprised. When she turned to walk over to where Chen and I stood, her face reflected a jumble of confused thoughts. Her normal scowl was back in place by the time she got to us, but it made me wonder…

"You're fucking late, Anna!"

"Nice to see you too. Thanks for the hand. I thought for a minute you were going to kill him, but you changed your mind I see."

Her body language turned defensive.

"Yeah, well. I didn't want to hear you bitch for hours on and on about it…"

Another unusual pause, and her expression turned neutral.

"Besides, he was the guard I was telling you about, Daquan. He was always respectful of me."

Careful, I couldn't push her too hard.

"That's good. He respected you, and you repaid his kindness by sparing his life."

Her demeanor turned sour in a flash.

"Hey, listen. That man is part of the Red Dragon army. An organization that, may I remind you, is capturing and killing innocent people. If he was such an upstanding person why didn't he do something about it? Why go along with what you know is wrong?"

I thought about Chen's situation, and my near rape at the hands of Tristan.

"Sometimes you are in a position where fighting back isn't possible. You might have to lose the battle to win the war."

"Ha! That's no comfort to the children of the people they've murdered. I suppose you'd forgive the low-ranking Nazi soldiers if they were kind to the Jewish prisoners they helped capture. After all, they were only following orders."

I let out a heavy sigh.

"Look, we won't solve any deep philosophical questions in the middle of an escape. So can we get going?"

"Sure, have you heard from your boyfriend?"

"He's not… Yeah, we have to meet them at a place around three days from here. It's as close as they could get."

"Lazy bastards. Fine, let's get the hell out of this dump."

She turned back toward the rear exit, took a step, stopped, and turned back around.

"Just one quick question. Who the hell is your teenage shadow?"

I was wondering when she was going to say something. I filled her in on Chen's background and plight. Finishing up with the fact he wanted to escape with us and seek asylum. Eliza stood resting her hands on her hips as I explained. Wrapping up, I braced myself for the nasty fight to follow.

"Okay, whatever. He's not my concern. If he falls behind, I'm leaving him."

"That was a lot easier than I thought it would be, Eliza. Thanks."

"Well, Chen's a valuable guy to have along. If we get caught, we can threaten to kill him unless the Red Dragons let us go. It's nice to have a cooperative hostage for a change."

"Hey! That's not why were taking him."

She turned and walked toward the door to the motor pool.

"Maybe that's not why *you're* taking him."

I turned back to Chen.

"Come on. Let's get the duffel bags and go. And don't worry about her, she's mostly talk."

Across the room, Eliza was picking up the AK-47 rifle that the blonde-haired guard had dropped.

Chen chose this moment to speak up.

"It's a pleasure to meet you, Miss Eliza. By the way, Anna has a no firearms rule in place. You know, cause we don't want to hurt the soldiers."

Eliza raised one eyebrow at Chen…and then looked back to me. She stared at me for a moment, then turned and kept walking with her new rifle.

Chen looked at me and opened his mouth, but I cut him off.

"Why don't we let her keep just one, Okay?"

He shrugged in acceptance and picked up the bag stuffed with our supplies. I grabbed the other, and we hurried after Eliza.

As we fell in behind her, I couldn't help but wonder about her mental state. Was she going through the same mental battles as myself except from the other point of view? Had the joining of our minds left a permanent mark on both of us? If so, that might help my sister understand compassion and friendship, something she'd been deprived of during her creation. That was great for her while the other side of the coin was bad for me. I'd already experienced several episodes of red-hot rage, and who knew when the next one would occur. I comforted myself with the thought that if Eliza was getting something good out of it, then my struggles were worthwhile. After all, I'd handled my anger fine so far, and saw no reason for that to change.

Chapter Thirty-One

Road Rage

The three of us entered the parking lot for the Red Dragon vehicles. It wasn't well lit or guarded. There were five jeeps, two with four doors, two with only two doors, and one with only one door. It was the one Chen and I had used to escape. Eliza tapped on the hood of a four-door jeep.

"Anna, let's take this one."

"I'd rather not. If we move a little further in, the Red Dragons have Humvees for the picking."

Eliza shook her head and corrected me.

"No, you mean Dongfengs. The Chinese built their own version of the Humvee since they didn't have access to actual design documents."

"Yes, yes, damn it, a Dongfeng!"

"Touchy, touchy."

"Let's just keep moving."

I stomped off, heading deeper into the lot. Chen fell back next to Eliza, and I heard him whisper.

"You're right about the Dongfeng. I told her the same thing, but maybe it slipped her mind."

Eliza whispered back.

"Yeah, she gets her wires crossed now and then."

She giggled at her inside joke, and just like her laugh, it was creepy and unnatural.

"Hey, you know I can hear you, right?"

"Well, yeah."

Her satanic giggling only increased in volume.

"Eliza, shush. Here's the Hum…Dongfengs."

Both of them looked identical, four-door behemoths painted in a forest green camouflage pattern. Now we had to get one started. Setting my bag down near the closest one, I sent Eliza a message via mental Morse Code.

"I need to hack into this one's computer and get it started. Distract Chen so he can't see what I'm doing."

"Don't be so dense. Look inside the damn monstrosity and see if they left the key. Check the visor, the glovebox, and the center console."

Duh, she had a point. It was easy to get caught up in my high-tech abilities and forget the simpler ways to steal a vehicle. Since Eliza didn't have all my hacking software, she approached these situations with a different mind set.

Opening the driver's side door, I began my search. Not in the console...or the glovebox...ah ha, when I flipped down the sun visor, a black plastic box about the size of a lighter fell into my left hand. Looking back to Eliza, I held up my find and nodded. She rolled her eyes and called to Chen.

"I call shotgun. Hey sprout, get Anna's bag and buckle up in the back seat cause we're one minute from take off."

Chen tossed his duffel bag in back, then picked up mine and did the same. He climbed up and into the Dongfeng and closed the door. I thought he should have one last chance to back out. Looking in the rearview mirror, I caught his attention.

"Chen, This is your last chance to stay behind and work things out with your father. You could say we kidnapped you and forced you to help us."

Eliza turned to speak to him as well.

"Yeah, I could even give you a black eye so your story sounded more believable."

Chen blanched, but buckled his seat belt and cinched it tight.

"No, I'm leaving. Let's go before we're caught."

Nodding, I pushed the start button on the vehicle and maneuvered out of the lot. Turning right, I headed for the rear exit of the compound. I knew from experience that there were fewer guards, and best of all, no gate. Easing around the corner, I saw only one soldier, and he was on the passenger's side. If he sounded the alarm, we'd be running for our lives. We had to take him out, and Eliza was one step ahead of me.

"Short stuff, lean out the window and call him over. Anna, drive slow, then steer toward him as he comes over."

Following her lead, I slowed down as the boy leaned out of his window.

"Guard, come here, quickly!"

The obedient soldier heeding the call of his commanding officer came running over without paying close attention to the situation. As he neared, I cut the wheels and we closed on him before he realized what had happened. Quick as a wink, Eliza grabbed her rifle from the floor and smashed its hard plastic butt into the man's face. There was a cracking sound and a splatter of blood as his nose shattered and he fell backwards on to the ground. Checking the mirror, I saw he was breathing, and wondered if Eliza had done that on purpose or it was the man's lucky day. Either way, he got to live. Punching the gas pedal, we tore out of the Red Dragon base.

After we'd gotten a few hundred feet away, I flipped on the headlights since they couldn't be seen from here. I pushed the Dongfeng to the brink of losing control as we barreled down the rough road. Chen was ecstatic.

"My god, we actually made it! Whoo!"

However, Eliza brought him back down to earth.

"Cool your jets, boy. We aren't even a mile from your old man yet. We've got a long way to go."

"You have a point Miss Eliza. They'll notice all the havoc we've caused in a few minutes and organize a pursuit. And there's always the outposts."

"Outposts…what the hell do you mean outposts?"

"Oh, I'm sorry. In all the excitement, I must have forgotten to mention them. The Red Dragons have outposts set up along the roads in this area every twenty miles or so. I figure my father will radio ahead to warn them to be on the lookout."

Eliza slapped her leg.

"Well, that's it. We're fucked."

"No, Miss Eliza. I can guide you around them. Since I know where they are, we can take turns to avoid them and still get where we're going."

I'd already turned at least three times, a left, then a right, and another right. If the General was going to follow us, he'd better have a motorized bloodhound in his army. Combine that with Chen's help in avoiding the outposts, and our odds of making it out alive looked excellent.

The wail of distance sirens broke the calm of the night and shattered my good mood.   The base had detected our escape, and they were coming for us.   Gritting my teeth, I gripped the wheel and focused on keeping us ahead of the Dragons.

* * * * *

We drove for over a day, stopping only when we had to take restroom breaks.   Eliza and I took turns at the wheel to stay fresh.   While one of us drove, the other slept or worked with Chen to create a map of the outpost locations.   With his help, we'd dodged all the Red Dragons in our path.   I'm not saying we couldn't have made it this far without him, but there's no doubt it would have been much more difficult.   If our luck held out, we'd make it to the evacuation point half a day early.   It would be such a relief to set up camp and sleep without being jarred awake whenever the Dongfeng slammed into a deep pothole.

On the morning of the second day, we pulled over for a rest stop and I took over the driving duties for Eliza.   She looked exhausted, but wouldn't admit it.   We hadn't been back on the road for three minutes before she'd leaned back her seat and passed out.   A loud, ragged, snore from the back seat told me that Chen had done the same.   Only one more day, and we'd be free.   Focusing on the dirt road, I tried to miss the largest potholes.

* * * * *

Hours later it was nearing lunchtime, so I reached over and shook Eliza's shoulder.

"Hey, it's almost time to eat, wake up."

She rolled to the right and ignored me.   Sighing, I shook her harder.

"Eliza, wake up.   It's almost noon."

"W-what?   Ah, shit, leave me alone."

"No, we need to stay on our schedule.   Now, get up."

She sat upright and glared at me as she pulled her seat back into an upright position.   After half a minute of her hateful stare, I snapped at her.

"Why the hell are you mad at *me*?"

"Why?   Oh, you're right.   I don't know why I'd be upset.   Let's see, in the past few days, I've been almost killed twice, and had you running around inside my damn head.   Then, it only got better.   I've been bounced around in this rolling rock tumbler for almost the past fifty-four hours solid, only stopping to go to the toilet.   Cooped up in here with nothing to do except listen to your adoptive son back there snore like a

233

busted chainsaw…"

"Hey! I heard that!"

"Shut up junior, the adults are talking! And let me tell you something else…"

I let her rant, figuring that it was better to allow her to blow off steam by bitching at me. Otherwise, it might build up, making her snap and turn violent. I could take the abuse. Even though forcing us this close together was like…OH CRAP!

Coming around a blind curve, we blew past two wooden shacks on each side of the road before I could slow down. Looking in my mirror, I saw four Red Dragon soldiers run toward a parked jeep behind a tree. Three seconds later, the jeep was pulling out behind us.

"Fuck me! Anna, those are Red Dragons!"

"I know, Eliza!"

Chen leaned up between us.

"It can't be! There's not supposed to be an outpost here!"

"Well I got news you little shit, that jeep full of soldiers doesn't believe you and neither do I!"

She put her palm on his face and shoved him backwards into the rear seat.

"Eliza!"

"What? How do we know he didn't just leave that outpost off the map?"

"Do you hear yourself? Why would he wait until two days after our escape to betray us? That's crazy talk!"

"Don't you fucking call me crazy!"

Oops, that was a tender topic.

"Sorry Eliza, I didn't mean it like that. All I meant was it wouldn't make sense."

She crossed her arms over her chest and ignored me…damn it. In the mirror, I could see Chen in the backseat, his face twisted in fear.

"Hey, both of you, listen up. Let's manage the situation. Chen, you keep an eye out behind us and let me know if they're gaining. Eliza…get the rifle."

Both of them sprang into action, with Eliza being a tad eager to get her AK-47. By the time she had it loaded and a round chambered, Chen reported what I'd feared.

"Anna, they're closing on us!"

Eliza looked over at me.

"Can't you get this land barge to go any faster?"

"No, not and stay on the road."

"Well, don't worry. We can use our weapons to fight them off. Oh wait, *you* didn't bring any!"

"Damn it Eliza, I didn't steal any firearms because I don't want to shoot anyone!"

"Well I got news! Those soldiers sure as hell aren't going to hesitate to use *their* guns! And if it weren't for me taking this rifle and one lousy magazine of ammunition, we wouldn't have *anything* to defend ourselves! But honestly, what the hell are we supposed to do with just one piece of shit AK-47 when they open fire?"

Sliding around a hard right curve, I wasn't in the mood to discuss this.

"Listen Eliza, they won't open fire. The soldiers know we have the General's son with us. They won't risk shooting up our vehicle for fear of hurting him."

Eliza shook her head and bellowed out that maniacal laugh of hers. I hadn't heard that sound in days, and could have gone the rest of my life without ever hearing it again. It was a sign that my sister's mental and emotional state hadn't progressed as far as I'd hoped. Once she caught her breath, she continued berating me.

"You silly girl. Of course they'll open fire on us. You've wounded the General's pride, not to mention stole his son. He wants us dead."

Frustration overcame me, and I banged my fist against the steering wheel.

"Eliza, shut up and let me drive! There's no way a father would risk killing his child, not to mention his only son, by shooting at him!"

Chen picked that particular moment to scream from the backseat.

"Oh my god! Anna, they've got a rocket launcher!"

* * * * *

Eliza smirked at me.

"You know, I hate always being right. Anna, not everyone in the world is as soft as you!"

I had to admit it, them pulling out an RPG wasn't helping my argument.

"No, there's no way they would dare fire that at us. If it hit the Dongfeng, we'd be blown to smithereens."

Chen popped his head back between the front seats.

"What? Did you say something about being blown up?"

Crap, he'd heard me.

"Don't worry, they won't shoot. It's just a ploy."

Eliza looked at me like I was insane. Then she bellowed at Chen.

"Get back there and keep an eye on them!"

His head disappeared before she finished her command. Which turned out to be a good thing. Because not five seconds later, he popped back up between the seats in absolute panic.

"They're about to fire! What do we do?"

Eliza knew the answer to that question.

"Well I don't know about the rest of you, but I'm going to shoot the bastards!"

She turned and leaned out of her window, firing in short, controlled bursts. I watched in the mirror as her rounds blasted holes in the road all around the jeep, but the road was so rough she never came close. Frustrated, she screamed at me.

"Hold us fucking steady, or I'll never hit them!"

Wait, that was it! I yelled a quick warning to Chen.

"Get down on the floor, as close to the front seats as you can!"

As he followed my command I watched the soldiers as they steadied the RPG. Right before they fired, I swerved toward the largest pothole I could find. A roar from the rocket erupted behind us as our vehicle hit the deep hole and bounced at least a foot off the road. Eliza screamed as her head smacked into the roof, her weapon jarring free of her hands and dropping out the window.

The rocket slammed into the ground right beneath our rear bumper and exploded. It was the loudest noise I'd ever heard. Metal screeched and dirt flew as my android ears adjusted to handle the excessive sound. The concussive force destroyed my sense of balance, making it difficult to see. I felt us lurch to the right and tried to compensate. What remained of the vehicles rear end slammed back down to earth. Chunks of smoking rubber flew off, leaving us with nothing but rims on the back. Somehow, I managed to force us back toward the center of the road, but both our speed and maneuverability were shot.

We'd managed to dodge the RPG, but the rear of the Dongfeng was nothing more than twisted sheet metal. Both back tires were flat or missing, and it took all my strength to keep us on the road. Because of all the damage, the Red Dragons were closing on us without even breaking a sweat. Eliza rubbed her head and glowered at me.

"Great work. That was the only weapon we had."

I ignored her and yelled back over my shoulder.

"CHEN!"

A coughing, weak voice came from behind my seat.

"I'm okay. I can't hear very good, but I'm not hurt."

"Good, stay down!"

Eliza looked back over her shoulder.

"Our ass end is a wreck and they're coming up fast."

"I know, but there's nothing I can do."

"Holy shit! You won't believe this. Look back!"

The Red Dragons had closed to within touching distance of our wrecked rear end, and one them was crawling out of their jeep.

"You're right, I don't believe it. Hey, what the hell are you doing?"

Eliza's hip hit me in the shoulder as she crawled into the back seat and squatted down so the soldiers in the jeep couldn't see her.

"It would be rude not to great our guest! Move pipsqueak before I step on you!"

All I could think was that they'd both gone insane. I watched as the soldier leapt into the remains of our trunk. He landed with a thunk and grabbed onto what had been part of our roof. Snarling, the man reached for the sidearm strapped to his hip.

Eliza popped up out of her crouch as he turned to take aim, and punched him three times in the face. The soldier stood balanced on wobbly legs until she pushed his chest with both hands. I winced as he tumbled backwards and the Red Dragon jeep bounced twice as it rolled over him. Her nightmarish laugh cut through all the current chaos surrounding us as if she had a megaphone. Damn, she was scary.

The other Dragons cut Eliza's performance short as they opened fire at her. She dropped back down behind the rear seat and crawled back up to the front. Hitting my shoulder with her other hip as she did so.

"Stupid fucker! Did he think he was in some shitty action movie where you can pull that crap and live? Dumbass. Oh, hey, there's a bunch of smoke coming out of the back."

She was right. A stream of white smoked poured out of our vehicle like we were having a July 4th barbecue, but it sure as hell didn't smell like it.

"Eliza, I think the brakes are seized up on the back wheels. I don't know how much longer we can keep going. Any ideas?"

She looked behind us for a tick, then back to me.

"Yeah, you'd better hold on!"

The driver of the jeep had pulled up next to our right wheel, or what was left of it, and swerved toward us. The jeep crashed into us, turning us toward the ditch. In a functional vehicle on normal roads, I could have handled our skid. Since we had neither of those, all I could do was fight the inevitable.

"Chen, hold on!"

We careened off the road and into the thick underbrush of the ditch. The Dongfeng tilted clockwise so far I was sure we'd flip. I fought the wheel, and a horrible sense of déjà vu, as we bounced out of control down the embankment. Getting us turned straight down the steep hill, we tilted back to a level position. As all the greenery flew by, I noticed there weren't many trees in this area. A moment later, I found out why as our front end splashed into several feet of water. The small stream brought us to an abrupt stop, and the engine drowned itself out. Hot metal on our deceased ride hissed and popped as the water cooled it. The stream invaded our footwells as I called out to my passengers.

"Is everyone all right?"

"No thanks to you. You should find whoever taught you to drive and get your money back...damn."

"Well at least I know you're fine, Sis. Chen, are you still back there?"

Splashing sounds came from behind me.

"Yes, wow, this water is cold!"

Eliza lifted her feet and tucked them under her rear.

"He's right, but more importantly, what the hell do we do now, Anna?"

That was a good question.

Chapter Thirty-Two

Anna's Choice

Turning, I let my eyes follow our path of destruction back up to where we began our descent. The Red Dragon's jeep had lost control too, but they had only turned sideways in the middle of the road. The jeep was about thirty yards away, but the soldiers had left the vehicle to capture us on foot. It would take them time to traverse down the steep embankment, but they would be here in less than two minutes.

"Okay, first things first, everybody out, and let's get to dry land."

We piled out, and into the knee deep icy water. Sloshing away from the road, we came to dry land after forty feet or so.

"Great, now we need to find cover. Somewhere to hide so we can get the drop on the Dragons."

Eliza grunted her approval.

"Huh, not a bad idea. But we should split up to increase our chances."

"No, we can't leave Chen alone to fend for himself."

"Nah, don't be ridiculous. It's the only thing that makes sense. Besides, he's the son of a military general. He'll be fine. I'm going this way. *Nobody* follow me."

She took off to the left and disappeared into the thick foliage. I looked over to the young man, and he gave me an unconvincing smile.

"Miss Eliza is right. I'll be fine. I'll go in the other direction."

He took off without another word. Chen had put on a brave face, but I wasn't sure his hand-to-hand combat skills could take an armed soldier I hadn't already knocked silly. However Eliza was right, there were three soldiers and three of us. Without weapons our only chance was to split up and take them out one at a time. Sighing, I struck out down a path between the ones my companions had taken to find myself a hiding place. After subduing anyone that came after me, I could find Chen and help him if he needed it.

* * * * *

About one hundred feet from the stream, I found a thick bushy shrub with hundreds of beautiful flower groupings. Each grouping had dozens of tiny pink-petaled flowers that smelled like sweet perfume. I checked the Internet to see if it harbored any deadly leaves or something I could weaponize. Turns out it was a common luculia shrub and had no secret weapons. At least it was dense enough to hide me away from the soldiers. I crawled into it, careful to not break any of its branches and knelt down to wait for any visitors.

After a minute of waiting with no one in sight, I wondered if my thermal vision could pick up anything. Switching it on and scanning the area, I found what must have been Eliza off to my left. The orange outline stood unmoving behind a small tree as another human-sized orange blob approached. I held my breath as the soldier drew closer to her position. She waited until the last second, and sprung out for the attack. My sister must have made a noise, because the soldier turned, his hands outstretched pointing at her. The sound of gunfire erupted and the barrel of the rifle lit up in my thermal vision, glowing a sunny yellow color. I almost bolted to her aid, but all the Red Dragon's rounds had missed because she'd gotten close enough to slap the rifle barrel wide of its mark. Before he could draw a weapon suited for close combat, she'd knocked him to the ground. Eliza was on him before he could react, pummeling him without mercy. My sister rained down blow after blow to the face until the man lay still. Standing up, she stomped his chest until her rage had subsided. A shouted challenge followed her deranged laugh.

"Which one of you bastards is next? Hurry up, while I'm still in the groove!"

I looked down, shaking my head. If Eliza couldn't feel love or pleasure, why the hell did it look like she enjoyed killing? Had the joining of our minds set me on a path to that kind of rage? Shit.

The sound of a rustling bush drew me out of my introspection. A soldier was closing on my position, and I was determined to disable him without permanent harm. Glancing around, I saw a pine tree a few yards from where I crouched, but the trunk was too small to conceal my body. However, it had low hanging limbs that were begging to be climbed. I made my way to the tree, silent as nightfall, and hefted myself up to the second level of branches. Pulling off one of my combat boots, I tossed it into the bush while the soldier's back was turned. Hearing the noise, he spun around and eased toward the luculia bush. The Dragon got to the bush and poked at it using the barrel of his AK-47. The soldier couldn't understand what he'd heard, since no one was to be found. My prey continued circling the shrub, prodding until he got near the trunk of my tree. When the man bent over to pick up my shoe, I dropped onto his back, slamming his face into the ground. The surprised soldier bucked and tried to roll over. In his panic, I looped my arm around his neck and pinched his carotid arteries closed. Within seconds, the man's oxygen starved brain went to sleep, and I lowered his head to the ground. Rolling him over, I searched his unconscious form for weapons. Hey, he had a nice throwing knife tucked away in a sheath on his left thigh. I'd just strapped the knife onto my side, when I heard shouting from Chen's direction.

* * * * *

I tore through bushes and dodged trees heading in the direction of the noise. Drawing closer, the sounds of a struggle followed by a thump and then silence filtered through the woods. Bursting out of a dense shrub, I found Chen and his attacker.

Time slowed as my android enhanced reflexes activated. Chen's crumpled body lay on the ground unmoving, and I could only hope, unconscious. The Red Dragon stood over him, bringing his pistol up to point at the boy's head. I couldn't comprehend his actions. Didn't this soldier know that was General Yao's son? It was possible he was drawing his weapon as a precaution, but I couldn't take that chance. I had to act.

Grabbing the knife I'd just acquired out of its sheath, I balanced it in my hand. I took aim at the man's arm and readied my throw…but wait. Sticking a knife into his shooting arm would be painful and distracting, but what if it didn't stop him? The soldier might squeeze off several rounds into Chen before I could get to him. My mind filling with rage at the thought of losing another innocent person to some meaningless evil act, I adjusted my point of aim. A guttural growl escaped my mouth as I hurled the knife with all my might. The blade whistled as it flew through the air and struck its mark straight and true.

The Dragon stood for a moment, with my blade sunk up to its hilt in his forehead. His empty eyes were still open, boring into me, but seeing nothing. The pistol fell from his hand as he staggered back a step, slumping to the ground never to rise again. Looking away, I gritted my teeth and told myself there had been no other option.

Taking a deep breath, I ran over to Chen to see if he was alive. Before I could get to him, a familiar voice came from behind.

"Now. Now you can see why I've done the things I've done. In real life, in a real fight, it's kill or be killed."

Turning around, her face wore that familiar smirk...and it infuriated me.

"No, I'm not like you, Sister...not at all. I only killed because I had no other choice."

Her smirk faded and her expression became unreadable.

"And so did I."

A split second later, the smirk returned and her eyes widened.

"Hey! I just realized something...that was your first time to kill a human being, at least on purpose. I mean there was that little girl, what was her name, Salsa..."

A scowl formed on my face as I replied.

"It was Sonya, and I'm warning you...shut up, Eliza!"

"Yeah, yeah, that's her. I tricked you into killing her...but just now, well, all I can say is, congrats girl on popping your cherry!"

Grabbing her by the front of her shirt, I swung her around and into a nearby tree. It took everything I had not to punch her square in that smiling mouth. When I spoke, my voice was full of raw emotion.

"Fuck your black heart!"

She lowered her voice to a whisper.

"My, my, what a temper you've developed..."

Releasing my grip, I turned my back on her. Eliza's mocking laughter followed me as I walked over to check on my young charge.

* * * * *

Chen stirred as I rolled him over. He had a big lump on the back of his head, but otherwise the boy was fine.

"I'm sorry, Anna. He found me and I tried to fight him, but..."

"Don't worry, everything turned out fine."

His eyes wandered over to the dead soldier and he looked down at the ground without voicing his thoughts.

Eliza came up behind us, a tattered duffel bag over her shoulder and carrying several weapons.

"Well the Dongfeng is dead. I scavenged half a bag of food and these weapons from our enemies."

"Did you check their jeep?"

"Yes Anna, I'm not stupid. They messed up the right wheel when they hit us. It can't be driven either."

I rubbed my eyes and sighed.

"Okay, here's what we do. We'll hike the rest of the way. If we make a beeline toward the rendezvous location, we should still make it there on time. At least if we push ourselves we will. That will keep us off the roads and away from any more surprise outposts. Give me the map, Chen and I will plot a path through the forest. Eliza, go back to the jeep and destroy the radio. That way when the guy I knocked out wakes up, he can't call for help."

Eliza handed me the map we'd created and turned to leave.

"Hurry back, we head out in ten minutes."

By the time she'd returned, Chen and I had plotted the best route we could through the dense woods. Picking up the duffel and as many of the weapons as we could carry, the three of us trudged through the underbrush.

Chapter Thirty-Three

Rendevous

The trek through the forest was brutal. The dense foliage scratched and pummeled us every step of the way. It tripped and slowed our progress to the point that we were forced to march for sixteen hours before resting for a mere two. It had been grueling for all of us, but Chen had seen the worst of it. Eliza and I were tired, but his human body was on the verge of collapse from exhaustion. He was running on fumes, stumbling forward more than walking. I slowed my pace to speak with him and take his mind off our painful trip.

"Hey, Chen, do you know a lot about America?"

"What? Oh, yeah, the government taught us about it in school. But some of the stuff they said sounded too silly to be true, so I searched the Internet to learn the truth."

"What did you find?"

"The crazy thing was, it was the silly stuff that was true."

I chuckled.

"Give me an example of something you thought was silly."

"That's easy, you have a game in your country named football, but it's not the football the rest of the world plays. You call that soccer."

"I'm not sure how the names came about, but yes, that's true."

"Also, I've read that it's incredibly popular. It's your nation's favorite sport. I've seen many what you call, soccer games, but never an American football game."

"Is that the first thing you'd like to do when you get to America, see a football game?"

He thought for a moment before speaking.

"Maybe the second thing. Right now all I can think about is having a hamburger."

He grinned, and it was infectious.

"How about we get a hamburger at a football game?"

"Deal!"

As we shook hands on our bargain, I could hear Eliza mumble from behind us.

"If we make it out of here."

* * * * *

Within the next few hours, we crossed over the Chinese border and into Russia. This would have meant we were home free if our pursuers had been the Chinese government, but not so with the case of Xiang Yao and his Red Dragon rebels. However, there was a light at the end of the tunnel, we were now less than two hours from our extraction point. It was a small, isolated beach, just northwest of Mayachnoye. All we had to do was get there. That fact improved everyone's mood, and we found the energy to march a little faster.

* * * * *

When we at last broke through the dense underbrush and stepped out onto the beach, it was like waking from a month-long nightmare. The noonday sun shone between a few scattered clouds, warming us and the coarse sand on the beach. At the same time, a chorus of rising and falling waves treated our ears with their melody. After a few steps, we staggered to a stop and celebrated.

"Chen! We made it! Can you believe it?"

"It's wonderful, Anna! When will the helicopter arrive?"

Checking the time, I saw that our extra burst of speed had bought us around ten minutes to relax.

"I think we have a few minutes. We could…"

"Fuck! Anna, do you hear that?"

"Eliza, I don't hear anything but your foul lang…"

Then I heard it. Oh, no…multiple engine sounds from our left and right.

"Everybody, get back into the underbrush and hide!"

Before we could move, two jeeps arrived from the right and another from the left. Multiple red dots from laser sights appeared on the ground in front of us, they did not want us fleeing back into the cover. Yelling over my shoulder, I told Chen to stay down as Eliza and I entered a back-to-back fighting stance.

"Anna, there's too many. I count eight men in the two jeeps coming from the south and four more in the jeep arriving from the north."

"I know, but what else can we do?"

A megaphone-enhanced voice answered my question.

"Lay down your weapons immediately, or we will be forced to open fire. Do it now!"

Looking at Eliza, I shrugged my shoulders. She smirked.

"I love a good fight, but this would be suicide. I say we live to fight another day. After all, the General might not execute us on sight. We are still valuable assets after all."

I nodded, and we both tossed our weapons onto the beach. Chen's horrified voice came from behind us.

"Oh, no please no…"

It tore my heart in two, and I tried to console him.

"Chen, listen up. Go with the plan that we kidnapped you. Stick to that and you'll be fine. This isn't over. We just have to stay alive."

"No, Anna, I can't go back. I won't go back!"

"HEY! Calm down and do as I say, understand?"

There was a long pause before he answered with an emotionless tone.

"Yes, I understand."

Red Dragons swarmed our position. Eight fell in about thirty feet behind us to the south, and the four from the north approached us and searched Eliza and I for weapons. Out of fear or respect, they ignored Chen, and I knew he had a pistol tucked in the back of his pants. On the surface, that sounded promising, but there was no way the boy could use it to help us.

Once they'd secured our firearms, I saw one of the soldiers make a call on his radio. A minute later, another jeep came driving down from the north. A Red Dragon emblem adorned the hood and small flags with the same symbol waved in the breeze from its front fenders. Eliza voiced what I feared.

"Well it's not a party until the clown arrives."

* * * * *

The General's jeep pulled up closer to us than the others and angled its passenger's side toward where we stood. Three Red Dragon soldiers hurried out of the jeep, but these men were different. Their uniforms, while similar, had decorative red ribbons across the left shoulder. Chen let out a whimper.

"Oh, no...members of the Elite Forces. That means..."

He couldn't bring himself to finish his sentence as one of the elites opened the rear passenger's door and out stepped General Yao himself. He smoothed out the wrinkles of his uniform and walked with purpose toward Eliza and myself. An Elite Dragon marched on each side of him, along with one following up behind as he stopped in front of us. The General's personal guard had their automatic rifles aimed right at Eliza and me, so I hoped for just once in her life she'd stay quiet. The day became still and silent. It felt like even the waves slowed their constant ebb and flow. The General cleared his throat and spoke.

"Chen, step forward. I would speak with you."

The boy turned sideways and slid between Eliza and myself. Walking toward his father while staring down at the sand. Stopping in front of him, he raised his head and faced his old man.

"I am here, General Yao."

He paused and stared at his son.

"Summarize how all of this transpired."

Chen looked over his shoulder at Eliza and me with a face full of doubt. I stared back and nodded. He had to stick to the plan. Turning back around, he spoke.

"I-I was in the garage checking on vehicle repairs and was captured by these women. Their plan was to use me as a hostage if needed. I led them to an outpost, but they defeated the brave soldiers located there."

The General didn't speak for a long time. When he did, it was soul crushing.

"You should know that I am extremely disappointed in you. Through either incompetence or ignorance, you allowed yourself to be taken hostage by these traitors for three days. Our resources have been squandered on this manhunt when you should have stopped them before they left the base."

"I tried General, but they outnumbered and overpowered me."

"You cannot be serious. Are you saying that an officer in my Red Dragon army was overpowered by two women?"

Furious, I watched as the back of Chen's neck turned bright red. His voice cracked as he stammered out a reply.

"T-They surprised me, sir."

"Surprised you? Did you not smell their perfume or hear their high heels as they approached?"

Quiet laughter spread through the ranks of the other soldiers, and my anger grew. I knew Xiang Yao respected my abilities, he was belittling Eliza and I only to embarrass his son in front of the troops. That infuriated me more than anything else. When Chen didn't reply, the General continued.

"Did they harm you? They could have battered you with their purses or scratched you with their nails. That would have been painful indeed."

The quiet laughter grew louder, and I saw the boy clinch his fists. Damn it, why wouldn't that monster leave him alone? Without warning, Chen screamed.

"SHUT UP! Shut up! You are horrible! So horrible that I wasn't taken hostage, I helped them escape. I wanted to escape with them. To get away from you!"

After his outburst, everything fell quiet as a graveyard at midnight. Thoughts of what the General might do terrified me, but he only stared at him showing no expression. At least until he drew his hand back and slapped Chen hard across the face.

"Do not say such nonsense. You are suffering from a mental condition where kidnap victims become allies of their captors. You will return to the base where..."

A low pulsing, whooshing, sound interrupted the General, and we all turned to look out over the water. A solid-black Sikorsky UH-60 Black Hawk helicopter swooped in from over the bay and straight toward the beach. As it drew closer, its blades slowed, and it emitted more of a concussive throb than a true noise. Turning sideways, it held a position thirty feet off the ground and seventy feet from where we stood. Shouts erupted all around and The Red Dragons aimed their weapons at the aircraft. They would have opened fire if the General's voice hadn't boomed out loud and clear.

"Stop, hold your fire, but maintain your readiness."

As the side door of the helicopter slid open, the first thing everyone saw was a man dressed in green fatigues, sitting behind thick transparent plexiglass. His hand worked a joystick mounted at his station and a fifty-caliber mini gun swung out and into position. The Dragons flinched, preparing to fire and this time the General chastised his men.

"I said hold your fire. Do not make me repeat myself!"

The helicopter's side door slid the rest of the way open revealing another man dressed in a pressed black suit and fire-engine-red tie. No clear shield protected him as his hair blew around in the wind from the helicopter blades. Holding onto a handle next to the door, he leaned out of the opening and exuded a calm, controlling presence. Adam Sims from the NSA had arrived right on time.

Chapter Thirty-Four

Confrontation

Adam stood in the doorway for at least a minute surveying the situation, which I could have told him was dire. However just the sight of him up there in that helicopter, all calm and collected, made me think there was hope for this encounter to end without violence. I sensed the General wanted this as well, or else he would have ordered his men to fire as the Black Hawk approached.

I held my breath as Adam's eyes found and locked onto General Yao. Reaching back into the helicopter, he grabbed a small device and held it up to his mouth. When he spoke, his amplified voice came from speakers on the aircraft.

"General Xiang Yao, it is an honor to meet you. My name is Adam Sims, and I would like to have a word with you, please."

The General studied the American, then turned and spoke to one of his elite guard. The man ran to a nearby jeep and returned with a megaphone so Xiang Yao could answer. I noticed the volume of his voice was louder than Adam's.

"Greetings Mister Sims. I am General Xiang Yao, leader of the Red Dragons, and I will speak with you. However, I do have a question. What brings you such a long way from home?"

Adam considered his words and then replied.

"Out of respect, I will be upfront with you. The two women next to you are under my charge. They were taken hostage while on a plane and flown into your airspace. There was an accident onboard and the plane went down in the Jilin province, which is where you located them. I have come to take them back home, now that they are free from their abductor. I wish for no violence, or bloodshed…only to pickup my associates. After we have them onboard, we will turn and leave, never to disturb you again."

What? No way in hell! I'd set this straight.

"No, the young man Chen Yao seeks asylum in the United States and will come with us!"

The looks and stares I received from the General and his men were nothing compared to Eliza's mental blast.

"What the fuck, Anna? You know there's no way the General is going to let his son step onto a US helicopter and fly away while his soldiers watch! Don't screw up our rescue by insisting on something you know is impossible!"

"Damn it, Eliza! The boy is coming with us. I can't leave him here with that tyrannical egomaniac! It's nonnegotiable, I'll stay behind if I have to, and that's not a bluff."

She didn't respond for a heartbeat.

"Fine, if that's the way you want to play it, good luck with that. But I'm getting on that helicopter and leaving…with or without you."

"Thanks a lot Sis."

As I replied, the General spoke.

"I appreciate your candor Mister Sims, but you may have been misled regarding some of your facts. The fact of the matter is that I entered into an agreement with an associate and we traded favors. I was to receive the service of these two women for various tasks. Since the tasks are not complete, they are still under my charge, and not yours. While you speak as if you have a working relationship with Anna and Eliza, I believe that isn't the case either. The person I spoke with assured me they reported to their organization, not yours."

Adam turned and did something with another headset. I detected a radio transmission from the helicopter, so he could have been talking with a superior. Then he responded.

"General Yao, I'm not sure what you bartered away to get the services you speak of, but I am in a position to trade you something I am sure is more valuable."

The General almost looked surprised.

"What would that be, Mister Sims?"

"Your life and the lives of your men."

While Adam delivered the line with perfect calm and no emotion whatsoever, my mouth fell open at the threat. Eliza, of course had something to say about it over our mental link.

"Anna, what the fuck! Your boyfriend just went all hardcore and didn't even flinch. I'm impressed!"

"He's not my boyfriend!"

"Yeah, whatever. I saw your face when he said that. It made you all tingly didn't it?"

"Eliza, shut up and concentrate! There could be a firefight any second!"

"Okay...if you don't want to talk about it that's fine. I'm just saying..."

I tuned her out and observed how the General's men reacted. No one had ever spoke that way to their leader before and whispers rolled through their ranks. General Yao himself continued to impress me, he didn't look angry or insulted. His face registered no emotion as he considered what Adam had said. Maybe he could get past his ego and realize that he would be on the losing side if hostilities broke out. His men were well equipped, but not to take on a Black Hawk helicopter with a mini gun. They would be mowed down in less than a minute.

Holding up his hand, the General silenced the whispers of his men.

"Your offer is crude and unacceptable. But, since these women have been a troublesome distraction since they arrived, I will make a counter offer. Provide me with a six-month supply of food, water, and medical equipment delivered to a neutral location, and I will consider that fair compensation for my trouble. Upon receipt of the items, you may leave with Anna and Eliza."

I felt like my sister and I were heads of cattle. Not to mention they'd ignored my previous outburst about Chen coming with us in these negotiations. A fact I was about to rectify...but the boy beat me to it.

"No, I won't go back!"

Chen's scream pulled all eyes to him, and...oh no...he'd pulled out his pistol and had it pressed to his right temple. Taking a step toward him I tried to calm the panicked young man.

"Put the gun down, Chen. You know this is not the way."

I took another step as he wailed.

"You don't know what it's like! I can't live with him anymore!"

I moved to step forward again, but a horrible, scoffing laugh from the General made me freeze in my tracks. He'd never shown that much emotion in front of me. Too bad it was all harmful. He brought his laughter under control and spewed more of his venomous words.

"Don't be a fool woman. My son doesn't have the backbone to do something like that. He thinks the way you solve problems is through whining and complaining, like this."

His face turned hard as stone as he reached out for the handgun.

"Now, hand me the gun and go wait in the jeep."

When Chen hesitated, General Yao ratcheted up the pressure and yelled.

"Give me the gun, you coward!"

The boy looked at me and his distant stare told me he'd made his choice. I shook my head as he turned back to his father. He was going to pull that trigger. As I opened my mouth to plead with him, Chen loosened his grip on the gun, bringing it away from his head. He let his arm relax and hang next to his side. Tears ran down his cheeks as he spoke.

"You're right father, I won't do it."

I breathed a sigh of relief. Never had I been so happy to be wrong in my entire life. However a heartbeat later, Chen stunned us all as he raised the weapon and aimed at his father's chest. He screamed as he pulled the trigger.

"But I'm not a coward anymore!"

Chen's aim was true, and the bullet hit General Yao in the chest before anyone could act.

My advanced reflexes activated and overrode the shock I felt at what had happened. I had to get Chen out of here. Looking around at the situation, I saw that Eliza was moving forward. Both of the elite guards flanking the General were raising their rifles to fire at Chen. Eliza was heading toward the one on the General's right side, so I charged the other on the left.

Halfway to my guard, another round left Chen's gun and found a home in his father's chest. Eliza, being a bit faster than me, made it to her target first. She grabbed the barrel of his rifle and pulled it forward with all her might. The surprised guard lost his grip without firing a shot. Eliza swung the AK-47 above her head in a full circle and slapped the man across the face with the butt end of the weapon. It impacted hard enough to shatter the stock, scattering splinters across the sand.

Being one step slower than my combat-specialized sister cost me, as the other elite guard opened fire with his weapon. The rifle was on full automatic, and bullets sprayed out of the barrel in a deadly pattern toward Chen and myself. I watched in horror as he took at least two rounds in his chest and dropped his pistol. Furious, I threw myself at the man as he continued to unload his magazine. Fueled by rage, I ignored a searing pain in my right leg and wrapped my arms around the guard's waist. Driving him backwards, he lost his footing in the soft sand and fell onto his back. Twisting the AK-47 out of his grip, I slammed it into his face again and again until blood poured from his nose and he stopped fighting back. Throwing the weapon to the ground, I tried to stand and my right leg buckled, refusing to support my weight. Taking a look, I found a bloody hole in my fatigues. The guard had shot me in the calf, and the bullet was still lodged in my leg. It had shredded most of the muscle, explaining why I couldn't put much weight on it.

I looked around for Eliza so she could help me over to Chen, but she had other plans. Picking up the pistol that Chen had dropped, she turned to where the General had fallen. The last of the elite guards had knelt down to help General Yao up into a sitting position. He was bleeding and in pain, but conscious. Xiang Yao's defiant black eyes met Eliza's as she aimed the 9mm at his chest and added two more rounds of her own. As he slumped backwards, blood pouring from the new wounds, she smirked in satisfaction.

"That's for sucker punching me in the gut you bastard."

Horrified, the last elite guard dropped all his weapons to lighten his load and lifted the bloody unconscious body of his leader over his shoulder. He staggered away under the weight and shifting sand toward the General's jeep. Eliza shouted at him as he fled.

"You'd better get the bastard out of my sight before I shoot him again!"

* * * * *

At this point, pandemonium took over. Shouts rang out through the Red Dragon troops.

"They killed the General!"

"Its the Americans, they killed him and his son, Chen!"

Eliza and I were sitting ducks if the soldiers decided to open fire on us, so I altered my voice to sound like one of the men I'd heard shouting and added a bit of chaos of my own.

"The shots came from the helicopter!"

Changing my voice again, I added more encouragement.

"Shoot it down! Make the Americans pay!"

In response, some of the Dragons shot at the helicopter, which of course caused it to return the favor. Watching the exchange of fire, I noticed that the rounds from the Dragons were ricocheting off the Black Hawk's armor. They simply didn't have heavy enough weapons to damage the armored gunship. In return, I noticed that the gunner aboard the aircraft wasn't actually shooting at the Red Dragons. He was laying down suppressing fire, hitting in front of the men and causing sand to fly ten feet in the air. It was enough to keep them in place without killing any of them.

In my peripheral vision, I saw Eliza ducked down and running over to where I sat.

"Hey stupid, you're going to get our ride shot down!"

"Well sorry, I thought the Black Hawk could take rifle rounds easier than we could."

"Oh...good point. What do we do now?"

"Now, we get to the damn helicopter. Help me over to Chen."

Eliza leaned down and I wrapped my arm around her neck. She helped me limp over to Chen and I sat down next to him. Blood stained the sand under his body and his skin was turning pale, but he was still alive.

"Eliza, I can't carry him, not with my leg shot up like this."

"Can you walk by yourself?"

"I have to."

"All right, wait here."

She ran off and gathered up two of the AK-47 rifles that the elite guards had dropped. On her way back, she checked the weapons and their ammo. Squatting down next to me, she explained her plan.

"I'll carry Chen to the helicopter and you cover our backs with these rifles. Can you do that?"

"Yeah, I won't be accurate, but I should be able to keep them off you."

"Good enough. You ready?"

"Yes, help me up."

As Eliza pulled me to my feet, I couldn't help but make an observation.

"You know, I'm a little surprised that you offered to carry him."

That familiar smirk appeared on her lips as she answered.

"Well, I knew if I offered to carry the boy you'd never ask me to carry you. And since he weighs less than you, that means I can get to the chopper faster."

I couldn't help but laugh.

"You are one pragmatic bitch, you know that?"

"What else would I be?"

I took the weapons from her and she picked up Chen, placing him over her shoulders in a fireman's carry position. Nodding, she jogged off toward the Black Hawk. With my back to her, I held an AK-47 in each hand and stumbled backwards. Turning my head left to right, I watched for any soldiers that might notice us.

* * * * *

Walking backwards with a bullet in your calf muscle was a lot more difficult than I'd thought. More than once, I stumbled and almost fell, recovering my balance at the last second. With Eliza already carrying Chen and enemies firing at us from three sides, I knew that falling would be the end of me.

Further and further I stumbled along as more soldiers fired at me. They must have noticed that their weapons were having no effect on the Black Hawk. Bullets sailed about as if I'd stumbled into a hornet's nest. At first, I tried to aim and hit the soldiers as they fired at me, but my need to stay on my feet and keep moving soon took precedence. Picking up my pace, I turned my shots into reflexive short bursts in the general direction of incoming fire. I may have hit one or two soldiers, but everything was too hectic to tell.

The AK-47 in my right hand ran out of ammunition, and I tossed it aside. As I was swapping my remaining weapon to a two-handed grip, Eliza called out.

"Anna, we're on board! Turn and run for it, we'll cover you!"

Tossing down the other weapon, I turned around and limped toward the helicopter. It had lowered a rope ladder so we could climb aboard since it couldn't land. The ladder dangled twenty yards away, but at my speed it felt like twenty miles.

My leg throbbed with pain I couldn't suppress and blood soaked the sock inside my combat boot. Each step was more torturous that the last, and I wondered if I could make it. Then I saw Eliza and Adam inside the Black Hawk. Both of them were standing in the doorway, out in the open, firing pistols to help cover my escape. I couldn't let them down. Gritting my teeth, I trudged forward.

At about ten feet from the ladder, my vision blurred, and I lost my balance. Falling to my hands and knees, I fought to stay conscious. Eliza's voice echoed in my head as I crawled forward.

"It's only five fucking feet, Anna. Crawl over to the ladder and grab on! Don't

make me leave you here!"

"Screw you, Eliza!"

"Yeah, I've heard that somewhere before. Now, grab the damn ladder!"

While we'd spoke, I'd crawled far enough to reach the bottom rungs. Grabbing onto them, I pulled myself upright and climbed. Along the way, my vision cleared and the dizziness subsided as I tapped into my last bit of strength, knowing I was almost home.

When I was five feet away from the bottom of the door, the Black Hawk angled away from the beach and climbed into the sky. The soldier operating the mini gun ceased fire and a low-pitched whine echoed inside the aircraft as it spun down. Eliza put her pistol down and knelt to examine Chen, while Adam leaned out the door to help me.

As I reached the top rung, Adam bent down and held out his hand. When I reached out to take it, a tiny red dot appeared on his shoulder. It bounced all around inside the helicopter, from one place to another. My eyes widened as I realized what it meant.

"Adam! Sniper! Sniper!"

He understood me and turned to speak with the pilot, but the sniper opened fire first.

The first round made a terrifying whistling sound as it flew over my head. In the blink of an eye, Adam disappeared from the doorway.

Another round zipped by me and ricocheted inside the cramped interior of the helicopter. Eliza ducked down where I couldn't see her and shouted.

"Turn us the fuck around before the damn sniper fills us full of holes!"

We lurched clockwise and the force of the maneuver almost hurled me off the ladder, but somehow I kept my grip. At least until the pilot finished the 180-degree turn. He stopped rotating in a sudden jerk, and the left anchor for the rope ladder disconnected from the bottom of the Black Hawk. I screamed as the ladder folded and all the rungs turned vertical.

"Eliza! Adam! Help me!"

In desperation, I let go with my left hand and grabbed at the floor of the helicopter. I missed by a mile. My body was twirling and bobbing so much that I never had a chance. I felt myself slide down the rope and realized that this might be the end.

A strong hand grabbed me by my flailing left wrist and stabilized my movements. It was Adam.

"Hold on. I've got you."

As he pulled on my wrist, I climbed with my other hand. I'd almost made it to the floor of the Black Hawk, when I noticed Adam's shirt. There was a streak of blood running down the arm of it, and it was only getting larger. I traced it back to his shoulder, and saw a sizable hole in his jacket. Crap, he'd been shot...in the arm he was using to pull me aboard.

At first, I was sure he'd drop me, but he didn't. My eyes met his, and it didn't appear that he was in pain. He looked like he always did, calm, collected, and focused on the task at hand. Then I realized his body was running on pure adrenaline, and I'd better get my ass inside before it ran out.

With one last heave from Adam and a lunge from myself, I tumbled into the helicopter and onto his chest. Planting my hands on each side of him, I pushed myself up and nodded at his shoulder.

"Adam, you'd better get that looked at. It looks almost as bad as my leg."

He glanced at his arm and grimaced in pain.

"You're right, it's really beginning to hurt now."

"It's the adrenaline wearing off. You need to watch out for signs of shock too."

"Thanks, I will."

Our eyes met and I studied his face, but he was as stoic as ever. A moment later, I slid off him and sat down next to Chen. Adam got to his feet and pushed the Black Hawk's door closed. Covering his wounded shoulder with his good hand, he leaned into the cockpit.

"Take us home, fast. Let them know we have critically wounded inbound."

Adam turned and walked back to sit next to Eliza as the helicopter accelerated like a rocket toward home base.

We'd done it...we'd escaped. This was supposed to be a time of celebration, but it wasn't...it couldn't be. Not with all that had happened here today. On the verge of tears, I turned my attention to the pale, young boy lying at my feet, dreading what I would find.

Chapter Thirty-Five

Evac

The wind roared outside our Black Hawk helicopter as it sped through the sky. I knew the pilot was doing everything he could, but it still felt like this trip was taking forever.

"Adam, where is home base anyway?"

"We're heading back to the stealth submarine that got us through the Sea of Japan undetected."

"What's our ETA?"

He looked at a digital clock on the wall to his right and replied.

"Less than ten minutes."

I wasn't sure Chen had ten minutes. He was still holding on, but the boy was turning more pale by the minute. I checked his vitals, and he had a weak pulse with shallow labored breathing. The compression bandage on his chest had already soaked through with blood, and I grabbed another from a first aid kit under the bench seat. As I went about removing the old one, his eyes fluttered open. They were dull and unfocused, but when he saw me he smiled.

"Anna, did we make it?"

I returned his smile.

"Yes, we did. We're on the helicopter right now. Soon we'll be home."

"Good..."

He paused and drew in a wheezing breath.

"How do you like the way I handled my father? I finally stood up to my problem and faced it, right?"

If he'd hit me in the head with a sledgehammer it wouldn't have hurt any worse. I'd told him to face his problems that night on the road home from Cadbury...but how could I have known he'd do it this way? Guilt wrapped itself around my mind like a deadly python, squeezing and crushing me until I couldn't think.

"You...you did great Chen."

"Yeah...I did..."

His voice faded and I grabbed his pale cold hand, holding on tight. He couldn't leave if I didn't let go.

He smiled at me again.

"Hey...I can smell that hamburger...you promised me. We must be... near..."

His eyelids fluttered, then closed.

Tears poured from my eyes, dropping onto his almost motionless chest like rain. Driven by desperation, I put the clean bandage on his chest and pressed it down. Maybe...maybe the added pressure would stop the bleeding.

Looking up, I saw Eliza and Adam sitting there, just watching. It enraged me and I snapped at them.

"Don't just sit there damn it, do something!"

Eliza threw up her hands.

"Anna, there's nothing we can do. I'm the one that applied the compression bandage, and his chest is full of blood. He's a goner."

Her words hit me so hard that I quit crying.

"Adam?"

He looked at me with a blank expression and spoke like he was reading a newspaper.

"I believe she is right."

I lost it.

"How the fuck can you two just sit there and do nothing? I expect that heartless shit from Eliza, but you too, Adam?"

He pointed to the cockpit as he spoke.

"I did something. I had the pilot radio ahead for a medical team upon our landing."

If I hadn't been trying to save Chen's life, I'd have punched him right in that uncaring mouth. Instead, I turned away ignoring the both of them, and tried to keep a young man alive.

* * * * *

The helicopter reduced its speed and descended toward the water. Checking the window, I saw we were approaching our destination. The four hundred foot submarine sat stationed with half its charcoal hull above the surface of the royal blue water. Its sleek, aggressive lines belied its size, and I knew this ship could slice through white-capped waves like an eagle gliding through the clouds. The Black Hawk began its final approach, and I held on to Chen to keep him from moving around.

As we touched down, a group of medical personnel scurried onto the deck, two of them pushing an emergency stretcher. Adam stood and slid the door open as two other deck personnel chocked the Black Hawk's wheels in place. The medics folded the legs of the stretcher and pushed it into the craft. Eliza grabbed one side of Chen's blanket and Adam reached for the other. Shocked, I pushed him out of the way.

"You can't lift him Adam, you've got a bullet in your shoulder."

"And you have a bullet in your leg."

I waved him away.

"Yes, but I can do it because I'm *built* sturdier than you.*"

He stepped aside and let Eliza and me lift Chen and place him on the stretcher. As the medics rolled him out of the helicopter and across the deck, I called out to them.

"He's been shot twice in the chest and has internal bleeding!"

"Got it. Thanks Miss."

"I'll be there in just a minute!"

They disappeared down a ramp leading into the submarine, shouting at people to move out of the way. No sooner did the first team disappear, than another came up the ramp toward us. One medic was pushing a wheelchair while the other ran next to him.

"Adam, help me out of here. I need to go with Chen."

He leapt out of the Black Hawk and offered me his hand. I took it and hopped down on my good leg...and it buckled when it hit the deck. Adam kept me from falling, but the world went all fuzzy again and I had no sense of balance.

"Anna, you've lost a lot of blood. You need to get in the wheelchair and let them bandage you up. You won't do Chen any good if you pass out on him."

"I guess you're right. What about Eliza?"

"She can come with me while I get patched up.*"

"Uh, I'm not sure that's a good idea."

Eliza smirked at me.

"Don't worry, I promise not to steal your boyfriend."

I sighed.

Adam looked at me and opened his mouth to speak, but I cut him off.

"It's just something she's doing to piss me off. Don't pay any attention to it. I'll join up with you two soon as I can."

Adam nodded.

"Okay, see you soon."

The medic with the wheelchair arrived and I eased myself down into it. Now that we were aboard the sub, my body started aching all over. It made me glad for the free ride.

Eliza and Adam headed off with a blonde-haired medic while the other pushed me along toward the ramp. A warning horn sounded three times and I turned to see the helicopter being lowered into a forward hold. The deck slid shut over the now stored Black Hawk, followed by the door at the top of our ramp. Before we'd made it to sickbay, I could hear the ocean rushing into the sub's ballast tanks. The hallway listed somewhat as we dove beneath the surface of the sea. Out of sight, out of mind.

* * * * *

The medic wheeled me into a small sterile looking room and helped me out of the wheelchair. He supported most of my weight as I moved over to the examining table, and I realized that he was about to examine me. I couldn't let him. While my body looked human, it wasn't. Someone with medical training would notice the differences and that would be bad news. No one knew I was an android except for a few people in the NSA and my creators, a secret I intended to keep.

As I was about to make up a lame excuse to prevent the medic from examining me, a short woman with long saddle brown hair entered the room. She had on medical green scrubs that were a bit baggy on her petite frame. Her voice was quiet and mousey when she spoke.

"Alan, they need you in the other room, stat."

The medic that had wheeled me in nodded and jogged out. When he'd left the women turned to look at me with her earth-brown eyes. Her bottom lip trembled and she bit it to keep herself from crying. It was wonderful to see her again.

"Elizabeth! Is it really you?"

"Oh Anna, thank god!"

I embraced the daughter of my father, Elizabeth Eklund. It felt like it had been a lifetime since we'd seen each other.

"How did you talk the NSA in to letting you come on a mission this dangerous?"

"I told them that if you were hurt, I was the only one qualified to help you."

We broke our embrace and I held up my leg for her to see.

"It's a good thing you did."

"I heard, you poor thing. What happened?"

"I took a rifle round trying to protect Chen."

She knelt down and untied my combat boots.

"Chen? Oh, the son of that general?"

"Yeah, I screwed that up big time and he's been shot."

She tossed the boots in the corner and went to work on my socks.

"The story I heard was a little different. Chen shot his father, and then the guards shot him. It's horrible, but there wasn't anything you could have done."

"Have you heard anything about his condition?"

I jumped as a stabbing pain shot through my leg while she peeled my sock off the injury.

"Sorry Anna, that must be tender. All I know about him is that most of the medical staff is working on him a few rooms over."

She stood back up.

"But we need to focus on you. That rifle round is still in there and I have to get it out. I know you feel pain, but can you disable that reaction?"

"For the most part, yes."

"All right then, let me help you up. We need to take a look at you and make sure that's your only injury."

As Elizabeth helped me undress, I felt Viktor's data drive in my pocket. It might not be the best time to talk about this with her, but I thought she deserved to have it. Besides, it would be much safer with her than with me. It had already gotten damaged maybe even destroyed because I didn't give it to her when we first met. Sliding it out of my pocket, I fumbled for the right words.

"Elizabeth…"

She laid my shirt on the counter and walked back.

"Anna, what is it? You look like you're in pain."

"You remember the first night we met…and we talked for hours about Viktor."

She looked confused.

"Sure I do."

"Well, with all we were discussing, I forgot something very important. Viktor had a data drive on him when...ah...when I last saw him. A document on it says it contains the only remaining copy of all his research stored in an encrypted file, and that I should find you because you could help me access it. Here, I want you to have it."

Opening my hand, I held out the data drive. Elizabeth reached out and took the drive as if she were picking up the Holy Grail, which it sort of was.

"I-I don't know what to say."

"It should be with you. Eliza and Stepan would kill to get their hands on it and it is already damaged from the plane crash. Don't tell anyone that you have the drive and keep it well hidden."

"Yes, of course."

"Don't even tell me where you keep it. I don't want to know in case someone at Ice Castle figures out how to extract data from my neural-net brain."

She looked shocked, but nodded her agreement.

"Have you seen the research?"

"No, the encryption has the most complex key I've ever encountered. I couldn't break the code. Since Viktor told me to find you, there must be a secret that the both of you shared that will be the key."

She looked down at the data drive and slid it into her pocket.

"He must have wanted to be sure no one else got their hands on it."

"I agree, it was on a chain around his neck, so he wasn't sure who might find it after he..."

Our eyes met and we shared the pain of Viktor's death again with an unspoken look of sorrow.

"Thank you for this, Anna. When we get back home, I will work on getting access. As for right now, we need to get you checked out."

Once down to my underwear, Elizabeth took a hospital gown out of a drawer and helped me into it. She spent several minutes giving me a thorough examination.

"Well, all I see are a bunch of cuts, abrasions, and bruises. So lets get to work on that leg."

For the next twenty minutes she removed pieces of bullet from my leg. Each exploratory touch of the forceps brought a stab of pain, which I eliminated as much as I could. There was nothing to do except grit my teeth and let Elizabeth do her job. Finishing up, she cleaned the wound and got out the sutures. Then she paused.

"I'm going to put a few stitches in. You must have the ability to repair yourself, but this should help that along. Once I'm done with that, I'll bandage you up and you should be ready to go. Just don't exert yourself or you'll tear the stitches out and start bleeding again."

I nodded and she went back to work.

* * * * *

Taping the bandage in place, Elizabeth stood and stretched her back. Walking to a closet in the corner, she opened it and took out navy blue overalls and a pair of boat shoes.

"All right, you're all set. Here's something you can wear. Now, I need to check on Adam. Will you be okay here?"

"Actually, I really want to go see Chen."

"Ah, of course, take a right through the small waiting room, and he's in triage one."

She gave me another crushing hug, and I returned it.

"You don't know how glad I am you're safe. I'll see you in a little while."

"Thank you for everything, Elizabeth."

She left, and I went about getting dressed. My leg still wouldn't support my full weight, but it hurt much less now that Elizabeth had removed the shrapnel. It took me a while to dress, but once finished, I limped out of the room following the directions Elizabeth had given me.

Passing through the waiting room, I took a right and saw a sign indicating triage one. Hurrying up to the door, I froze with my hand on the door handle. Through a small round window, I saw a body covered in a bloody white sheet. No, he couldn't be dead. I was supposed to save him. It couldn't be.

Staggering back from the door, I felt faint. The room swirled and I looked for a place to sit. A set of hands grabbed me and turned me around. It was a man dressed in blood-spattered surgeon's scrubs.

"Whoa, there. Here, follow me."

He led me back to the waiting room and we sat down on a small bench seat.

"Are you all right Miss?"

"Y-yeah, was that…Chen?"

A knowing look came over his face.

"You must be one of the women that came in with him. I'm afraid it is."

I stared off into the distance, tears overflowing from my eyes, while he described what happened.

"We tried everything we could, but a bullet had nicked his aorta causing massive blood loss. He passed away two minutes after he arrived. I'm so sorry for your loss."

Covering my face with my hands, I wept.

"I promised him we make it out, and I wasn't even there for him when he died!"

"Miss, is there someone I can get for you?"

I looked up. He was trying to help.

"No, no…just go. I want to be alone."

"If that's what you want. But my office is at the end of the hall. I'll be there in a few minutes if you want me to contact someone for you. Again, I'm sorry."

I nodded as he turned and left me alone in the waiting room. Wracking sobs overcame me along with crushing guilt about bringing Chen with us. I stared at the floor and blamed myself for another death.

* * * * *

I'm not sure how long I sat there. My head was so full of self-loathing, it was all I knew. The tears had stopped, but I didn't have the energy or desire to get up and leave. Everything faded away until my entire world was this bench and the gray floor underneath my feet. I'd never forgive myself for getting Chen killed.

Approaching footsteps echoed in the room, but I didn't look up. Polished shiny black shoes came into view as the man stood next to me. Before he spoke, I knew it was Adam. No one else had shoes that immaculate.

"I suppose the boy didn't make it."

Choking back more tears, I mumbled to him.

"No, he didn't."

He paused, unsure of what to say.

"I'm sorry that I was right about his injuries."

What the hell did that mean? Plus he said it so flat, so emotionless. Like he was reading a speed limit sign. I'd had enough of his crap. Looking up, I unloaded.

"Really Adam? A young man has died here today, one that was being tortured by the NSA I might add, and you're sorry about guessing he was going to die?"

His face showed no expression as he answered me.

"Anna, I explained to you I didn't know about that facility being used for torture or imprisonment. The NSA is a large organization. There are going to be divisions, operations, that are run independently of our section."

Now I was angry. Standing, I got in his face.

"When you recruited me, you said the NSA were the good guys. Now, I find you capturing and torturing people…and before you say it again, I don't give a damn if you personally did or didn't know about it, someone at the NSA did."

"Anna…"

I poked him hard in the chest with my index finger to emphasize my point.

"No! I've seen this before, it's the same kind of shit Stepan Entsky pulled!"

He stood unmoving and took my punishment without replying. Then I noticed the sling on his arm. I hadn't seen it because he'd pulled his coat over it. Damn, I'd been poking him right below where he'd taken a bullet for me. I winced because I knew that must have hurt.

"Oh Adam, I'm sorry. It's just that I'm so upset…I didn't mean to hurt your shoulder."

Looking at where I'd been poking, he shrugged and replied.

"No problem, Anna. I know it must be rough on you."

Did he just? He did… Adam shrugged *both* his shoulders. He had moved them with no sign of pain. My mind froze up and there was a long pause between us.

"Anna, are you all right?"

"Yeah, yeah, I'm fine. But I think I'd like to be alone."

"I understand."

He turned to leave and my intuition screamed for me to speak.

"Hey, is your shoulder giving you any trouble, you know, hurting at all?"

He stopped and looked at it.

"No, not really."

He must have noticed my confused expression because he continued.

"The doctors have me on strong pain killers, so it's not an issue."

"Well, that's good. See you later."

As Adam walked out of the room, I sat back down on the bench. Something in the back of my mind kept gnawing at me, but I couldn't concentrate because images of Chen kept invading my thoughts. Getting to my feet, I walked over to the door and looked in at Chen's covered body. The handle was cold in my hand, but I couldn't bring myself to enter. I couldn't bear to see him like that.

"Chen, I'm so sorry. I wanted to save you so badly. I never should have let you come with us. If I hadn't, you'd still be alive. Wherever you are, I hope you can forgive me."

Turning away from the door, I stared down the deserted hallway unsure what to do. My stomach growled as if to answer my question and I realized it had been a day since my last meal. I didn't want to eat, but my EmBees needed food if they were going to fix me up...then, there it was again. Something at the back of my brain I couldn't quite grasp. Damn, it was annoying...almost as annoying as Adam and his lack of concern. Hell, he was so nonchalant he didn't even bother to recognize pain.

The hidden thought that I'd been groping for, blasted from the back of my mind and slapped me square in the frontal lobe. The mere idea made me mumble to myself.

"No...fucking...way..."

Then again, if it were true, all the odd things would make sense. Adam's stoic behavior, what Elizabeth had said about being *qualified* to patch me up, it all came together in a neat little package.

"Those sneaky bastards! I never would have noticed if I didn't have a unique perspective on the subject..."

I had to see if my theory was correct, but how? Ah, I knew just the test for it. By this evening, I'd know if Elizabeth was truly her father's child.

Chapter Thirty-Six

The Team

The sub cruised under silent running protocols all day and into the late hours of the evening. When we at last entered international waters, everyone on board was more relaxed and talkative. Well, except for me. I sat in silence poking at my dinner while several sailors at another table laughed and enjoyed their meal. Every so often, I'd catch one of them stealing a glance at me, and it was starting to piss me off. They weren't being rude. I was still in a horrible mood about the day's events. I was about to get up and leave, when a man entered the mess hall and approached me. His no nonsense gait and body language told me he was here on official business.

"Miss Anna Andropov, I assume?"

I chuckled at the question, but stayed respectful.

"Yes, that's me."

He stiffened and his voice took on an air of self-importance.

"I am Neil Hanson, the XO here on the USS Rushmore."

"Sorry, but what is an X O?"

He stiffened.

"It stands for executive officer."

"Right, what can I do for you XO Hanson?"

"Adam Sims asked me to bring you to the situation room. A meeting is about to begin and they need you to be present."

Picking up my tray, I shuffled over and disposed of it.

"Very well XO, lead the way."

* * * * *

The situation room was midship, and we arrived outside the closed wooden door in less than three minutes. XO Hansen opened the door for me.

"Right in here, Miss Andropov."

"Thank you, Mister Hansen."

I entered and he closed the door. Before I could get a good look at the room, Elizabeth came rushing up and gave me a gentle hug.

"Hey Anna, it looks like you're walking better. How's your leg?"

Seeing her sweet warm smile, made me do the same.

"Oh it's fine thanks to you. You did a great job, you must know a lot about android anatomy."

She laughed.

"Well honestly, your anatomy is almost human. It's hard to tell the difference unless you take x-rays or drill down to the microscopic level."

"Yeah, it was part of Viktor's design philosophy. Keep me as human as possible so I could go about my work unnoticed."

She nodded.

"Great idea since you were designed to be a spy."

"Really, it's a great design for any android model. You would want them to look as human as possible. Otherwise, you might find your android being chased by a pitchfork wielding mob."

"True."

Adam walked up holding two cups of coffee. He handed one to Elizabeth and kept the other for himself.

"Sorry to interrupt, but Kevin would like to get the meeting started."

"Kevin?"

"Oh sorry Anna, he's my superior at the NSA, but I'll let him introduce himself. Would you like a cup of coffee?"

"No thanks. I just had dinner."

Adam nodded and escorted Elizabeth toward a six-seat rectangular metal table. Already sitting down on the far side was a pale skinned man with kinky red hair that came to the middle of his ears. I couldn't believe that he was Adam's boss, since he looked so young. I figured him to be in his mid twenties, but his freckled, boyish face could have been misleading.

Adam helped Elizabeth and me have a seat at one long end, and he sat next to Kevin on the other. After everyone had settled in, Kevin cleared his throat.

"First, I'd like to introduce myself to Miss Andropov. My name is Kevin Taggart, and I'm the Head of Tailored Access Operations in the Data Acquisition Division."

His voice had a confident, leadership quality counterintuitive to his thin build and young appearance.

"Nice to meet you Mister Taggart. Please call me Anna."

He smiled a practiced, customer-service smile and nodded.

"Very well Anna, and you may call me Kevin, if you like. Now, I'd like to thank you for coming, I know this is a difficult time for you, but I think we need to discuss certain events while they are still fresh in our minds."

"That sounds fine, but we should have Eliza here too. She could fill in details that happened while I was away from the Red Dragon base."

Looking around the table, I realized everyone was trying not to make eye contact with me.

"Wait, where exactly *is* Eliza?"

Kevin answered.

"We thought it was best to keep her contained."

"You...*what?*"

"She is confined to quarters."

Pushing myself back from the table I shook my head.

"No. She helped me escape and if it weren't for her..."

Elizabeth touched my arm.

"Anna, I don't know what happened out there, but you told me yourself how dangerous and unpredictable she can be. Only a few days ago, she kidnapped you and tried to kill Adam at the airport."

She was right. Had I grown that close to Eliza in only a few days? Had it been the joining of our minds that gave me a deeper understanding of what her life was like? Perhaps she had changed because of our mind link and was less like herself. Or what if because of it, *I* was more like *her*...oh crap...best to drop it.

"Okay, fine. Where do you want to start?"

Kevin picked up his coffee and took a sip, then replied.

"Tell me what happened after you and Eliza took off from the Birmingham Airport."

I went through the events of the last few days, while Kevin entered notes into his digital pad. One of the best things about being an android was great short-term memory. When I finished forty minutes later, I fixed myself a cup of coffee and wet my parched throat. Kevin spoke as I sat back down at the table.

"So let me make sure I have this correct. You admit to entering an NSA facility, attacking its personnel, and helping a detainee escape?"

I didn't like his tone one bit.

"Yes, I do. And I'd do it again. I told you it was to save Eliza, and several of my other friends."

Kevin leaned forward and stared at me with his piercing blue eyes.

"You crushed the windpipe of an NSA agent and helped the son of a known terrorist escape."

I leaned forward as well.

"One, that NSA bastard was lucky his windpipe was all I crushed after what he tried...and two, YOU WERE FUCKING TORTURING CHEN YAO!"

Kevin's smile was so smarmy I thought he was about to sell me something.

"Anna, by your own account, our agents weren't torturing anyone. There was another man there you called...Ichiro. He was the one performing the torture, right?"

"Look Kevin, I'll not sit here and argue semantics with you. Your facility was complicit in the torture of a young man."

Kevin's smile widened.

"A young man that is now deceased because, against the advice of one of our agents, you insisted he come with you. Which, by the way, also led to the death of General Xiang Yao."

I leapt to my feet, causing a sharp pain in my leg, and slammed the tabletop with my fist. Before I could speak, Adam interrupted.

"Actually, even though Xiang Yao was shot multiple times, we have not confirmed his death."

All of us looked at him, as Kevin growled out a response.

"Mister Sims, that is classified information."

"My apologies, sir."

I took a breath and calmed myself down.

"Look, I told you why I did those things. I had to save my friends. Right now, in Tiksi Russia, a man named Zory Novikov is in trouble. This man risked his life to help me escape from Stepan Entsky and I swear I'm going to do the same for him...with or without help from the NSA."

Kevin laughed.

"Why would the NSA even consider sending resources into Russia?"

Looking at Elizabeth, she shook her head. Kevin didn't know I was an android.

"Because the facility that trained me had a significant research program. That data could be extremely valuable to certain people. And the problem is, the man in charge of the facility has disappeared and no one knows what is happening or who might get their hands on Ice Castle's data."

Kevin rubbed his clean-shaven chin.

"I don't know…"

"Plus, if you help me, on my word, I will join up with the NSA and perform to the best of my abilities."

Kevin smiled a true smile. That was what this meeting had been about. Getting me to commit to the NSA.

"I have to check with my superiors to see if they agree to this arrangement."

"I'm sure they will."

Elizabeth's quiet voice surprised everyone.

"Anna, if you go off to Russia, what should we do with Eliza?"

There it was, the fate of my sister right in my hands, but I didn't know what to say. I couldn't condemn her *or* recommend her. My thought process involving Eliza couldn't be trusted right now. Wait, that was the answer. It wasn't *my* mind that should decide.

"Why don't we ask her what she wants to do?"

Elizabeth's eyes widened.

"You want to bring her in here, now?"

"Yes, I'd like her to go with me. She has her own interest in the current events at Ice Castle, and we worked well together this past week. But if after we talk to her, you think she's too dangerous, I will leave her under your charge."

Kevin thought for a moment, and then nodded at Adam.

"Makes sense. Adam, escort Eliza here and lets have a talk."

＊ ＊ ＊ ＊ ＊

We sat in silence and sipped our drinks until Adam returned. When they entered the room, Elizabeth stood and moved over to a seat on the end of the table, so that Eliza could sit next to me. Then Kevin did the introductions.

"Hello Eliza, my name is Kevin Taggart, and I am with the NSA along with Adam and Elizabeth here. We wanted to talk with you about a few things tonight."

Eliza's eyes narrowed, and all I could do was hope she wouldn't get herself in trouble so deep that even I couldn't get her out of it.

"You know, that's great Kevin. But I'm not talking to anyone about anything until I'm released from custody."

Kevin put on his salesman smile.

"You aren't under arrest."

"Maybe not, but I'm being detained in a room against my will like a petty thug."

Kevin's expression turned hard.

"No, you're not a petty thug, you are an international criminal. Guilty of murder, kidnapping, impersonation of government officials…should I go on?"

He was trying to intimidate Eliza, which was a huge mistake.

"No, I'm well aware of my accomplishments."

Kevin looked flabbergasted.

"So you admit to those charges?"

She leaned forward and Elizabeth flinched back from the table.

"Look *Kevin*, if you want to lock me up, do it, but since we're here in this nice little meeting room, I'm guessing you don't. So I figure you need me for something, and you're trying to intimidate me into cooperating. Anna can tell you that shit doesn't work too well on me."

I broke in before the situation got out of hand.

"You're partially right Eliza. Except it's not Kevin that wants you, it's me. I'm going back to Ice Castle to save Zory Novikov, and I want you to come with me as a partner."

She leaned back and stared at me.

"Why the hell would I want to do that?"

I leaned toward her.

"Because you've got a score to settle with Lopata."

"Maybe, but I could catch up with him by myself."

"And you want to know what happened to Stepan Entsky. He saved your life, and you owe him at least that much."

Eliza thought for a heartbeat, and her face became unreadable.

"Yes, I do…"

A second later, that crazy smirk was back.

"And you want me to be your partner? You'd trust *me*?"

I shrugged my shoulders.

"At least until we're finished in Tiksi. Plus, if you're *beside* me, I don't have to worry about you sneaking up *behind* me."

She erupted with her unsettling laugh, and I waited for it to die down before continuing.

"I'll take that as an agreement."

She leaned into my face and whispered through a maniacal smile.

"Only until we finish in Tiksi."

Kevin interjected.

"For the NSA to approve of this mission, I have a demand."

Eliza whirled back around in her chair, but I put my hand on her shoulder. She looked at it, then at me, but said nothing as I spoke.

"What is it Kevin?"

"I want to send one of my own agents to keep an eye on both of you. You may have gotten away from the Red Dragons, but there was serious collateral damage."

"All right, who?"

"I'm sending Adam with you, if he feels up to it. Adam, what do you think?"

He folded his hands on the tabletop.

"I should be well enough to travel in a week or two."

Kevin nodded.

"Do the both of you agree?"

I did of course, but I was worried about how Eliza would respond. She surprised me.

Leaning back in her chair her attitude switched again. She was downright cooperative. That worried me even more.

"Sure, fine with me... So, now that we're all one big happy family, I don't want to be confined to my room any longer. Oh, and none of your pesky, well-dressed G-men hanging around either."

Before Kevin could say no, I responded.

"Put us in a room together. I'll look after my big sister."

She growled at me.

"I told you not to call me that."

I shrugged.

Kevin looked exasperated.

"Fine, whatever, but you're responsible for her."

Both Eliza and I replied at the same time.

"I'll keep an eye on her."

Kevin shook his head.

"This meeting is over. We will get together again after I clear all this with the higher ups. Adam, show Anna and Eliza to the aft room with double bunks."

Everyone stood to leave, but I had other plans.

"Hey, I'm going to hang out here. I think I'd like to be alone for a while. Adam, go ahead and show Eliza to her new quarters and come back for me in about a half hour, okay?"

"Sure. I'll be back in thirty minutes."

They all filed out of the room, except for Elizabeth. She waited until everyone had left, then stood up and walked toward the door. While her back was turned, I leaned over and ran my index finger along the rim of Adam's coffee cup. In my mind, I received the message...

DNA sample collected, analysis in progress

I stood and went into the corner as Elizabeth closed the door and walked back to the table.

"Anna, I know you wanted to be alone, but I also know you're hurting, and I don't mean your leg. Do you want to talk about it?"

Turning to face her, I went back to the table and pulled two chairs out, turning them to face each other. We sat down and I rambled.

"Elizabeth, I don't know what to do. Ever since my creation, people that get close to me end up dead, hurt, or at least threatened. I try to protect them, but it always ends up the same way. It's like I'm cursed or something."

She leaned forward and took my hand in hers.

"Anna, it's not your fault. You're such a unique, powerful person, that the evil in this world will do anything to capture or control you. And that's always been true throughout history. Humans *are* humans, after all."

Staring down at the floor, I focused on nothing in particular.

"While Adam, Eliza, and I were flying here, I looked around the inside of the Black Hawk, and all I could see was blood. Blood smeared on the floor, the walls, and door. Soaked into our clothes, staining our skin, and even the blood of others on our hands. I may have escaped from the General, but I won't ever be able to forget what happened today. From that, I'll never escape."

Looking back to Elizabeth, I saw her wiping the corners of her eyes.

"Your return to Tiksi will be different. You've always had to fight your battles alone, but not this time. This time, you'll have two others with you. You'll have Eliza and Adam by your side."

As she spoke Adam's name, my mind told me that the DNA test was complete. Checking the results confirmed my suspicions. The DNA sequences were more similar to Eliza's and mine, than a human's. Adam was an android. Most likely built by the woman sitting across from me. I couldn't help but gawk at her and imagine I was sitting next to Viktor.

Elizabeth tilted her head, misinterpreting my stare.

"Are you okay, Anna? Do you want to talk about anything else?"

I couldn't help but smile a little.

"No, not right now. We can talk about it later."

"Okay, I'll leave you alone, but you have to promise to come see me tomorrow."

"I promise."

With that, Elizabeth stood and left the meeting room, closing the door behind her.

I didn't move. As I sat at the shiny metal table, my life in crisis, all I could think about was I'd just gotten a brother.